I0742469

Chaos Reigns Vol 1: The Hand of God

True Tree Press
TrueTreePress@gmail.com

Chaos Reigns, Vol 1: The Hand of God
by G. S. Scott
The True Tree Chronicles: Book Two

Cover by Colleen Nye
Editing by Genevieve Scholl

Published by: True Tree Press
PO BOX 81168 Lansing, MI 48908
TrueTreePress@gmail.com

Copyright © 2019 True Tree Press & G. S. Scott
Printed in the United States of America
First Printing 2019

ISBN: 1-7337092-0-7
ISBN-13: 978-1-7337092-0-0

This is a work of fiction. All characters and situations appearing in this
work are fictitious. Any resemblance to real persons, living or dead, or
personal situations is purely coincidental.

For Sarah

Chapters:

Chapter 1
Betal

(502 years after the start of the Reign of Chaos -R.C.-)

Heartless squatted on the edge of his golden throne, his eye color changing wildly. A snarl played on his lips as he reveled in the power flowing from the Lord of Chaos through the bejeweled, multihued crown, entangled within his long black hair. At the foot of his dais lay the bubbling pool that used to be his herald—the man had the poor luck to bring him the spy. Heartless didn't dare kill his eyes and ears within the Council of Taneer so he took his rage out on the herald.

A voice whispered in the back of his head.

He glanced at the spot where the spy's gateway closed when the man left, the lingering scent of burnt ozone still in the air. "What were you holding back?" he asked, his voice echoing in the vast, dust-choked chamber. The light from mangled, crystal chandeliers and rush torches, along with the sparse rays peaking in through boarded windows left the castle in perpetual dim, earning it the name, the Black Keep.

Heartless clenched his fists, the knuckles whitening. It didn't matter what the spy withheld, the news he brought was bad enough. His face twisted. "Gabriel thinks he can take what is mine? The gall! I won their damned Game. Edis—Chaos himself—chose me, and I won. The world is mine. And now the Arbiter expects me to step down over some time limit? A *time limit*?" Heartless hurled his golden scepter across the room, the crystal top shattering on the rippled, uneven marble floor. Taking a deep breath, he chuckled. "A Rebirthing? Why would Gabriel do such a thing? Why be a mortal when he's already a god?"

Next to the bubbling pool, the chamberlain trembled on his knees. Sweat dripped down his face and soaked his mottled vestments singed from the proximity of the blast that destroyed the herald. "He—he said they were the rules of the Great Game, My Lord."

"Rules? What do I care about rules?" Heartless bellowed, stabbing a finger at the chamberlain. "You dare blaspheme before me?"

"No—no, My Lord. But, the Council, the Arbiter, they are gods, all of them, gods. How—" When Heartless snarled, the chamberlain threw himself to the floor. "Forgive me, Lord."

Chuckles from his Yurken guards filled the room, but Heartless paid them no mind as he fingered his chin. "That imbecile spy may not know *where* Gabriel will show up, but we at least know *when*."

"How—" The chamberlain swallowed. "How does this help us, Oh Great One?"

"It's simple. We—" Stopping short, Heartless tilted his head. "What are you doing down there? Up, my good man, up, on your feet. That's more like it. You're my chamberlain—one of my most trusted. No need to grovel like the rest." His eyelid twitched. "Where was I? Oh, yes. We know when the Arbiter will be born—sometime within the next two years. All we must do it prevent him from growing into his power. And as a mortal, he'll be weak—easy to kill. But how to find the *right* child?"

The voice whispered once more, an answer so obvious it made him giggle.

"I have an edict, chamberlain," Heartless pronounced. "Proclaim it to all, that to honor the Great Lord of Chaos there shall be a… a *Cleansing*, a sacrifice befitting the Great Lord, in celebration of his reign." He shrugged. "The Lord has already granted me extended life. With this gift to him, he'll give me the means to rule forever." His laughter filled the nearly empty chamber. "Oh, how the hordes shall revel in the coming slaughter."

John Simmons, Master of the village of Cool Winds, strode into the fields with an ax over his shoulder in his sturdiest pair of black pants and a blue shirt—though they'd both seen better days. The wide-brimmed hat atop his sandy-blond hair shaded his eyes from the late-morning sun. Birdsong, along with the buzz and hum of insects mingled with the scent of the forest on the light breeze from north of the village.

"Going to clear us out another field?" Erin Cruchfield asked with a laugh as he approached. "Or are you just looking to add to your house?" The village's Master-at-arms matched Simmons six-foot height but was blade lean rather than John's large frame and a barrel chest.

John smiled. "Neither, unless you intend to lend a hand for the next few weeks."

"Not likely." Erin clasped John on the shoulder.

"I thought not." John chuckled. "No, sheep broke out again— the pens needed repairing. Plus, I'm low on firewood."

Erin rubbed his arms. "It does seem to be getting cold early this year, doesn't it?"

"Just count yourself lucky we don't live in the south. The weather changes ten times a day—one moment it's snowing and the next you're dripping with sweat from the heat."

Erin shook his head. "Don't tell me you believe those stories?"

John shrugged. "I've heard it from far too many peddlers in the trader caravans to doubt it at this point. How are the boys and little Mattie? She'll be walking soon and—"

A wolf's howl from the trees ahead ruptured the tranquility, followed by the screams of terrified children.

John stabbed a finger at Erin. "Gather men, bows, and blades. There's always more than one." He bolted toward the forest's edge. The villagers already in the fields sprinted ahead of him with their hoes and spades in hand to ward off the pack. Through the irregular rows of corn and wheat, the children scrambled toward them, still screaming and crying. The villagers did their best to collect and calm them.

"Get them out of here," John said. "I'll need five of you to follow me."

They broke through the crop, reaching the grassy area where the children had been playing. Stopping, John peered into the heavy canopy of oak, maple, and brushwood, but saw nothing.

The howl rang out again, a single crackling cry filled with mourning and sorrow.

It sent a chill down John's back. "I don't think it's a pack. It sounds like just one." He'd heard the wolves' howls hundreds of times in his life but never like that. It was the sound his heart made when he lost his beloved Janell to Withering Fever three years earlier.

He shook off the melancholy. "The kids are safe. Let's not tempt Chaos, and head home."

As they started for the village, Erin ran in their direction with a dozen armed men. John lifted his hands to wave them off but stopped as the plaintive cry of a toddler pierced the air. He turned back to the forest. "Why would the kids bring one of the little ones out here?" He crept back to the trees, ax held tight in his hands. "Spread out. It could be a grunkin." Beasts born out of Chaos Storms, grunkin could imitate the sounds of others to lure the unwary—or so he'd heard.

At the edge of the tree line in the grass, lay a small, naked boy with jet-black hair. He wailed and pawed at the air with his hands and feet.

"He's as pink as a newborn," John muttered.

Adam Killington approached, his gray eyes searching the woodland. "How did it get all the way out here?" The anxiety in Adam's high-piped voice matched how John felt.

Erin, holding his broadsword at the ready, glanced down at the child, then back to the forest. "I don't recognize him. Do you?"

"No," John replied. "He's not one of ours. And there's been no strangers about that I know of."

Adam gazed at the baby and jumped back with a shout. "By Chaos, look at his eyes."

John nodded, unable to look away from the child's eyes, shifting between brown, blue, and gold. It brought excited talk amongst the surrounding men. "Fetch Dithiyar," he said. "He needs to see this. Chaos is at work here." Three villagers darted for the temple at the center of town. "The priest will know what to do."

John knelt next to the toddler. The child was special beyond its color-shifting eyes. His anxiety melted, replaced by a calm assuredness, a feeling everything was right in the world. With Chaos somehow involved, he doubted the others would take it in, and he couldn't just leave it. He wouldn't. *I'll die before letting any harm come to him.*

"How can you say that?" Erin asked. "It's touched by Chaos."

John hadn't realized he'd spoken aloud. "I don't know. I only know it's true. I'll take him as my own." His chest tightened. Janell always said he'd make a good father.

In the village temple, Dithiyar slumped in his favorite chair, the ever-present stink of must and mildew clinging to his study. "Lord, I despise these people," he muttered, staring out the dirty window at the villagers who went about their dreary business. He hated them nearly as much as he hated his life. "I've grown stagnant in this piss-hole."

Standing, he scooted closer to the window with a spryness that belied his appearance. His rail-thin body and ever-present stoop obscured his true height, and his lanky, steel-gray hair added to his apparent frailty. He peered at the Green in front of the temple where children scampered about while their mothers clutched infants to their chests and babbled.

"I'm never getting out of here," he grumbled. He belonged in the Black Keep, sitting at Lord Heartless's side, rather than a dump on the other side of the world. He blamed Hogar for his predicament. "I'm in this shit-hole till I die. How could I—"

Power erupted from the outskirts of the village, a wave of ethereal energy so strong that had it been physical it would have leveled the village. Dithiyar staggered away from the window clasping his head. With a shake, he darted from the room, down the hall, and out the temple's front doors. He sprinted across the Green, ignoring the screams and yelps of the worthless peasants as he weaved his way around the hovels, through the cut in the berm surrounding the village, and out to the fields. A group of the villagers ran toward him, shouting something, but he paid them no mind and headed to the center of the disturbance.

A group of armed men surrounded the epicenter of the blast, so Dithiyar slowed his pace. *No need to seem alarmed,* he thought, even if it was a bit late for it. Whatever caused the eruption was corporeal, otherwise, the peasants would not be staring at it. However, that didn't mean it wasn't dangerous, quite the contrary. Visual manifestations of the Great Lord were often exceedingly so. "What is it you've found?" he asked, his voice oily. "What is it? Let me see."

He pierced the wall of people and stopped. His eyes widening, he tilted his head. A young child lay naked upon the ground, its eyes shifting color every few seconds and emitting surges of power upon each change—not as strong as the initial burst, but strong nonetheless.

Edis has shown his hand for certain, he thought. *He sent this child to free me from my bondage.* At least, that was how he planned to use it. "Step back. Don't get too close."

"But, he's only a child," one peasant said.

"It's far more than that. It's a gift from Chaos, a sign of the Great Lord's power and might upon this world." Dithiyar smiled, staring hungrily at the squalling toddler—his weapon to be, and the means of his escape. *Thank you, Great Lord. Thank you.*

Hogar led a contingent of thirty warriors down the lane to the little village of simpletons he controlled. At seven feet tall and four hundred pounds of muscle and sinew, the Yurken paladin sat astride his black warhorse, his red eye—set deep in his gray-skinned, angular skull—smoldered like twin pits of fire. As they cleared the western wood, he thought of Dithiyar and chuckled. Centuries before, the wonderfully pathetic priest taught Hogar the ways of The Great Lord along with its highest mantra, the heart of the doctrine of Chaos: do as thou wilt. You can do anything you want, so long as you're strong enough to deal with the consequences, and as long as that remained true, all would be right in the world to Hogar.

As the village came into sight, the aether within the region changed—it quivered and crackled like the air before a lightning strike. The following burst of power sent his mind reeling. Even he couldn't wield such a massive amount.

"Continue to the village," he barked. "You know what to do." He then cloaked himself in Chaos, rendering him invisible, and spurred his horse toward the disturbance.

A large group of villagers, along with Dithiyar, stood around something upon the ground. He considered it a *something* because, even though it appeared to be a human child, no human possessed the power pulsing in this creature. "What is this then?"

His booming voice caused the villagers to scream and jump. Some even ran for their homes. He snarled. *How pathetic.*

Kneeling next to the creature, Dithiyar bowed to him. "I've discovered a blessed child of Chaos. I was about to take him to the Lord High Priest at Gate Hall."

Yes. I'm sure you were. Hogar uncloaked himself. "That's not necessary. I shall inform Karados myself when I am done here."

Hogar was not there on a pleasure trip. He was to initiate *The Cleansing* upon the village. He examined the child and judged it to be within two years of age. Not that it mattered. Hogar was not about to kill it. Not out of some misplaced sense of pity—he was already up to his neck in the blood of infants. No, this child was special. It was a powerful gift from the Great Lord of Chaos, and he would use it to further his dreams: to become the High Lord Paladin to Heartless.

"His name shall be Betal," Hogar said.

"Betal?" Dithiyar tilted his head. "That means 'The Hand of God' in the ancient tongue."

"Precisely. You are to raise the child and train him. He shall be a boon to us all." But Hogar didn't intend to tell anyone about the child—certainly not Gunther Karados.

"The rest of you, gather all your kin and go to the temple's main hall. I want every man, woman, and child there by the time I arrive. If you're not there, my men drag you there." A smile spread across Hogar's face. "I have an edict from Lord Heartless to pronounce."

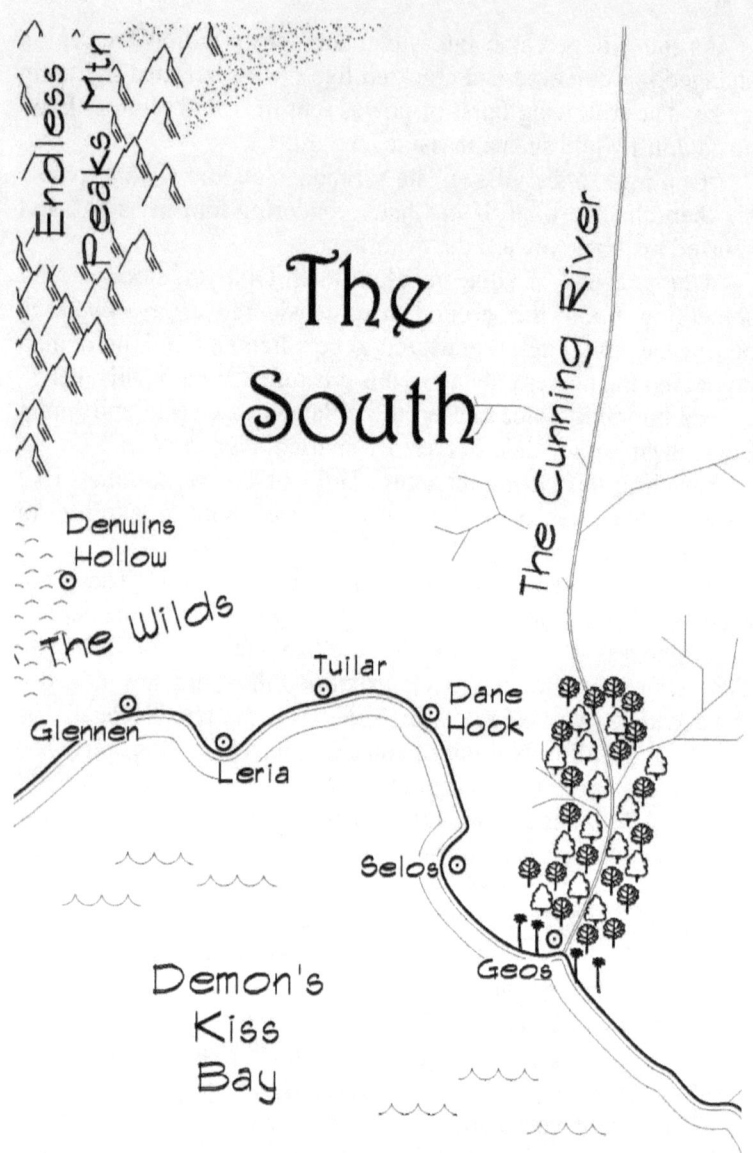

The South

Endless Peaks Mtn

The Cunning River

Denwins Hollow

The Wilds

Tuilar

Dane Hook

Glennen

Leria

Selos

Geos

Demon's Kiss Bay

Chapter 2
Fleeing Chaos

(Year 504 -R.C.-)

Daniel Conduit sat at a table going over the ledgers by the light of a single candle. As Village Master of Denwins Hollow, it was up to him to make sure they prospered, though one wouldn't know it from the modest single level home he shared with his wife and child. He was tabulating the village's grain stores when someone knocked.

Daniel opened the door. "What can I help you with, Marty?"

"Travelers," the young herdsman blurted out, practically dancing on his toes and wearing a huge smile. "I saw them coming down the road! They'll be here any minute."

With their village so isolated, it had been decades since they'd seen a troupe of musicians, singers, and acrobats. "Wonderful. Go on; spread the news. I'll be right out."

Daniel grabbed his light, dark brown cloak from the peg by the door. "Marsha, Travelers are coming in. I'm going out to greet them."

"That's delightful," Marsha replied from the back room. "I'm bathing Ellis. I'll be out as soon as I can."

Stepping out, Daniel stopped short. A host of people filled the green-space at the village's entrance, and more ran to join them. "That young man works fast," he said with a chuckle. Standing a head taller than the rest of the villagers, he nudged his way through the crowd. His bright red hair shone in the noonday sun as he awaited the traveling show's arrival.

The wagons rumbled toward town, looking like little houses on wheels, all brightly colored and trimmed in gold or silver. Large plumes adorned the horse's heads, seeming to dance with every step. The people themselves were awash with color or bright sequins flashing as they caught the sun.

The people oohed and aahed as the Travelers made their way to the center of town, but Daniel's elation soured as he examined the entertainers. The troupe didn't look right—none smiled. They looked bone weary, their eyes sunken and haunted. "What's going on here?"

"What is it, Daniel?" asked Barek Dona, the village's cobbler.

"Why were they pushing so hard?"

"What do you mean?"

"It's said the Travelers have no fear of the wilds. They make camp wherever they feel because bandits never attack them. They're protected by Chaos."

Barek shrugged. "What's your point?"

"Well, look at them." He pointed toward the Travelers. "They're exhausted, and froth covers their horses. Why?"

"Perhaps they had a run-in with a Chaos Storm or a pack of grunkin."

"Perhaps," Daniel said with a shake of his head. Barek may have been right, but a shiver ran up his spine, nonetheless.

Upon stopping his team, the driver of the lead wagon—a tall man in loose, brightly colored clothes, and long gray hair—jumped down. He called out in a strong, deep voice, "I must speak with the Village Master, at once."

"I am the Village Master." Daniel stepped forward from the crowd.

The troupe leader marched up, took him by the arm, and spoke quietly, "It is of the utmost importance that I speak with you in private."

Confused, Daniel nodded and led the man through the crowd to his home. After they entered, Daniel offered him a seat and asked the man his name.

"There's no time for that," the man replied gruffly.

Daniel scowled. "What is the meaning of this? What's going on? You look as though you've been chased by a host of demons."

The man closed his sharp green eyes and took a deep breath, calming himself. "I'm sorry. My name is Duncan. Forgive my bluntness, but there is something of the utmost importance I must ask you." Pausing, he pursed his lips. "We just came from your neighboring village, Kettering. Folk there—and others before that—said there was a 'miracle child' born here within the last two years. Is it true?"

Daniel was puzzled. "Yes; it's true. Why do you ask?"

"The child must come with us, at once."

Daniel shook his head. "What game is this? What are you going on about?" The man started to say something, but Daniel overrode him. "Yes, Ellis is a miracle, but only to us here in the Hollow. If you're thinking of taking my child and putting him on some kind of display, you can think again." Daniel's hand went to the knife at his belt. "No one is touching my child."

The Traveler's face firmed. "It's not we who want your child, sir. It's the Lord of Chaos who wants him."

Daniel's eyes went wide. "Are you mad? What in the Lord's name are you talking about?"

"As I said, we just came from Kettering." Fatigue filled Duncan's voice. "As we were readying to head out, a priest entered the town with a large contingent of soldiers. The priest said he had an edict from the Lord of Chaos, calling it the 'Cleansing.' They gathered all the children under the age of two to the center of town where they'd be 'blessed by The Lord.' Once they searched our wagons, they told us to leave—which we were more than happy to oblige." The man shook as he told his story, so Daniel offered him a seat again. With thanks, Duncan sat, his shoulders slumping as if they held the weight of the world.

"As we reached the top of the hill on the way out of town, we saw their 'blessing.' The soldiers surrounded the children, drew their swords, and slaughtered them—every child. Parents rushed in to stop it and were struck down." The Traveler let his head drop. "After the butchery, the priest raised his hands and engulfed the carnage in flames."

Daniel's legs wanted to give out under him. He gazed about his home, lost in thought, trying to grasp it all. *How could the Lord have done such a thing?* By its very nature, Chaos was random and unpredictable. But this was simply evil.

"Why are you telling me this?" Daniel asked. "Why come here and offer to take in our child? If what you are saying is true, they'll likely kill anyone trying to harbor him."

The man stared up at Daniel. His face firmed, and he stood. "There is no love for Chaos in my heart any longer—nor in my troupe. We accepted him in the past for his tepid protection, but this?" He glowered. "We've seen much of the world, and it is apparent Chaos's reign is destroying it. And after what we just witnessed, it must end."

"And how would protecting my child do that?" Daniel asked.

"I believe your child is special." He took a step toward Daniel. "You all call him a miracle, and I believe it. I've heard the stories of how Chaos cursed this village—everyone stricken sterile."

"Yes, but that's passed. As I said, it's only a miracle to us. We're past that affliction."

"Are you? Tell me this, how many births have followed your boy?"

"None," Daniel replied uneasily.

"Precisely. There have been no more births because you're all still barren. Your boy is a true miracle—one outside the realm of Chaos."

Daniel held up his hand. "There's nothing outside of Chaos."

"Yes, there is. Most have forgotten it, but before The Great War, there were gods aplenty. Chief among them is The True Tree, The Mother of Creation."

"A tree?"

"Yes. All life springs from the Mother. There's also a prophecy dating back to the end of the War, the prophecy of *The Ancient One*. It speaks of the end of Chaos."

"How is that possible?" Daniel asked.

"Think about it," Duncan said. "There's a reason The Lord of Chaos is killing children. This isn't on a whim—it's systematic. I think he's looking for one child, the promised *Ancient One*." His voice firmed. "I believe the gods of old sent us your son to end the time of Chaos."

"You're mad." Daniel retreated.

"Aye, I may be. But are you willing to take the chance I'm wrong?"

"I don't know." Daniel's stomach churned. Even in his wild youth, he disliked the way of the world, with everyone out for themselves and bloodshed only a heartbeat away. Was it possible there could be another way of life, one without the Lord of Chaos? "I just don't know."

Marsha, her shoulder-length blonde hair disheveled, rushed out from the back bedroom clutching little Ellis, still wet from his bath and wrapped in a towel. "You don't know?" Her tan blouse lay open to her belly, exposing her bronze sun pendant, and her blue eyes burned with intensity. "This man has just told us The Lord of Chaos wants our child dead—a story I know you believe from the look it in your eyes. And you're still not sure we should flee?"

"I did not say we should stay. Of course, we need to go. I'm simply saying we need not go with them." He turned to Duncan. "No offense. But you travel slowly, and we need speed. I wasn't always a Village Master, and I know of a place to start—a way for us to escape. I also know how to live off the land for a time. I've done it before."

"And where would you go?" Duncan asked. "Where would you take your child to escape Chaos? You can't live in the wilds forever. So, what will you do? Go to one of the cities?" He shook his head. "We do travel slow, but we're always on the move and in that, there's a measure of safety. We're also masters at disguise. We can secrete him among us; hide him away from any who'd wish to do him harm."

"Dada?"

Daniel looked down at Ellis, his red-blond hair wet from the bath. The boy seemed to sparkle in the afternoon light shining through the window, and his blue eyes glimmered as he smiled. "Nice man. We go with, Dada?"

Daniel's uncertainty melted. The man was right. Daniel couldn't take a chance on his son's safety, or their own. "Very well. We'll travel with you." Turning, he started for the door. "I'll tell the village we are leaving. They need to hear this. Take your troupe through the village and out the other end through the fields to the west. We'll take to the north, then turn and catch up to you once we are out of sight."

An hour later, Daniel sat on the bench next to the troupe leader, the wagon heading west through the tall grass. A cold, light rain fell, one hinting at snow. "There's a dry riverbed five miles from here," he said. "We can follow it north. About a mile from there, we'll come to a hidden path."

Duncan raised an eyebrow. "Hidden path? You do realize it's quite difficult to hide our wagons, don't you?"

"That won't be a problem." Daniel smiled. "It's enchanted. No one else knows or remembers it. It conceals any who travel upon it."

"And how do you know about it?"

"Because that's what the Tebu told me when I stumbled upon it."

"You met one of the Tree-folk, the protectors of the wild? It's said they kill on sight."

Daniel laughed. "He took pity on me though some would say I didn't deserve it." He patted the long sword hanging at his side. "As I said, I wasn't always a Village Master. In my youth, I led a small band of raiders in these parts."

"You were a brigand?" The troupe leader's eyebrows shot up. "What made you stop?"

Daniel lowered his head slightly. "Marsha. One day, we waylaid a small wagon train. Marsha sat at her father's side in the lead wagon." A grin bloomed into a smile. "It was like she'd cast a spell upon me. Without a second thought, I slew my compatriots before we could spring our trap."

"You killed all your friends?"

"They weren't friends so much as cohorts," Daniel explained. "There's never any trust when you are in that kind of life. And truth be told, I'd grown weary of it. I wanted a calm, quiet life, and I saw it in her." His voice took on a sense of wonder. "It was as if someone spoke in my mind and showed me what I needed to see. It was all so clear." He shook his head. "So I killed the others in my party and walked out as bold as you please."

"Cocky."

"That was me. I told her father what I'd done, with a swagger in my step and a smile on my face."

"What happened next?"

"Well, that little stunt nearly cost me my life." Daniel chuckled. "If not for Marsha, her father would have put a bolt through my chest."

"Why did she do that?"

"I asked her sometime later. She said it was because she liked my smile." Daniel shrugged. "Within a year, we married. A short time later, her father passed, and the rest of the village looked to me for leadership."

Duncan laughed again. "Quite the fascinating tale—from loathsome robber to respected leader. I believe I could make it into a grand saga. I must hear more of your life, my friend. Something tells me you're holding back."

Daniel sat back in thought as snow fell. The man spoke true, which didn't bode well for what lay ahead. To a youth, these things were an adventure, but now, older and much wiser, he saw them for what they were: a heartache, the true cost of living under The Lord of Chaos.

"You should think about changing your names, you know," Duncan said.

"Yes. Marsha and I discussed it as we walked. From now on, you should all refer to me as Cord. Marsha chose the name Tasha after her grandmother. We'll drop the last name altogether."

"Good thinking," Duncan said with a nod. "What about the boy?"

"We decided not to change it—I doubt the priests know it, anyway. Regardless, we don't want to confuse him with a new one. His life's going to be difficult enough as it is."

"Very true, my friend. I fear life will be more difficult for all of us from now on."

Calidos Flint rode his large, black gelding into Denwins Hollow at the head of his own forty-man army. His long, jet-black hair hung loosely about the shoulders of his colorful priestly robes. A smile played on his lips. He felt ripe with pride knowing The Lord of Chaos had given him this duty—The Cleansing, God's gift to the world.

Denwins Hollow was to be the last village in the stretch of worthless holes, and the words 'miracle child' lay on many lips who talked about it. *Well, I'll be the judge of just how miraculous this child is.*

The first thing he noticed about the village—other than its unusual cleanliness—was everyone appeared to be awaiting his arrival. Over one hundred people stood near the entrance, talking quietly, scrutinizing him and his men filing in.

His dark eyes narrowed. "They knew of our coming." That meant they would be hiding their children. *The fools.*

The second thing he noticed was there wasn't a single person below the age of twenty. *Why hide their teens as well as the children?* He smiled. It was going to be a messy search to find all those needing Cleansing.

At the edge of the village, he shouted out with his piping voice, "Where is your Village Master?"

A short, broad man with curly black and gray hair stepped forward. "I am Barek Dona, Master of the Hollow. What is it you want, priest?"

"I want everyone gathered here on the Green—every man, woman, and child—and I want them now. I have an edict from The Lord of Chaos."

He turned to the head of his troopers. "Cranston, help these peasants assemble. They have an obstinate look about them."

Cranston nodded, dismounted, and with a wave of his arm, led half the men into the village to root in every home.

"We have no children here in the Hollow. What you see is all we have," the broad man replied in a strong voice, his eyes shining defiantly. The crowd joined in, adding their voices to give their Master's statement weight.

Calidos snarled. "I don't care what you may have heard from that troupe of vagabonds. I'm here to do The Lord's work. And if you don't wish to aid me, you shall pay for it in pain." Reaching out with his will, Calidos grasped Chaos. The pure essence of The Lord of Chaos coursed through his veins. Calidos had an affinity with fire—he loved the flame, and the flame loved him. He funneled his fire into the Village Master.

The large man screamed and flopped to the ground, writhing in pain. "There are no children here! I swear it!"

An older woman leaped down to help the Village Master. As soon as her hands touched his now steaming face, she hissed and pulled them back. "Please, my Lord. He tells the truth! We have no children! Twenty years ago, The Lord cursed us, leaving us all barren."

With a yelp, she flung herself backward as the Village Master's body burst into flames. His screams reached a crescendo and ceased.

"Do not lie to me, hag!" Calidos roared. "I know you are hiding at least one child! The last three villages all spoke of your *miracle*. Every one of them swore to it! They said the child The Lord wants lives here. They begged me to take your *blessing* so I might spare their own." His eyes burned with hate, and a cruel smile sprung from his lips. "But The Lord does not want one child. He wants them all. And I shall see the Great Lord of Chaos gets what he wants."

Calidos sent waves of Chaos into the woman. She shrieked as fire burst from her eyes.

Two hours later, Calidos's hatred still burned hot. They'd not yet found the child, but it was only a matter of time. They tore apart every house and building in their search, and every villager had cried out the same lie—even as the flames took them.

However, his lips still held a spiteful smirk. He'd put the entire village to the flame, leaving it a smoldering wreck. He even roasted their livestock. The men would enjoy the meat in addition to their normal field rations.

"Reverend Flint." His guard captain saluted as he approached. "We've found tracks leading away from the village. Several wagons headed west of here across the plain. They lead to a dry riverbed..." Uncertainty filled his eyes. "We lost their tracks there."

"Don't worry, Cranston. Jantos will have no trouble picking up their trail." His smile broadened. "The Lord has gifted him."

Jantos could see the ethereal trail left by anyone, so long as the priest held something belonging to their prey.

Upon reaching the riverbed, Jantos led them down the dry bed. Their trail reached a wide, earthen path at the edge of the woods where Jantos frowned. "I'm sorry, Calidos, but the trail ends here."

Calidos screamed in a rage. "How could their trail simply vanish?"

"I don't know. There must be some kind of ancient warding. The trace ends at the tree line, and every man who entered became weak and loose of mind."

Anger and shame filled Calidos—along with a small amount of trepidation. He'd lost them; he lost a child needing to be Cleansed. "The High Priest will not be pleased."

Calidos snarled. "It would appear this child truly is something special."

"Come now. It's a coincidence, nothing more."

Calidos shook his head. "There are too many signs for it simply to be another lamb for the pyre. Think it out, Jantos. Not one person in that damned village would tell me where they went—before or after they burned. It speaks of a higher power at hand."

"I will find the child!" he bellowed at the road, his voice reverberating off the tree line. "Do you hear me? I will find him and roast him in the glory of God!"

Chapter 3
Foresight

(Year 507 -R.C.-)

Sitting in the driver's seat of the lead wagon of the troupe, Cord shook off the snow from a sudden squall as the clouds cleared and the baking hot sun returned. The troupe asked him to take over as their head after only a year. He'd asked Duncan why, and the man replied, "You're a natural leader, Cord, and a man of great wisdom. You instill confidence and pride in the people. You don't lie to us, you say what you feel, and, above all, you keep your promises. That's rare in a world run by Chaos." For three years, their tour avoided the large coastal cities, choosing instead to visit the villages on the edge of the northern frontier. The area was so rough the troupe needed to add a fair number of guards.

"What's the world coming to?" Cord said and concentrated on the road ahead. Brigands were common, with a plethora of places for them to ambush the unwary. Most wouldn't bother Travelers—they had little to steal. But then, some marauders didn't care about the coin or the supposed protection of The Lord. They attacked simply for their love of death and pain.

Her voice like a dove, Tasha sang to little Ellis as she went about readying the midday meal in the back of the wagon. Cord couldn't sing a lick. Everyone said he sounded like a bullfrog in heat, which made him laugh.

"So, tell me, my love," Cord called back to her through the small, open doorway. "When are you going to take the stage? It's selfish, you know; to hold back such beauty from our most deserving patrons."

"Hush now, husband. You know I get stage fright."

Ellis piped in, his voice high yet soft, "Mommy has the prettiest voice in the world."

"Aw. Well, thank you, my little sweet-ling."

Cord heard her open a cupboard and lift the cover off a pottery jar. "Here, my love, a sweet for the sweet." Cord laughed. She loved to spoil the boy.

Upon topping a hill, the two-track, gravel road dipped through the center of a large hollow with a thick copse at its center. Movement from within the thicket caught his attention. His first thought went to brigands, but his tension melted when Evan, their lead scout, rode out on his brown gelding. When they came abreast, Cord pulled the horses to a stop. "What news?"

"The road's boggy through the stand," the tall man replied.

Cord checked out the shin-deep mud on Evan's horse, as well as on the man's brown pants. "Will it cause us trouble?"

"It's not too long a stretch, so it should be all right. But we'll need to take it easy." Evan flexed his grip on his bow, a sudden gust tugging at his brown and green tunic. The best shot in the troupe, Evan often led the hunters whenever they needed to range for their supper.

"Any chance we'll be eating fresh meat tonight?" Cord asked with a smile.

"Not unless you want to wait here for a while."

"That's all right. We'll be fine. We'll take the wagons through one at a time. Daylight's burning, and this could take a while." Cord nodded his head to the rear. "Pass the word and hurry back. We should be up to the tree line by then, and I'll want you to help lead us through." Cord gave the reins a twitch, starting the team down the decline.

"Papa," Ellis spoke up from the back. "Papa, we need to stop."

G. S. Scott   - 20 -

Cord shook his head. "Hush now, son. We've a rough road ahead of us."

"But, Papa, we have to stop," the child said louder.

"Hush now," Tasha chided the boy. "Don't bother your father."

"We have to stop. We have to stop." Ellis continued over his mother's hushes. He then screamed, "Stop! Stop!" The child's little fists beat at Cord's back.

Cord looked back into the wagon. "What in all the hells has gotten into you?"

Ellis wrestled with his mother and broke free. He clawed his way next to his father and tried to grasp the reins, screaming.

"Knock it off, boy!" Cord fought off the scrambling boy.

Cord's anger turned to alarm when Ellis jumped out of the wagon, tumbling into the high grass next to the road. Cord sawed back on the reins, causing the horses to scream and rear. By the time Cord kicked the brake lever, Ellis was already up and running back up the road.

"Stop!" the boy screamed, his arms flailing as he ran.

Cord leapt from the wagon, turning his ankle in the process, and limped after his crazed son. He was halfway up the wagon train when the boy fell in front of Evan, who'd turned back at hearing the ruckus.

The gusts of wind tugged at Cord's shirt as he knelt to his boy. "Ellis, what's wrong?"

His son thrashed on the ground, mumbling incoherently with his eyes rolled back in his head.

"What d'you do?" Cord asked Evan.

"Nothing, I swear. He just fell as I rode up." The man's hair flailed in the increasing wind.

"Get Tasha!" Cord yelled, trying to hold the thrashing boy down.

Before Evan moved, Tasha dashed to Cord's side. "He's having a seizure. Roll him on his side."

"Should we put something in his mouth so he doesn't swallow his tongue?" Evan asked.

Tasha shook her head. "No. That's a myth."

Within moments, Ellis calmed, but he continued to mumble with only the whites of his eyes showing.

"What's wrong with him, Tasha?" Cord panted. "What happened back in the wagon? What made him so scared that he'd go berserk?"

"I don't know, dear," she replied. "Let's put him to bed and let him rest. Perhaps it'll pass."

The wind gusted, nearly flinging Cord to the ground, and caused the others to stagger. "What the—"

The hair raised on Cord's neck as the wind took on a higher pitch, becoming an ear-piercing wail, as though the air screamed in agony. The sky darkened as clouds blotted out the sun. Ahead, at the bottom of the hollow, the black clouds condensed and swirled.

Cord's stomach clenched. "Chaos Storm."

He picked up Ellis. "Get the wagons turned around! Now, people, now!" He then turned to Evan as the scout mounted. Once in the saddle, Cord handed him Ellis. "Get him out of here. Tasha, you go with him. I'll get the team."

Cord sprinted to their wagon, the horses rearing and screaming as he grabbed their bridle. "Hush now, hush," he said, trying to calm the team.

Drawn into the hollow behind him, the wind struck Cord full force. Like a giant hand, it solidified, grasping him about the chest. Feet slipping, he tightened his grip on the bridle as the wind lifted him in the air. As if changing its mind, it suddenly relented, dropping him to the ground. Still gripping the bridle, he scrambled to his feet and dared a quick look back. He wished he hadn't.

Black and red clouds swirled above the hollow. Jagged strokes of black lightning stabbed into the woods, setting fires in over a dozen places. Four slender funnel clouds extending out of the storm like gnarled, twisted fingers, tearing into the trees and road. What they didn't destroy became warped and deformed. The trees turned a blackish-brown and warped into knots. They coiled and flailed of their own accord, lashing out at anything nearby. The ground cracked and turned molten, shining in a multitude of colors. Animals fled in all directions. A herd of deer charged up the road toward Cord, but didn't make it far as a lightning bolt struck at their heart, blowing them to pieces.

Those are the lucky ones, Cord thought. *At least they won't turn into—*

An ear-piercing screech split the air. The carcass of one deer lurched and twisted as its headless neck jutted into the air. With a tearing sound, the neck split open, black fangs sprouting from the new gaping maw. A long forked-tongue snaked out, whipping through the air. The thing's fur grew shaggy and green as its back bulged. With a pop, two spikes jutted from its back, grew into legs, and stabbed into the ground on either side of its body. The thing hissed, jumped up, and skittered toward Cord like a giant green bug.

"Grunkin," Cord croaked. He wanted to run, but fear rooted him in place as death scurried his way.

Vines shot out of the flailing trees with the sound of whip-cracks and ensnared the grunkin. The beast of Chaos hissed and squealed, its legs tearing at the ground as its razor-sharp fangs snapped at the vines. But for each vine cut, two more took its place. The grunkin thrashed, clawing at the ground, but the vines dragged it back into the flailing forest.

The horses screamed again and reared, ripping the bridle out of Cord's hand. He snatched it back, and with all his strength, yanked the bridle down to the right. The jolt startled the team, settling them enough to turn the wagon about. He clamped down on his anxiety and soothed the frightened animals as he made his way to the bench. Cursing himself for his stupidity, he shook the reins hard. The horses didn't need the urging as they fled up the road, doing all they could to put distance between them and the hell they left behind.

Chapter 4
A Song and a Sword

(Year 507 -R.C.-)

At a clearing by the side of the road, Cord called the troupe to a stop. After setting the brake, he jumped down and with tranquil words and a light touch, soothed the still agitated team. He then went around the back of the wagon, lowered the steps attached to the back, and opened the door. His wife knelt next to the side bed, caressing Ellis's damp forehead. "How is he?" he asked.

"Better," she replied without turning. "He came to a short time ago, but cried himself back to sleep."

Cord climbed in the wagon and stood behind his wife, placing a hand on her shoulder. "Any ideas as to what caused the fit?" He caressed his boy's head.

She craned her neck to look up. "I've no idea. I checked his head for any marks or bumps, and there's nothing. Hells, there's not a mark on him." She turned back to their boy, taking his little hand in hers. "I just don't understand it."

"I love you, wife." Cord leaned down, kissing her head. "I've faith in you." He then bent over to do the same with Ellis's forehead and quietly left the wagon, closing the door behind him.

He made his way to the center of the wagon train, deep in worry. *Is this some strange touch of Chaos?* he wondered. The boy acted up just prior to that Storm hitting. *What does Chaos want with my son?* Upon reaching the center of the train, Cord called the rest of the troupe to gather. They needed to talk about what to do next.

"How is the little one?" Duncan asked.

"As well as can be," Cord said, doing his best to keep his voice strong and sure. But he knew they heard the trouble laying behind it. "We cannot continue forward. So, I put it to you. Where do we go from here?"

"Can we go around?" asked a tall, spry, flautist.

Cord looked to Evan, who replied, "No. I know this terrain. It's far too steep and rocky for our wagons. That's why the brigands love this stretch. There's no good way around."

"What do we do then?" Duncan asked. "It'd take us three to four months to reach the other end of the circuit if we go backward."

"We have, at most, two months of supplies," Evan said. "We could do our best at foraging, but let's face it; few of us are apt at hunting."

"Can't we just go back to some of the last villages?" asked Kirk, the eldest of the five Kosimov Brothers. Many troupes had acrobats and tumblers claimed to be kin, but the Kosimovs actually were brothers—dark-haired and stocky, strangers often found it difficult to tell them apart.

Duncan shook his head. "We can't. The last five towns gave generously. I doubt they've anything left to spare." He turned to address the rest. "We must face it, friends. For the next three to four months, we're on our own."

That only brought cries of "what to do then?" and "where should we go?" from the troupe.

Cord spoke up, "We go to the coast."

The statement brought an explosion from the others. "What?" "Are you mad?" "That will take us toward Chaos. Not away from it!"

"Cord, we cannot. What about Ellis?" Duncan asked.

"Perhaps they're no longer chasing us?" Dandle the Jape said. The comment brought them all up short, so Dandle continued, "Everyone knows I've an affinity for Chaos. I understand it, and it's what helps me read the crowd. So, I say to you, when was the last time we heard of Chaos sticking with any kind of dogma for more than a few months, let alone years? Perhaps they've moved on."

"He has a point," Kirk said. "Not all of Chaos is bad. We are Edis's most favored after all."

Duncan's mouth twisted as though he'd bitten into a sour berry. "Perhaps, but do we take the chance? Chaos has changed, and not for the better."

"We'll continue to keep him out of sight," Cord said. "He's growing fast and already looks closer to seven than five." He raised a finger. "Here are our choices as I see them. We can go back until the ground is less hilly and rocky. Then, we hope to find a way to cut across the Barrows country—some way we can navigate and live off the land if our provisions run out before we find our way through."

The troupe dropped their gaze, shifting their feet while shaking their heads.

Cord raised a second finger. "We turn back around and do the route in reverse. It'll likely take at least three months before we reach the first town who'd have recovered enough to pay us. We can hope that the closest can look after us, but, again, I doubt it." Using his other hand, he grasped the two fingers. "Just remember that with either one of these choices, we'll still have the same problem until the road is passable. The only other choice is to make for the coast."

"But, what of Ellis?" Duncan asked. "Can you really risk his exposure? It's said that every city and many of the towns have priests."

"We'll do what we can," Cord replied. "What say you?"

In short order, the troupe agreed, but a part of Cord wished they hadn't.

Two days down the southern road, Cord spotted two people trudging along the lane toward them. Despite the current pleasant weather, they wore the hoods of their cloaks pulled up, hiding their faces—not that Cord blamed them, as it had been raining hard only an hour before. The shorter of the two had a lute slung across his back, while the second, standing head and shoulders above the first, sported a sword strapped to his side.

The blade caught Cord's attention. *Brigands?*

The road stretched flat in both directions, and what trees there were lay at least a mile away. That meant nothing. Brigands could easily lie low in the tall grasses by the side of the road. He dared not take a chance. Giving a short, sharp whistle, he pulled the wagon to a stop. Reaching behind him, he picked up the loaded crossbow he kept just inside the wagon, and waited.

Their lead guardsmen, Lem, rode up. "What is it?"

"Pass the word to keep a sharp eye out. We have a pair of men coming our way. If they're a distraction for an ambush, I want us to be ready."

After Lem rode away, Cord took up the reins with his left hand and urged the team to a slow walk while holding the crossbow low in his right, hoping to keep it out of sight.

Shortly before reaching them, the shorter of the two men threw back his hood, exposing long flowing blond hair. He called out, spreading his arms wide, "Ho, friend. We mean you no harm."

So much for keeping the bow out of sight, Cord thought, his mouth twisting as he pulled the horses to a stop again. He called out to the stranger, "What can I help you gentlemen with?"

With a laugh, the blond man threw back his cloak, exposing bright red pantaloons and a flowered white silken shirt. He swung the lute about and played. "I am Jacob, the minstrel, and I mean you no harm. Merely a weary traveler on the road of life, seeking to bring a bit of entertainment to all that I can." His playing picked up speed, and he sang:

> *"Oh. The road is a very weary place to be*
> *going 'bout a world full of hostility.*
> *With death and strife both near and far,*
> *surely it's safer to stay where you are.*
> *Ah, but this I must confess.*

It's a life I dearly love best.
For all the world I would dearly love to see—"

"You can stop now," Cord interrupted. "You can clearly see that we're Travelers. So you're either singing to stall for time, or you're auditioning." He laid the crossbow across his lap, pointing it the general direction of the two men. "Which is it?"

Again, with a laugh, the minstrel bowed to Cord. "Why, an audition, of course." He slung his lute back across his back and slowly approached Cord's wagon. "I meant what I said about it being a dangerous world. And as I see it, it's better to travel with like-minded friends in some form of safety than to trek the world alone."

"You're hardly alone. Jacob, was it?" When the singer nodded, Cord continued. "Who is your friend with his face still covered and lacking any kind of instrument? He doesn't look the type to bring the crowd to their feet in applause."

"Hardly," Jacob said. "This is my dear friend, Dirge." He looked back to the tall man. "Come now, old friend. No need to be uncivil. Throw back your hood and show these good people we mean no harm. We've no need to hide our faces from them."

The swordsman lowered his hood. Dirge's dark-skinned face held little to no fat, his skin stretched tight over his skull causing his cheekbones and chin to appear sharp. He wore his jet-black hair cut short, and his slate-gray eyes seemed to loom out of two dark caves. The swordsman crossed his large, dark arms, apparently trying to appear casual, but he looked like a coiled spring, ready to strike.

This man is dangerous, Cord thought. "Why have you need to hide your faces?"

"Ah. Well, you see," Jacob said with more than a bit of flair, "my friend and I are not well liked by the people of a certain city-state on the coast. There was quite a bit of disagreement some years ago, and Dirge and I were on the losing side of it. So we mostly keep them hidden out of habit." He eyed several of the troupes' guards as they approached on horseback. "So I ask you, good man. Will you let me perform for your troupe; to prove that my skill is not only worthy, but would be a good addition to your group?"

Something about it all didn't fit well with Cord. *We'll need to keep a sharp eye on them.*

He nodded his head back to the wagon train. "You can walk with us until we reach good ground to camp upon. Once we're set, you can show us your skills."

"Wonderful," Jacob said with aplomb. "I know of a perfect place. We passed it not but an hour from here." He made to climb aboard Cord's wagon but stopped short when Cord raised the crossbow. "Ah, yes. Of course. You did say 'walk', didn't you?" He waved to his friend. "Come, Dirge. It would appear that you give our good Troupe Master a case of the jitters." He laughed again. "Not that I blame him, of course."

As they walked back into the wagon train, Cord heard Jacob pat the swordsman on the shoulder. "Dirge, my friend, you must learn to smile more if you are to make more friends."

Cord frowned, gave the reins a jiggle, and got the team moving again. But he kept the bow handy while keeping an eye on the high grasses. *No use taking unnecessary chances,* he thought.

As night fell, they all sat about a large fire in the middle of their camp. Jacob's word had been more than good; the campsite was perfect. After the troupe put on a show for him and his friend—to show them their worth—Cord gestured to the young man. "So, my friends, you have seen our wares. Let us see yours."

Standing, Jacob bowed to Cord, and stepped before the fire. The members of the troupe sitting on the other side of the fire moved to get a better view. Jacob bowed to the group, pulled out his lute, and played. The song was soft and sweet, containing such tenderness that Cord couldn't help but feel moved. Then Jacob moved on to a ballad. One of valor, of marching forth to war, and to all the wondrous things victory would bring—as well as the pain and loss that came with it. He sang songs of gallantry and courage, as well as songs of sorrow, and lament. He had the ability to captivate an audience, let them see the world through his eyes. Near the end, Jacob pulled out a flute and soon had everyone's feet stomping and dancing.

Once done, Jacob bowed to raucous applause. He sat at Dirge's side once more, accepting a large mug of ale from Jeanette.

"You did wonderfully," she said, then turned and slunk away, her hips undulating with each step.

Oh, I know that look, Cord thought with a smile.

"When did you start playing a flute?" Dirge asked quietly.

The question surprised Cord, as it was more than apparent the two men knew each other a long time.

After taking a long pull of ale, Jacob replied, "This thing? I've had it forever."

Dirge tilted his head slightly, his brows furrowed.

"No. I mean it," Jacob said. "I never played it at the inn because Katlyn didn't like the flute. She said they were for children. Truth is I always thought she was right since it was my mum who gave it to me and taught me to play." Taking out a pipe, he filled it with leaf and lit it, then smiled at Dirge.

With a frown, Dirge stood and walked to Lem, who stood at his leisure against a wagon where they struck up a conversation.

What are these two up to? Cord wondered. Against his better judgment, Cord found himself liking the dark-skinned, brooding man. He gave off an air of strength and... discipline, of all things. He watched the two of them talk for some time. *Whatever it is, Lem should worm it out of him.* Eventually, the two shook hands, and Lem went out to the take his turn at Watch. Cord smiled. *Well, he's earned Lem's respect. It looks like there's hope for the young brooding man.*

He turned his attention back to the singer. "So, tell us, Jacob. Where did you and Dirge meet? Was it in an army? It's more than apparent that you were a piper, as well as a common-room bard."

"Ah. Very true, my good friend," Jacob said around his pipe. He nodded toward the swordsman. "Dirge and I go way back. Why, I've known him my whole life. We grew up together in Tuilar, a city on the coast. Do you know it?"

"No," Cord replied. "We've never been this far south."

"Ah. The coast is wonderful, so long as you like the smell of salt and dead fish." Jacob sat up and looked over Cord's shoulder. "And who is this now?"

Twisting, Cord spotted Ellis just out of the light of the fire. The boy was staring at Jacob with his head down, his body turned slightly, and a large frown on his face.

Damn it, son. You're supposed to stay out of sight.

"Ah. This is my boy... Dennis." Something told Cord that until he knew these strangers better, it was best not to use his son's real name. "Come here, boy. You've nothing to fear." He waved his son to sit at his side, but Ellis didn't move.

Jacob's eyes narrowed. "How old is he, if you don't mind my asking?"

"He's eight," Cord said, his speech well-rehearsed at that point. "He's a little small for his age, I know. He just hasn't hit his growth spurt yet."

When Ellis started forward, it surprised Cord that the boy didn't come to him. Instead, his son padded around the fire—all the while keeping his eyes on the new minstrel—until he reached the apparently ever brooding, Dirge. He gazed up at the tall, dark man-at-arms, seeming fascinated by the powerful warrior. He then smiled and gently patted Dirge on the leg. "It's all right," Ellis said in his piping voice, full of reassurance. "I understand. It will be all right." The boy beamed. He yawned, rubbed his eyes, and walked back to the wagon without another word.

Dirge blinked several times, his eyes casting about, and then violently shook his head. "It's time for my watch," he said in his rough, gravelly voice, and heading into the darkness.

"What was that all about?" Duncan asked.

"I have no idea," Cord replied. "That boy is always a wonder, as well you know."

"Your friend is a man of few words," Jeanette quipped.

"Aye. He's a quiet one all right." Jacob still had a questioning look in his eye before he laughed. "Why, that man will go days and not say a word to anyone. Not even me. But then some say that I talk enough for the two of us. And I suppose it's true."

"Perhaps you talk so much that he can never get a word in," Henry said with a laugh.

Jacob laughingly replied, "Very true, my good man, very true. But then, what I have to say is often far more interesting."

"Tell us, what news have you from the south?" asked Jonathan.

Jacob replied with a casual wave of the hand, "Oh, nothing... other than the war."

The troupe erupted with shouts. "War!" "We're headed into a war zone?" "We could always turn back." "We cannot. They'll still have nothing for us at the villages." "What do we do, Cord?"

"Calm yourselves, my friends," Cord said in a raised voice. "By the look on Jacob's face, he has more to say on the matter. Come now, Jacob. I see your smile. Stop trying to play us and speak the rest."

Jacob smiled broadly. "I'm sorry. I just couldn't help myself. My nature sometimes gets the better of me. There was a war between Tuilar and Leria a couple of years ago, but it's long over. Leria was the victor, and Tuilar is now a smoldering ruin."

"Didn't you say you were from Tuilar?" Evan asked.

After Jacob nodded, Cord said, "And that is why you two have kept your heads down. Do you fear reprisals?"

"No. Not at all," Jacob said. "You've nothing to fear. As I said, it's mostly out of habit. We did not desert our army. There was no real army left to desert from."

"So why did the two cities go to war?" Tasha asked.

"It was The Cleansing," he said in a low voice, filled with dread. "One day, the Masters of the city announced that the priests of Chaos had come to them and told them of the proclamation. It took several months for the aftermath of that day to percolate through the people. One day, a strange man came to town, speaking of the ancient God of Order. He said that Chaos's time was done. With his help, the people rose up, slaying the priests, and several of the city Masters in a rage. Afterward, they declared war on Chaos itself." He shrugged. "How one declares war on a God, I'll never know."

"So, you rose up and joined the army?" asked Jeanette.

Jacob snorted. "Hardly. Dirge and I were born in the slums of Tuilar. We cared for the Masters of the city about as much as they cared about us. But once the new Master declared war, he had every man, woman, and youngling that could hold a weapon—from the highest Lord to the lowest urchin—join their army. We didn't have much choice, did Dirge and I. We were puppets in a war of the gods." His voice was wistful, but gained strength and certainty as he continued. "We did well at first. The new Master had doctrines from the old God of Order and passed it out among the people to inspire them." He chuckled. "Many took to it quite strongly. Along with the religious canons, they had ancient manuscripts of how to wage war from the time before Chaos. They placed us in groups and ranks. It was an amazing feeling. We were going about our preparations with a true sense of order. Order in a world of Chaos. We felt inspired."

Cord nodded. Jacob was good at his job. He had the entire troupe enraptured by his telling.

"As I said, we did quite well in the beginning," Jacob said while striking a pose. "We marched into war with our nearest neighbor, Leria. They'd heard of our proclamation against The Lord of Chaos and thought to destroy us. They met us on the field of battle—thousands of men and women driven mad by Edis. They slammed into our line, like a never-ending wave of insanity. Our line buckled and bent from that Chaos infused mass. It seemed as though nothing would stop them from wiping us out. But we had something they lacked, a leader, the Capitan of the Warriors of the Righteous. The captain rushed to the forefront, carving a swath of death into that mass. Anyone that came near him died. Inspired, our army pushed forward in unison, each step a thunderous march of death. The mob didn't have a chance. They broke and scattered, but there was no escape from our righteous campaign. We slaughtered them all."

"Yay!" Jeanette shouted and clapped. She wasn't alone.

Jacob's eyes turned haunted, and his voice took on a hush. "And then *they* showed up."

A shiver ran up Cord's spine. "Who?" His stomach fluttering, he tasted bile because he already knew the answer.

"The Chaos priests—three of them. The things they can do in battle..." Jacob stared off into the distance and shuddered. "The head priest threw out his hands and called forth a Chaos Storm that stretched for miles—a thing of nightmares that swallowed men and spit forth grunkins. A second army poured forth from behind the priests... our army was shattered. Everyone ran, screaming. Well, except for Dirge, that is." Jacob shook his head with a crooked smile, his eyes bewildered. "The fool wouldn't quit. We both saw what was happening. We both saw the fires and explosions and the twisting masses of bodies strewn about the field. But the man wouldn't quit. He's stone stubborn when he gets an idea in his head, and all he could think of was his war on Chaos."

Cord asked, "If he'd not run, how is it he's still among the living?"

"He's alive because I clocked him across his thick skull and dragged him off that field," Jacob said with a chuckle. "It's a miracle we're still alive, I tell you."

Cord shuddered—the man's story put him on edge. "I think it's time we are to bed. We will want to make an early start in the morning. You and Dirge are welcome to ride along with any of the others that will let you. But until you get either a tent or a wagon of your own, you'll have to make do by sleeping under one of the wagons. We simply don't have the room."

Taking Tasha's hand, they headed to their wagon. Ellis had fallen fast asleep, as usual, so they quietly disrobed and climbed into their bed, but it took some time for Cord to fall asleep. He just couldn't get his son's reaction to the two newcomers out of his head.

Jacob lay under the dulcian player's wagon, deep in thought. They'd trekked with the troupe for a mere three days, entertaining a town only the day before, and his routine went well—as it always did. Jacob considered himself a master at not only singing but also storytelling. He had entranced the townsfolk with his stories almost as easily as he had fooled the troupe. Already, they thought him and Dirge as one of them. He wanted to laugh. Tasha asked him as they left the town why he hadn't bought a tent to sleep in. He told her that it had simply slipped his mind and that he would get one at their next stop. But the truth was he didn't want to be weighed down. Also, the wagon he lay under was next to Cord's.

Just before they left town, Jacob saw the coins Cord received from the townies, watching the Troupe Master put them into their moneybox. The rest of the troupe may not know it, but they carried around a small fortune. Why they possessed all that gold, Jacob didn't know. Travelers didn't need much in the way of coin. Cord was up to something. Hells, they all were. He had never seen a group of Traveling people who guarded their secrets so closely.

And then there was the boy, Dennis. On the rare occasions the boy looked at him, it felt as if the child stared into his soul. The boy was not natural and gave him a case of the shakes.

It was deep into the night, and he'd not slept—as planned. Dirge had ensconced himself within the guard, and he would have sent the rest of them to bed—Dirge now kept the late-night watch. As Dirge's light footsteps approached, Jacob quietly rolled out from under the wagon with his pack and nodded to his friend, who wore his pack as well. The plan was simple. Take the moneybox, race back to the town where they would steal a pair of horses, and make for the Cunning River. From there, they could go anywhere.

They crept up to the lead wagon. As Jacob put his foot on the bottom step, quietly drawing his short sword, he was shocked when Dirge grasped his arm. "What?" he hissed.

"No killing tonight," Dirge replied, quietly.

Jacob shook his head and snarled. "Whatever happens will happen. If they awaken, they'll not just let us walk away with their gold. You know that. Now stop screwing around and keep an eye out."

Jacob froze as he saw his friend's eyes look over his shoulder, his face troubled. A cold shiver traveling up Jacob's spine, he spun around and there stood the child.

"What are you doing?" the boy asked. His high, piping voice sounded deafening in the quiet night.

"I should ask the same of you, little man," Jacob replied, still keeping his voice low. "What are you doing up at this late hour?"

"I had to pee," the boy replied matter-of-factly. "You're a bad man. You should go away."

Jacob kept the sword low and crept closer. "Now why would you say such a thing as that?" It was time to silence the unnerving little shit.

"I'm sorry," the child said, his voice somber but assuring. "But it has to be done."

Jacob, having no idea what the kid was blathering about, lunged for the boy. Snatching Dennis by the arm, Jacob yanked him closer. With his other hand, he slashed at the child.

His wrist exploded in pain, and his sword clanged to the ground. He raised his right hand up to his face, but only a bloody stump remained. Then his back and chest bloomed in agony. Bewildered, he gazed down at the sword blade protruding from his torso.

As he fell forward, the sword slid from his body. Surprisingly, the wound no longer hurt. He hit the ground with a grunt and curled up in the fetal position. His vision blurred, but he still saw the bloody sword in the hand of his best friend. Jacob's eyes begged the question that he could no longer bring to his lips.

"I am sorry," Dirge said. "But it has to end. No more needless death and destruction. This world *must* change, Chaos must end, and this boy can bring that about."

Kneeling, he closed Jacob's eyes forever. "I am sorry, my friend. I will see you on the other side one day."

Chapter 5

A Proposition

(Year 508 -R.C.-)

Hogar stalked through the halls of the citadel in Gate Hall. The High Priest, Gunther Karados, summoned him, and one did not openly defy Karados without repercussions. Possibly the most post powerful being in the ways of Chaos next to Lord Heartless, Gunther Karados was strong willed, highly intelligent, and disciplined—nearly heretically so. The man was perfect to oversee The Lands of the Dead.

Hogar didn't like taking orders. But he hated being so far from Cool Winds. Even after six years, he didn't trust Betal in the hands of that old relic, Dithiyar. The man might kill the boy out of spite.

As Hogar approached the High Priest's office, Gunther's pair-bond, Koren Laylear, stepped out from an alcove near the door. "Hello, Hogar," she purred, her smoldering green eyes boring into him.

Most fools only saw her bright red hair, smooth, supple-skinned face, and hourglass figure. But Koren was devious, possessing a quick wit and agile mind, her schemes often took people by surprise when they thought her nothing but an object of lust. She was powerful as well. Hogar found her in a worthless, rundown village years before. He saw great potential in her; someone he could exploit to raise himself higher. He discovered her innate ability to manipulate the minds of the weak and taught her how to expand upon it. In some ways, her ability even outstripped his own at manipulating the mind. While he had to make physical contact with the person, she could do so from afar.

She glided toward him. "No need to disturb Gunther. He's quite busy." She wore a loose, nearly transparent, white silk top, and forest green skirt slit up the side. Her hair hung loosely about her shoulders and bejeweled rings sparkled on her fingers.

"Why don't we retire to my apartments and you can fill me in about all that happened?" She sashayed down the side corridor, glancing over her shoulder at him. "Come along. I promise I won't bite."

What is she playing at? he wondered. His sharp nose picked up her flowery perfume. With a grin, he followed. *Whatever it is, I think I may enjoy it.*

They entered the suite she shared with Karados and their two children. "Would you care for a drink?"

He shook his head. He wasn't about to let her poison him.

She laughed. "You need to loosen up." After pouring herself a drink, she slinked across the room, her hips undulating, and lazed upon a chaise lounge in the middle of the room. "Come, my old friend. Sit." She pointed to a chair near her feet. "We've much to talk about." She sipped her wine, her eyes following him like a hawk as he approached.

He stood at the foot of her lounge. "Did we come here to talk, or to fuck?"

"Hogar, no need to be so vulgar. I simply wish to talk."

"About what, exactly?"

"Well, my darling life-mate plans on sending an envoy—along with several promising young prospects—to Borromar.

They're to be presented to Lord Heartless." She frowned. "But he doesn't want me to go along." Taking a sip, she added under her breath, "No matter how hard I try to convince him."

Hogar chuckled. "So, he's found a way to block you from completely manipulating him." He barked a laugh when her lovely face contorted in anger. "What would you have me do? He'll not listen to my suggestions on the subject any more than your pleadings."

She whipped the scowl from her face and smiled once more. "Well, as to that. Once the envoy and his company leave, you could secure me to them somewhere on the road. If you gave them the word, they'd listen."

"And why would you want to meet Lord Heartless?"

"Why, to pay homage to his greatness, of course."

"Yes. I'm sure you would. Do you really think you could twist his mind like you do Gunther's?" Her eyes lit with anger again, but he continued before she could speak. "And why would I do such a thing? What have I to gain from it?"

She leaned forward. "To keep me from telling Lord Karados about your little pet in Cool Winds."

Hogar's face turned to stone. "What are you talking about?"

"Come now, Hogar. Things of that magnitude are bound to get out. You seriously thought you could keep it a secret?" Her laugh was musical, full, and rich. "It didn't take long before word reached here of a 'blessed child of Chaos.' But fear not. It didn't take much for me to… *convince* everyone that it was nothing more than a monster on the loose."

Hogar smiled; the knots in his back loosening. "Thank you, my dear. I'll be forever in your debt for that. As to your request, I think you already know my answer."

She snatched Chaos and whipped it into his mind. It delved deep… and dissipated. Her eyes went wide and her mouth gaped.

Laughing, Hogar grasped Chaos and lashed out at her, binding her in place and closing her mouth so she couldn't scream.

"Do you really think that your ability with the mind outmatches mine?" He snarled. "I've been in The Great Lord's service long before you were born. I was weaned and ready for battle when The Great War broke the world. I was there when the abyssal demon, Dekriot, infused himself into The Chaos Sphere to create The Lands of the Dead."

He advanced, his voice rising in volume and intensity with each step. "I was there when Raven the Black plunged his dagger into The Champion of the Lord of Order. His death destroyed an entire continent, sinking it to the bottom of the sea. I have *reveled* in the glory of The Great Lord of Chaos for over five hundred years. I'm no simple human, like you. I'm Yurken, born and bred to serve The Great Lord of Chaos! You think that your meager ability can outmatch my mastery of the mind?"

Throwing a ward at the entry door to prevent any noise escaping, he released her gag. He wanted to hear every sound she'd utter. He grasped her head, and she whimpered in pain at his grip. He sent his tendrils of The Lord's Breath into her brain, and she squealed in agony. He barred her thinking about fleeing the room, and made her forget how to touch Chaos—he wanted her to know she could stop him, but not remember how.

"What are you going to do?" she panted.

"I'm in the mood to play a game. It's called 'who leaves this room alive?'"

A door opened behind him. "Mommy, what's going on?"

Without looking, he encased the child in Chaos and dragged him over. "I do believe this is yours," Hogar said as the child screamed.

"No!" Koren shouted. "Not my son!"

"What is he? Three?" Smiling, Hogar knelt behind her son.

She shrieked as he pulled out his dagger. "No! Please, I'll do anything. Just don't hurt him!"

Hogar smiled at Koren and slowly sliced the child's throat. Blood flowed from the wound and fanned across his paralyzed body as his mother cried and thrashed on the floor.

Hogar knelt next to Koren. "You actually thought you were smarter than everyone else, didn't you?"

She spat in his face.

Without wiping the spittle away, he continued, "You thought yourself untouchable. But, you forgot that I was the one who found you. I was the one who made you. And I will be the one to end you because you're of no more use to me."

Placing his dagger's point against her belly, he pushed it in. She bellowed and convulsed. Once up to the hilt, he ripped the blade up, opening a large gash, then he stood back and released her bonds. He reveled as she crawled across the floor toward her boy, leaving a trail of blood and entrails. The life in her eyes faded with each inch. With a whimper, she stopped a hand's-breadth from her dead child.

Karados stared at nothing. "Assassin?"

"Yes," Hogar replied. "I believe it was one of The Brotherhood. Only assassins could have done this."

"Yes," Karados said numbly.

"She made many enemies here within the sect. And I believe they're not finished."

The High Priest's eyes shot to Hogar. "What are you saying?"

"I'm saying that your daughter is still vulnerable."

"Mangin? But she's only nine."

"Yes, and she's shown to have the same innate ability as her mother. She'll likely draw comparisons."

Karados shook his head. "What do you suggest?"

"Let me take her away from here. I'll hide her with Dithiyar Mardoon in Cool Winds. He can teach her. Few have lived as long as he, so he could teach her much."

"Yes," Karados nodded absently. "That makes sense. Few even know he's still alive. Go fetch Mangin and bring her here. I'll explain it to her."

As Hogar exited the High Priest's office, he smiled. Having Dithiyar raise and train Mangin would be a good way of keeping the old man in line. Dithiyar might be stupid enough to kill Betal out of spite, but not if he had to watch over Karados's girl as well.

The paladin chuckled. "This trip has turned out far better than I ever expected."

Chapter 6
Hunted

(Year 512 -R.C.-)

Betal shifted in his padded high-backed chair in Dithiyar's small, cluttered study. Its musty scent, mixed with the smell of dust and stale lamp oil clung to his nostrils. The modicum of light from the lamps—along with what little shined through the single dirty glass paned window—left the room perpetually dim and oppressive. He liked to tell himself it was the reason for his having difficulty grasping Dithiyar's teachings, but the truth was he felt uncomfortable wherever he went.

The old priest told him repeatedly that he had it in him to be a priest of exceptional power and ability, but Betal had his doubts. He was well behind Mangin in his training. Betal had difficulty with the simplest of spells and manipulations. He desperately wanted her help at that moment, but she was off visiting her father.

"Open yourself to the flows of Chaos," the priest intoned, his voice slick and oily, as he started again with one of the basic exercises. "Chaos will not just come to you. You must grasp it—dominate it—as is the way of all things. See the flows all about you. Smell it in the air. Taste it on the wind."

Betal closed his eyes, trying to open himself to Chaos, watching it swirl around him with what Dithiyar called his third eye. But it was elusive when he reached for it, like grasping at motes in a gale.

His concentration snapped as the priest's hand struck him across the face, leaving his head ringing and seeing stars.

"Open your eyes, damn you," the priest yelled while rubbing the back of his hand. "You think the world will wait for you as you dawdle your time away with your eyes shut?! I don't care that you're only twelve. Life is a battle—a never-ending war with death. Close your eyes to it and the world will strike you down no matter your potential."

Dithiyar took a deep breath. "Hogar bade me train you in the ways of Chaos, and I'll not have his wrath befall me for your failures."

Betal bit his lip, curbing his anger. It wasn't the first time he'd been struck by Dithiyar, nor was it the twelfth, nor even the hundredth. The elder priest seemed to harbor a hatred and resentment toward him that he simply couldn't understand.

"Forgive me, Dithiyar," Betal replied, rubbing the side of his face. "I am doing my best." He adjusted himself in his chair, trying to empty his mind and open himself to Chaos. He reached out with his will to grasp Chaos, and again, it eluded him.

Dithiyar turned away with a snarl on his face. "Pathetic. You're better than this. You have it in you to be a true power in the world." He strode to his small, dark hardwood desk, and sat on its edge. "There are many types of magic in the world, and many ways to manipulate them," he said with an impatient sigh. "Take what many hedge mages do. They manipulate the essence of life that emanates from the world, and use that manipulation to weave what they will." Dithiyar waved his hands in front of him and then swatted it away like an imaginary fly. "Paw! It's slow and weak, and can affect very little directly."

"There are others who draw upon their own inner reserves." He gestured at his head. "They use their minds to draw out that inner power to control the surrounding elements, or to reach into another's mind."

With a hint of malice in his eyes, Dithiyar stalked back toward Betal. "But what is moving a few rocks or reading someone's thoughts, compared to tapping into The Lord of

Chaos himself?" He reached out as if grasping something out of the air. "What is drawing from the trees, compared to wrestling with the Breath of God? They are nothing compared to the power of The Lord."

Dithiyar strode back to his desk and turned, eyeing Betal with a hint of questioning. He crossed his arms over his chest and tapped a finger on his lips. "Perhaps I've been going about this the wrong way. You seem to make it more difficult than needs be. But there are many other ways to manipulate the Lord's Breath."

He slowly crisscrossed the small room, seeming to think aloud. "Perhaps we need to teach you the more subtle ways of manipulation first, rather than the brute strength method—though I know you have it in you to wield it that way."

His voice took on more than a hint of condescension. "So, we will take the lesser route of simply having you guide and cajole the current. It's called, 'The Fine Art.' It has a subtlety that escapes the most powerful. Perhaps if we start you down this path, you can later learn to be more direct. The Fine Art is often for those who work from behind the scenes as it has its limitations. To reach the highest levels of power and influence in the world, you must learn dominance. If you want to control the world, you must take it."

He stopped in front of Betal and straightened his shoulders. "The Fine Art is approached quite differently…"

Several hours later, Betal emerged from the study an exhausted wreck, but enthusiastic. He'd made great strides with his Master's new techniques, pushing himself farther than ever before.

It looked to be a glorious afternoon from the study, so he decided to spend the remaining daylight outside, but first, he needed to get a bite to eat. His hunger was gnawing a hole in his belly, so he stole to the kitchen. Ronald, the cook, pointed Betal to a half loaf of bread in the pantry. He wolfed it down with a cup of cold milk from the crock. Once finished, he headed out the back door from the kitchen and into the temple's stable yard.

He decided to first head for the Village Green. The road that meandered through the town from the front gate crossed right in front of the temple and circled back around along the houses. It encompassed a roughly round section of grass and short weeds with a large two-foot high stump at its front. There was something about the simple patch of grass... It helped Betal think, and held a serenity the rest of the village lacked.

Betal started down the walkway that separated the stable yard from the temple by a split-rail fence, but stopped before reaching the front corner. Something didn't feel right. He put his back to the wall and peered around the front of the temple to an empty Green.

Where is everyone? He wondered.

Betal inspected the homes and storehouses that edged the Green. A dozen boys crouched in the shadows of many of those buildings, and more than a few of which held rocks ready to throw.

"I guess they're no longer afraid of me." His raw innate ability that held them in check had failed to show itself. He'd become a toothless lion.

He considered returning to the temple, but that would only raise Dithiyar's suspicions. The priest would want to know why, and that would lead to many of those young men's deaths.

Even though they hated him, he felt no animosity in return—not really. In truth, he wished he were one of them. Every day, he'd watch them from his window as they played in the Green, or ran in the streets. They wanted nothing to do with him. To them, he was a freak and a monster. Who would want to play with that?

So Betal thought it best to go elsewhere. He'd hide in the fields or forest for a while and give them time to cool their heels. After a while, they'd grow bored, or perhaps one of the village elders might spot them and send them on their way with a few swift kicks.

Betal smiled. They may have thought him toothless, but he knew how to defend himself. Though still tired from his studies, Betal reached out to Chaos. He caressed it, fanning it toward him like smoke off an incense burner. As it flowed to him, he spun it out in filaments around his body like a cocoon. It refracted most of the surrounding light, making him invisible—it was something Hogar used, earning the paladin the name The Ghost of Death. The remaining light left the world a dark, dull mist, but it was better than the alternative. But, unlike *Hoga*r's, Betal's gave off a shimmer, like heat off the hot and dry summer fields.

Shrugging, Betal ghosted away from the corner of the temple, down the fence line of the stable yard, and away from the Village Green. He crept along the edge of the road, following the fence line, trying his best to keep out of the taller grasses where their movement might give him away, yet not in the road where the gravel would crunch beneath his boots.

As he neared the first house that fronted the temple's fence, he stopped. He wanted to be sure no one hid in the shadow between the fence and the house. Crouching, he diverted a portion of the Chaos forming his cloak, and sent it ahead of him, weaving it into a tunnel. When it reached the end of the house, he turned it around the corner, allowing him to see what lie behind. There was nothing. Relief flooded him, as did elation. He'd not tried to form two separate and intricate constructs before. Even more thrilling, he'd not learned the trick to look around corners form Dithiyar; he'd constructed it without thought.

Maybe I do have what it takes.

He continued along the edge of the house, turned the corner, and flattened himself against the wall in near exhaustion. The exertion of keeping up the cloak became too much, so he released it.

So far so good, he thought. *Now all I have to do is make it to the berm without them spotting me.*

He crept from house to house. It took twenty minutes to reach the berm surrounding Cool Winds. Ducking behind the last house, he checked if any of the youths followed.

"Dung," he murmured with a scowl. Two boys were on his trail, peering behind each building they passed.

He felt too weak to try another cloak, let alone do anything to protect himself from the rocks they carried. *At this point, I doubt I could even muss their hair.*

With his pulse racing and his mouth dry, he took a deep breath, and quickly scrambled up the earthen berm. Lying low, he crawled over the top and slid down the steep backside to the bottom of the ditch that fronted the berm. He wove his way through the chest high, sharp, wooden stakes, and scampered up out of the ditch. He headed out to the fields, staying low through the uneven rows of wheat, oats, and barley, and into the forest beyond.

A few feet into the forest, he ducked behind a large tree, pressed his back to the trunk, and counted to twenty. He cautiously peered back toward the village, having difficulty making out the spot he'd crossed over the berm.

It didn't take long before one boy—Cobb Cruchfield, the eldest son of Erin, who led the village militia—crested the berm right where Betal crossed. Although only fifteen and rail thin, Cobb stood nearly six feet in height. His shaggy brown hair waved in the wind as he scanned the field erratically. He turned his head to his left as another boy topped the rise next to him— his younger brother, Lucas. Cobb yelled at Lucas, pointing toward the west. Lucas merely nodded, scrambled down the berm, and sprinted off through the fields to Betal's right.

Betal crept deeper into the forest until the trees obscured Cobb. With a sigh of relief, he strode deeper, finally feeling safe.

The villagers said no part of the forest was safe, claiming a grunkin lived there. But Betal doubted it. He'd been exploring it for as long as he could remember. In all his forays, he'd seen no evidence to back up the claim. Besides, no one had seen a grunkin in his lifetime. They were a rarity in The Reach, even rarer than Chaos Storms.

He'd once asked Dithiyar why that was, but the man claimed not to know.

"These simpletons are all fools; scared of their own shadows," the elderly priest had said. And Betal was inclined to agree.

I could be wrong, he thought. *Anything can happen in The Lord's world.*

He kept his magical senses alert, forging deeper into the forest, where he felt more relaxed with every step. The forest felt like home to him. Whenever Betal stood in a crowd, he felt isolated and alone, but not there. With a smile, he stretched, luxuriating in the lush canopy of browns and greens, the musky scent of deep earth and moss, of downed trees and fallen leaves. It felt right. But his smile slipped. A part of him often felt out of sorts while he roamed the forest, as if he wore the wrong skin.

A mile or so into the forest, northeast of the village, Betal stopped. The boys would tire of their hunt before long, and he doubted they'd follow him that far into the wood. He'd take his rest, and, in a few hours, head back around the same time the adults would finish their work in the fields.

He sat in a patch of moss, his back against a large oak. "Why are they doing this?" he wondered. "I know they hate me, but what's different about today?"

The only answer he could think of was Mangin—or more to the point, Mangin's absence. She left over a week before and hadn't said when she'd return—if at all. Mangin's father sent her to Cool Winds five years before and wanted to know how she'd progressed.

"Why do you have to go?" Betal had asked her.

Mangin laughed, patted him on the cheek, and turned back to her trunk, her bright red hair glinting in the morning light from the window. "He's not about to come to this flea-bitten hole in the middle of nowhere, now is he."

Betal shrugged. "As fun as it is to watch you pack, I think I'll take a walk in the forest."

Mangin scowled. "The woods are dirty. Honestly, I don't know what you see in it."

Mangin preferred they take horseback rides into the pastures nearest the village whenever they weren't at their studies. And the day she left, Betal wondered if he'd ever see her again. Her father might well decide she was old enough to enroll in the citadel in Gate Hall.

The village boys must have decided the same thing. She intimidated them with her guile, beauty, and devious nature—not to mention, her family connections. Plus, she always stood up for Betal. But with Mangin gone, he'd lost her protection. "Please Mangin, don't abandon me," he said under his breath as he squeezed his eyes shut, laying his head back on the tree.

A sound cut short his introspection. He couldn't tell from how far away, or for that matter, even what it was. It wasn't the rustle of leaves or the snapping of a twig, but it was... something. He listened closer, but nothing made a sound. Then, realization dawned. He heard no sound, nothing at all. The forest had gone completely silent. Opening his magical senses, he sent them out, searching the forest. It didn't take long. A few hundred yards away, something waited, dark and malevolent, and filled with hatred and pain.

"A grunkin," he whispered. "Here?"

He considered cloaking himself again—he'd recovered enough of his strength that it would be easy—but if it was indeed a Chaos Beast, he dared not. According to texts, they could sense any manipulation of God's power, and it would draw the thing like a fly to shit.

He headed back toward the village. *Better to face the boys than something driven mad by a touch from The Lord.*

A good half mile from the village—slipping from tree to tree—he still felt the presence deeper in the woods, shadowing him, so he picked up his speed. If he made it to the fields filled with villagers, the thing might not follow.

A sense of foreboding grew in him the closer to the forest edge he came; it gnawed at him like a giant tick burrowing into his back. The presence was still out there keeping pace. It didn't feel as twisted, but it grew stronger in his mind with each step. He also felt it growing more agitated—it didn't want him to leave. His heart hammered in his chest and his skin prickled. Panic seized him by the throat. He ran.

Brambles tugged at his shirt as he sprinted through the forest, and limbs slapping him in the face. His biggest fear was catching his toe on a root. The thing would have him for sure, then. With the edge of the forest in sight, he finally heard the thing behind him. It panted and snarled, as it tore through the underbrush, a hulking thing of white fur with a mouth full of fangs. Out of the corner of his eye, Betal saw Cobb standing at the forest edge. He also saw the rock leaving Cobb's hand.

Betal screamed, but it cut short as he tripped and fell. The root had snagged him. The rock flew over his head and struck a tree behind him. Betal tumbled to the ground, bruising his shoulder on a tree root, rolled head over heels for ten feet, and landed on his back in the first row of barley.

He heard Cobb's blood-curdling scream and looked up, expecting the Chaos Beast to be at the boy's throat. But the grunkin had disappeared. Cobb stood stock-still, staring at the ground just inside the forest, his face white, and his eyes wide.

Betal got to his feet as several of the villagers ran toward them. He crept back to the forest edge and realized what Cobb was staring it. Betal hadn't tripped on a root. He'd stumbled over a body—Cobb's mother. She lay on her back just inside the forest, her milky-white eyes staring blankly at the sky. Blood soaked the ground all about her. Betal doubted she'd much left in her. Her throat was torn away, and her belly ripped open with her intestines strewn all about. Much of her blonde hair, now tinged red with blood, had been torn out, and her shredded clothes exposed deep gouges in her chest. Whatever attacked her wasn't interested in food. It mutilated her just for the sake of it.

"The grunkin." Betal's voice sounded cold and distant in his ears. He felt numb, but shook nonetheless.

Betal's voice seemed to break Cobb out of his trance. The boy flung himself at Betal, his fists flailing, screaming incoherently. Betal threw up his arms in protection, but it lasted only a moment as a pair of adults separated them.

"Stop it, you two." Betal found himself in his father's arms. John cupped Betal's chin and raised it to look into his somber eyes, his deep voice tinged with worry. "Is everything all right, son? Are you hurt?"

Betal nodded. "I'm all right."

"What happened? You can tell me. It's all right. You're safe now"

Shaking, tears filled Betal's eyes. "The grunkin. It chased me through the woods. I tripped over her. I didn't see her."

John raised his eyes to where the rest of the villagers stood, staring at the woman on the ground. "Myrial," he said in a shushed, shaken voice. "Gods no, not Myrial." He spoke to the rest of the villagers, "Harl, you and Zak cover her body. Albert, Finly, go fetch a stretcher. Angela, take Cobb. Tessa, Mat, you two go get your bows and a pair of spears. The rest of you keep a sharp eye about you. That grunkin can't be far."

Taking Betal by the hand, his father started toward the village. "Erin just arrived from Cross Corners. He said Adam and Mangin got there as he was leaving. They'll be here soon." He lowered his voice as though speaking to himself, "Erin needs to hear this from me. I owe him that much."

Chapter 7
Birth of Power

(Year 512 -R.C.-)

Betal stared out his bedroom window, thinking about the funeral for the mother of the Cruchfield boys. it started in the Green and wound through the village to a plot on the eastern edge. Dithiyar found it silly that the villagers had a singular spot dedicated to the burial of the dead.

"These peasants are sticklers for odd, ancient rituals," the old priest had said with a sneer.

When everyone returned from the burial, Erin Cruchfield stood in the center of the Green with his crying boys clutched to his chest. One by one, the rest of the village clasped him on the shoulder, spoke a few words, and moved on.

He wanted to feel sorry for the Cruchfield's, but he couldn't, and a lack of sympathy had nothing to do with it. He simply felt nothing but numb, as if something bottled up his empathy, leaving him an empty husk.

Rattles and squeaks from outside drew Betal's attention. A coach rounded the corner of the Green and stopped in front of the temple. The door opened and Mangin stepped out, her bright red hair sparkling in the sun as the wind caressed it.

"Take the carriage around back." She jumped down and hurried up the temple stairs with a beaming smile.

Betal dashed out of his room and down the steps to the main floor. As he entered the Grand Hall, Mangin greeted him at the entrance.

"Oh, Betal I had such a wonderful time." Grasping his hands, she drew him into the Hall. "It was so good to see Father again. I forgot how big the citadel is. Oh, and you should see Cross Corners. We must go there sometime. I met such a wonderful young man there. His name's Kenja, and he... well, he showed me things I never knew. It felt so amazing. And—" She frowned. "What's wrong? You look like you're about to cry."

He grabbed and hugged her tight. "I'm just glad you're back." Tears streamed down his face as everything came rushing back to him.

"What happened?" She walked him to the dais steps, and they sat.

Sobbing, he told her everything.

"A grunkin? Are you sure?" Mangin asked.

"Yes," Betal replied with a sniffle. "What else could it have been? It wasn't a rabbit."

She hugged him close, rubbing his back. "Well, it's over now. You needn't worry about it. If you ask me, it was The Great Lord showing his hand. Those boys attacked you, and Edis slew their mother for it."

Taking Betal by the hand, she stood—her smile broad and her eyes alight with joy. "Come on. Let's go for a walk. There's so much I must tell you about Father and Gate Hall." Her hair seemed afire from the light shining through the dirty windows behind her.

"All right." Betal wiped his tears and followed her out of the temple.

Three steps onto the Village Green, a group of boys, led by Cobb, came rushing around the corner of a house. "Murderer!" Cobb shouted.

Betal raised his hands "Cobb, enough. I had nothing to do with it."

"You had everything to do with it!" Spittle flew from Cobb's lips. "You, the priest, that bitch next to you; all of you are to blame!"

"Bitch?" Mangin said with more than a touch of malice and took a step toward Cobb. "You dare use that tone with me, peasant?" Her voice took on a crooning quality, and Betal saw her caress Chaos and direct it toward Cobb. "You've quite the nerve to speak to me so." As she sauntered up to him, she smiled wickedly. With a lick of her lips, she took a finger and grazed it along the underside of the large boy's chin. "It would be a shame to seal up such a lovely mouth."

Lucas rushed up behind her and struck her in the back of the head with a rock. Mangin crumpled to the ground like a puppet with its strings cut.

Betal screamed, "No!"

One boy slammed his fist into Betal's face, knocking him to the ground. He curled up in a ball as the rest kicked him mercilessly. Several blows to the head left him dazed, and a kick to the sternum had him gasping for breath.

"Help me." Mangin's faint cry carried over the screams and taunts of the boys. "Help me, Betal. Please, God, help me."

Betal desperately wanted to go to her aid, but he couldn't even help himself.

After a time, the kicks blessedly stopped. His mind in a daze, Betal thought it might all be over. But then someone turned him over on to his back. It was Lucas. The younger Cruchfield boy sat on Betal's chest and rained blows down upon his face. The world turned muffled and warbly, Betal's head spun, and his vision thinned by the time Lucas finally stopped hitting him. Through blood-filled eyes, Betal saw Lucas smiling down, his face filled with a mixture of malice and triumphant as he held a large rock over his head with both hands.

Betal laughed. Not about dying—he could do nothing to stop Lucas from crushing his skull, so it didn't matter. He laughed because he saw the thing for which he'd searched so long and hard. Through his third eye, a bright light pulsed, hammering like the heartbeat of God. He desperately wanted to touch that light, if only once, before he died. Time slowed as he reached for it, stretched with all his might. The light was so close. His mind strained from the pressure.

Please, God, he thought. *Please, just this once—*

The light grasped him, flooding into him with the force of a galactic tidal wave. It washed the world away, turning it white—burning everything in rapturous agony. Betal floated in a place of snowy wonder, a glowing universe where light flowed in vast rivers all around.

Oblivious to any other world that might exist, he wanted to explore his wondrous new existence, yet felt constrained, as though a weight lay upon his chest. He wanted to remove the burden, so he pushed.

John slumped in his favorite chair in his home near the Green. He stared into the fire burning low in the hearth, filled with worry and sorrow. He'd just helped bury his best friend's wife.

After interring Myrial, John saw murder in his friend's eyes. Erin blamed Betal for Myrial's death—if not directly, then by association. "See reason," John said. "Betal had nothing to do with it."

"Get away from me," Erin growled.

John sighed. "Go home, Erin. Go home and mourn with your boys."

Erin's eyes burned. "Ukase take you, John! You're a spineless, Chaos loving piece of dung. You've always protected that monster. Well, to the hells him and Chaos. He's your god. Not ours! I still believe in Ukase, and Order will one day prevail!" Tears flowed down his face, and he screamed.

The accusation stung. John was no lover of Chaos. The truth was he didn't know what to believe. He clasped his friend's shoulder. "I'm sorry, Erin. I truly am."

Erin spun about, shaking with clenched fists. He took deep breaths and calmed himself. After a few moments, he turned back to John. "No. I'm sorry. I didn't mean what I said."

"I know, Erin." They hugged each other tight. "I understand."

"You raised him as a son. As a father, I understand why you protect him. I'd do the same for my own boys." Yet resentment still burned heavy in Erin's eyes as they left the gravesite.

John sighed. "I hope I convince him not to do anything stupid." He then shook himself. "It's no good sitting here stewing." He needed to get to work—it helped clear his mind.

As he stood, the sound children fighting erupted from the Green. It was nothing new. They often fought for position, just as their parents did. But with the adults, it rarely came to blows. He became alarmed though when he heard Mangin, calling out to Betal for aid.

If those boys hurt her, there'll be bloody retribution.

He hastened out of his house and stopped in shock. Mangin lay on the ground, moaning, her face covered in blood, while Cobb knelt next to her, his face set with a wicked grin. Betal lay on the ground some fifteen feet away near the center of the Green, surrounded by the ruffians as they screamed in a murderous rage. Lucas sat on Betal's chest, his fists covered in blood, beating upon Betal's face.

John sprinted toward the fight. "Stop! Do you hear me? Stop it right now!"

John grew horrified as Lucas reached down and picked up a rock the size of his head. The boy raised it with both hands while Cobb exhorted him from afar. John sent a silent prayer to whoever would listen, pleading for them to stop the madness. But he knew it was futile as the rock descend toward Betal's face. John was about to watch his son die.

That's when The Lord of Chaos showed his hand.

A blinding flash of light, followed by a thunderous blast, sent John hurling back as if struck by a mammoth hammer. He hurled end over end like a rag doll until he succumbed to blackness.

When he came to, the world spun, his head rung, and his ears whined. He fought for breath as he opened his eyes to a blurry world, but when they cleared of tears, dust, and haze, he wished they hadn't.

The children lay about Betal in a wide circle, the closest being over ten feet away. Leaves scattered about the Green, stripped from a young stand of trees twenty feet away, along with many of their branches. The doors and window shutters from nearby houses were torn off their hinges. Even the grass lay flat in a ring about Betal. The children groaned and cried. All accept Betal and Lucas.

Betal lay as before, bloody and beaten, but smiling, with a curious look as if he heard something he didn't quite understand.

Lucas, on the other hand, lay sprawled not far away, a charred hunk of twisted flesh from the waist up. What remained of his head—now facing John—lolled away from the body with his throat torn open, like a green twig snapped in half with only the bark keeping it together. Lucas's hair had been singed away, his eyes burned out of their sockets, and his lips scorched off, exposing blackened, cracked teeth.

John rolled over and retched.

Chapter 8
The Ghost of Death

(Year 512 -R.C.-)

Something clasped the nape of his neck as the deep forest trees rolled by like waves on the water. Anxiety filled whoever held him.

His ears wilted. *She's really angry with me this time.*

The forest stopped moving, and whatever held him, let go. He landed on all fours, his large paws easily cushioning the drop into the leaves. He danced about and gave himself a shake that traveled all the way down his black-furred body to his tail.

The large white wolf stalked towards the opening of a den beneath a downed tree. A black wolf lay at the opening of the den with its belly torn open. In its jaws was a chunk of gray-colored flesh, with gray-white fur that stank of rot. Dirt, mud, and blood lay scattered all about. The bodies of pups littered the ground, their bodies torn and crushed. Whatever attacked them didn't do it for food, but merely for the thrill of killing.

The white wolf lifted its head and howled in anguish.

Betal bolted upright out of the dream filled with an overwhelming sense of grief and loss. The dream faded as his head burst in pain.

It'd been three days since the *incident* and Betal's swollen face and body still ached. He thought about that day, pictured his brush with a greater power. In his mind's eye, he saw the veil lifting, exposing the most beautiful light in all of creation. He remembered how it flowed through his veins like rivers of fire, and seeped into his bones—power, pure and sweet. It was as if a something tore a heavy gauze from his senses, laying bare the entirety of creation. He'd never felt more alive.

Groaning, he put a hand to his head. The light still burned, only dimmer, and it no longer called to him. When he tried to touch it, it felt like putting his hand through shards of broken glass. It frustrated him to no end.

Shouts erupted from outside the window, as though the entire village had gathered out front in the Green, haggling over something. With a groan, he sat up and turned so his feet were on the floor. The world wobbled and pulsed. Taking a deep breath, he stood, needing to grab the headboard to steady himself. When the world stopped spinning, he slowly made his way to the window overlooking the Village Green.

It really looks like the entire village is out there, he thought.

The villagers were split into two groups. The smaller, led by his father, stood with their backs to the temple, barring anyone from entering it, while the village elder, Victor Cargo, headed the much larger group. Standing on the Old Stump at the edge of the Green, he exhorted the crowd, gesturing dramatically.

Betal cracked open the window.

"I said, step aside," the elder shouted, strong and loud, belying his feeble bearing. "You'll not stop us! We don't want to harm you, but we will if you force us to." He turned back to the crowd, urging them on again. "We must kill the beast now, while he's weak! Kill him and rid the world of the demon!"

The mob screamed louder, shaking their spears, axes, and bows—some even held hoes and scythes. However, the men standing with his father, many of which were armed members of the militia, stood fast.

Surprisingly, Betal couldn't find Erin Cruchfield among either group. "I guess he decided to sit this one out."

"Give over, Victor," Betal's father shouted back. "No good can come of this. You'll bring Chaos down on all our heads. You'll curse us all." He pointed back toward the temple. "Do you think Dithiyar will just forgive and forget? I guarantee you he won't look aside if you go through with this."

"We'll rid ourselves of all of them," the old man shouted back. "That pathetic priest can't stop us all! And the bitch is unconscious! We'll kill them all and burn this cursed place down!"

Betal chewed his lip. He was in no shape to protect himself. And if Mangin was still unconscious, the elder was right. Dithiyar would do nothing to stop them. In fact, the old priest was most likely on his horse, halfway to Cross Corners. He needed to get Mangin and himself out of there without detection. But how?

Hoping no one saw him open the window, Betal took a step back but glimpsed something near the back of the crowd with his third eye—a slight ripple in the air at the edge of the last house bordering the Green. Against his better judgment, Betal returned to the window for a better look. At first, he suspected it was Dithiyar, trying to make his escape. But the longer he looked, the more he doubted it. The shape was simply too big. When the Chaos cloaked figure moved into the open, away from the houses, Betal got a better look. The shape was that of a massive man upon an equally massive horse.

He gasped. "Hogar."

The Ghost of Death had finally made an appearance, and it didn't bode well for the people of Cool Winds.

The paladin ghosted his way between the gathered people— the few he bumped muttered and looked about in confusion. He came to a stop directly behind Victor just as the old man reached the peak of his vitriol.

"Out of the way now, all of you," the boney old man shouted. "I've had enough. We'll kill you all and throw your bodies into the fire to show your *God* what we really think of him!"

"Will you now?" Hogar's rumbling, malevolent voice echoed off the surrounding buildings.

The gathered people screamed and then went deathly quiet.

Hogar uncloaked himself, encased the village elder in Chaos, and lifted the old man several feet to look him in the eyes. The paladin wasn't wearing his helm, and his eyes glowed a hellish red. "That would be interesting to see. I've never seen sheep with teeth so sharp and willing to bite."

The village elder shook, unable to speak. But he could piss himself.

"No," Hogar went on. "I don't think you'll harm your shepherd. Dithiyar may be a fool, but you are still his flock." He then cast his gaze at the rest of the villagers, sending shivers through the crowd. "It would appear it has been too long since your dear priest sheared his sheep." He drew a long, dead black dagger from his belt. "I shall now remedy that." Hogar then meticulously shaved off the old man's clothing, exposing his bone-white, splotchy skin. The old man's scant body hair, as white as that on his head, glowed in the sun.

Shivering, the old man lost control of his bowels. With shit and piss running down his legs, he finally found his voice. "Please, my Lord," Victor squeaked. "No more! I implore you. Have mercy. I repent my blasphemy. I do. I swear I do!"

Hogar smiled, his skin looking like gray leather stretched over a sharp, angular stone. "I'm sure you do. But I'm not done shearing you." The paladin raised his dagger once more and slowly flayed the man's skin from his body.

Howls of agony filled the Green as skin, blood, and shit piled up on the ground. The villagers screamed in horror. Those who didn't run were too busy vomiting or had fainted. Betal wasn't immune to the scene. He trembled, his eyes wide and his breath ragged as Hogar, with a smile on his face, slowly removed every inch of skin from the old man—the very picture of a man going about the job he dearly loved. After removing every inch of skin below the neck, Hogar dropped the remains of the old man, and rode his horse around to the back of the temple.

Betal, in a state of shock, stared at the bloody pile of offal. He jumped when his door opened and Hogar entered the room.

"Hello, Betal. How is our star pupil doing today?" The paladin's voice held none of the malice it had down on the Green. In fact, he sounded quite pleasant. "Come, lad. Come away from the window. Let me have a look at you." Hogar smiled, his red eyes beaming with pride, like a father beholding his favored son as Betal approached.

Betal shakily stepped into the middle of the room, his shock wearing off, but not his fear or his weakness. "Hello, Master Hogar. How are you this day?" He had difficulty keeping his voice steady. "That was an interesting… um… display you put on out there." Betal knew Hogar was chief of those who saw great things in his future. He hoped that never changed, considering what had just transpired.

"That was nothing." Hogar waved his hand dismissively. "They'll not bother you again, I'm sure. Enough of this. Sit down, boy." Hogar waved at his bed as he grabbed the large padded chair at Betal's study desk. It groaned under his massive weight when he sat. "So how are you feeling? How are your studies going?"

"I'm feeling much better," Betal lied. "I'm sure I'll be fine in a day or two."

He told Hogar of his struggles in his studies and how he'd used Hogar's cloaking spell to escape the boys earlier. "I considered using it in the woods. It worked almost perfectly with the villagers, but I realized it would never work against a grunkin or another magic user."

With a frown, Hogar tilted his head. "Why do you say that?"

"Well, the texts say grunkin can sense the Lord's Breath."

"That's very rare. Most are simply too mad to care about anything. Personally, I doubt it's possible."

"Why?" Betal asked. "I saw you on the Green when you were cloaked. Why wouldn't a grunkin be able to?"

The paladin's eyebrow cocked. "You can see others manipulate Chaos?"

Betal nodded. "Yes, sir."

"Not just during training?" Hogar asked with a smile.

"No, sir. Always." Betal frowned. "Should I not be able to?"

"No, you most certainly should not." Hogar chuckled.

Betal's eyes widened and his jaw dropped.

Hogar continued. "To see it during training is one thing, when a student and master are in sync, but it's very rare for someone to see the ether being influenced. It's a rare talent that will suit you well." He tilted his head. "So, you are having trouble with the higher focus?"

"Yes, sir." Betal lowered his head. "I can't seem to grasp it no matter how hard I try."

"Give it time, son. You can do it. I know you can." Hogar's smile shone with confidence.

"I don't know." Betal shook his head. "Maybe it's all a mistake? Maybe I'm not meant to be a higher user?"

Hogar leaned forward in the chair, causing it to creak severely. "What you did to those boys was no minor feat. Few in the world could have done that. And none, not even Lord Heartless himself, could at your age." The paladin waved his hand. "Hells boy. I was a hundred miles away when I felt you unleash that."

Betal scowled. "All I did was push him. I didn't mean to kill him."

"You 'pushed him' with pure power. You didn't caress or cajole it. You didn't turn it into something tangible, like lightning of fire. You tapped into the very essence of the Lord and unleashed it on the boy's face."

Betal still had his doubts. He explained how it felt to duplicate what he'd seen and felt.

"The Lord's Breath is treacherous, my boy. It affects everyone differently. Don't worry. You'll figure it out." Nodding, Hogar smiled. "And when you do, it'll be like dipping your hands in pure ecstasy. You'll never want to let it go."

They talked for a few more minutes. Hogar then left him with a pat on the shoulder and a smile. Betal stood there for a few moments, trying to take it all in. *How could someone so brutish and cruel act so benevolent?*

Shaking his head at the thought, he immediately regretted it. With a groan, he leaned up against his bedpost, and put a hand to his head, waiting for the pain to subside. Once he felt better, he heaved himself up with the bedpost then gingerly made his way into the hall and down to Mangin's room. After lightly knocking on the door, he wasn't surprised by the response.

"Go! The hells! Away," Mangin yelled on the other side. "I told you, old man, leave me alone, and let me sleep!"

"It's Betal."

"Oh, I'm sorry. Come in, come in."

As he opened the door, his fellow acolyte scooched into a sitting position in bed, causing her white nightshirt to fall open in front. He did his best not to stare, so he focused on her face. She had a large bandage about her head, causing her hair to puff out the top like a scarlet bush. The bandage seemed clean and fresh.

"How are you feeling?" Stepping into the room, he went to her bedside.

"Like someone cracked my head open with a rock," she said with a mixture of chagrin and amusement. "You look like a mule kicked you in the face." She smiled, but it faded as she continued. "If you've lost that pretty face after the swelling goes down, I'll have those mules skinned."

"Too late." He described Hogar's appearance and actions out on the Green.

She sneered. "Oh. I do wish I could have seen that."

The look on her face, combined with his recollection of the scene, sent a shudder through Betal.

Mangin laughed. "Don't be such a priss. His actions may not have been subtle—not that anyone would ever call Hogar subtle—but I'm willing to bet they'll be effective. They'll not try a stunt like that again in our lifetime." A frown crept across her face. "I wonder why he didn't come to see me."

Hogar's voice boomed from the door. "Oh, but I have, my dear."

Chapter 9
Glennen

(Year 514 -R.C.-)

"I know what you're thinking, mister." His mother glanced at him over her needlework." So, don't even try it."

"But, Mom." Ellis huffed, furrowing his brows as he peered out the front of the wagon at Glennen's high stonewalls. Unlike past cities, Glennen beckoned to him. He scowled at the floor. "I'm ten; not two. Why can't I work the crowd just like the others?"

"I know very well how old you are, but you're still too little. You might get hurt." She put down her work. "I know you feel put-upon, my dear, but it's for your own good."

"But the others make fun of me and complain I don't do my share." He often felt ostracized by the other kids in the troupe. None of them were quite his age—they were all at least five years older than him, or a couple of years younger. It frustrated him to no end. "And, besides, I'm not that little. Everyone keeps telling me I look big for my age."

His mother's eyes took on a keen look of displeasure. "*Who has been telling you this?*"

He lowered his head and pouted, putting his hands in his lap.

"Ellis, you tell me right this minute, or so help me…" Setting her needlework aside, she stood with her hands on her hips.

"Villagers," he mumbled.

"Damn it, Ellis!" she yelled. "How many times have we told you not to talk to any outsiders? You know they're not to be trusted. You don't see the other children blathering with them, do you? No!" She took a deep breath. "I swear, boy, I'm starting to think we are going to have to lock you in here till you come to your senses."

Tears welled up in his eyes. "You are going to lock me in?"

She scowled. "No. It hasn't come to that yet. Not *yet*."

Sighing, she took his face in her hand. "I love you, son. We all do. But you are a sick child, and you know it."

"But I can't even remember the last time I had a fit."

Her eyes held skepticism. "No? Well, I can. And I won't risk you having another."

He pouted even harder from his lie. He'd experienced two fainting spells within the last six months. Three months earlier, he froze in place while stepping into the wagon at bedtime. As with every spell, he felt a sudden dizziness, a severe feeling of vertigo that quickly turned into a half-waking dream.

As usual, he saw a massive white conical spire, hundreds of feet high, flickering between ghostly mist and granite-like reality. The tower shone bright as though encased in glass. It seemed so real he felt like he could reach out and touch it even though it didn't exist.

But the most recent dream was different. A week before, he dreamt of a dirt-covered girl with long brown hair, standing next to a massive shaggy black dog. The girl was pretty, but she had a strange, sad look in her eyes—eyes that changed color from one moment to the next.

He told no one about these dreams. They scared him, feeling far too real, like the memories of things he'd not yet experienced.

His mother walked back to her knitting. "We don't know what causes these fits of yours – not yet, anyway. I know they're little more than fainting spells, but that first one almost killed you. And until I find the cause, you're not to get out of my sight."

Crestfallen, he sighed, knowing he lost his chance to get out. Then an idea came to him. "Mother, can I do my studies with Mister Whisp?"

His mother gave him a stern look. "All right. I doubt He'll be doing any shows here. So, I'm sure he'll have the time."

With a grin, Ellis dashed out the back door.

"But I want you to go straight there, you hear me?" she yelled behind him.

Whisp was the troupe's hedge mage. Apart from being a minor conqueror of magic and illusions, he was also the only one in the troupe who knew how to read and write—something his mother pressed Ellis to learn.

The hedge mage's blue and black painted wagon lay close by, in a direct line of sight from his own. Ellis sprinted around the red and black painted wagon of Loma, the Fire-breather, whose stage stuck out some five feet where it attached to his wagon. He dodged several members of the troupe and ran up the old man's steps.

Upon reaching the top, he shot a look back to his family's wagon. True to her word, his mother was leaning out the door, eyeing him. Ellis turned back and knocked on Whisp's door with a smile. He loved the moons, comets, and stars covering the old man's wagon.

"Who is it, and what do you want?" the old man called from within.

"It's Ellis. Mom wants me to do my studies." Once the old man bid him enter, he waved to his mother and dashed inside.

Whisp lounged in one of his two large, padded chairs along the wall that opened out to form his stage. A pair of candleholders protruded from the sides of the chair to illuminate his reading. With his windows closed, he had a few scattered candles, causing the room to smell of smoke, beeswax, and incense, to light the dark interior.

He Lowered his book and waved to Ellis. "And how are you doing today, my fine young man?" A large smile split his wide, weathered face, and his piercing blue eyes, beamed through long, curly gray hair. "So your mother figures you're over your latest episode enough to come spend time with this lonely old soul, eh? Well, bless her."

Ellis changed what he was going to say. "Aren't you going to perform, Master Whisp?"

The elderly man quirked his mouth. "I don't do shows near the cities, my boy."

"Why?"

"They'll be Chaos priests in the city. And I don't want to draw their attention."

"Why?"

"They don't like me."

Ellis shook his head. "Why?"

Whisp growled a little. "You're not going to let this go, are you?"

He blew out a puff of air, causing his long whiskers to wave. "Well, you see, priests tend to find us hedge mages… contemptible. They often abuse us when the mood struck them, which is quite often."

"Enough talk of priests." He waved Ellis to take the other padded chair. "So, what book would you like to learn from today?" He pointed to the books in the case built into the opposite side of his wagon. "There's pre-war history: the legend of the dragon lying beneath the 'Great Swamp Sea.' I know! How about, 'The Tales of the Elves of Talendor?' It's quite fascinating. Or, better yet…" He stood and pulled out a large, dusty tome. "How about, 'Tales of The True Tree, The Mother of All Creation?' I acquired it only a few days ago. It cost me a pretty penny, too. Books from before The Great War—before the Time of Chaos—are scarce."

The last one made Ellis pause. *The Mother of Creation?* It pulled at him, but he dashed it from his mind. He had big plans today and wanted to throw the old man. He needed to come up with a book Whisp hadn't heard of. That way, he'd be able to tell Whisp he had it back in his wagon—something his father just bought. Then instead of going back home, he'd be able to make his escape. It was flawless!

"Do you have anything about a land covered in darkness with a great white tower covered in mist, but still shines like glass?" He grinned, knowing Whisp couldn't have a book about something he'd dreamt up.

The old man's face soured. "Where did you hear about that tower?"

When Ellis didn't answer, Whisp became agitated. He clenched his fists, his face a thunderhead. "I asked you where you heard about it, boy. Answer me!"

He shrunk in on himself and lied, "From one of the guards."

Jumping to his feet, Whisp bellowed, "Don't give me that! Who told you about the Tower of Time?"

He grabbed Ellis by the arm in a painful grip. "I must know who told you! Our lives may hang in the balance!"

Shaking, Ellis squeaked out the truth. "It's not real, I swear! I saw it in a dream!"

The old man's eyes grew wide. He let go of Ellis and took a step back, his mouth agape.

Ellis sprinted for the door, flinging it open. He scampered down the steps and ran. But, he didn't run home. Instead, he made for the nearest gap in the circle of wagons, not caring if anyone saw him. He just wanted to get away.

He dashed out of their camp and into the maze of others camped about the city walls. Ducking between two tents, he slammed into a large man in the dirty brown clothes of a woodsman. He bounced to his right and continued on, heedless of the man's screams behind him. He tripped and stumbled over tent lines. After crashing through a line of people waiting for food, he dodged a man on horseback—causing the animal to scream and sending its rider to the ground—and then weaved through a herd of sheep.

Yet, he saw none of it. He saw only a glowing white tower in a sea of blackness, a tower from his fevered dreams, a tower that couldn't possibly exist. Yet, from the way the old man reacted...

After a while, he slowed and stopped, panting hard, drawing fearful, ragged breaths. Running wasn't good for him. He needed to calm down and think, but it proved difficult with his heart pounding in his chest and his mind still racing.

How could it be real? Why did Whisp react that way? What does it mean?

He stood in the middle of the road, shivering and staring at the ground where a swarm of red ants ate a small lizard. "What's wrong with me?" he mumbled.

Ellis gave himself a shake and looked about, realizing he didn't know where he was. He put the fears of the tower aside and took a deep, calming breath—he needed to decide what to do next. "I can't go back. Mom'll lock me up for sure."

A strong gust of wind tousled his blond hair as he stared at the high, bright-white city walls. He'd wanted to get away, to get his look at the city, and this would be his only chance. He was going to catch hell for today regardless, so he figured he might as well make the best of it. Turning, he raced for the city gate he saw through a gap in some ramshackle shacks.

A river of people—comprising mostly dirty people afoot, with a few carts and wagons—flowed toward the open gates. Once in the flow, he reached the city gates in short time. Jostled in the thickened crowd right before the gate, he avoided being trampled while staring at the high, stucco coated, stone wall. Up close, he saw the wall was actually in rather poor shape. From afar, it appeared pristine, but now the cracks and breaks were clear. Parts of the wall were crumbling, despite the multiple layers of stucco trying to hold it together.

Once he was through the open, steel-bound gates, passing several crossing streets and alleys, the crowd scattered into the city, allowing him to step aside and decide what to do first. Picking a direction, Ellis wandered about the city at random. He kept to the streets, avoiding the dark and narrow alleys stinking of shit, piss, and death. He gawked at his surroundings, marveling at the tall wooden buildings as he wandered, wondering why they swayed back and forth. The sound made him want to cover his ears, a raucous mixture of people and animals that bounced all about, confusing his senses. And the smell—he didn't know *what* to make of it. It was like the city walls bottled up the entire world's collection of dust, smoke, and feculence. Not that anyone seemed to notice as they ambled about, shopping at the small stalls and carts lining the streets.

"How can they stand the stink?"

"They're used to it," a woman said behind him.

Ellis spun and his eyes went wide—woman's age surprised him. By her voice, he thought her young, but she looked old, much older than his mum. Gray, stringy hair hung out of a faded bonnet, and her dress was so tattered it looked to be little more than rags.

"How can that be?" he asked.

"Well, when you're around somethin' long enough, you get used to it." She shifted the large sack on her back with a greasy smile. "You surely not from round here. Where you from?" The woman had a darkness about her as though she stood in shadow.

He shied away. "My troupe's camped outside."

Her smile slipped. "Troupe? You're a Traveler?"

When he nodded, she took a step back. "Great Lord, forgive me. I didn't know."

She placed a trembling hand before her face. "You shouldn't be here alone. City's not safe for one as little as you, if you don't know it. Run along now, lest someone try doin' something to you without knowin' better. Go on now, shoo." She shuffled off, nearly tripping in her haste.

Ellis distanced himself from the woman and dashed off, delving deeper into the city. He kept to the larger streets heading toward the center. The woman may have frightened him, but he wasn't about to go back yet.

He passed a large crossing street where the road changed from dirt to cobblestone. Once he reached the building on the other side, he glanced up. The buildings were stone rather than wood, much taller, and sturdier, each one plastered white or painted in bright colors. It reminded him of their own wagons, only not as cheery. Lightly trafficked, everyone seemed to overflow with wealth. The smells were far less foul as well—a pleasant mixture of cooking food, incense, and the smell of salt from the ocean filled the air. He loved it. He loved it all. The beauty and variety titillated his senses.

He lost track of time on those cobbled streets. Some folk gave him odd looks, and others yelled at him to be on his way when he stopped to peer in windows, but to most, he seemed beneath notice. Few children—none anywhere near his age—walked about on their own. As he thought about it, he'd seen *no* children his age. Everyone was either much younger or much older. *I wonder why that is?*

Relaxing, Ellis slowed his pace, doing his best to take in the splendor. Just before passing yet another stone building, he saw an open, cobblestone space. On the far side, lay a huge building, shining with every hue imaginable in the late-morning sun. Its domed roofs and tower tops sparkled in gold, silver, copper, and bronze. It was both the most beautiful and garish thing he'd ever seen.

He sprinted toward the building for a better look, dodging around a gaggle of women with brightly plumed hats, he ran right into the back of a middling sized man in bright, multihued robes. He bounced off and tumbled to the ground, bruising his seat in the process.

"What the hells?" Upon whirling around, the man's piercing black eyes examined Ellis through long, jet black hair. His hard-angled face held a cruel snarl. "What's the meaning of this, you filthy urchin? Do you have any idea who I am, boy?"

The man's mouth took on a wicked, twisted smile. "Perhaps the dogs would like a new play toy?"

Blood drained from Ellis's face, his breath seized, and his heart skipped a beat. He scrambled backward on his hands and feet. This man was evil. He didn't know why, he simply knew it to be true.

The man's smile melted, and he stared harder, hatred filling his eyes. "How old are you, boy?"

Terror raced through Ellis's soul. With a yelp, he jumped to his feet, turned, and sprinted back down the street he'd come from, dashing in front of a fast moving carriage. The driver yelled, and the horses whinnied, their hooves clacking on the cobbles. Then came a loud snap. The whinnies turned into screams, followed by a crash. Ellis ignored it and ran.

Reaching a small, nearby alley, he turned without looking back. He sprinted down the alley, twisting this way and that, his feet pounding the cobblestones, as his arms pumped, his heart slammed, and his lungs labored. The alley opened out to a smaller street where he took a quick left. He'd no idea where he was going. He only knew he needed to get away. He dashed down alleys and streets until reaching the poorer section of the city where his running slowed. He simply couldn't keep up such a frantic pace while dodging through the crowd.

Upon exiting one of the smaller dirt streets, the great, white wall loomed above the buildings to his left. Headed toward it, but found he couldn't get there directly—most of the streets in the poor section didn't seem to run in straight lines, they turned and twisted like the alleys. He made his way to the gate as indirectly as possible, zigzagging back and forth, and making turns leading him back to the city.

As he neared the wall, the street dead-ended, forcing him to take an alley. Having regained some of his breath, he sprinted down the dark, narrow passage. Things squished and popped beneath his feet, giving off the most horrid smells. He didn't care. He just kept running.

Finally, he burst onto the main street and saw the gate to his right—the traffic seeming lighter than when he'd entered. He raced for the gate, ducking between a pair of guards questioning the driver of a heavily laden wagon. The guards cursed at him as he sped by. Once out of the city, he ran another hundred yards where he came to a stop, panting while doubled over in exhaustion.

This is the last time, he swore to himself. *I'll never leave the wagons again.* He didn't know how many times in the past he'd made that same oath, but he told himself he'd hold to it this time.

Taking a quick guess as to the direction of the camp, he paused. He was going to catch hell for running off, and needed to find a way to sneak back to the camp, then duck beneath one of the wagons. "I'll just tell them I fell asleep there and lost track of time."

Short of breath, he straightened and looked toward the cam. His heart sank. Some hundred yards off, both Dirge and his father sprinted toward him. His father's red hair whipped as he ran, his face filled with worry. While Dirge, on the other hand, looked ready to chew nails.

With a sense of foreboding, Ellis stared toward them, but a hand grabbed him by his shoulder from behind.

"There you are, my little imp," said a man in a high, piping voice as he spun Ellis about.

Ellis's jaw dropped. It was the man from the city.

"Don't look so surprised." The man's eyes squinted slightly while a sneer spread across his lips. "You certainly weren't a local boy, by the look of you, and that meant there's only one way for you to go—you don't look like a ship rat, after all.

The man's eyes took on a somewhat dreamy look as he continued. "Now, what should I do with you? You made me quite cross back there. I actually snapped that horse's leg in half while trying to snare you. But then, my dander isn't as high now.

He tilted his head. "The truth be told, I'm more fascinated than angry. You were both quick and smart to run the way you did. And that means you've potential." He held up his free hand to his lips. "But potential for what?

The man's black eyes took on an evil glint again. "I think I'll still give you to the hounds. I'm sure you can give them quite a chase, and they need the exercise. And who knows, if you live through it, it just might prove you're meant for greater things." The man cut his cackle short, his smile slipping as he raised his head to peer over Ellis.

"Please, good priest," Ellis's father yelled from behind him. "Whatever it is my son did, I'm sure it wasn't meant to be disrespectful."

When his father and Dirge ran up, his father's statement struck. Dennis quivered. *He's a priest?* He gave his father a pleading look but didn't get much in the way of comfort. Dread filled his father's face. The swordsman's face, on the other hand, was hard as an anvil, his eyes firming with determination as he rested a hand on the sword-hilt at his side.

"This one, he is yours?" the priest asked. When his father nodded, the priest continued. "Tell me, why should I let you have him back?"

His father placed his right hand upon Dirge's sword arm without taking his eyes of the priest. "Please. We are Travelers and have only just arrived. We would be more than happy to perform for you whenever and wherever you wished.

His eyes shot to Ellis and then returned to the priest. "I'm sure my boy would be happy to serve you and yours during our exhibition. But, please, I beg of you, let him come back to us during the interim."

Relief flooded Ellis when the man let go of his shoulder.

"You're Travelers? Wonderful!" The priest threw his arms wide. "The Lord does so love your kind. And I do as well." Stepping back, he raised his head even higher, staring down his nose at his father. "But I must decline. I have much more important things to do.

The priest's eyes went back to Ellis. With a smile, he placed his hand on Ellis's head. "For one who is so small, I do find you fascinating." He plucked a couple of hairs from Ellis's head.

"Until we meet again." The man then whirled about and headed back toward the city gates.

Ellis looked to his father. "I'm sorry—"

Ellis didn't get a chance to finish his apology as his father met Dirge's eyes and nodded. He then grabbed Ellis by the hand and ran to the wagons. Tired as he was, Ellis had difficulty keeping up with his father while Dirge sprinted ahead. When they reached the rest of the troupe, he heard the large man-at-arms yelling, while everyone rushed about.

His mother sprinted up with a mixture of fear, anger, and questioning in her eyes.

"A priest," his father said.

With a gasp, his mother seized Ellis's hand.

"To your wagons," his father yelled. "We leave in a quarter of an hour. Anyone not ready by then, we leave behind."

Many questioned his father, but when they saw Ellis being ushered toward their wagon by his mother, their faces took on a look of determination. They set upon the task of leaving.

As Ellis climbed into their wagon, Dirge ran up to his father. "Where are we going?"

His father hesitated. "North. Far north. We make for The Reach. We've plenty of coin and supplies to get us there. It's said Chaos's influence is weak there. Quickly now. I fear we've little time."

Ellis heard no more as his mom pushed him into the wagon, slamming the door behind them.

Chapter 10
The Lord
Delivers

(Year 514 -R.C.-)

Calidos Flint quickly made his way back to the temple. He'd considered taking the child with him but thought better of it. There was no need raising the ire of The Lord, who had an affinity for the Travelers. They were the epitome of the good things he bestowed upon the land, presenting joy, creativity, and freedom wherever they traveled, and it pleased The Lord greatly. Moreover, those who trespassed against any mirth-maker often suffered terribly for it.

Only a month before, he witnessed a member of the city guard kill a local poet. The poet had been screwing the guardsman's woman, and she told him the guard was less than well endowed. The poet made a song of it: *The mighty-mighty man with the wee-wee willy.* He played his new song to all who entered through the city gate that day, and in a fit of rage, the guardsman killed him with his own lyre.

Calidos remembered laughing at the irony of the poet's death. He also laughed because he knew the whims of The Great Lord were often cruel. And on that day, it proved he could be swift as well. The guard didn't even have time to wipe the blood from his hands when a large piece of the wall broke loose and crushed his skull.

Besides, Calidos didn't need to bring the child back to find out more about him. A small part would suffice. Asan Dent—a fellow priest specializing at delving objects—was in residence at the temple. Many said he was the best in the world. But then, Asan was the one making that claim.

Let's see just how good you are, he thought.

As Calidos entered the temple, he scowled. He hated that building. Calidos had been stuck there for the past three years. Hannibal, The Lord High Priest of the whole of the southern continent, had called him to heel for continuing his search for the only child to escape his grasp.

Hannibal had said, "It's unnatural to pursue something for so long, and speaks of a dedication that is unbecoming."

How dare the pompous ass speak to him that way? He was only doing what The Great Lord called upon him to do. So now, he wallowed in that worthless city, barred from doing The Lord's bidding.

But, no matter, he'd moved on. He was a vessel of The Lord of Chaos, so if something struck his fancy it must be something The Lord wanted him to see. The boy was a puzzle, and Calidos dearly loved puzzles.

Calidos made his way up the marble stairs and through the temple's large colorful double doors. Making his way deep into the fortress, he fidgeted at his favorite robe—a mixture of reds, yellows, and blues, it make him think of fire—while his shoes made soft whisking sounds on the multihued tiles. On the fourth floor, he went to Asan's apartments. With no glyphs on the door indicating Asan wanted privacy, Calidos entered.

Slouched at his writing desk like a sticky wet sack of suet, Asan's rotund body overflowed his voluminous robes. His greasy hair looked as if he'd soaked it in butter, and the room smelled of feet and body odor, making Calidos wrinkle his nose in disgust. He doubted the man ever partook in the baths.

The only time his body sees water is when he gets lost walking in the rain, Calidos thought. The man rarely left his rooms.

Asan looked up from the papers on his desk. He blinked at Calidos as though not sure if what he saw was real. "Calidosh Flint, is that you?" His voice garbled as though his tongue fought with his cheeks. "I must shay, I've not seen you in quite shome time."

"What can I do for you? I'm sure you're not here on a social visit. Not that anyone ever is," he finished, somewhat under his breath, his jowls wobbling as he shook his head.

Taking the few strands of the child's hair out of his pouch, Calidos handed them over. "What can you tell me about this person?"

"As abrupt as ever." The fat priest eyed Calidos's hand with a measure of uncertainty mixed with curiosity. With a shrug, he took the hair and rolled them into a ball with the stubby thumb and forefinger of his right hand. He closed his eyes in concentration. "Hum... human, male... in good health..." Tilting his head to the side, he arched an eyebrow. "He has the potential to be quite powerful." His eyes opened and locked on Calidos. "There is much this one could do. If you were to bring him in and teach him the ways of The Lord, I believe he'd do well."

"Powerful, you say?" Calidos paused. "Interesting. He didn't look like much."

"Truly?" Asan smiled knowingly. "Then why seek me out at all? There must have been something."

Calidos nodded. There *was* something else nagging at him. But what? "Is there anything else you can tell me?"

Asan again closed his eyes. "Well, he originally resided in the northwest—somewhere near the frontier. The only other thing I can read is—" The fat priest's eyes grew wide. "This boy shouldn't be alive. He's twelve years old."

Cursing, Calidos dashed out the room. *How could I've been such a fool?!* He'd been looking for the little bastard for years, and The Lord delivered him up like dinner on a platter.

Calidos sprinted toward the guardsmen sector. He needed to gather men, and ride. There was no way the troupe still sat outside the gates—they'd know Calidos would discover the truth. As he reached the first floor, he headed toward the back of the citadel. A short distance ahead, he saw a dust-covered ranger, apparently returning from a patrol. "You, stop!"

The man eyed Calidos through hooded brows. His shoulders slumped and his face sagged as though he longed for bed. "Yes, sir?"

"Fetch me a squad of your best and have them meet me in the stables at once. Then, I need you to find a tracker named of Jantos. He lives up on the third floor somewhere. Have him meet me there as well. We're going on a hunt that may take some time, so have everyone pack accordingly."

Without looking back, Calidos headed straight for his apartments to fetch his own traveling gear. "You're not going to slip away from me this time, you little spawn of Ukase," he cursed as he ran. After ten years, he'd finally be able to fulfill The Lord's call.

He arrived in the stables less than half an hour later, happy to see thirty men awaited him—several of whom he'd ridden with on his crusade. His good mood soured when he realized Jantos wasn't among them.

"He wasn't in his rooms," the ranger said.

"Find him! I don't care where you look or who you have to disturb. You find him and bring him here at *once*."

Two hours passed before the tracker showed up with a glib look on his face.

Calidos raged. "Where the Hells have you been? So help me, Jantos, if your delay has let this child slip through my fingers again, you'll not live to see the morning!"

Sighing, the tracker shook his head. "Where I was, is not of your concern, Calidos. You're no longer my superior. I'm here as a favor to you. Nothing more."

Calidos's anger rose even higher. He felt his skin tingling as his inner fire neared its peak. Taking a deep breath, he moderated his tone. "Yes, Jantos. You are no longer under my command. But just remember that my failure in culling this child in the first place is your failure as well. Hannibal knows this."

"Calidos, we both know the High Priest doesn't give two shits about this child. You must learn to temper yourself. What will happen, will happen as The Lord dictates." He held out his hand. "Now, do you have something of his for me to sample?"

Calidos handed him the remaining pieces of hair.

Jantos smiled broadly. "Excellent. This will do wonderfully." Sniffing the hair, he rolled it into a ball between his hands. Jantos then directed Chaos into his hands, focusing it on the little ball of hair until it burst in smoke. The tracker inhaled the smoke, closed his eyes, and concentrated.

Smiling, he opened his eyes. "Yes. The residue is quite strong. I'll have no problem following the boy's trail. Worry not, my friend. We'll have him in hand before the day is done."

Chapter 11
Death Comes

(Year 514 -R.C.-)

Pots clanked in the cupboard as the wagon bumped and rattled through the tall grass of the open plane. Ellis rocked back and forth and bounced about in the back, filled with a sense of foreboding. Doom approached like a swift and savage storm. And it was his fault. For some reason, that man in the city didn't like his father, and Ellis let him right to them.

He glanced up at his father in the driver's seat, not knowing what to say. Turning to his mother, he quivered at her cold eyes as she chewed her bottom lip. "Momma, I am sorry for—"

"Don't you dare speak," she snapped. "I've told you—*we've* told you, time and again, to stay with the wagons! And what do you do? You run off like an addlebrained fool! Didn't you even *think* there might be a reason we told you to stay out of sight?" She threw up her hands in disgust. "Of course not! You just run off and do as you please!"

He sat back in a huff. It wasn't fair! They always told him to stay close because of his being *sickly*. How was he supposed to know there was more to it? But he didn't dare bring that up. He'd just end up across her knee again. His bottom still smarted, and he didn't want to add to it.

A horse galloped up. "Cord," Dirge called out.

"What news?" his father asked.

"Riders, coming hard from the city." His gravelly voice held urgency. "Two dozen at least, and it looks like a priest is amongst them."

Ellis quivered as the dread in his heart grew, pressing down on him like an anvil. His eyes rolled into the back of his head, and he fell to the floor, his arms flailing. As the fit overtook him, Ellis didn't experience the usual waking dream. This was as stark and clear as waking life—a vision of blood and destruction, and the end of all he knew. "Death comes! Death comes! Death comes!"

His world was ending. He saw it in his mind: oceans of blood surrounding the men following them. The men pursued him, not his father, but *him*. Chaos swirled around the man leading their charge—the man from the city. Chaos was fast approaching—coming to kill him.

His mother and father yelled, but he couldn't tell what. He was lost in his vision and fear. The wagon stopped, and the voices of the members of the troupe added to the din, but they were but a dream to him. Only *that man* existed, and the swirling essence surrounding him.

Someone lifted him off the floor, hugging and whispered to him, but he heard none of it. They placed him upon a horse in front of its rider, who hugged him closely. Yet, still, he only saw his horrific vision over and over again.

The horse lurched into motion. Wind blew over his face and through his hair as he bounced and jostled in the rider's grasp, his arms thrashing, threatening to break the rider's grip and send him tumbling. A strong hand clasped over his mouth, trying to stifle his screams, while in his mind, the Chaos riders butchered and killed everything in their path.

Suddenly, the vision ceased, his world turning into a vast, black void. From deep within that emptiness, a soft, yet all-encompassing voice called to him, *"QUIET. YOU MUST REMAIN QUIET. CALM YOURSELF."* The voice echoed to him from the vastness, distinct and true. He'd never heard it before, yet he felt he should. It was like a spirit, speaking to him from beyond.

He calmed; the voice a balm he clung to it for all his worth. He saw nothing after that. The vision did not return, nor did his eyesight. He floated in a sea of blackness. From time to time, he heard the spirit's voice talking to him, murmuring *left* or *right* at random intervals. Left and right, right and left, stop and go, all at random.

After a time, he realized the quiet voice now came from his own mouth. "Left... left... right... left... right... right... stop... wait... go now." It was not his own voice, but that of the spirit, speaking through him.

It should frighten him, but it didn't. He held onto that balm and floated in the endless void, peaceful, losing track of time in his dream-like state. As he fell asleep, he still heard the spirit's voice. *"Left... right... right... left... right..."*

Calidos Flint snapped at Jantos, "What are you talking about? The tracks are right there, plain as day."

The tracker smirked. "Most observant, Calidos, but someone placed an Obstructment here. Those tracks are authentic, but it hides others, and I can't make out how many. It's faint, but I believe the one you seek has veered off to the east."

"You *believe*?" Calidos snarled. "Is it possible they used the Obstructment to lay a false trail?"

"Quite possible, yes."

Frowning, Calidos felt as though the Lord conspired against him—first, the delay in finding Jantos, and now this.

"If I may suggest," Jantos continued, "follow the caravan tracks, but have some of the men fan out. I'll follow this one."

"Why that trail?" Calidos asked.

Jantos shrugged. "It has a strange feel to it. Besides, the caravans will be easy to follow. Leave this one to me."

"So be it." Sighing, Calidos pointed at two guards nearest to the tracker. "You two, go with him. I want that boy's head. Bring it to me. The rest of you, follow me!" He rammed his heels into his horse's side, taking up the tracks once again.

Several minutes later, he spied the Travelers ahead. Brightly colored and looking like little houses on wheels, the things rocked and jumped as they traversed the rough terrain. His face twisted. There were only six. *They said there were at least twenty in their caravan. Where's the rest?*

Drawing in The Lord's Breath, Calidos created a ball of Chaos laced with fire licking and swirling within the mass. Arching it high into the air, the ball struck ahead of the lead caravan. The ground erupted, spewing dirt and rocks. Their horses screamed, turning hard to the right, and sending the carriage tumbling sideways. It rolled several times, wheels and bits of wood flying about, until finally coming to a stop. As the other wagons peeled away, Calidos sent several balls ahead of them, bringing them to a halt.

Riding forward, he spotted the red-haired man—the one claiming *the child* as his son—leaning over and touching the face of a blonde-haired woman. The woman wasn't moving. The man kissed her on the forehead, rose, and slowly approached Calidos—his face a mixture of anger and resolve—before stopping next to his overturned carriage.

"Everyone, out of the wagons," Calidos shouted.

His men prodded the sniveling Travelers, yanking them off their driver's bench when not fast enough.

Calidos stared at the red-haired man. "Where's the boy?"

The man crossed his arms. "What boy?"

"Do not try me!" Calidos trembled. "Where is your son? I want him now!"

The Traveler smiled. "I have no son."

"Do not play games with me!"

Calidos stabbed a finger at one of their women—a pretty thing with a heart-shaped face and shoulder-length brown hair—blasting her with a bolt of fire-infused Chaos. She burst into flames. Shrieking, she flailed about, dropped, and fell silent. The people screamed and shook as the hisses and pops of her cooking flesh filled the air.

Another of the Travelers women, tears streaming from her bright blue eyes, fell to her knees. "Please, leave us be! We are favored by the Lord. How can you do this?"

Calidos grinned. "I do as I wish." Not wanting this one to die as quickly as the first, he spun a fine thread of fire into the woman's belly.

She flopped face-down, shrieking as her innards cooked.

Spittle flew from Calidos's lips. "Tell me where the boy is!"

"Please, no more!" A dark-haired, blocky man knelt to the screaming woman. "I'll tell you what you want. Just leave her alone!"

"Kirk, you mustn't," an older man, with sharp green eyes, yelled.

Kirk spat. "I wanted none of this, Duncan!" He turned back to Calidos. "Please, just stop hurting her and I'll tell you. There's no more need—"

A dagger sank into Kirk's throat. Gurgling and thrashing, he fell forward, dead.

Calidos spun to where the dagger came from. He found the red-haired man smiling as another dagger left his hand, flying straight at Calidos. He threw himself from his saddle, the blade scoring his cheek as he fell, and hit the ground with a grunt.

Shaking his head, he got up on his knees, warmth spreading across his cheek. When he wiped at it, his hand came away red with his blood. "Damned Traveler!"

"I wasn't always a Traveler." The man laughed from behind the wrecked wagon.

"I'll kill you!" Calidos sent a bolt of Chaos at the man. It struck the caravan's overturned bottom, blasting a head-sized hole and sending chunks of wood flying.

Some Travelers dashed off into the tall grass, screaming and shouting, while others grabbed clubs and axes from their nearby driver's benches and attacked his men.

One of his soldiers knelt over him. "Are you all right, Great One?"

Calidos shoved the man. "Get away from me and kill them!"

He started to stand but slipped and fell back down. Something buzzed past his ear. The soldier let loose a high-pitched scream and flopped to the ground, grasping at the crossbow bolt now protruding from his crotch. Calidos spun about as the red-haired man jumped behind cover with a crossbow. Getting up on one knee, Calidos thrust his arms forward, funneling Chaos through him. Fanned and stoked from the flames in his soul, a massive ball of fire erupted from his hands, and struck the lead-Travelers' wagon.

It exploded. A conflagration of fire, wood, and metal knocked nearly everyone to the ground. Fiery debris rained down as his men—those that survived—scrambled to their feet and relieved the groaning Travelers of their weapons.

With a smile, Calidos strode to the wreckage, searching for the red-haired man. Calidos found him, blackened and bloody, some fifteen feet away, lying face-down next to the dead blonde woman from earlier.

He rolled the Traveler over. "Now, where is the—"

Dead, vacant eyes stared back at Calidos, the man's ghosted smile mocking him.

Chapter 12
Lost

(Year 514 -R.C.-)

When Ellis awoke, it was nearly dark out, and it had grown cold. He lay on moss-covered ground beside a small fire tended by Dirge. They were in a hollow roughly twenty feet across beside a felled tree and surrounded by tall shrubs. He shivered, both chilled and afraid, but he dared not cry, even though he desperately wanted to. The clearing held only himself, Dirge, and his horse—not the troupe, not his mother, not his father, just him and Dirge alone in the world. But he didn't dare cry. He knew if he started, he'd never stop. So, he forced it down into the pit of his stomach where it churned and soured.

"Where's Momma and Poppa?" he asked quietly, knowing the answer, but fearful of hearing it.

"You're awake. Good. Here, lad, take this." Dirge handed Ellis a canteen. "Drink. You'll need to keep your strength."

"Where's Momma and Poppa?" he asked again, his voice strained.

"I said take it—"

"No! Where's Momma? Where's Poppa?" His voice rose with each question, and then screamed, "Where is everyone?"

"Hush, boy," the tall guardsman snapped. With a sigh, he lowered the canteen. "I don't know. Your folks bid me take you somewhere safe, and that's what I aim to do." The big man hesitated. "No crying now."

"I'm not crying." Ellis wiped his eyes with the back of his shaky hand. "What happened?"

"The caravan was attacked," he told Ellis in hushed tones, "led by at least one Chaos priest."

"I saw him, in my mind," Ellis said absently. He gazed up at Dirge, who had a strange look on his face. "He was the one from the city. But why? Why are they trying to kill me?"

The swordsman's expression remained uncertain, as though he were looking at Ellis for the first time and wasn't sure what to make of him. "How do you know they were after you?"

"I don't know," he replied. "I could just see it." He told Dirge everything—the vision, the voice, all of it. "I just don't understand why."

"Your folks didn't want you to know the truth, about The Cleansing. They feared the stress would cause a fit."

Dirge stared into the fire. "I remember when it came to Tuilar. It was a very pious city, overrun with the devout. When the priests declared The Cleansing, the streets ran red with the blood of children. Some parents didn't even wait for the priests to come by and perform the sacrifice. They simply walked out in the streets and slew their babies with their own hands, all in the name of The Lord of Chaos." Dirge eyes burned with hate. "I was only fourteen at the time, but I knew the reign of Chaos had to end.

"A couple of years later, a strange wanderer came to the city, calling himself The Prophet. He preached about the need to end the time of Chaos and restore the glory of The Old God of Order, Ukase. My fa—" He cleared his throat. "My *friends*, didn't agree with him, but I saw that The Prophet spoke the truth. It didn't take long before people in the city were listening. We met in secret where The Prophet taught us the difference between 'right and wrong.' He showed us what the world needed."

"And what's that?" Ellis asked, hunkering in on himself.

"Order," Dirge replied, his face as hard as stone. "The world needed law and order, and The Prophet was to lead us to it.

Dirge stared into the flames, his voice taking on a touch of sadness. "It seemed so simple then. The Prophet saw into a man's soul and knew what lay there. He knew if we were true or false.

His voice firmed once again. "When the time was right, we rose up. Led by The Righteous, we slew them all—every priest, warrior, and City Master who had Chaos in their hearts. Then came our own *Cleansing*." He sneered and fell silent.

Ellis leaned forward, sensing the turbulence within Dirge, a mixture of righteousness and shame. "What happened next?"

Dirge's eyes went back to Ellis, shining with unshed tears. "We *Cleansed* them. All those who gave up their children to the slaughter, died as their children died."

"Did *you* do any of that?" Ellis asked.

Dirge ignored the question. "Those closest to The Prophet, he anointed as 'Warriors of the Righteous.' He placed us in command of each unit, charging us to never falter and always be true to Ukase.

Dirge's head fell to his chest. "We failed him. The Prophet, the army, my friends... my wife... all died." He squeezed his eyes shut. "I lost my faith."

"What happened next?"

His eyes snapped open and went to Ellis, burning with an inner light. "You happened."

"Me?"

"I'm devout to The Lord of Order. I'm an anointed Warrior of the Righteous, the Right Hand of Ukase." His voice grew stronger as he spoke. "So believe me when I say that I see The Lord's touch in you. Ukase's fire burns within you. I've known it for some time."

"What are you talking about?" Ellis drew away. "I don't know what you're talking about. Stop it!"

He couldn't take much more. He didn't know if his parents lived or died, and the only person left in his life was going insane.

Dirge held up his left hand, moderating his tone, "It's all right. Don't worry.

He hesitated. "Look. When you were much younger—just a wee lad—my friend Jacob and I came across the troupe. We'd been wandering for some time. The only thing I had left in the world was Jacob. He was my brother in all but blood, and he saw the troupe as a mark." Dirge sighed. "He was not one of the anointed—he had too free a spirit. Nevertheless, we always stuck together. He saved my life. So I did as he wanted—to my everlasting shame.

"That first night, you came out to join us at the fire, and my life changed. You came up to me, a lost soul in pain, and told me everything would be all right. I saw The Lord in your eyes that night though I didn't want to believe it. But as time passed, I became convinced." He reached out and clasped Ellis on the shoulder. "Chaos must be stopped. And you, Ellis, *you* are the means to see that happen. I knew it then, and I know it ever more now, because of what happened today."

Ellis shook as tears streamed down his face. "What? What happened? I don't understand any of this."

"The Lord spoke through you today, my boy. His voice came from your lips," Dirge said, his voice filled with fervor.

He shook his head when Ellis looked away. "Think about it. You said yourself that it was like a voice from far away, a voice that wasn't yours. What else can it be?

Dirge knelt next to the boy. "Listen to me, Ellis. You're not just another random child of the world. You've a destiny. Your father told me that on the night you came into this world, he saw a portent in the sky—a great star burst forth and fell into your village. He said you glowed when you came from your mother, as if the star itself were being born. Everyone said he'd imagined it, just an overly proud father talking up his progeny. But I believed him.

"You are touched by God, my boy. I believe He sent here you to end the time of Chaos." Dirge drew his sword and placed it, point down in the ground before him. "I pledge my life to you, Ellis, son of Cord. Wherever you go, I go. Until my last breath, I will defend your life."

Ellis's mouth opened and shut like a fish out of water. He didn't know *what* to think. "I'm tired, Dirge."

"Lie down and rest, my boy. When you're ready, we'll go check on the others."

Ellis began to lay down, but froze when something rustled in the shrubs at the far end of the camp. Their horse, tied to one of the dead roots of the downed tree, whinnied and jerked its head. Dirge spun about and moved to get in front of Ellis.

Ellis quaked. "What is tha—"

Dirge hushed him.

A dark mass formed at the shrub line. Two yellow dots sprang forth from a darkness and hovered at the edge. The glowing points slowly moved up and down, left to right. Ellis did his best not to scream as he shook. The darkness moved toward them. It broke through the shrubs and came into the light of the fire. It was a large, black wolf.

Ellis whimpered, and Dirge set his feet, his eyes darting about, looking for other wolves.

The wolf stopped inside the edge of the shrubs. It raised its muzzle and sniffed the air, but came no further. It sat down on its haunches, opened its mouth, and panted, its tongue lolling out to one side. Dirge's horse whinnied again and stamped ground, its eyes wide and flaring as it snorted a warning.

"Is it gonna eat us?" Ellis asked.

"It'll choke on my sword first," Dirge said.

The wolf tilted its head, looked back, and with a slight whimper, returned to the darkness.

Dirge cast his eyes about. "I don't like this." With his left hand, he motioned behind him, palm out. "Get back in the roots. They'll likely try and come at us from the sides."

"There aren't any others," came a voice from the darkness—a girl's voice, high and melodious. "It's just me and Vir. May I join you at your fire? I swear, we mean you no harm."

Dirge snarled. "What trickery is this?"

"It's not a trick," the girlish voice replied. "I'm just cold and I'd like to sit by a fire."

"You may enter," Dirge yelled back, his voice hammer strong, as he hunkered down to better cover Ellis. "But come slowly, and I want to see your hands as you do.

He pulled his dagger from his belt and handed it to Ellis, behind his back. "Just in case," he whispered.

Ellis took the dagger in his shaky hands as he eyed the edge of the opening—his rapid breath sounding thunderous in his ears.

He wanted to be brave like Dirge, as brave as his parents would want him to be.

A moment later, a young girl, only a few years younger than himself, walked into the clearing. She had long, dark hair, curly and unkempt. Her dark brown eyes had a fierce look to them, but her face was pretty, albeit layered with dirt and dust. She wore a light brown dress that fit her like a sack; with several holes and a torn hem, it was even dirtier than her face. Her skinny legs stuck out like a pair of mud-covered sticks.

"I don't have any weapons," she said. "Can I share your fire? It's getting cold, and I don't want to spend another night in the cold if I don't have to." She continued slowly toward the fire, flopping down in front of it. She stuck out her hands to warm them, but didn't take her eyes off Dirge, who'd yet to put away his sword.

"Where're your friends?" Dirge asked uncertainly. "You said 'we.' Are your friends going to join you at our fire?"

The girl smiled. "Oh. You don't have to worry about Vir. He's not a big fan of fire. Besides, his fur keeps him warm." Breathing into her cupped hands, she rubbed them together before sticking them back toward the fire.

Ellis's fear fell away as he stared at the young girl. For all her apparent confidence, her eyes still held fear… and a great deal of sadness. He lurched forward and stared in wonder as he watched the girl's eyes slowly change color from brown to blue to yellow. *It's just like the dream. The little girl and the shaggy dog—well, shaggy wolf—and her color changing eyes.*

Ellis was about to ask her about her eyes when her last comment came to mind. "Fur?" his voice squeaked. "You said his fur. Are you talking about that wolf? Your pet wolf named 'Vir?'"

She laughed.

Ellis found it musical.

"Don't be silly," she said. "Vir's not a pet. He's my friend. And I didn't give him his name. He told it to me." She glanced over her shoulder. "We look out for each other."

Her mouth quirked, and she rolled her eyes. "All right. Fine. He looks after me, and I just keep him company." She turned her head back to the brush line. "Is that better?"

"It looks like our little wood nymph is a bit touched in the head," Dirge said under his breath to Ellis.

The girl scowled, peering at Dirge through heavy brows. "I'm not *touched*. You take that back!" She stood up, her hands clenched into tiny fists at her sides.

"And I'm not a nymph! I'm a girl, and I have a name. It's Daylin." She held her head high with pride. "Daylin Dragonvein."

Ellis scampered past Dirge—he still felt too light headed to stand and walk. "Mine's Ellis," he said, and sat across the fire from her. "Please, sit down. It's all right."

He liked the girl and didn't want Dirge to scare her off. "Frowny face here is Dirge. He didn't mean to hurt your feelings. You said the wolf *told* you his name? You can talk to him? Could you get him to talk to us? I'd dearly love to see that. Heck. It would be great for the show, wouldn't it, Dirge?" Ellis realized he was rambling, but couldn't help himself.

Daylin shook her head at the onslaught. "No. It doesn't work like that. He doesn't actually talk—not with his mouth. It's more like he talks to my head." She held up her hand as Ellis tried to interrupt. "And, no, I can't get him to talk to you. He can't talk to just anyone. Only to me."

"Can you talk to other animals?" Ellis asked.

Lowering her hand, she smiled shyly. "Yes; I can talk to all kinds of animals. Of course, some talk better than others. Most of the small ones don't really talk at all. It's more like… I can sense how they feel and I can tell what they want. Though, Master Ruddick had a really smart hare once." She lowered her head, her face filled with sorrow. "He could talk better than I could."

She has such a pretty voice, Ellis thought. *I could listen to her all night.*

"Who's Master Ruddick?" he asked.

Her voice sank and her face darkened. "No one."

"No one? You said this Ruddick is your Master." Dirge frowned. "So, you're a runaway then. We can't get involved with runaway slaves. We've enough trouble as it is."

"I'm no one's slave," she snarled. "Not anymore." She grinned wickedly. "Ruddick is *dead*. Vir saw to that."

She swung her hand at them as if to swat a fly. "I only came here because Vir said you were running from Chaos priests and he thought I should help. If I had my way, they'd *all* be dead."

Dirge smirked. "And how can *you* help us?"

"Well," she replied tartly with a mocking grin. "For one thing, you need to stop burning green wood in your fire. It's sending up smoke. It's a good thing for you Vir killed the ones tracking you."

Dirge's head snapped up. "What? Where was this?" He stood and kicked dirt on the fire. "When, girl? Tell me! I must know if there are more."

"Stop that. I told you, they're dead." Daylin jumped to her feet. "Vir killed them about a couple of hours ago, about a hundred yards from here. The rest are far from here, scattered about, trying to run down the other wagons.

She knelt and fixed the fire. "We'll need the warmth before long. Just stop using green wood." She cast her gaze about the campsite and then back to Dirge. "You've found a great spot to hide. You really knew what you were doing there."

Dirge hunched his shoulders. "Thank you."

"You didn't actually know what you were doing, did you?" With a chuckled, she shook her head. "I don't get you. You twisted all about to confuse anyone tracking you, but then you don't hide your tracks. And *then* you make a fire with green wood."

Dirge scowled at the little girl.

Ellis felt confused. "I don't understand. What are you trying to say?"

"I'm saying you don't make sense," she snapped. How did you end up in my camp?"

"*Your* camp?" Dirge looked dubious. "Stop playing games, little girl. There were no signs that anyone had ever been here— no fire pit, no bones, no leavings. I know enough to know a *campsite* when I see it, and there was no such thing here."

She smirked. "That's because I know how to make a camp that doesn't draw *attention*." Frowning, she looked at her feet. "I've been living out here for a while. They've hunted us for six months, and you go and lead them right to me.

Her head shot up, staring at Dirge. "You don't know anything about the wild. So how did you find this place?"

Dirge glanced at Ellis. "God led us here."

"Chaos," she spat, jumping to her feet.

"Ukase." Dirge redrew his sword and stepped in front of Ellis.

The girl hissed and backed away from the fire as Dirge advanced.

"What are you doing?" Ellis asked. He then saw motion to their left at the edge of the camp. He staggered to his feet and flung himself at the swordsman. "No. Stop! She's just scared!"

"She could betray us." Dirge stopped, glancing to his left. He'd seen the wolf.

"She won't. I promise." Ellis spun about and fell to the ground with a grunt, flinging his hand toward the still retreating girl. "Please, don't go. *Please*. He's telling the truth. The Lord of Law spoke to me. He told us where to go." Tears fell—he couldn't help it. His vision blurred, and he sobbed. "Please don't go. My parents are dead. I know it! I don't want to lose you, too." The statement made no sense to him, but he knew it to be true all the same.

The girl scampered out of the camp without a word.

Dirge knelt next to Ellis, caressing his head while keeping an eye out for the wolf. "Hush, boy. You don't know that about your folks. The wagons were scattering as we left, and there's a good chance they got away."

Ellis couldn't stop his tears. He knew the truth. While deep in his sleep-like state, he felt it happen. He heard his parents' screams in his mind. He felt them pass. He was alone. Dirge would never abandon him, but the man had a coldness—he held himself apart and let no one in. Dirge's rigidity was all Ellis would ever know from now on. Try as the man might, he couldn't replace Ellis's parents.

The girl, on the other hand? There was something about her. From the moment he saw her, Ellis felt a kinship. Sadness filled her and knew he could help. At the same time, a part of him screamed he needed her in his life. Without that girl, he'd be lost, never be whole. And now, she was gone.

Chapter 13
Make for The Reach

(Year 514 -R.C.-)

A sense of despair engulfed Daylin as she crept away from the camp—her former camp. It had been her home for half a year. The only place she'd ever felt safe. She and Vir had been running and dodging priests and their lackeys for six months after escaping Ruddick and his horrific experiments. Vir told her the old felled tree still held a strong connection to The Mother, and it helped shield them from the minions of Chaos. She'd been happy in that hollow, the only refuge in a world of pain and sorrow.

Now the fates presented her this boy, someone so weak he couldn't even stand. Why did she feel a pang of hope when she saw him? It was like something clicked in her head the moment he spoke. Was it a bewitchment? Master Ruddick had many priests at his dinners, and after what happened with Sam...

"They are not with Chaos," Vir said as he crept up to her side.

"I know." She sensed as much from the big man—he was far too rigid to be with Chaos. But when he said their *God* brought them...

"You should go to them," Vir said.

"I can't. The big man won't allow it. He doesn't trust us." She flopped down, wanting to cry, but shook it off. "Besides, why should I? We don't need them. We have each other, and that's all we'll ever need."

"You are just being stubborn, little pup. The little one will talk the man into allowing it. There is great *Spirit* in him. I can feel it."

"There is? I couldn't feel anything."

Ever since Ruddick... *succeeded*, with her, she could feel people's emotions, and get a sense of their intent. Yet, with that boy, she felt nothing. And it bothered her.

Vir nuzzled her neck. "I would not want you to be alone."

She looked Vir in the eyes. "What do you mean, *alone*? I have you."

"I will not always be here. The time will come when The Mother calls me home."

"Oh, shut up. You're not going to die." She kissed him on the top of his huge head and hugged him, his thick, coarse fur tickling her nose. "I won't let that happen."

"Listen to me, pup. We do not live as long as you humans do. Not even those of us born with The Mother's touch. I am old, little pup. My spirit longs to go *home*, and I don't want you to be alone when that happens." He stood. "We must join them now, before the boy returns to their wagons. Because once it happens, the rest will never allow us to be among them."

He licked her face, causing her to giggle.

"I love you, little one. And I want you to live long and happy. That can only happen with your own kind." He nudged her with his head. "Go now. I will check on the rest of his people and make sure the priest and his men have left."

Standing, she trudged back to the hollow. She heard the boy crying as she drew near, and it tugged at her. He lay curled up on the ground, the large man caressing his head. She may not be able to read his emotions, but she knew the desolation in those tears, the anguish in those sobs. "Please stop crying. I'm sorry."

The hard man's eyes jerked toward her, and he raised his sword.

The boy lurched toward her. "You came back!" He staggered to his feet as she entered the clearing and ran to her, throwing his arms around her. "Thank you! Thank you! Please don't leave me again. I couldn't stand it." His voice quivered, tears flowing from his bloodshot eyes.

"It's all right. Calm down." She helped him to the fireside.

Sitting next to each other, they held hands, and talked as if they'd known each other their entire lives. At one point, they stopped and simply stared.

Somehow, in her heart, Daylin knew this strange little boy. Her eyes welled up. She'd not cried in months—tears brought pain—but there was no stopping it. They huddled together, holding on to one another so tight breathing grew difficult. But she didn't dare let go.

Tended by Dirge, the campfire grew, giving off heat and light, until they both fell asleep. She'd dreamt about Ellis for much of the night.

The swordsman woke them at dawn, and they ate some of the food she'd stashed away in the roots of the overturned tree. The children talked and laughed. Daylin couldn't remember ever being so happy.

"All right, lovebirds, we need to get going," Dirge grumbled. "We have to find what's left of the troupe and keep heading north."

She read the big man and discovered what the statement meant. Grabbing a nut, she tossed it at him. "It's not like that."

"As you say," Dirge said dubiously. "We need to be on our way and find the wagons as soon as we can."

Daylin got to her feet. "They're camped about ten miles north of here. For some reason, the priest and his men can't find them."

"How do you know that?" Ellis asked.

She brushed the leaves from her dress. "Vir told me."

Dirge rolled his eyes. "Oh, right. I forgot. You can *talk* to your pet wolf."

"Hush." Ellis waved a hand dismissively at the swordsman and then turned to Daylin. "How far away can you talk to him?"

"A long way. The bigger the animal, the farther away we can talk." She stuck her tongue out at Dirge.

The older man chuckled. "Well, come along, you two. Let's head back and see to our people as best we can. Those still alive will need our help and *your* guidance," he said to Ellis.

Ellis scrunched up his face. "What do you mean?"

"You're now the leader of the Traveling Show, Ellis. It's what your parents would want."

"I wouldn't know what to do."

"No worries there. I'll guide you until you're old enough." He reached down and took the boy's hand to pull him up, but Ellis fell once more. "Come now, lad. You can do this."

Ellis started to stand, but failed. "My legs are still too wobbly."

Dirge picked Ellis up in his arms and then looked at Daylin. "I am sorry for being so gruff, young miss. We *could* use your help as well as that of your friend. We'll need all the help we can get from this day forward, I am thinking." He placed Ellis on his horse, and they left the hollow.

Fuming, Calidos fingered his cheek—it burned from the dagger slice and would need stitches. *Why is The Lord making this so difficult?*

After going through every wagon, he'd put the surviving entertainers to the question with glee. He so loved the feel of the flow of fire he funneled into each person, their insides rapidly heating until their blood boiled, and their skin crisped and crackled. Howling in anguish, they all denied knowing anything about the child. It was just like that damned village all those years ago. He raged as he burned the wagons, teams and all. He then waited there among the smoldering remains for Jantos to return, but the man didn't show.

Brushing soot off his sleeve, he stared south. "Where in all the hells is that man?"

Gathering his men, Calidos backtracked to the trail Jantos took. There, he ordered his men to spread out, and they all hunted for the tracker. It didn't take long to find him. In less than thirty minutes, Calidos spotted the head of his friend lying in the high grass, bloody and mangled as though something chewed it off.

"Grunkin," one man said.

"It's an omen from the Lord," another said. "He's angry with us for hunting his people."

Calidos wondered if they were right—the Lord of Chaos was fickle after all. Still angry, he gave up the hunt, and headed back to the city. "I'll find you, boy. No matter how long it takes, I will find you."

Daylin's jaw dropped at the sight of the wagons. Painted every color imaginable, they looked like little houses on wheels, and at their center, sat people in clothes looking even brighter and more colorful. Upon the trio's approach, the surviving members of the troupe jumped up and shouted, flocking toward them, overwhelmed with joy at seeing Ellis and Dirge's safe return.

An old man with a weathered face and long gray hair clasped Ellis on the back. "Thank the gods you're alive." He then nodded toward Daylin. "Who's the girl?"

"Her name's Daylin." Ellis then turned to her. "Daylin, this is Whisp."

He turned back to the gray-haired man. "She can talk to wolves. She helped us."

Rather than scoff, as Daylin expected, the man grinned, giving off waves of amazement. "That's *wonderful*."

The women rushed in and cooed at her, doing everything they could to comfort her. She wanted to shudder from the overwhelming wave of emotions and feelings the people gave off. She'd never been around so many people at once. *I don't know if I can do this*, she thought.

"You'll get used to it," Vir said.

With feelings of love and devotion, the women quickly ushered her away. They washed her with soaps smelling of sweet flowers and then heaped upon her the most beautiful clothes she'd ever seen. Dresses, blouses, pants, and hats, none of them were plain or simple. And none reminded her of the clothes Ruddick made her wear—all silk and lace with deep plunging necklines.

She scrubbed at her damp eyes, trying to block the memories. "Stop it," she said to herself.

These people were nothing like Ruddick or Celeste—who'd taken up the chase after Ruddick died. These people were different. At least she hoped so.

The next day, Vir led them to the burned-out wagon belonging to the boy's parents, along with the wagons of a half dozen other members. Little remained, but they buried what they could.

Once finished, Dirge stood atop one of the wagons, while Ellis sat on its stoop, clutching something in his hands—a bronze sun pendant.

Dirge called out to the troupe. "We must continue on. But not here."

"Where then?" someone cried out.

Another cried out, "Who will lead us?"

"I will," Dirge said.

The members mumbled with sour looks.

"When Ellis is old enough, he'll take over," the big man continued. "Until then, we head north. We'll make for The Reach."

"But that's a thousand miles away!"

"Yes, it is. We'll ride hard and fast. Chaos is weak up north. It's a place where order can gain ground, where judgment and rise up. Remember the prophecy. 'The reign of Chaos ends when judgment walks the land.'"

"That's not quite right," Whips said.

"It's close enough." Dirge waved the man off and turned back to the crowd. "Our trip won't be easy. I've heard many of you express doubt and remorse over what's happened. If any wish to leave us, you may."

He cast his gaze about all the faces staring back at him. None took him up on his offer.

"The priest knows Ellis's last name, so we must change it. I've already spoken to him, and he wants to go by Ellis Concord."

Her new friend stared at the pendant in his trembling hands. "I wanted to honor my father." He wiped tears from his eyes.

"They're still after us," Dirge went on. "We won't go near any towns or villages, and we'll stay clear of the

Cunning River. Once we make it to The Reach, you can go back to doing what you do best."

A man in motley punched his fist in the air. "We shall put on the best show in the world!"

The people cheered.

The sounds and feelings of joy and pride surrounded Daylin. It emanated from the Travelers like water gushing from a river. She'd never heard nor felt the like. *These people are strange,* she thought. *Only a short time ago, sorrow filled them, and now, this.*

"Travelers are a queer folk," Vir said. "But I've found them to be some of the best humans I've ever witnessed. The Mother loves them, for they know only love."

Daylin clutched to her doubts, but it was difficult in the face of all that joy. Closing her eyes, she soaked it up like the dry earth after years of drought.

The first day of travel, though easy, quickly drew irksome for Daylin. The women were wonderful, heaping compliments upon her. They admired her for how well she did all by herself. "You've so much strength and ingenuity to survive out in the wilds at such a young age."

They also praised her for her beauty, which made her a little uncomfortable—it made her think of Ruddick and the things he did.

The men, on the other hand, she found infuriating. They took her for an invalid, particularly the younger men. Just because she was skinny, and some bones stuck out, they treated her like a baby, wanting to do everything for her and hoping she didn't "overexert" herself.

In the early afternoon of the third day, she sat beside Ellis on the lead wagon—a guardsman at the reins as she and Ellis eyed the countryside and made idle chat. "There are almost no trees around here," she said.

Ellis raised his head and put on a strange voice. "We're in plains country, comprising mostly high grasses, except where there are rivers and lakes present."

She eyed him sideways. "Why are you talking like that?"

He lowered his head and blushed. "It's how Whisp sounds when he teaches me."

"I don't like it here. There's no place to hide, and the sun's so hot." She peered into the vast sea of brown and green grass. In the distance, the air seemed to shimmer. "And it looks funny. Why does it do that?"

"Do what?"

"The air. Why does it seem to wave back-and-forth way out there?"

Ellis shrugged. "I don't know. It just does. Haven't you ever seen grasslands before?"

She shook her head. "Mast—Ruddick's house was in the woods, and Vir said it was easier to hide in the trees."

"Where is Vir?" Ellis asked.

"He's behind us, making sure they're not following." She reached out to Vir. He was many miles away, and she needed to strain to keep in contact.

"Does he see anything?" Ellis asked.

"No. Nothing but rabbits and mice. He said he'd bring a nice fat rabbit for us for supper. He's already had his fill."

"So how come you can talk to animals? Were you born with it?"

Daylin dropped her head, her voice becoming mousy. "I don't want to talk about it." She still had nightmares.

"You can trust me." Ellis sat up straighter and tried to firm his voice. "If we are going to be working together, we need to be forthright with each other."

"Do you even know what that word means?"

"It's something Whisp said to me. It means we need to work together."

"Well, I don't care. I don't want to talk about it."

"*Please.*"

"I said no!" She jumped out of the wagon.

"What are you doing? You can't do that," Ellis yelled.

Several of the men hollered to her, asking what was wrong. Some of the boys even jumped down to run after her.

Dirge rode up. "Where do you think you're going?"

"I'm going to tinkle. Is that all right with you?" she shouted back. "Since when do I need your approval, anyway?"

She ran off into the high grass, flinging her hands in the air. "Boys!"

Chapter 14
Mangin

(Year 516 -R.C.-)

"Time for a ride," Mangin said to herself as she strutted out of the temple. She hated staying indoors for too long, no matter how well her studies progressed with the decrepit old priest.

She paused in front of The Green, her eyes on the Old Stump, stained dark brown with blood from where Hogar taught the villagers a lesson four years before—since those little bastards dared lay hands on her. Now seventeen, Mangin contemplated how much she'd changed, both mentally and physically. She slid her hands down her pale blue, cotton blouse, opened to expose the uppermost of her firm breasts, enjoying the feel as it hugged her narrow waist.

"Hmm... where is Betal?" She loved riding through the countryside, but they were ever so much more enjoyable with Betal at her side. "He'd better not be out in that stinking forest again." She'd already checked his room to no avail.

Maybe he's with Simmons, she thought.

She crossed the Green, her loose white ankle-length skirt dancing on her broad hips. Her high black riding boots crunched the dry grass. She wore no undergarments, as usual.

She sashayed over to the house of John Simmons and entered without knocking. No one was home. "He must be out in the fields."

"Where is that boy?" She twisted her mouth.

She set out down the main street, taking her time, observing the people going about their daily routine. Spotting Cobb Crutchfield coming down the road toward her, she smiled.

Well, if it isn't my second favorite person in this shit-hole. Mangin admired Cobb's audacity. He spoke his mind and stood up to her. She respected that in a village full of cowardly mewing cattle.

Cobb wasn't alone. On his right strode Jason, whom she thought might be his best friend – if cattle even had friends. On his left, was a young woman holding his hand.

Mangin frowned. *She's not from here.*

The girl stood a good head shorter than Cobb, with long, straight blonde hair. She had an adorable face, with sweet, puffy cheeks, full, ripe lips made for kissing, and bright blue eyes that dazzled in the light of the day. But the young woman's attire caused Mangin to twist her mouth in disdain. She wore a simple white cotton dress buttoned up neatly to her neck and hung to her ankles, covering her completely.

"But I do like how it hugs her," Mangin muttered, running her tongue over her teeth.

As the trio came closer, the young woman noticed Mangin first. She froze, her eyes going wide and her mouth hanging open.

Well, she clearly recognizes me, Mangin thought with a chuckle. *But then, who doesn't?*

Stopping, Cobb frowned at the young woman. "What's wrong?" When he turned his head and discovered Mangin, his face firmed.

A shiver up Mangin's spine—she reveled in his disdain.

Jason tried to emulate Cobb's anger, but his eyes twitched and he licked his lips. Cobb placed his hand on the woman's back and turned them around to head back the way they came.

"Stop," Mangin said.

They continued walking at a steady pace.

"The insolence," Mangin muttered and grasped Chaos. "I said stop." She created a ten-foot-high wall of fire in front of them.

The woman screamed as they jumped back. She trembled, her hands to her face as she leaned into Cobb. The surrounding villagers cried out and froze as well.

"Turn around," Mangin said, her mouth quirking playfully as she let go of the fiery wall. "Let's not be rude now, Cobb."

They complied.

"Why don't you introduce me to your lovely friend? Is she new to Cool Winds? I think I'd remember seeing someone this exquisite." Mangin approached them slowly, each step measured and crisscrossed, causing her hips to sway.

Cobb puffed up, and his eyes burned, but he kept his voice steady. "This is my woman, Adel. Her family moved here from Cross Corners a few months ago. My Lady," he added belatedly. "Now, if you don't mind, we've much to do today." He briskly started past her.

Mangin stepped in front and placed her hand upon his chest, bringing him up short. She moved closer to Cobb, their faces inches apart. "Tell me, Cobb," she cooed. "Why do you hate me so? I only wish to be your friend."

Cobb jerked back. "You know why I hate you." The anger in his voice grew stronger and louder with each word. "And I don't want to be your friend. I want nothing to do with you. None of us do!"

"You shouldn't say that." Mangin put on her best wicked smile. "You know that's not true, Cobb." She knew how much he hated her, and she'd no desire to change that. But, she also wanted more. She relished the fire in his eyes. *I wager he'd make a passionate lover.*

Mangin gently manipulated Chaos and caressed his mind with it. She opened him to the possibilities of her, of being with her. She made him see her in all her glory and fanned the flames of desires. From that day forward, he'd want her. He may hate her, but he'd never lose the desire to take her and ravish her to her heart's content—not his content, only hers.

"Now tell me again, my dear Cobb, how do I make you feel?"

The light of lust sparked in his eyes, but he refused to say it, refused to give in to his newfound desire. His continuing defiance thrilled her to no end.

She swung her eyes to the young woman at his side. *Perhaps a little push is required?*

"Well now, let's take a good look at your friend here." Mangin stepped in front of the lovely young woman. "You say she is your woman? Are we talking exclusivity then?"

"Yes," Cobb spat, his voice trembling. "She's mine and I'm hers."

"We will see about that," Mangin breathed, as she gazed deep into the woman's eyes. "I never will understand why anyone would ever do such a thing. This 'exclusivity.' Why limit yourself to all the possibilities The Great Lord gives you?"

Cobb snarled. "Don't you dare touch—"

Mangin raised her finger at him and encased his mind in an entrancement spell. He'd be able to see and hear everything, but unable to say or do anything about it.

Mangin reached out with her index finger and gently placed it under Adel's chin, raising it up to look her in the eyes. The young beauty quivered, as Mangin moved forward and kissed Adel on her full, sumptuous, trembling lips.

Not reciprocating, Adel held herself stiff.

Mangin pulled back slightly. "Come now, my dear. You've no reason to fear me," she said in a caressing voice. "Well, that's not entirely true, is it? I am someone to fear." She ran the back of her hand across Adel's cheek. "But you need not fear me for this."

Mangin again bent forward and kissed Adel. Only much more firmly. She felt the young woman's lips soften and become more accepting. Emboldened, Mangin's hand traveled down Adel's body. Mangin teased the girl's right breast, producing an ever so slight moan, and then lowered her hand further to cup and caress Adel's womanhood through her sleek white cotton dress.

Adel snapped out of her stupor and shoved Mangin away. "No! I don't like—I don't like women. Not like that. And I don't like *you*."

Mangin scowled, and her eyes smoldered. But, ever so slowly, her wicked smile returned. "Are you sure, my dear? Are you *sure,* you feel that way, my little lovely? I think, deep down, you feel quite differently." Mangin delved deep into Adel's mind, searching for what she knew lay there. "You want me, don't you?"

Adel's face froze, and she panted. She slowly shook her head, mouthing the word no.

Mangin's eyes grew bright, and she smiled broadly. "There it is." She found the woman's hidden desire.

She brushed the young woman's mind and crooned, "I think you want me. I think you want to have me here and now... don't you?"

Lust bloomed in Adel's eyes. She lunged forward, grasped Mangin's head, and kissed her passionately. After several moments, Adel broke the kiss and sunk to her knees. Those of the crowd that hadn't slunk away in fear, gasped as Adel crawled forward and ducked under Mangin's skirt.

Mangin's threw her head back and gasped as Adel noisily ravished her womanhood. For a naïve young woman, Adel was a natural. Her tongue took Mangin to the height of ecstasy.

Jason's eyes shifted from Cobb to Adel, between his friend—frozen and controlled—and the woman his friend loved, who pleasured Mangin in front of the entire village. With a snarl, Jason shifted to the side. He crept up behind Mangin, pulled a dagger from his belt, and thrust it forward.

Yet, however enthralled Mangin might have been, she always remained alert to her surroundings. With barely a thought, she cocooned Jason in Chaos—inches before his blade struck home—and held him in place until she fulfilled her sexual gratification.

After several minutes, Mangin groaned as her orgasm washed through her. She shuddered and shook, then sighed and gently pulled the young woman from beneath her skirt. She drew Adel to her feet, and with a wistful smile, kissed her ever so lightly on the lips.

"Thank you, my dear," Mangin said. "That was wonderful. I shall have to return the favor one day... soon."

"Enough, Mangin," Betal said, his deep voice rumbling as he gently pushed through the crowd. "You've had your fun."

Mangin smirked as she turned. Betal had a way of showing up when she was at her most decadent. "Hello, Betal."

"Release them." Betal crossed his arms over his chest.

"As you wish, my Lord," she said, sarcastically, as she bowed her head ever so slightly. She loved it when he was forceful. Mangin didn't take orders well, yet she yearned for a strong hand, someone dominant she'd need to fight.

Where's the joy without a struggle? she thought.

She waited a full five seconds, all the while staring a challenge at Betal, before turning to Cobb and Adel. "You two go on now." She released the spell upon them both. "Go on about your day."

Cobb shuddered and snarled, but swallowed his bile. He lovingly took Adel in his arms and walked through the crowd to his home. "Everything will be all right," he told her as he stared balefully at both Mangin and Betal.

Adel merely nodded as she went, but the look in her eyes—a mixture of wonder, understanding, and guilt—spoke volumes.

Mangin thrilled as her nethers tingled. She chuckled. *Oh. The fun we shall have.*

Her eyes hardening, Mangin turned her attention to Jason. "But this one goes nowhere. This one thought he could poke me from behind with his little steel dick."

Red-faced, she snarled. "Cobb is a man I can respect. He's a man that'll face you and tell you what he really feels. You, on the other hand, are a coward. And I can't abide a coward." She cocked her head slightly to the side. "Why do this? Why attack me? Because of what I did to Adel?"

"You forced yourself on her," Betal said.

She turned to Betal. "You can be such a prude at times, my dear. I did nothing but open her mind to other possibilities. I saw her hidden desire for women and let her know she could have more than a single man thrusting into her for the rest of her life. You needn't worry. What I did will have no lasting effect… for the most part."

She turned back to Jason. "But what I will do to you…"

Mangin wove a complex net of Chaos, a spinning, twisting matrix to cover Jason's mind. Once satisfied, she pulled the net tight. As it slowly sank, infinitesimally small filaments of Chaos sliced into his brain. Jason thrashed in his cocoon and screamed. Spittle flew from his mouth, and his eyes rolled back into his head. The crowd looked on in horror, their eyes glued to the tubule before them. Once the net reached the core of Jason's brain, it snapped shut. Jason's screams cut off like a knife, and his face went slack.

"What did you do?" Betal asked. His head cocked to the side with a bewildered look in his eyes. "I saw everything, but I seriously doubt I could ever copy it."

"I'd be surprised if you could, my dear," she told him over her shoulder. "It was something I got from my mother—a *gift* if you will."

"But what did you do?" Betal asked.

"I wiped him." She swung back to the listless young man. "Jason is mine now. Mine for the rest of his life. Isn't that right, Jason?"

"Yes. Jason is yours," he said woodenly.

"Yes." Mangin bounced on her toes. "In fact, I think Jason is too good a name for you." She tapped her lip with her finger. "You need a different one. A better one. I know. How about Worm? Yes. Worm will do nicely, won't it?" Her wicked smile was back in full force.

"Yes," Worm said. "I am Worm. I am yours."

Betal sighed and shook his head. "Now that you're finished, I take it you want to go for a ride?"

"Of course I do, my love," she said coquettishly while slowly twisting at the waist.

Betal hesitated. "So, you're in love with me now?" Wearing a subtle frown, he turned his head slightly to the side.

Mangin spied him out of the corner of her eye. She turned and took a deep breath, causing her breasts to heave in her blouse. The lust for her burning in his eyes made her giddy.

"You're my best friend. What's not to love?" She grinned. "But I never said I was 'in love' with you. It's just a term of endearment. Don't get too big a head now."

Betal's eyebrows sank at her reply, and his frown became full blown.

It tugged at her heartstrings, but she stayed resolute. In truth, she'd been in love with him for some time. *But why tell him that? It's far more fun this way. No. He must first admit he loves me. Only then will I reveal myself.*

"Come now, Betal. Let's have our ride. You, too, Worm. Follow me." She spun and headed back to the temple, exaggerating every step so her hips swayed and her ass popped. She felt Betal's eyes on her behind with every step, and it sent a thrill up her spine.

Once they reached the temple's stables, Mangin turned to Worm. "Stay here until we return." Her eyes went to Betal for a moment with a sultry smile on her succulent lips. "I'm sure Betal is more than capable of protecting me on our ride."

This should be easy coin, Durrend thought as he knelt behind a large tree at the edge of the copse. *Just make sure you keep your head about you.*

Normally, ambushing a pair of rich snots while out on their daily ride wouldn't be a problem. However, these weren't ordinary targets. Priests required extraordinary care.

Years before, when Durrend joined The Brotherhood of Assassins, Dillon Slade told him, "A crossbow bolt to the heart or head and you're dead. I don't care how close to God you are."

Durrend took a quick survey of the situation to reassure himself. Thad and Qian, fellow Brotherhood members, lay in a hollow they'd dug out behind a fallen tree at the other edge. Each held a heavy crossbow, and wore brown and green leggings, tunics, and cloaks to blend in. He'd covered them in fresh-cut brush to conceal their prone bodies even further – one could never be too careful in their line of work. He did the same with himself with cut shrubbery stuck in the surrounding ground. That way, he'd remained hidden while still having a good view of the surrounding area.

The location was important. Their quarry often rode by the thicket on their way out to check on the herdsmen's fortifications several miles east of their village. Their client, who'd contracted The Brotherhood in Cross Corners, gave them more than enough details regarding the two.

Apparently, the man had been hounding Dillon for weeks to get the job done. The man hated the pair with a passion and wanted them dead. But Dillon knew it wasn't something you rushed. It took finesse and caution when priests were involved—especially those two.

Durrend took a quick glance at the crossbow he held low to the ground to make sure the bolt was still well in place. He didn't dare take any chances on the job.

Voices in the distance drew his attention. Slowly, he raised his head and peered to his right beyond the trees to confirm his suspicion. Durrend turned to his companions and made a low clicking sound, like the chittering of a squirrel, to let them know the young priests were in sight. Thad replied likewise, signifying their readiness to take the priests from behind.

Durrend took in the pair as they approached. The young woman, Mangin, sat high on a tall, sleek, gray stallion that frisked as they rode.

It wants to run, Durrend thought. He dearly loved horses, and one of these would soon be his.

The woman appeared tall and slender. Her freely flowing scarlet hair hung about her shoulders, framing her porcelain-skinned, oval face. Her petite nose, eyes like fiery emeralds, and sweet pink lips curling in a sensual smile, emphasized her stunning beauty. He thought she was the most beautiful woman alive.

And by the look on her face, she knows it.

She rode with her skirt hiked up well above her knees, showing off a great deal of lovely pale leg, and her blouse hung open, exposing copious amounts of bosom.

How could a creature so vile be so breathtaking?

Her laughter was musical, and her eyes smoldered as she gazed at her companion.

If she'd not bed this man already, she will be soon, by that look, Durrend thought. *If I'm lucky, one of the boys will take her through the heart.*

He wanted to be able to look upon her perfect face as he fucked her corpse. There was no way he'd be able to have a woman like her while she still lived—not even a whore. He simply couldn't afford it.

The young man sat on a dappled stallion, with a large chest and strong legs. Though it didn't look to be as fast as the woman's horse, it was quite impressive. Unlike the man who rode it.

Betal was nothing like what he expected. He seemed to be only a teenager, tall and slim, but quite plain looking. His short black hair, dark brown eyes, and a long face made him look rather like a fox.

No. Not a fox, he thought. *More predatory. The client's right. This one's a wolf at heart.*

It was obvious to Durrend the woman didn't want him for his looks; it must have been for his station and money. He wore tight black breeches, a bright white shirt unlaced at the top, knee-high, polished black leather boots, and a dull gray cloak of high quality. Durrend also noticed he didn't have a sword, only a jeweled dagger hanging from his belt.

That should fetch a pretty penny or two, he thought with a sneer.

It surprised Durrend that for all the woman's coquettishness, he seemed unaffected by it. If he was smitten with her, he hid it well as he held up his side of the conversation with his deep voice. If anything, the young wolf seemed agitated. He kept staring at the woman as if she was a puzzle.

"Honestly, Betal, I don't know why you're still upset by it."

"I understand what you did to Jason..."

"His name is Worm."

"But did you have to do that to the young woman? In front of everyone?"

She threw her head back and laughed. "Truly? Oh, darling, I really need to broaden your education."

What a fool, Durrend thought. To have at your taking such a scrumptious morsel and not want to sample it was beyond his thinking.

Durrend held perfectly still as the two rode past, daring not even to breathe. Flies tickled his nose and buzzed about his head, but he refused to notice. He remained focused. Once they were about one hundred feet away, he slowly brought up his crossbow and took aim at the back of The Beast's head...

Suddenly, the air about the corpse rippled like summer heat off the dry plain seen at a distance. A massive man appeared directly in front of Qian, standing head to toe in black scale-mail armor. He wore a dull red cloak that seemed to swirl and writhe chaotically, twisting his eyes so much so it pained to look at. He held a large, grayish black sword raised to shoulder level.

Durrend squeaked. "The Ghost of Death."

Hogar struck first at their crossbows. The sword cut through wood and steel with ease, causing both bows to explode from the strike. Bits of wood and metal flew, sinking deep into the faces and shoulders of his compatriots. Whatever pain they felt was short-lived, as the backstroke sliced through their necks. Blood sprayed everywhere as their heads rolled upon the ground, yet not a drop touched that terrifying figure.

Hogar raised his head to Durrend. The red glowing eyes peering out of that black helm seized Durrend's throat with fear. He took a shaky shot at the paladin with his bow. The bolt flew true, struck its target, and ricocheted back. The bolt landed within a yard of Durrend, a twisted mess.

Durrend threw down his crossbow and fled. He didn't make the wood's edge before he stumbled and fell as the ground beneath him softened like a bog. He struggled and thrashed, desperate to reach the edge of the wood, yet the earth continued to engulf him. Deeper and deeper, he sank into the mire. When he reached shoulder depth, the ground re-solidified, trapping him fast. Heavy footsteps approached him from behind as the sound of his blood pounded in his ears. He screamed.

"They can't hear you," Hogar said, his deep voice sounding raspy and warbled. "I want us to have some privacy."

"Wha... wha... what do you want?" Though he knew full well what The Ghost of Death wanted. "Please don't kill me," he panted. "I'll tell you anything. Just don't kill me!"

Leaves and twigs crackled and snapped as the paladin knelt directly behind him. "Yes; you will." The mirth in his voice chilled Durrend to the bone. "Give me your mind, pathetic human," The Ghost snarled, his voice like ice.

The giant paladin grasped his head, and all was pain, screaming white-hot pain, as Durrend lost all sense of the world.

Cutting through the agony, The Ghost's voice reverberated in his mind. *"WHY ARE YOU HERE? WHO PAID YOU? SHOW ME HIS FACE."*

The answers came unbidden as though the giant's hand rummaged through his skull and tore out the name and face of Erin Cruchfield.

After what seemed an eternity, the pain ended. He panted; his lungs working hard for breath. His head spun, but, thankfully, the pain abated.

"It would appear the sheep are sharpening their teeth again," Hogar said under his breath.

The paladin stood and walked away, but quickly returned. Durrend held his breath, awaiting his fate. When something landed heavily in front of his face, he screamed. It cut short at the sight of the heads of his friends.

"I'm taking these two with me," Hogar's voice rasped, "to send a message to the rest of you vermin. I think I'll have them mounted in your tavern." The paladin chuckled before leaning over and taking up the heads once more.

"I'll be leaving you now. And I wouldn't expect any help from your intended prey. I doubt they would be as nice to you as I. Enjoy the rest of your life." Hogar laughed as he walked away.

"He didn't kill me," Durrend said in shock. He needed to get out.

He struggled for over an hour trying to free himself from his partial entombment. He'd loosened the ground with his arms, giving him hope.

"I'll get out of here yet, you monster. No one can keep Durrend down for long." He laughed wildly, hoping it to be true.

The stench of damp fur and rotten flesh assailed him, and he caught motion out of the corner of his eye. The heavy padding of feet rushed up behind him. He never even got out a scream before it tore out his throat.

Upon returning to the temple's stable, Mangin dismounted and stretched with a shiver—the feel of the silken, heavily padded saddle on her bare flesh left her charged and amorous. She bid a good afternoon to Betal and sauntered into the village with Worm to her rear.

After twenty feet, she took a glance over her shoulder and smiled. Betal stood watching her, taking in every inch of her from behind. He shook his head and entered the temple's gardens.

She mulled Betal over in her mind. At fifteen, he already stood as tall as most of the men in the village. True, he was a bit lean, but he'd fill out. Moreover, he possessed a sharp and agile mind—even if his thinking was still too linear for her liking. In truth, it perplexed her to no end. How could a being of Chaos not be more frenzied?

"Just imagine what he'll be like when he reaches his potential," she said aloud. The Lord loved to give his world puzzles, and, in Betal, he gave them a wonderful one.

"Are you keeping up, Worm?" she asked over her shoulder.

"Yes, my lady. Worm is keeping up," he droned.

"You are going to be my bodyguard. From now on, whenever you are not guarding me or my door, you will train for that job." She paused. "Amend that; unless you need to eat, sleep, drink, or relieve yourself. We'll clear up the details later. We can't have you dying of neglect, now can we." She chuckled.

"Yes, my lady. As you wish, my lady."

She passed two more houses deeper into the village when another thought struck her. These were houses. Not hovels. When had that happened? When she first arrived, the people lived in broken down rickety shacks, all laid out at random. They leaned against trees that used to dot the village, just to keep them standing, and many of their thatched roofs were in serious need of repair. Now, she saw well-built houses lined up in neat rows. The farm animals that used to run amuck were now behind pens and fences of wood and neatly placed mortared stone. It resembled Old Town, in Cross Corners, an area built before The Lord laid claim to the world.

It doesn't even stink anymore, she thought. *When did this happen? It must have been gradual, or else I'd have noticed long before.*

With a grin, she decided to consider it later as she strode up to the home of Cobb Cruchfield. *I've much better things to do at the moment.*

She opened the door and walked in. It took a moment for her eyes to adjust to the dark. Cobb sat at what she presumed was the dinner table.

He jumped to his feet. "What in the name of Ukase are you doing in my home?" Stabbing a hand toward the door, he yelled, "Get out! Adel's not here. You can't have her."

Mangin's eyes burned, and she snarled. "Ukase? You dare use Order's name around me? You best watch your tongue."

She sighed and smiled. "Anyway, I'm not here for her, dumpling." She sauntered into the room, her hips swaying. "I'm here for you."

"Me?" He took a step back and turned his head. "What do you want of me?"

"You know what I want." Crossing the room, she extended her arm and laid her index finger upon his sternum. "I want you." She eased in closer, her voice husky. "And you want me. The need burns in your loins."

He shot a look past her. "Jason, what's going on. Really? What's she up to?"

"His name is Worm, darling," she quipped. "And Worm does whatever I tell him. From now on, he's the head of my personal guard. Granted, he's the only member, but I will remedy that in time."

Cobb's eyes went back to Mangin, still burning with hate... and lust. "My father will be back from Cross Corners any time now."

"Worm, go outside and close the door behind you." She lifted her blouse over her head. "We don't want to be disturbed." She pushed down her skirt, exposing all her splendor.

Sweat beaded Cobb's brow, and he licked his lips. He shot a look at Worm's back as his former friend walked out the door and then back to Mangin. His lips quivered and his hands shook. With a snarl, he lunged forward, grasped her head, and kissed her for all his worth. He tore open his shirt, and Mangin undid the laces of his trousers, while Worm closed the door.

Betal lay on his bed, staring at the ceiling, deep in thought about Mangin. She made his head spin. He so badly wanted to take her every night, but she was a woman in full bloom—a stunning piece of perfection. And even though he was only a year younger than she was, he felt more like a boy. She was also his best friend—only friend, really—and she made it more than apparent she wanted to keep it that way.

At least I think she does.

He wished she'd stop tormenting him. The steamy looks, the coquettish smiles, the gentle and insinuating caresses on his arm or back or face, caused his blood to boil. Not to mention the way she flaunted her sexual conquests around him.

Yet, he still questioned. Was her flirtation anything but jest? Every time he reached for her, she pulled away, rebuking him. Every time he brought up the subject of them being together, she called him silly.

"We're friends, Betal, and I don't want to lose that," she'd say to him.

The events of the day twisted his mind even more. The lust in her eyes when she spied him at the back of the crowd thrilled him. He knew she did it for his titillation as much as her own gratification. And the look she gave him when he interrupted her…

He groaned and rolled over to face the wall, but still couldn't get her off his mind.

She'd said she loved him, and, for a moment, he'd believed it. But he knew she meant it as only a friend. They were kindred spirits in a sea of disdain. Besides, who'd want a monster for a lover? He was the "Beast of Cool Winds," the creature everyone feared.

His thoughts drifted back to the look in Mangin's eyes as Adel ravished her. It played out in his mind, again and again, searing it into his memory. Mangin quivering, her eyes fluttering, her breath coming in huffs and moans, the way she licked and bit her lips while clutching Adel's head through her silken skirt...

With a groan, Betal rolled on his back, hastily untied the laces on his trousers, and took matters into his own hand.

Chapter 15
The
Westlands

(Year 522 -R.C.-)

The low hills of the Westlands rolled by as an invisible rope pulled Ellis forward. He sailed high above, yet he felt neither wind nor mist on his face. Below, trees, streams, and small lakes dotted the land, and a ridgeline spread across the fast-approaching horizon. A large river appeared beyond the rise with a broad floodplain between. At a bend in the river, lay a small walled town atop a large hill.

His heart felt heavy as the rope dragged him toward the small town. For beyond the river, a vast forest loomed, dark and menacing like a beast ready to strike. Above the forest, the sky flashed with faint miasmas of yellows and pinks, like oil on the surface of a pond. A hiss and warble filled his ears, twisting his stomach into knots until he wanted to scream.

An overpowering sense of need filled him as thoughts floated across his mind. *Why do I have to come here? Where is this place?*

The vision faded...

Ellis lay in the back of the lead wagon, idly fiddling with his mother's bronze sun pendant. The cacophony of *Concord's Grand Traveling Show* lulled him—dulcimers, zithers, lutes, tambourines, and flutes, the roar of the lions, the growl of the bears, and the squawks and tweets of the myriad of birds. Even the ever-present rumble of the people themselves helped Ellis overcome the headaches he received when his clairvoyant powers struck him.

During their travel north, he'd learned to focus and possess a modicum of control over his ability. He'd learned how to bring forth visions. Though often vague and painful, it gave him glimpses of what he needed to see, and a feeling of what to do next. He never divulged what he saw. Not even to Daylin. He didn't want her to fret.

"You can't keep pushing yourself like this," Daylin said from the driver's seat while shaking her head.

He grinned. Now nineteen, she'd grown into a beautiful woman with a lovely figure she often tried to cover. A bright red ribbon held her long, dark, curly hair in back, swinging from side to side every time she looked back at him. Her eyes were a reddish-brown at that moment—a sure giveaway to her anxiety.

"Don't smirk at me, damn it. I'm serious. I've never seen you down this long before. You've not been this weak since the night we met." She pointed at him as if trying to poke him in the ribs if she could only reach. "I swear, if you somehow kill yourself, I'll never be able to keep this rabble together."

Although difficult, Ellis refused to drop his smile. "If there's anything I've learned in my twenty years, it's there are no guarantees."

She huffed. After a couple of minutes, she spoke up again, her tone far too nonchalant. "So, are you going to tell me what you saw?"

She's still too blunt to pull off being sly, he thought. She often said she felt more comfortable around her animals than people.

He ignored her question for the time being. "What do the scouts say?" He needed time to think about the vision until he understood it better himself.

"All clear at the moment," she replied.

"Good," Ellis mumbled.

Ever since the troupe arrived in the Westlands, his life had changed. That feeling of the rope tied around his neck, always pulling them north, stopped one day—at least in the waking world. He took it as a sign that Ukase finally led them to where they needed to be, a wonderful place of relative peace and tranquility.

"You know," Daylin said. "Even after all this time, I still can't get over the weather here."

Ellis grunted a reply.

"It's so predictable," she went on. "Down south, you never knew what was going to happen next. But here, hells, they actually have seasons."

"Yup."

"And the people are so wonderful."

Ellis agreed. The troupe grew and thrived in the four years they roamed the Westlands. Amongst others, they'd picked up three separate animal acts, a quartet of singers, a trio of sword dueling japes, and an acting company. Their latest addition was a musical group calling themselves Serenity, comprising a pair of pipers, a lute player, a percussionist, and a singer.

Daylin sighed. "It's like Chaos doesn't even exist here. We're finally free."

Ellis wanted to agree about their freedom, but he held doubts. He still had something to do according to his vision, and some place to go. He just didn't know where.

"Is it even in the Westlands?" he mumbled.

"What was that?" Daylin asked.

Pretending to snore, he calmed his mind and focused inward—it often helped him decipher the visions. He reached deep into himself, trying to touch his core, the very center of his gift, a place of bright light and tranquility. His world spun as he closed in. It lay just beyond his reach. He stretched hard, focusing his mind on only that one thing, reaching the light. Yet, time and again, he failed. Sighing, he gave up and let himself drift off to sleep.

His eyes sprang open when Daylin rang the bell hanging from the ceiling. He'd been dreaming about a strange mammoth tree, but it faded quickly. With a groan, he rolled over, stood, and went to the driver's seat. "Well, at least my headache is gone."

"Good," Daylin said. "Just in time. We've reached the outskirts of Timsdale."

He thanked her, sat on the bench, and took in the sights of the upcoming town.

With bandits being an ever-present problem in The Reach, folk had learned how to keep them out. Several large fields and pastures surrounded the town, each one bordered with low stone walls and large, thick hedgerows for protection. The road to the town was wide enough for two wagons to pass each other and leave a good bit of space between them. Earthen berms surrounded the town proper, along with high, wooden palisades, and a large set of iron-bound doors. Next to the doors sat a tall watchtower with a view of several miles.

Ellis waved to the sentry atop the tower.

Daylin squinted. "Do you actually think he can see you wave? We're still a mile away."

"No," Ellis said, and waved all the same.

He gazed about at the bright-green hedges, the colorful fieldstone walls, and the wildflowers dancing in the high grass as the wind caressed it. He tilted his head up to the brilliant blue sky as the glorious day filled him with joy… along with more than a touch of melancholy.

They'd loved to have seen this, he thought. He sighed and tried to push the sadness back down.

"What's wrong?" Daylin asked.

"It's nothing." He scratched the short beard covering his chin and upper lip.

"Don't give me that," she replied, her eyes turning from brown to a dark yellow. "It's a beautiful spring day, and we'll be in Timsdale in no time. You know, I think they love us more than any other place in the world, and we've three new acts for them. It's going to be magnificent, and here you are moping with that hangdog look on your face."

"I am happy, Daylin. Believe me. It's just… on days like this, I miss them most. They should be here leading us. Not me." Under his breath, he added, "I'm the one that should be dead."

"You *stop* that. You hear me?" She jabbed her chin at him. "I don't want to hear any more talk like that. Hells, Ellis. Your parents gave their lives to save you and the others. You didn't kill them. That stinking priest did!" She angrily flicked the reins to urge the horses on faster. By the end of her diatribe, Daylin's eyes had turned black.

By the time they reached the wall, Michael Lyn, the Village Master, awaited them with open arms. The epitome of a jolly gent, Lyn stood well under six feet in height and his girth strained his bright-green doublet as well as his voluminous, brown breeches. His full gray beard partially obscured a puffy red face, and his equally gray hair lie hidden beneath a large pointed hat with a long, black feather at the brim.

"Ellis Concord," the man bellowed, waving Ellis over to join him. "It's been far too long!"

G. S. Scott — 127 -

Ellis jumped down just as Daylin pulled the wagon to a halt. "Master Lyn. How are you this fine dawn?"

"What kind of greeting is that?" he replied with false incredulity. He stepped up and enveloped Ellis in his massive arms and vigorously patting Ellis on the back. "Call me Michael. You know that. Gods, but it's good to see you, lad." He stepped back and waved his hand toward the gates.

"Come in and be welcome my good people," he shouted to the rest of the troupe. "The lads saw you coming, and we've already cleared the Green for you."

Ellis led the troupe onto town afoot with Master Lyn at his side. As usual, they put on the proper entering display, with the troupe's tumblers and jugglers following behind Ellis, just ahead of the wagons. Loma, the fire-breather, stood atop his wagon, bellowing fire into the sky. The musicians played their hearts out and the singers crooned at the top of their lungs.

The townspeople waved and shouted. Children sat on the shoulders of adults shouting and laughing. Folk looked out the windows of the two and three-story houses abutting the road, all pointing and gasping at what they saw.

Ellis simply nodded and waved back to the gathering crowd. He didn't like to do anything flashy. Even his clothes, though bright, colorful, and clean, were modest when compared to the rest in the show.

Master Lyn glanced at him out of the corner of his eye with a small smile on his face as he waddled next to Ellis, his eyes weighing.

"Out with it, Michael," Ellis said. "You were never a good one for keeping secrets."

"Very true," he bellowed over the din of the crowd, and again patted Ellis upon the back. "Tis nothing nefarious, I assure you. I was merely musing at how different you are compared to the other show masters. The rest of them are all brash and boastful, exalting everyone who could see or hear." Michael thrust his arms about in large, dramatic gestures as an example. "But not you. You are almost humble. But I will say this. You exude pride. Not pride in yourself, but in those around you. You love your people, and they love you. You're a born leader, my friend. Governance with humility is a rare trait in this world. Don't lose it, and let no one ever take it from you."

Ellis took it all in without comment.

Michael continued, "Now all you have to do is get that little fox of yours with child so you can keep this wonderful show of yours going for generations to come." He laughed heartily, his cheeks reddening as Ellis stumbled.

Ellis stared at the Village Master's back as the hefty man quickened his pace into town.

"What the hells is he talking about," Ellis muttered. He shot a quick glance back at Daylin. True, they shared the lead wagon, but they weren't intimate. Far from it. He didn't think of her that way. She was a sister to him. Nothing more. Besides, she'd likely laugh at him for even thinking of it—that or slap him. "Hells, most likely, both."

He shook his head and went back to waving to the townspeople, doing his best to smile. Michael's comment about his standing out among other troupe masters unnerved him; the last thing he wanted to do was stand out. He'd no illusions that Chaos had given up its pursuit, so he'd been consciously keeping himself reserved. It never occurred to him that by standing back, he was drawing attention to himself.

"I'll have to have a talk with Jaden," he said. The troupe's tailor and dressmaker worked marvels. He'd be sure to come up with something flamboyant.

Ellis led them to the middle of town. There, they set up in a large circle in the very center. The town's Green was large enough they could put up their high canvas walls. Placed twenty feet in front of the wagons, the walls allow intimacy for those performing in front of or within, while keeping a large common area for those who liked to roam while they performed. The wall had several breaks to allow the crowd to flow, and short enough so the stage acts and the guards standing atop the wagons could keep an eye on the crowd.

Ellis loved keeping watch. From his high vantage point atop his wagon, he took in all the acts at once. If he felt someone needed a little help in getting a larger crowd, he'd get one of the children to tell the jesters, Maxie, or Dandle the Jape to entice people to flow into those areas. He wanted to keep everyone happy.

On the first day, however, he walked through the show, getting a feel of the crowd. Just past mid-day, he made his way to the center where three acts shared the space. Each performed their act and moved on, allowing someone else to replace them. First up were the Celestial Sisters, four stunning women who, although not real sisters, had voices that were gifts from the gods. The second act was Steel Lotus, five belly dancers—of varying age—who worked with balanced swords upon their heads or snakes entwined about their bodies while they danced.

I'll never understand how they get used to that, Ellis thought, doing his best to suppress a shudder as the white snake wrapped its way around the neck of the lithe and lovely, Jess. Its tail slithered through her long blonde hair, and she never lost her glowing smile.

Ellis grinned. *She loves the crowd and the crowd lover her.*

And then he came to Daylin.

He stopped and watched her perform with her dogs— he never tired of it. Daylin's simple blue cotton dress, buttoned up to her neck and hanging to her knees, waved in the day's gentle breeze.

He'd been trying for years to convince her to wear something more revealing and dramatic, like a dress hanging open at the chest, or sequined pants and a shirt that dazzled in the light of the sun and hug her wonderful form. Yet, she refused every time.

"I don't want to stand out," she said. "The dogs are the stars. Not me."

Daylin started her show with her seven mutts, varying in type and size, all in a line before her. She never used the wolves—they had too much pride, she said.

"All right. Let's get this going," she said with a clap. She let out a sharp whistle and whirled her arms in front of her in intertwining circles.

The dogs simply stared at her.

"Come on, guys. Move it," she said with another clap and a whistle.

They sat there; some scratching themselves, some looking about at the crowd with their tongues lolling out, and the largest, Henry, licked himself before lying down, bringing chuckles from the crowd.

"Aww. What are you doing? Why are you guys doing this to me?" Daylin said with a huff. She pulled out small bits of dried meat she kept in a pouch at her belt and held them before her. "You know how this works. No tricks, no treats."

The littlest one, Mitsi, quickly leapt into the air and snatched the treat out of her hand, hurried back to the others, and sat down, scratching herself.

Dalyn threw her hands into the air and turned to the laughing crowd. "Please, don't go. They're just a little tired."

As soon as she turned her back, Henry got up on his hind feet and danced in a tight circle—his forelegs pawing at the air above him—while the rest ran in precise, intricate circles about him, leaping over one another in the process. The crowd roared in laughter while the children pointed at her dogs and yelled at Daylin to turn around. By the time she whirled about after understood them—or pretended to understand—the dogs had stopped and lazed about on the ground as though they'd nothing else to do.

It went on much the same way to the delight of the crowd. Daylin continued to plead for forgiveness while her dogs ran about one another, performed backflips, and danced—both separately and together. In the finale, the dogs climbed upon each other, forming a pyramid of six, while Henry tossed up a ball to Mitsi with his mouth. She caught it and balanced upon her nose. At the end, Mitsi tossed away the ball and leapt over Daylin's shoulder. Daylin caught the dog in her outstretched arms, bowed, and turned with her right arm extended to include the dogs in the praise.

The people loved it, as did Ellis. He smiled, filled with pride, and clapped as hard as the rest. When she looked his way while waving and thanking the crowd, he bowed to her. She nodded back and ran off the Green, her face flushed with an odd look in her eye.

That was strange, Ellis thought.

As he made his way to the acts before the wagons, he considered the Village Master's words regarding Daylin. A hotbed of social activity, the show's people seemed to switch up partners week to week—and that didn't include the folk who simply gallivanted around, never taking on anyone in a serious relationship. It caused some strife from time to time, but they'd lost only two acts due to any ill-fated emotional entanglements. In all those years, he'd never known Daylin to be with anyone. In fact, she often seemed quite timid. The only two people she interacted with daily were Dirge and himself.

I hope I didn't embarrass her with that bow, he thought. Or worse, take it as some kind of flirtation. He'd hate to think he might be leading her on.

He stopped in front the wagon the Portrayals Theater Company. The six of them were putting on a show about the gods—something about their dinner host feeding them his child for some reason. Their dramas often left him befuddled.

As he watched, the complexities of the relationships within the troupe came back to his mind. Bright, a lithe and lovely young man looking strident in his dark blue robes and curly white hair darted about from relationship to relationship. As did the diminutive Rikki, looking ravishing in a form-fitting white robe with her long brown hair fanning down the back, which highlighted her light brown skin. The other two men on stage were Mike and Leo. Distinguished gentlemen, they'd been in a relationship for years. The two remaining members were Angharad and Sarah, who frequented each other's beds, even though they were both in steady relationships with others in the troupe. Angharad perched on her toes in a light green robe, her curly, golden hair flowing down her back, and her piercing blue/green eyes seemed aflame—the personification of a righteous God. Sarah—a beauty in her thirties, with dark red hair and blue eyes—held herself high in her tight silken blue robe, her nose pointed up and her head turned slightly as she delivered her lines. One of the smartest people Ellis knew, Sarah wrote many of their plays, and worked as the troupe's herbalist.

Ellis never seriously considered getting involved with one of the troupe. It would cause only trouble. When he felt the urge, he enticed a local into bed. The village men and women gave him a sense of belonging in a far too tenuous world. He climbed atop their wagon with a chair to observe the shows for the remainder of their stay. On the second day, Canda caught his attention—the young man had a certain twinkle in his blue eyes. Ellis spent the rest of their nights in Timsdale in Canda's hot, sweet embrace.

After a week, Ellis decided they needed to move on. He went to Michael Lyn's large home at the edge of the Green, to bid the Village Master farewell. Lyn's wife, Rachel, greeted him at their door.

"Good morning, Ellis." She greeted him with a warm hug. "You're here to see Michael, I suppose. He's in his office." She ushered him through the house.

The large man stood from his desk and hastened to Ellis. "My good friend. What brings you here so early this fine morning?"

Ellis clasped Michael's large hand. "It is time for us to move on, my friend."

"Oh. That's a shame. I'm truly saddened to see you go. You'll be greatly missed, as always." He went back to his desk. "The gift you all have given us is immeasurable. I tell you, I've not seen my people this happy in far too long." He opened the top drawer and fished out a large leather purse. "I'll see that your people get all the food and supplies you need, right away." He handed the purse to Ellis. "And I want you to take this as well."

Ellis's eyes grew wide at seeing quite a few pieces of gold along with the customary silver and copper. He glanced up at Michael and raised an eyebrow.

The Village Master chucked. "Think nothing of it. We've been doing quite well lately. We've had bumper crops, and the sheep have produced some of the best wool we've ever seen. And what's more, we've not seen any bandits in years."

"That long? What do you make of it?" Ellis queried.

"Well, some say it's because of the Beast across the Cunning. They say it's frightened them all off." He shook his head in mirth. "I'm not one on that. That monster, whatever it is, is too far away to bother us. But we have seen an increase in Chaos paladins roaming around. I've heard the Ghost of Death was seen no more than ten miles from here."

Ellis had heard the same thing himself, from many lips.

"As for the crops?" Michael shrugged. "I think they are doing well because of the night lights from the north."

Ellis cocked his head to the side. "What do you mean by, *night lights*?"

"Well, from time to time, we see strange swirling lights to the far north during a new moon, when the sky is darkest. It's had some folk terrified. They think it has something to do with those Chaos storms they get down south. But after seeing the lights for several months and having nothing go awry, folks just dismissed 'em as nothing."

The big man looked Ellis in the eye. "*Others* may think they're nothing, but not I. Ever since we've seen them, there's been fewer creatures lurking about. And as I said, the crops have been booming. It's not natural, I tell you. I think that's why we've seen so many paladins about. Now I'm not a man to denounce the Lord," he said with a shake of his head, "but I think something else is stirring. Hells, Kirks Knob sees them every night, and people there have been acting all strange. And that's saying something considering where the Knob lays."

A tingling ran up and down Ellis's spine. Trying to keep his voice moderate, he asked, "Kirks Knob? I've not heard of it."

"You've not been to The Knob? Well, I suppose that's not too surprising. It is rather small, far to the north, on the edge of The Reach, west of The Barren Mounds and just before The Lands of the Dead." Michael shuddered. "It's on a bend in the Dourer River. If you're thinking about heading that way, my friend, just be wary. As I said, strange things happen there and they're not the friendliest of people. I would hate to see anything untoward happen to you all."

Chapter 16
Kirks Knob

(Year 522 -R.C.-)

Daylin fidgeted on the driver's bench, glancing at Ellis out of the corner of her eye. Five days passed and she still couldn't decide if Ellis had been playing with her. The bow hadn't thrown her; it was the look on his face. He used it whenever courting his lovers in the towns. His eyes held admiration and desire.

She bit her lip. *Why would someone as beautiful as Ellis look at me like that? Why would anyone?*

Shaking off the silly thought, she turned to Ellis. "I'm going to grab a bite of that amazing bread we got from Michael. Do you want any?"

"No, thank you."

Daylin climbed over the bench and went to the pantry. Opening the door, she drew her head back. Two mice—one gray and one white—eating into the bread. "Where d'you two come from?" She shook her head. "Well, no matter. I'll give you a piece but I'm hungry too." She tore off a small piece and handed it to them. "All right, run along now."

The white one bit her finger.

Snatching her hand back, she lashed out at it with her thoughts. "How dare you!"

The mouse stopped and shuddered. Squealing, its little feet clawed at the wood in fear as her thoughts held it in place.

She gasped and released it. "Oh, I'm so sorry. I didn't know I could do that. I swear I wasn't trying to hurt you."

The mouse skittered away into the cupboard. She felt it crawl through the tiny opening until it reached to outside where it jumped to the ground. It scampered no more than five feet before Bucky gobbled it up.

Daylin gasped. "Bucky, how could you?"

The half-wolf sent back confused thoughts. "Mouse hurt you. I eat it so it not hurt you again."

She scowled. "Yea, right. Why aren't you with the others?"

Shortly before Vir died, he led Daylin to a den of three wolf pups who'd lost their pack. Now fully grown, the wolves—along with her larger dogs—operated as guards and scouts for the troupe.

"They tell me to stay close to you. They not like the smell here. I protect you."

"Well, thank you." She grinned.

She'd picked Bucky up less than a year before. Something about the half-wolf always reminded her of her beloved Vir. "Are you sure The Mother didn't send you back to protect me?"

"What? *You* my mother."

"Well, that's very sweet of you. However, I think I'm plenty safe with our guards. I want you to—"

A vision from Kylee, the pack leader, filled her mind. In it, she saw a floodplain at the edge of a broad river. Beyond the river crouched a dark forest; the sky above looking like something out of a nightmare.

"Ellis." She scrambled for the driver's seat.

They topped the ridgeline overlooking the Dourer River. The road led straight down the decline and meandered through the floodplain to Kirks Knob. What Ellis saw concerned him as the stonewalled town atop a steep-sided hill, so they'd have no place to erect their camp. He doubted the town had a big enough Green, and the marshy land around the hill would give them even more trouble—their wagons would sink up to their axles in no time.

He called Evan over to him. "I need you to go to the town and let them know of our coming. And I want you to get a feel of the people themselves. Also, I need you to check the land around the bottom of the hill. Tell me if there's any place for us to set up. Take Lem and Hoak with you."

As they left, he jumped down from the wagon. His eyes drifted back to Kirks Knob like iron filings to a loadstone. A thick blanket of gray clouds hung over the land. Bands of swirling colors flickered above and within the ominous clouds, and a hiss and warble filled the air. It sent a chill up his spine.

"Can you feel it, lad?" Whisp asked.

Ellis jumped; he'd not heard the old magic user approach. "Feel what?"

"The Chaos. That swirling miasma is the essence of the Lord of Chaos. It's the visible element of the prison encompassing The Lands of the Dead." Whisp appeared uneasy as he gazed at the distant lights.

"What's in there?"

"You know what's in there, lad. You've seen it in your visions. Outside Glennen, you told me of a story you wanted to hear. You described the Tower perfectly."

Ellis squeezed his eyes shut to hold out the guilt. "But what *is* it?"

"It's the Tower of Time. It's why they created the prison, and why it's on constant guard. You see, there's a prophecy about that tower. It goes:

> *Time stands vigil, a spire of white in a sea of black.*
> *The Mother's child cries as love dies*
> *While the Slayer's blood does battle.*
> *Awaken and pass judgment, Ancient One*
> *For the Abomination blackens the quivering heart."*

Ellis rubbed his arms as a chill ran through him. "What does that mean?"

"No one really knows."

"Have you ever been in there?"

The old man pursed his lips. "Yes. Once. And it's something I'll never do again."

Whisp pried his eyes away from the hellish lights above the distant land, pulled out his pipe, packed it from the pouch tied to his belt, and took a long drag. "Near the end of my training, they summoned me to Gate Hall. While I was there to be tested, someone breached the border. The High Priest dispatched several us to fetch them. I guess they figured it would be as good a test for me as any." He chuckled wryly. "Gunther Karados, the High Priest, has always been a vigilant man, and he takes his charge of guarding the prison very seriously. Truth be told, he's the only disciplined priest I've ever met. I guess that's how he won the job."

"But the border is so large. How would you be able to tell where they crossed, let alone when?" Ellis asked.

"As I said, those lands are a prison, my boy. No one's allowed in, and nothing gets out. There is a powerful physical and spiritual force behind those lights. The only way in, the only place where the boundary is weak enough, is in the lands around Gate Hall. The shield's focus is in the citadel at the heart of the city. Due to the very nature of the shield—a manifestation of the Lord of Chaos—it has inherent inconsistencies. The closer one gets to the focus, the easier it is to breach the shield."

"Every so often, a hole will open near Gate Hall that's large enough for a person to pass through." He demonstrated by blowing a smoke ring and poking his finger through it. "But, doing so leaves a trace that can be located and followed." He struck his finger through the side of the smoke ring, breaking it and leaving a residue following his finger.

"Did you ever find them?" Daylin asked from her seat atop the wagon.

"In a way." The old man closed his eyes and trembled. "There were three of us that went after them – myself, a paladin I didn't know, and my master, Abram Kelly. It didn't take us long to find them. It turned out to be a pair of young acolytes wanting to see if the tales about that hellish land were true. They also wanted to prove their bravery and manliness."

Whisp spat on the ground. "The fools. It's called The Lands of the Dead for a reason. There's nothing living there, not animals, nor plants. Hells, even the water isn't fit to drink. Nothing lives there, and those residing there resent it."

A crowd gathered to hear Whisp's story. Karen, one of the Celestial Sisters, stepped forward. "What does that mean?" she asked in her high, delicate voice. "If there's nothing living there, how can anything resent it?"

"You have to understand, my dear," Whisp said. "The stories of wandering spirits in there are true. The ghosts lingering there are not benign wandering apparitions. They're living beings, trapped in a timeless world. Most are simply mute specters, lashing out at everything they come across, but since they're in the ethereal realm, they cannot touch our world, and therefore only ravage each other."

"But there are a few, my dear, which can reach into our world. And if one of those touches you, they can pull you into the ethereal realm where they'll flay you for an eternity." He lowered his head, his voice soft. "It is something I know firsthand."

"What happened, Whisp?" Angharad asked, her delicate voice quivering. "Please, tell us."

"We found them, but something else found them first." He took another draw on his pipe and shook his head. "It happened just as we reached them. They were kneeling down, investigating a sword on the ground next to a large pile of stones. As we approached, one of the young men picked it up and showed it to us. 'Look what we found,' the fool shouted." Whisp chuckled dryly before his frown returned.

"An apparition came from behind the rocks and grabbed hold of him. His shout turned into a scream. I watched that thing pull the boy into their realm, like a fish plucking a fly from atop the water. His screams thinned and went silent, but I could still see his mouth agape, screaming silently. The thing took the sword from the boy's hand, and with one swing, took his head off. That poor boy's head lay upon the ground, his eyes wide, searching about frantically, his mouth still screaming, while his body lurched about, its arms flailing."

Whisp's eyes filled with incongruity, as if even he couldn't believe what he was saying. "The boy lost his head, but did not die."

When the old man didn't continue, Ellis asked, "What happened next?"

"What happened? I did the dumbest thing I've ever done in my life. The thing turned on the other boy, and without even thinking, I jumped the thing from behind."

Whisp's eyes seemed to look inward. "I could actually feel it pulling me in. I felt my life draining away, my body... going thin. Abram hit it with a bolt of Chaos and the thing fled." He looked at Ellis, his eyes haunted and lost. "But it took part of my soul with it. I lost most of my touch of the Lord's Breath that day. They cast me out for my stupidity."

"The odd thing was: in taking part of my soul, it seems it gave me a gift of sorts in return. I realized if I concentrated, I could mask myself from the minions of Chaos." Whisp shook his head in disbelief. "Who would have thought a thing of death could give me a gift I'd need to use later in life?"

"So I fled Gate Hall and headed south. I never wanted to be near that land again. Truth be told, lad, even being this close turns my stomach." He turned and headed back to his wagon without another word.

The crowd dispersed with much muttering—many of them gazing at the skies above Kirks Knob. Ellis didn't blame them. He was at a loss for words himself. He sat back and awaited word from the scouts, and stared at those swirling, colorful clouds.

Several hours later, Evan and the guards returned, and the news they brought was not good. "Thems folks are crazy," Evan said. "I had Lem and Hoak scout the lowlands, as you requested, and I went straight to the town. They'd closed and barred the gate, even at this time of day. When I asked to come in, the gatekeepers cursed at me, telling me to shove off. When I told them who I was, and about the troupe, they damned near turned white. One of them yelled at the other to go get the mayor, and then he aimed his crossbow at me, telling me to stay where I was."

He ran his hand through his short-cropped black hair. "I'm telling you, Ellis, if I had moved a muscle that man would have tried to put a bolt in me. Of course, the way he was shaking, he likely would've missed, but I didn't want to take that chance, if you know what I mean. So's, anyway, it took about an hour before some fat, greasy haired fellow came to the top of the wall. He told me his town wanted nothing to do with us and to—now these are his words—'take your stinking, Chaos infested horde as far from here as you can, or I'll set the armsmen after the lot of you.'"

Evan shook his head. "I'm telling you, Ellis, I think he would. By the time that fat, ugly bastard showed up, I could see at least two dozen bowmen on the wall and I heard the shouts of more. On top of that, I heard a fair number of them askin' each other whether or not they I was even alive! I mean, what kind of crazy dung is that?"

Ellis didn't know what to say. It wasn't unprecedented that a town turned them away, but he'd never heard such open hostility before. "Thank you, Evan. You did well. Go back and let everyone know we need to turn around and head out as quickly as possible. If they're as volatile as you say, then we best put as much distance between us and this town as we can before we make camp for the night."

They traveled hard and made camp as late as possible with Ellis deep in thought the entire way. Once stopped, Ellis told the guard to keep sharp just in case those townsfolk decided they weren't sufficiently far away.

"Why in the world were they acting that way, do you think?" Daylin asked as they got ready to bed down for the night.

"I don't know," Ellis replied with a shake of his head. "Perhaps they are being affected by the prison. Maybe The Lands of the Dead are spreading. You heard Evan; they were asking each other if he were even alive or not."

The entire thing perplexed him. Why the hells were they acting so crazy? And more importantly why had his vision told him they needed to go there if not to perform? He needed to find out.

He stripped, removing even his small clothes, and settled down in his small bed on the other side of the wagon from Daylin. Closing his eyes, he took relaxing, deep breaths. He calmed his mind and focused inward, reaching deep into himself. The world spun the deeper he reached. That place of bright light and serenity lay before him, just out of reach. He stretched and strained while focusing his thoughts on those colorful, shimmering clouds beyond the town. The answers were there, within that chaotic prison.

He pushed and stretched, and the world thinned. His mind strained and trembled, like a thin sheet of glass ready to shatter. The light drew closer. Screaming in pain, he made one final lunge...

The light filled him, and the world fell away.

He opened his eyes to a universe of nothing but white, a place of utter tranquility. In the past, he'd only touched the surface, only felt the barest breath of the serenity he now knew—a world of peace.

He thought of his vision of Kirks Knob, and the town popped into existence below him. He hovered above it and the world spread out beneath him: the town, the river, the floodplain, and the prison wavering beyond.

"Where do we need to go?" he asked the whiteness. "What do I need to see?"

His head rang like a softly struck bell. The world fell away once more, and the old vision returned. He floated over the large, walled city of Gate Hall. He'd never been there, but he knew it all the same. To his left lay a broad river and the massive, rolling hills beyond it. To his right lay shallow hills leading to a great chain of mountains in the far distance. Before him, lay utter desolation.

He lurched forward and flew directly into that devastated land. Far above him, roiling black and gray clouds that never let through the light of the sun filled the sky. Intermixed within those clouds, the mass of miasmic Chaos swirled and pulsed. A thin, unnatural gray fog, holding no moisture, shrouded the land below. The vegetation, consisting of short, gray-green grasses, shriveled bushes, and gnarled trees, seemed neither alive nor dead. No wind blew in the desolate land, nor did it rain, and the temperature never wavered, always staying cool as a late autumn night. Scattered cities, towns, and fortifications passed beneath him as he soared above. People filled the land, looking like statues mimicking everyday life. They weren't the only people he spotted. Misty forms roamed the land, wandering semi-corporeal spirits attacking each other in a never-ending war. A vast hellscape mimicking both life and death spread all the way to the horizon. It was The Lands of the Dead.

His flight seemed to take an eternity, yet only lasted an instant as he raced toward something far to the north. At the foot of a massive mountain chain sat a tower, a ghostly white spire shrouded in darkness. The air around the tower seemed to writhe and shake, causing it to pulse white light intermittently in both intensity and duration. That light drew him. It pulled so hard he feared it would rip out his soul.

He raced to the tower. The light grew in his eyes, expanding until it engulfed him in its frigid purity... then all went black.

Time stretched out to infinity until the emptiness faded and warmth returned. He heard a voice in the distance, faint yet persistent. The voice, soft, trembling, and most assuredly feminine, slowly grew louder.

"Come back to me," the sweet voice said. "Please, come back. Don't leave me. You can't do this to me." The woman was crying, the pain evident in her voice. "Just come back and everything will be all right. You're the only person here who means anything to me, so don't you dare leave me."

She caressed his head and ran her fingers through his hair. It hurt. His entire body ached like someone dragged him behind a galloping horse. He tried opening his eyes, but the light blinded him, causing even more pain. He thought his head might well crack open from the agony.

"It's all right, Daylin," he croaked. "I'll be all right. I just need some sleep."

"All right? *Sleep*? You've been asleep for three days!" The anger in her voice melded with relief and joy—and love.

A man could die happy in her arms... but she only sees me as a brother, he thought with a hint of sorrow before slipping into unconsciousness.

The next morning, he woke with a groan, but not from the pain—although that remained. He felt the *pull* once more. That ever-present rope drawing him north so many years ago had returned. But instead of wrapping about his chest with a gentle, steady drag, he felt it tied about his throat, wrenching him hard from the east.

He knew what he needed to do. The vision told him to go north. That in and of itself, was no surprise. They'd been traveling northward since their initial flight from The South. But now he needed to go east to Gate Hall, to leave the Westlands and never return, before traveling north into the very center of The Lands of the Dead. And he wouldn't be alone.

Chapter 17
Cool Winds Blow

(Year 522 -R.C.-)

The bear-sized beast of Chaos stood with its back to the wall of stone half the height of the surrounding trees. It chomped its razor-sharp teeth and hissed while lashing out with the talons at the end of its snake-like second neck.

Blood oozed from Lakota's shoulder as he crept forward, slickening his gray fur. The surrounding pack bore similar wounds. They'd tracked the stinking thing for miles and finally had it cornered. "Get on its flanks. Don't let it escape."

The beast turned its head to Lakota, staring with its blue human-like eyes. It twisted its head; the sunlight sprinkling through the forest canopy glinted off the things twisted crown of horns. Opening its mouth, the beast of Chaos screeched, its breath smelling like fetid, rotten meat.

"Now," Lakota barked.

The wolves pounced. They snapped at the beast's legs and necks. Lakota's youngest brother, Danka, got hold of its rear leg, snapping it like a stick. The thing spun and bit Danka's ear off, who yelped and tumbled away.

Lakota lunged for the snake-like neck. It slid through his grip and sunk its dagger-like talons into Lakota's shoulder. He clamped down on the neck, refusing to give in to the pain. The thing's round head turned to him, shrieked, and attacked with its silver teeth. Lakota knew he might die, but he dare not let it go.

Three of his brethren slammed into its side, causing its teeth to snap on empty air. The snake-neck tore off halfway down as it rolled away. The thing howled and bulldozed its way through the rest of the pack and into the forest.

The pack started to follow, but Lakota called out, "No, that's enough."

"But that thing killed Alpha Tengay and the pups," White Cloud said.

Lakota shook his massive, shaggy head. "I know. But I'll not risk any of your lives further. Besides, it won't hurt any of us again after this. It's only a threat to humans now."

Betal's eyes snapped open. Covered in sweat, he jerked his head out the book lying on this desk. As the dream faded, he swore he could still smell the stink of the grunkin in the room's air.

He sighed. "Now it's too warm." Weeks before, Mangin showed him a technique to manage the temperature of his room without using the fireplace or the window. Yet, for the life of him, he couldn't get it right.

He crossed the room and cracked his window, letting in the strong, cool wind. The sun stood near its zenith in the bright blue sky with nary a cloud in sight. With most of the villagers out in the fields, the Green held only a handful of children at play, and a pair of men.

"Ho, Cable. What news from Tapers Pointe?" the Blacksmith called out.

"Not good, Gordon." The herdsman shook his head as he approached on horseback. "A grunkin attacked a young woman, not two weeks back. Folks said it ripped her to pieces and spread all over the field."

Gordon shivered. "Did they find it?"

Cable only shook his head.

"Curse them," the Blacksmith growled. "Curse them and everything Chaos."

Cable shot a glance up to Betal's window. "Not so loud. He might hear you."

"I don't care what that ugly monster hears. He doesn't belong here. This is our village. Not his."

"I don't disagree with you. You just need to—" Cable swiveled his head. "The Ghost may be around. I need to get going. Mary worries."

As the two men went on their way, Betal glanced at his reflection in the glass. "Ugly?"

He looked harder at himself. He'd grown considerably in the last few years. Now twenty-two, he stood a hand taller than six foot and his face had filled out some. But he hadn't realized he'd grown ugly.

"No wonder Mangin only wants me for a friend."

He shook the thought away.

As of late, something troubled his thoughts. Something felt wrong, and he couldn't quite put his finger on what. Fluctuations in the world—something outside the Breath of the Lord—tugged at him. Even the day's brisk winds whistling through the window carried something ominous. A feeling he shouldn't be there—not anymore.

"Why do I have to leave?" he mumbled. "And where would I go?"

What little he knew of the world—other than a few tidbits he'd garnered from overhearing the townspeople—he'd learned from Mangin and Dithiyar. However, they only talked of the things they cared about, and told him nothing of the common people and the places they lived. Trying to pry information out of Dithiyar was nearly impossible—he'd have a better chance to get a stone to speak. In the realm of Chaos, if you wanted something, you had to take it. And the priest wanted to keep him in the dark about a great number of things. Mangin was quite the opposite. She went out of her way to educate him in the ways of The Lord, His power, and the politics therein, but didn't care about the regular people.

"Maybe she can help." Mangin excelled at interpreting the fluctuations of Chaos.

Leaving his room, Betal set a ward upon it to prevent anyone else from entering and strode down the long empty hall, his boots echoing off the bare walls. He approached Mangin's door and saw a ward upon it. Not knowing if it was a physical barrier or one against sound as well, Betal sent a small pulse of power into the room. Unless Mangin were either deep in meditation or asleep, she'd sense it. After waiting a few minutes without a response, he set a glyph on the door to tell her he'd called upon her. He then went up to her personal study on the third floor. Again, he detected a ward and repeated his pulse, and again garnered no response, so he left another glyph.

Next, he chose the temple's library. Books and scrolls haphazardly filled its shelves stretching from floor to ceiling. The twenty by fifty room smelled of beeswax polish, dust, and the musk of yellowing pages of theories, academia, and stories, all growing dusty from disuse. Reading was widely discouraged—knowledge was power, and people with no power were much more pliable.

He hustled to the far wall where several comfortable chairs with end tables and lamp-stands sat next to the large exterior windows and the fireplace. The two library cats sunned themselves in the windows next to the cold hearth, and dust motes swirled in the sunlight, but Mangin wasn't there.

"Where are you?" He considered asking Dithiyar, but dismissed it. He didn't feel like dealing with the pompous ass. "Maybe she's in the village."

Exiting the temple's main entrance, Betal paused on the top of the landing and gazed up at the sky. A few light, swirling clouds floated in the ever-changing blue sky. The heat of the sun soaked into his skin, but the wind kept it from being too hot. He loved it.

Is there a better place in the world? he wondered.

Quite a few people meandered about the Green. Scanning the villagers with no luck, he set out at random, taking a leisurely stroll in hopes he might run into her, or someone who knew where to find her.

As he ambled through the village, the people didn't shy away from him like usual. A young woman with long brown hair, Stacy Kendal, even approached him while holding a basket of apples.

"Good afternoon," she said with a nod. "Would you care for an apple, Betal?" Her thin lips held a pleasant smile, and her long, flowing white dress and slippers shined in the sunlight.

"No. Thank you," Betal replied.

He tilted his head slightly. "I don't think I've ever seen anything so white before?"

Her eyes sparkled, and her smile broadened. "Do you like it? Papa got it from a merchant a few weeks ago. I didn't dare wear it before for fear of gettin' it dirty. But there's just something about today. I had to put it on." She twisted her hips back and forth.

"There is something about today, isn't there?" He gave her a slight smile and a nod. "Well, a good day to you."

Her smile faltered. "Good day to you… Betal." As she walked away, her cheeks seemed a bit flushed, her eyes went to the ground, and she fiddled with her dress while biting her lip.

That was strange, he thought. For a moment, he believed she might have been flirting with him, but realized it was impossible. No one would flirt with an ugly monster.

"I guess I'm not the only one feeling the world stirring."

Stacy wasn't the only one acting odd toward him. The village cooper, Gerald Cain, also approached him. "Good day to you, my young master. How are you?"

"I am well, Master Cain."

"Oh. None of that 'Master' stuff. Call me Gerald. You are the true master here. Not I." He laughed.

"As you wish, Gerald," Betal said with a smile of his own.

"And how is your father doing?"

"He's well, the last I saw him. Though you've probably seen him more recently than I have."

"Well, that's most likely true. We hardly ever see you around anymore."

Betal frowned. "Most people don't *want* me around."

"Oh, posh." The man waved his hand. "To the hells with them. You're not to blame for what happened all those years ago, regardless of what Erin and his folk think. You're a good lad, thanks to your father. Unlike others." He paused a moment and glanced back at the temple. "At least I hope you don't mind me saying so."

"I understand," Betal said with a nod and a slight raise of his hand. "Speaking of which, have you seen Mangin about?"

The man grinned and lowered his eyes. "Actually, I was referring to the old man. The young miss is a fine one, in my mind. Oh, she may be more than a tad devilish at times, but she's not done anyone any real harm. Sure, some folks claim she's bewitched them into her bed. But me, I just chalk it up to plain ol' lust. She's a fine-looking woman, after all."

"Truly?"

Gerald nodded. "Deep down, she's a good heart. I can see it."

Betal wondered if she'd done something to convince the cooper of that, but he saw no obvious charm on the man. "Have you seen her?"

"No. I'm sorry. But if I do, I'll let her know you're looking for her." He bid Betal a good day.

Betal continued down the lane, and as Chaos would have it, around the next turn stood his father talking to one of those Betal knew hated him, Erin Cruchfield. As he approached the two men, the militia head made a comment to his father and briskly stalked off while staring daggers at Betal.

If a look could kill, I'd be dead many times over by now, he thought with a shake of the head.

"My boy." John threw his arms around Betal in a hug.

"Hello, Father," he replied just as warmly.

"How are you?" John asked. "It's good to see you out and about. It's been days. You shouldn't stay so cooped up in that musty old temple all the time."

John stood about a half a head shorter than he did, but to Betal, his father would always loom large. "I get out when I can. Study time is hit-and-miss so I like to keep close and not miss out."

Glancing in the direction Cruchfield went, he frowned. "Besides, there's some who'd rather never see me again."

"I know, son. I know. It's always weighed hard on Erin, but it's not your fault. You hear? So, what brings you out this fine day?"

"I'm looking for Mangin. Have you seen her?"

John thought for a moment. "No. Not in some time actually; at least two days. She was walking back to the temple with Jason in tow."

Betal frowned, his eyes sad. "I'm sorry, Father, but you know that's not his name anymore."

"He was born Jason Connor. I was there on his name day, and that's what he'll remain to me."

"I know, Father, but it doesn't change the fact that he's not Jason. Not anymore. I don't know what Mangin did to his mind, but it looks to be permanent." He dearly wished it weren't the case. Nevertheless, Jason was now Worm.

"Well, if you see her, Father, just let her know I'm looking for her. I'm going to get my horse. Maybe she went for a ride."

He gave his father a hug and bid him a good day.

John always felt uneasy whenever Betal left. When he stood near his son, he felt overwhelmed with a feeling of tranquility, that everything would be all right and nature was taking its course. But as Betal left, the world came crashing back in a swirling vortex.

"How do you stand being near that monster?" Erin said behind him.

John jumped. "Gods, man. Don't creep up on a man like that." He moderated his voice. "Was there something else you wanted, Erin?"

"I want that thing dead." Erin snarled. "My little Mattie is dead because of him."

"Watch your tongue." Taking a deep breath, John continued, "Again, was there anything else you wanted to talk to me about?"

"Yes. The Ghost of Death has come back to town," Erin said, his voice still filled with anger. "As I turned the corner of the Davis's house, I saw him coming down the lane toward the temple."

"And yet you *still* talk like that? Do you have a death wish?" John took another deep breath and shuddered. "Just stay out of his way, Erin. Whatever he's here for, it's none of our business."

Erin spat and walked away.

John scowled. *So much for this being a beautiful day.*

Chapter 18
Signs of
Order

(Year 522 -R.C.-)

Hogar rode slowly down the lane, his helmet on his pommel and a smile on his face. He so enjoyed days like that. He was about to unleash a storm upon the too-cozy village, and the bedlam it brought would indeed please The Lord.

Hogar noticed many changes since his last time there, and none for the good of The Lord. The day before, he ran across three separate groups of villagers on what looked like a regular patrol. Additionally, the villagers constructed a gate at the opening in their berm, cleaned out the dry moat of underbrush, and clear-cut the forest another two hundred yards.

It's looking like a Westland town, he thought with a frown. *These sheep have grown more than teeth. They've grown orderly.*

As he entered the Village Green, he saw Betal riding out from the temple stables, and counted it a good omen. His favorite instrument in the world would be there when he gave his news to Mangin.

Betal urged his horse forward with an air of uncertainty. "Good afternoon, Hogar," Betal said, his voice hesitant. "What brings you to our little corner of the world?"

Pleased the boy still felt uneasy around him, Hogar replied, "Great things, my boy. Great things. Have you seen Mangin? I have word from her father." The paladin dismounted.

"No," the strapping young man replied as he dismounted as well. "I've been looking for her for a while now with no luck."

"Well, I've no time to dawdle." He handed his reins to Betal. "Take them to the stables and hurry back."

He smiled lazily as Betal ran with the two horses in tow. *Oh. The plans I have for you, my boy. With you as my tool, there's no telling how high I'll climb.*

When Betal ran back, the paladin waved him away. "Not too close."

He closed his eyes and brought his fist slowly to his chest, focusing his energy, gathering Chaos about him. It twisted, churned, and coalesced in his clenched fist, causing it to glow like the white-hot coals of a blacksmith's forge. When satisfied, Hogar opened his eyes and thrust his hand above his head, releasing all that power in one massive bolt. The flare soared into the air, warbling and bubbling like a boiling cauldron, and exploded. The Lord's Breath rippled across the sky in a rainbow of colors, like oil on a clear pond, before dissipating.

"That ought to bring her running," he rumbled. "Won't it, my boy?"

He smiled wickedly. *It should also do a fair job of seeding the area for a Chaos Storm.*

Mangin lazed bare upon her large feather bed—the fine linen sheets strewn on the floor—with one arm behind her head and the other around an equally unclad Adel cuddled up next to her. The aroma of sex permeated her third-floor study.

She cast a gaze at her sweet, sweat-covered lover, and smiled. *What would I do without you?*

Adel was far from Mangin's only lover, but the others, like Cobb, came to her because of her bewitchments. The villagers were little more than frightened cattle, so she had to take matters into her own hands when the mood struck. Adel, though, came of her own free will, and Mangin loved her for it.

"Tell me, my dear," Mangin said. "Why is it you insist coming here in secret?"

"The rest would think ill of me. I'd be outcast."

Mangin scowled. "You're too smart to care what they think. Are you sure it's not because of Cobb?"

Adel frowned and lowered her chin. "He's my life-mate."

She sniffed. The very notion of two people being mutually exclusive baffled Mangin. "So be it. I'll continue to keep our relationship clandestine."

Outwardly, she showed dissatisfaction, but inside, she smiled. Cobb was Mangin's favorite sexual disciple. She loved toying with him, often summoning him right after she'd had her way with Adel. It gave her an extra thrill when Cobb ravished her in the sweat and sex-soaked sheets she shared with the love of his life only moments before.

Mangin lifted her lover's chin and kissed her lips. "Have you given any thought about your future, my darling?"

It brought a pout to Adel's delicate face, but before she could answer, Mangin felt a pulse of power sent into the room.

What does Betal want? she wondered. Mangin ignored him. He'd leave a message, and she'd deal with him later. She loved making him wait. And, besides, she didn't want him to see her and Adel together like that. *Not yet, anyway. Not until the situation's just right.*

She realized Adel said something. "I'm sorry, my sweet. Something caught my attention. What was that?"

"I said I'm still not sure. I'd love to come with you when you go back to Gate Hall, but that would mean leaving Cobb. I just don't think I can do that. I love him so dearly." Her voice, both touching and plaintive, brought a frown to Mangin's face.

"You love *him*?" Mangin said. "And what of me? What am I to you then?"

Mangin disentangled herself from the nubile young woman and slipped out of bed. "Who's better to you? I don't hit you, or make you work in the dirt." She stood taller, jutted her chest out, and placed her hands on her hips. "Who would you rather have? Would you have *only* Cobb and his little dick—his rough hands groping and bruising you? Or would you rather be at my side?"

Adel's eyes went wide, and they flitted about the room a moment. She parted her lips, but closed them. Her eyes teared, and she reached out to Mangin. "I'm sorry," she said, her voice trembling.

Mangin sighed, lowered her head, and held up her left hand. "No. I'm the one who's sorry. That was not fair of me. I *know* you care for me." She smiled wickedly. "And I also know Cobb's prick is hardly small, and how wonderful it is to be taken roughly by him."

Dropping her smile, she sat on the edge of the bed. "That's all he is to me. A great time. You know that. I know what he means to you, and I love that you don't mind we share him."

She went to the desk and picked up her robe. "But the truth is the truth. When I leave, it will be forever. And you will have only him from then on. We both know how prim your people are, and it is very unlikely you'll find another woman to lie with."

Before putting on the robe, she peered over her shoulder at Adel, still in the bed. The girl's eyes drank in her naked backside. Mangin slowly put on her robe and turned, her wicked smile spreading across her face. "And we both know that even if you found another lovely woman, she could never compare to me."

Mangin sashayed back, sat on the bed, and stroked Adel's cheek. "It's as simple as this, my love. A life with me would be far easier and more enjoyable than one here. It would be ever so much sweeter, and full of The Lord's varieties. In Gate Hall, there are so many things to entertain you. They've theater, gladiatorial games, and oh so many balls. I will teach you to read and write, so you can enjoy the great library there. And who knows, I'm sure we could find us a wonderful lover to take us as roughly as we'd ever want—both apart and together." She winked.

Adel stared at Mangin, her eyes damp with unshed tears and her mouth agape. "You... you mean it? You'd teach me to read?"

"Of course I would, my dear." Mangin cupped Adel's cheek. "My mother taught me to read when I was only six. And I taught Betal when I was only twelve."

Clasping Adel's hand, Mangin led her out of bed and to a bookshelf on the far wall. "This is my pride and joy. These are my mother's manuscripts. Everything she ever learned about the mind. Some she learned from other manuscripts and masters, who knew much on the subject. But most were written by her, gleaned from her own experiments. The mind was my mother's play toy." She turned back to Adel. "And it's also mine."

Adel's eyes went to the books, scanned the rest in the library, and returned to Mangin. "You mean, you could teach me to read all this? How long will it take?"

"Not long. In fact, I could hasten the project by several years if you like."

"How... how would you do that?" Adel asked.

"Don't fret now." She patted Adel's hand. "It's a simple thing, and will cause you no pain. You see, at a young age, the mind is more open to learning language. It's a normal part of the process of development. But as we get older, it closes down so we can learn to do other things. All I will do is open that part of your mind back up and boost it a bit. You'll be able to learn at a much faster rate. I'll have you reading to your heart's content within a matter of weeks."

"And it won't hurt?"

"Not in the slightest."

"Have you done it before?"

Mangin turned and walked a short way away before continuing. "Well, not this, precisely, but I've done experiments like it, many times."

"You have?" Adel asked, surprised. "On who?"

Mangin turned back to her. "Why, on all of you, my dear. That's what I've been doing; furthering my mother's work. And you've all been my test subjects."

"Have you hurt many people?" Adel asked, her eyes wide while licking her lips.

"Not many. Certainly not anyone close to you." Mangin approached Adel and stroked her cheek. "I would never harm you or those dear to you, my love. Not without good cause."

"You mean… like what you did to Jason?"

Mangin's face firmed. Her voice took on a tinge of anger and her hand stopped. "What I did to *Worm* was brought on by his own doing." She softened her voice and gently caressed Adel's earlobe. "What I did to Worn was for the better. You must admit, he's far better at being my bodyguard than just a simple dirt farmer. Believe me; he's quite happy in what he does now."

Adel still held a small amount of doubt in her eyes. "And you're sure it won't hurt me?"

"Not at all." She took Adel in her arms. "Come, my love. Let's see what kind of culinary delights the chef has—"

Her mind shook from a powerful blast rocking the ethereal realm close to the temple.

"Betal," she whispered. "What have you done now?"

She released Adel and stalked to her clothes lying on the floor. "Something just happened outside." Throwing off her robe, she swiftly dressed in her loose white blouse and deep purple skirt.

"Get dressed, quickly, and make your way out the back. Whatever happened, it's going on right out front, and I want you to be as far from it as possible." Pausing, she gazed into Adel's eyes. "I can't have anything happen to you."

Adel yanked her dress over her head and did up the buttons.

Mangin gave her plump rump a quick smack. "Hurry up now. I have to be the last out. I need to reset the wards, and you don't want me to leave you in here."

Once out in the hall, Mangin put up her wards. As Adel started for the back stair, Mangin grabbed her by the hand and pulled her back into her arms. She kissed Adel passionately, released her, and gave her a little swat on the butt to set her going again.

She waited for Adel to reach the stairs before sprinting the other way to the grand staircase. "I swear, Betal, I'll tan your hide for interrupting me like this."

Chapter 19
The
Summons

(Year 522 -R.C.-)

Betal turned as the temple door flung open and Mangin stormed out, radiating beauty and power.

So, she was in one of her rooms, after all, he thought. *And by the looks of her, she wasn't studying—at least not her manuscripts.*

Her eyes locked onto him like a pair of blazing emeralds. "What have you done now, Betal? That blast was enough to wake the dead."

Her eyes shifted to the paladin. "I thought a dragon had just dropped in on us, but I see it's actually something less courteous." She laughed as she sauntered down the steps, her broad hips swaying. "Good morning, Hogar. Did you sneak up on our little prince here and goose him?"

Betal winced at the quip. To her, Hogar was simply an overly protective uncle. She simply didn't see him as Betal did—erratic and dangerous. Try as he might, Betal couldn't bring himself to trust the Yurken Paladin. By nature, the Yurken people were violent and tumultuous.

"Where've you been?" Betal asked Mangin. "I've been looking all over for you."

She raised her eyebrow and grinned. "Have you now?"

She stopped directly in front of Betal, but turned to Hogar and sighed. "He just can't get enough of me." Her brazen smile returned. "Not that I blame him."

She turned back to Betal. "For your information, I was deep in study and didn't want to be disturbed."

Out of the corner of his eye, he saw Adel, looking equally disheveled, sneak around the corner from the back of the temple.

How long has this been going on? He frowned. *I hope Cobb doesn't find out about this.*

"So, Betal," Mangin's voice firmed, "I ask again. What in the black abyss were you doing out here? Showing off? I don't like being disturbed in my ruminations."

Betal shook his head. "Don't look at me." He gestured to Hogar with a smile. "He felt it was the best way to get you to come running."

Her eyes flashed white-hot. "Come running?" Her eyes softened, and she laughed. "Well, that it did."

She turned to Hogar. "So, tall, dark, and grumpy, what's so important you needed to resort to that to ferret me out?"

"Not here," he replied, sternly. "This involves Dithiyar as well, and I don't want to repeat myself. We'll go to his study. He should be there cowering under his desk."

He stalked past them up the stairs, not looking back to see if they followed.

"What's going on, Betal?" Mangin asked with more than a hint of worry in her eyes. "Why does he have the look of death in him today?"

Betal shrugged. "I don't know."

Filled with a sense of dread, he slowly climbed the stairs into the temple. *Whatever he's up to, it will not be good,* Betal thought as he opened the door for Mangin, and followed her inside.

The empty cathedral and the dark hallway to Dithiyar's rooms only added to his trepidation. Mangin stuck close to him, even going so far as to take hold of his arm.

He glanced at her sideways. *What is she playing at now? When has she ever wanted reassurance?*

Upon reaching Dithiyar's door, he heard raised voices within and hesitated. "Maybe we should give them a moment."

Mangin pinched his rear and brushed past him. "Come now, Great One. Don't just stand out here in the hall like a statue. Let's join the game and see what all the fuss is about." She opened the door and glided in.

Shaking his head, Betal followed her into Dithiyar's study.

Dithiyar cowered behind his desk, staring daggers at the huge paladin. The look in his eyes reminded Betal that the old man was still someone not to take lightly. The skeletal priest sneered at Hogar, his nose large like an animal's horn. His enormous ears—seemingly taking up half the side of his head—were red, and his hands curled into fists as they clenched the arms of his chair like white gnarled roots of bone and sinew.

"They're here," the crotchety old priest spat. "Now tell me what this is all about and leave me in peace. I've lessons to give to Mangin, and you're wasting my time."

Hogar smiled broadly. "There *is* no more time, old man. Your time is at an end."

The priest shrank back even further into his chair, his face turning ashen, a mask of horror, as though seeing his own death stand before him.

Hogar laughed so hard he shook. "I've not come here to kill you, you pathetic wretch. I mean that your time as her teacher is at an end."

Hogar turned to Mangin. "I bring word from your father, my dear. It is time for you to go home. You're to pack up what belongings you wish to take and join him at Gate Hall where you'll enter the priesthood."

"Do you mean it?" Mangin squealed with delight. She ran to the paladin, jumped up, hugging him around the neck, and kissed his cheek. "Oh. Thank you, thank you!"

Betal's eyes widened and his mouth hung open. He looked to Dithiyar, but couldn't tell what the priest thought of the news, as he appeared just as poleaxed.

Mangin ran to Betal, grabbing him by the hand and dragging him out of the priest's study. "Come on. There's so much to do," she said as he numbly followed her out into the hall toward the back stairs. "We have to decide what we're taking and what we're leaving behind."

"We?" Betal stopped dead at the foot of the staircase and put his back up. "What do you mean, *we*? You want me to help you pack, and then just watch you *go*? Just like that?" His cheeks grew hot, and he trembled.

She tilted her head. "What are you talking about?"

He stabbed a finger at her. "You know *exactly* what I'm talking about. You're packing up your life and leaving me here alone with that worthless old shit!" He shook his head. "I don't think so."

He turned and stalked down the hall to the stables. The emptiness in his center grew with each step. She was leaving him behind to rot in a hell of contempt and hatred. And he thought he'd felt alone before? He planned to get on his horse and go as far away as possible—the where did not matter.

"Betal, stop. Stop, I said," Mangin yelled as she ran up behind him. She grabbed him by the arm as he reached the back door and spun him around. "What in Chaos has gotten into you?"

He refused to look her in the eye.

She brushed his cheek. "I'm not leaving you."

Betal dared a glance into her eyes; eyes filled with love and joy.

"I said *we* are going home." She cupped his cheek. "Both you and I are going home to Gate Hall, my sweet." She pulled back a bit and twisted her head. "You think I'd actually leave you in this shit-hole?"

His mind raced, and his hands shook. He tried to put his arms around her waist, but she quickly stepped back, pretending not to notice.

"Come now, Betal. I wouldn't think of leaving you. I may be wicked, but I'm not cruel. Certainly not to you. I love you."

Betal turned his head slightly, his heart fluttering. "You... love me?"

Her eyes went wide, and she smiled softly. "Of course I do," she said, her voice soothing. It regained its playful tone as her favorite wicked smile flashed across her face. "You're my best friend. Who doesn't love their best friend?"

She laughed and raced back down the hall to the staircase. "Come on, silly. *We* need to pack and get the hells out of here."

Betal shook his head. She enjoyed tormenting him. "I just wish she wanted me," he murmured. "I'd do anything…"

He started after Mangin. *Gate Hall. It'd be nice to be in a place where everyone doesn't see me as a demon spawn sent to torment them.* He'd still have to be careful there. According to Mangin, the currents of political intrigue ran deep. Life was going to get much more complicated from there on out.

Mangin felt like dancing. It was finally happening! She was going home to be with her father and her rightful place in the sect. The last time she saw him, five years before, he seemed so disappointed in her.

"Still too weak," he'd said with a shake of his head. "Too many still remember your mother. And those with hard feelings will take their displeasure for her, out on you."

However, that all changed. She was more than strong enough to handle anything they could think of. She'd honed her skills on these peasants, and now she'd put that knowledge to proper use.

Before she mounted the stair, Hogar stepped in front of her, startling her. She refused to let her upset reach her voice, though, as she addressed the paladin. "Is there anything else you wish to talk about, Hogar?"

"Nothing of import, my dear," he said with a smile. "I was just wondering if you'll be lonely at home. After all, life at the sect can be quite difficult, and you'll have no true friends there. I can tell you that."

"Why would I be lonely?" She tilted her head. "True, I expect that it'll be unwise to trust anyone new, but I'll still have Betal with me."

Hogar's smile slipped. "Betal is not going with you, my child."

Mangin's smile fell completely. She stood taller and tipped her head back to look down her nose at the large man. "Yes, he is."

"No. He is not," Hogar said, his face a thunderhead. "He's not ready. He's not prepared for life in the sect."

"The time to hold his hand is at an end, Hogar. It's time for him to sink or swim. He's not a child anymore." She smiled with pride. "I think I'm more than a fair judge of character, and I know he'll do well there."

Her voice became stern again. "He is Chaos clothed in flesh. You cannot hold him back from his destiny. He will, in time, take his rightful place at the right hand of God."

Anger burned in the paladin's eyes. "So be it. Who am I to hold back the will of God?"

He looked over her shoulder and smiled mockingly. "I bid you goodbye, Betal. May you rule as you see fit." He bowed his head ever so slightly.

Betal slowly approached, eyeing the two of them through slightly hooded brows. With a shake of the head, he asked, "Why goodbye, Hogar? Aren't you coming with us?"

"Unfortunately, no. I still have to continue my patrol. There've been reports of troubles to the south I must see to." The paladin smiled broadly as if a whimsical thought occurred to him. "But don't worry. I'll make sure you arrive home properly represented. Dithiyar shall accompany you. I want him to receive his reward of training you so well in person." The smile slipped. "Besides, it's past time he presented himself to the High Priest." Hogar bowed his head once more and stalked back down the hall to the old priest's room.

Thanks for nothing, Mangin thought with a scowl.

She turned to Betal, smiled, and held out her hand. "Come along now. Let's see what we'll be taking, and what we'll forever leave behind."

Several hours later, Mangin slowly crossed the Village Green, deep in contemplation. *This will be a long trip,* she thought, not for the first time. She and Betal had taken an assessment of their things and came to the same conclusion. They'd need several wagons to carry everything.

And with us saddled with that old ass, it'll likely take us three to four times longer than it should.

It was going to be a more dangerous trip without Hogar there to provide protection. They'd need a caravan guard made up of much of the militia. "But who to head that guard?"

The logical choice was Cobb's father, but she loathed the man, finding him repugnant. So, who else? Who would have the strength to keep the men in line?

She cast her gaze about the Village Green and caught sight of John Simmons's house. *Of course*, she thought. *Who better? He'll do wonderfully and have a nice soothing effect on Betal during his first days at the sect.*

She sauntered over. As she reached his door, it opened and John stepped out. He jumped about a foot. "Is everything all right, Simmons? You'd think someone goosed you." She smiled and placed her hands tight on her hips, knowing it pulled her top down to expose more of her bosom. "I'm not that scary to look at, am I?"

Settling himself, and obviously doing his best not to stare, the older man replied, "Of course not, Mangin. You look as lovely as ever this afternoon."

"Well, that's good," she purred. "I hate to look too out of sorts. I came to you because I have need of you."

"What can I help you with?"

"I'm going home. Father has called to have me join the sect at Gate Hall, and I'll not be returning. Oh. And Betal will be joining me," she added as if an afterthought.

"Betal is leaving?" A wrinkle of surprise showed on John's face.

"Of course he is. I couldn't just leave him here in the middle of nowhere."

"Walk with me," she said as she started back across the Green. "Hogar will not be providing us with an escort, so we will require many from the village militia to guard us. We think six to seven wagons should do to carry all our things. Oh. And that sack of dung, Dithiyar, is coming as well, but he'll likely return with you. So, that'll make it a much longer trip. We'll need more provisions and travel gear—tents and beds and such."

"I'll get right on it. I'll let Erin know so he can pick out his best men," he said at her side with perfect respect. However, Mangin saw in his eyes that he wasn't enjoying any of it; not one bit.

"I don't want Cruchfield to head the guard." She couldn't help smiling at the obvious uncertainty on his face. "I want you to."

He stopped dead. "Why me?" he asked guardedly.

She turned to face him. "Because, I wouldn't want to separate you and Betal. You're good for him. You helped raise the most powerful man in the world, and kept him safe," she said with pride. "You will be well rewarded, and I would have you receive that reward in person."

John hesitated and turned, looking at her out of the corner of his eye. He took a deep breath. "I am sorry, but I cannot. My place is here."

Mangin's jaw dropped. "What did you say to me?"

"I'm sorry, Mangin," he said, turning to her and bowing his head. "I said no. You said yourself; you're taking both Betal and Dithiyar with you, along with much of the militia. That will leave us vulnerable. I need to be here in case anything happens."

Her nostrils flared and her eyes burned. *The man dares say no to me, and then makes excuses.*

Mangin sighed and chuckled. "You are an amazing man, John Simmons. You're both strong and smart. The rest of the peasants here are very lucky to have you." She pursed her lips and looked him up and down. "For an older man, you're quite remarkable—tall, strong, and quite handsome. How is it I never saw it before?"

He cleared his throat and looked to the side.

Mangin moved in close to him and spoke softly. "Betal will miss you, John, and so will I." She tilted her head and gently ran her right hand up and down his arm. "When's the last time you had a woman?"

"What are you getting at, child?"

"I am no child." She pressed up against him. "As well you know. You lost your partner much too long ago, and I doubt you've taken another—or even bedded a woman, for that matter. I want to fix that." She grabbed him by the back of the head and kissed him.

He kissed her back, but his lips firmed. He put his hands on her shoulders and gently pushed her away. "No. I can't." His breath was short and his voice quivered before firming. "I'll not be one of your toys."

"You say no, but you're still holding me."

He snapped his hands back as though burned and took a step back. "Why do this? You know it would hurt Betal."

"Would it?" she mused. "Yes. I suppose it would. But what does he have to do with it, really?" She ran her tongue across her teeth. "No. I can see in your eyes it's still no."

How dare the man refuse me twice?

She caressed Chaos and curled it about John's head... and stopped.

"No. I think not. Betal might not like it if I lead you to my bed." She stepped further back. "But I'm sure he'd think poorly of me it if I *took* you."

She turned and sashayed away, speaking to him over her shoulder. "Erin Cruchfield it is then. Tell him Cobb is to be part of the guard. I expect the rest of what I need before sun up tomorrow. We've a lot of preparations to make, and I don't want to stay here one more day than I have to."

As she made her way down the lane, she smiled with glee. *Now to tell Adel.*

"How much longer till they get here?" Kark asked.

Mal, crouching at the edge of the woods, eyed the road. "They'll get here when they get here. Stop gettin' so antsy."

"Yeah, well, my ass is getting sore from sittin' in these bushes so long." Kark flexed his grip on his crossbow. "Tell me again why we're doing this?"

"Because the Kendricks paid us to," Mal said. "According to Fen, they'll come down the road sometime today. We hit them in the middle, hard—got to kill the priests first. Two'll be on horseback, so they'll be easy, then we use the firebombs on the black carriage. After that, we get those in front. But, remember, we leave the ones in back alone. Got it?"

"Why?"

"Because, they're the ones that paid the Kendricks. They ain't gonna fight us, anyway, so we don't have to worry about 'em."

"I still don't think it's smart attacking priests."

"There are fourteen of us," Mal gestured to the other men. "You ten hit 'em with your bolts, and there'll be no worries."

Kark eyed the forest. "What if The Ghost shows up?"

"Don't worry. Word is he's across the river."

"I'm with Kark," Emmitt chimed in. "This don't feel right. And it's too quiet."

"Well, if you'd all shut up, the critters will get used to us and start making their racket again," Mal said.

Emmitt shook his head and rolled his shoulders. "No. I'm tellin' you. We're being watched."

A sour stench wafted past Kark's nose. "What's that stink?"

"Very funny," Mal replied.

With a piercing screech, something grayish-white and the size of a bear burst in amongst them. It collided with Mal, sending the two tumbling to the ground where Mal let loose a bloodcurdling scream.

"Grunkin!" Kark swung his bow around and shot.

The bolt sunk into the grunkin's flank, but the beast didn't flinch. Blood and gore spewed as it ravaged Mal with razor-sharp claws. The others turned, firing hasty shots. Three stuck home, but again, the beast was unfazed.

Kark grabbed his lever and cocked the bow while the others drew their swords and attacked. They struck at the beast, but the blades couldn't penetrate its stinking, matted fur.

The Chaos Beast spun about to face its attackers. Using the twisted horns on its round head, it gutted Emmitt. As Emmitt fell, it grabbed Sam's arm with its jaws, clamped down, and snapped it off at the elbow with a loud crunch.

Kark's hands grew shaky with each shot. His heart hammered faster each time a friend died. His breath grew ragged and his feet itched to flee, but you don't turn your back on a grunkin. It will only run you down.

After biting Gerald's head off, it turned on Kark, ramming him in the belly. Kark's bow slipped from his hand and sailed through the air. He shrieked as the thing chewed into his stomach and gouged his face.

Chapter 20
The
Clutching
Darkness

(Year 522 -R.C.-)

Daylin's eyes burned with tears as she knelt, staring east at the city of Cross Corners in the distance. The Cunning River—a mile wide ribbon of sparkling, churning water—split the city and the horizon. "Are you sure you have to go?"

Bucky tilted his head. "Rest of pack afraid of water. They say to cross is to seek death."

Daylin sighed. "I know. They're afraid of the boats too."

He shook from head to tail, puffing out his black and brown fur. "Boats, things of people. They not trust people."

She felt Kylee and the others near the back of the troupe's caravan, waiting on Bucky. "But I'm people."

"You not people. You, Mother." His tongue lolled out. "Stay with us, Mother. Stay with pack."

"I can't. These people are my pack."

"But they head toward city. City not smell right. Much darkness there."

Daylin shuddered. "I know."

Kylee barked. "Are you coming, little wolf?"

Bucky took a step in their direction, but turned back to Daylin. "Please come, Mother."

"I can't." She buried her face in his long fur. "I'll miss you."

She called out the Kylee and the others. "I'll miss you all so much. I'll see you again, one day."

"We will see you again," Kylee replied. "Either in this world, or in the embrace of the Great Mother of All."

Bucky licked her face and dashed away.

"I love you, Bucky." Her thoughts drifted to Vir as she wiped away her tears.

The caravan rumbled down the heavily traveled road. Other than the normal creaks and groans of the wagons, only the animals made notice, and even that seemed half-hearted.

Daylin stared at the approaching city as well as the far bank of the river, fingering her favorite yellow flowered dress. *How could it be so wide?*

Ellis tugged at his wide-brimmed, rose-colored hat. "Any news from the scouts?"

She turned to gaze back down the road while chewing her lip. *Maybe I can ride back and find them.*

"Daylin?"

She said nothing.

He rose his voice. "Daylin?"

Dirge rode up. "Is something wrong?"

"We need to go back for them," she said, her voice soft and uncertain.

Dirge grunted, keeping his eyes out for trouble.

Ellis shook his head. "You said they refused to cross."

"We could find a bridge." She scrubbed at her eyes to wipe away the tears.

Ellis's voice firmed. "There are none."

"Not for a thousand miles," Dirge added. "And that one is to the south."

"What about the north?" She stared back down the road. "There's rumor of one near The Lands of the Dead."

"No," Ellis said.

She swung her head at the cold, sharpness of his voice. "No? That's all you can say? No?!"

"Daylin—"

"*Why*?" She flung her hand wide. "Why can't we at least look? You've been harping for years about having to go north. So why don't we?"

Tightening his grip on the reins, his voice grew stern. "Daylin…"

"Tell me!" She stabbed toward the upcoming city. "Why here? Why do we have to cross here? You know there are priests in there as well as I do. So why?"

"I have to!" Ellis seethed. "I feel the pull of Ukase about my neck so strong it's liable to choke me. It's pulled me all the way across the Westlands, and now it says I must cross here."

"We do as God commands," Dirge said, his voice iron hard.

Closing his eyes, Ellis lowered his head a moment. "Look. I know you miss them…"

Daylin scowled, turned away, and crossed her arms.

"…but it was their choice to leave."

She cried. "They're all I had left of Vir. It's like I'm losing him all over again."

"Daylin…" Ellis reached out and gently touched her shoulder.

She shied away. Even now, any type of familiar contact reminded her of what Ruddick did all those years before.

Ellis frowned and pulled his hand back. "Daylin, Vir's not gone. He's still in your heart."

She whipped her head around. "He is gone. Those pups were the only connection to him I had left, and now they're gone, too. They were the only family I had that wasn't taken away from me."

"That's not true," Ellis said, the hurt plain in his voice. "We're your family."

"It is true! You don't understand." She stared into his eyes, tears streaming down her face. "For years, I thought my mother sold me to Ruddick. But Vir showed me the truth—some damn fat priest locked it in my head. He showed me Ruddick killed my mother and took me."

Ellis's eyes grew wide.

"He took me and did this to me!" She pointed at her ever-changing eyes and trembled with rage. "He twisted and tortured me with Chaos. He made me a freak!"

"YOU KNOW THAT'S NOT TRUE."

The voice in her head brought her crying to an abrupt halt. It was like an echo, a memory of Vir's voice, yet vast and powerful beyond measure.

She closed her eyes and sighed. *Wonderful. Now I'm going mad.*

"You know that's not true," Ellis mirrored the detached thought. "You're not a freak. You have an amazing gift. You can speak with animals. You can feel people's emotions." He hesitated, bit his lips, and glanced down a moment while his left hand fiddled with his mother's bronze sun pendant. "And even if it is Chaos that lets you do it—"

Daylin shook her head and cut him off. "It's not Chaos."

Taking a deep breath, she dabbed her tears. "Ruddick twisted me with it, but it's not Chaos that lets me do it. Ruddick had screwed up. He tried to connect me to Edis, but instead connected me to Mother."

"I thought your mother was dead?" Dirge asked, frowning.

"Not my mother. It's what Vir called The True Tree, The Mother of Creation," she told him. "It was Mother who sent Vir to find me."

Daylin chuckled slightly while wiping away the rest of her tears. "I never knew why. I'm just thankful she did."

"I know why," Ellis said with a smile, his voice as soft and sweet as a rose. "She knew you were special." He reached out and caressed the back of her hand before picking it up and giving it a squeeze. "Just as I do."

She flinched a moment, wanting to pull away… but didn't. His touch was so gentle, and comforting, his eyes full of tenderness.

Ever since Ellis bowed to her back at Timsdale, something he'd never done before, she wondered if he'd started having feelings for her. Their entire way across the Westlands, he'd not taken a single person into his bed. Was he trying to tell her something? Did he want her, but was too afraid to ask because of her past? She hated not knowing.

Reading people's emotions was one of the gifts bestowed on her by Mother. Some people were easier to read than others, but she always felt something. Except when it came to Ellis. For some strange reason, he was a closed book, and it aggravated the hell out of her.

She never told Ellis exactly what happened to her while a slave to Ruddick. It was simply too painful. But he knew enough. He knew the priest hurt her in ways well past his torturous alterations.

I'm so tired of being afraid, she thought as she gazed into his eyes and squeezed his hand in return.

She yearned to be happy, to lie in someone's arms and not feel soiled by it. Ellis's touch was nothing like Ruddick's. It caused her heart to flutter. For the first time in her life, she considered being with someone, about tasting her first *real* kiss—what the priest did, didn't count.

She stared into his lovely eyes as a gentle breeze carrying the scent of wildflowers caressed her face. She leaned in. Her heart pounded, and her breath fluttered as she parted her lips...

Evan rode up hard, his horse throwing up dust as he pulled it to a halt. It caused the wagon's horses, as well as Dirge's, to frisk as Ellis brought the wagon to a stop.

"I've found us a good spot to camp near the river," he said, gesturing back the way he came with his head.

Daylin shot Evan a glare so strong the scout pulled his head back and sawed at his horse's reins.

"I'm sorry," Evan said with a grin and a slight shake of the head. "Did I interrupt something?"

Daylin dropped her gaze. "No." She smoothed her dress as her face burned.

"We were just talking," Ellis said with a quick shake of his head as he shifted in his seat.

"What would make you think that?" Daylin adjusted the light blue scarf hanging around her neck.

"You know, about the city and all," Ellis added as he fiddled with his pendant.

Evan's head snapped back and forth between the two of them as they prattled on at the same time. His grin grew wider and wider. "Are you sure?"

"Of course I'm sure," she snapped, challenging him with a stare. "Now what do you want? And wipe that smirk off your face before I smack it off!"

The scout looked truly taken aback, and Daylin couldn't blame him. She'd never spoken like that to anyone before.

"I'm sorry, Evan." She raised her hand slightly before letting it drop. "You didn't deserve that. I'm... I'm just all out of sorts today."

Evan's eyes saddened. "I understand, little one. They'll be sorely missed, believe me. To be honest, I'm surprised Bucky went with them. He always struck me as more dog than wolf. But I'm sure the other dogs will fill in nicely."

Daylin wasn't surprised. Bucky adored his full wolf cousins, and when they said they were going, he stuck with his pack.

"And who knows," Evan added, "you may even find a wolf on the other side you'll take a liking to."

"That would be nice." She gave Evan what she hoped was an encouraging smile.

"I do hope you don't mind taking up much of the slack," Daylin continued. "There's still Henry, but the rest of the dogs simply aren't cut out for long scouting."

"Where's the campsite?" Ellis asked.

"Through the city, right next to the docks," Evan replied, gesturing the way he'd come with his head. "They've a big area set-aside for large caravans and Travelers." The scout frowned and shook his head.

"What's the matter?" Dirge asked at the man's uncertainty.

"Nothing really," Evan said. "It's just..."

Ellis leaned forward a tad. "Just what?"

"Well, it's the queerest city I've ever seen." Evan tilted his head slightly. "Much of it—the dockside anyway—is all laid out in straight lines. It's all quartered off and, well, *orderly*."

"Orderly?" Dirge said with a quirk of his eyebrow. "Perhaps it is an omen; the reason God is sending us here?"

"Perhaps," Ellis said. "That does sound strange for a city run by priests. There are priests, right?"

"Oh. There's plenty of them about," Evan said. "From what I gathered, there's a fair-sized temple on the other side."

Daylin shot a glare at Ellis, who pretended not to notice.

"It doesn't matter. Good job, Evan," Ellis said with a nod. "Go back and inform the rest—I'm sure they'll be relieved to hear we're stopping—then take us in."

The past several weeks had been tough on everyone. They crossed the entire Westlands in what Daylin suspected to be record time, stopping to perform at only half the towns they passed.

Daylin continued to stare hard at Ellis as he flicked the reins to get the wagon moving again. She crossed her arms and fumed, clenching her fists. She continued to do so after Evan returned and took the lead. She glowered at him, her temper growing hotter and hotter, and Ellis continued to ignore her. The man didn't even have the common courtesy to squirm in his seat.

As they approached the outskirts of the city, the wide road filled up with traffic. Dirty people hustled about, dodging traffic, selling their wares, and coming and going from two and three story wooden buildings.

Not that Daylin noticed any of it. She continued to glare at Ellis as she kicked her skirts. She was about to give in and say something when he stiffened and his eyes went wide.

"What is it? Did something finally occur to you?" Daylin asked with a hint of a sneer.

He scanned the crowded streets. "Something's not right."

"What is it?" Dirge asked.

"Of course, something isn't right," Daylin snapped. "I thought that would've occurred to you long before—"

She felt something tickle the base of her neck. An alien presence emanated from the crowd, and it caused her skin to prickle and writhe.

"It feels foul," Ellis said, still searching. "It's almost like…"

Daylin shivered. "Like something clawing at the back of your skull."

The horses snorted and yanked at their bridles; even Dirge's and Evan's horses bucked and reared, nearly throwing them to the ground. Daylin reached out with her mind to calm the animals and bring them under control. She tried soothing them with words, but that did nothing. She clasped hold of their minds hoping to shield them from the alien presence. It worked, but only enough to keep them from kicking and pawing at the air in attempts to break free from their harness and be free to run.

She tried desperately to get Ellis to stop the team, for as the caravan moved forward, more horses reacted to the evil presence. She tried to scream to him, but it came out as only a whimper. She felt laden as though a hundred-pound quilt covered her body. Slowly, she twisted her head toward Dirge hoping to get his attention, but he, too, was staring at something in the distance.

The caravan continued forward.

She strained under the pressure and quivered as her mind screamed in agony from the exertion. Her heart hammered in her chest, and her consciousness began to slip the thinner she spread her mind. The light dimmed as Daylin's vision tunneled, but she refused to give in. Daylin *had* to keep the horses from breaking. She didn't matter; only they did.

Suddenly, the horses calmed. She still felt the malevolent presence, but the horses no longer seemed to care. She let them go and slipped into darkness.

She felt herself falling, tumbling into nothing; an emptiness she could not fathom. Yet the grotesque manifestation remained. It grew stronger and colder as she fell into that black abyss. Time made no sense there. It could have been years or only an instant.

The core grew closer; the very center from which the malignant emanations derived. Something lay there in the deep, something vast and evil beyond measure. It twitched and squirmed, its movements seeming to crackle, like the charred remains of oblivion. And it wanted her. It yearned to make contact. Its entire terrible will focused on that one thing.

Daylin panicked, knowing if it touched her, she'd be no more. Trying to scream, she made no sound. She clawed at the nothing all about her to stop her descent into annihilation. Yet still plummeted. She felt the thing's mirth at her attempt to escape the inevitable.

Something touched Daylin's mind, something soft and pure. It caressed her, stopping her descent, and she began to rise.

Denied her soul, the void quaked with the demon's madness and rage as she rose.

She rose until the darkness fell away, becoming only light, an all-encompassing and loving embrace beyond measure. Daylin felt at one with the light. She was at last in the arms of her Mother and didn't want it to end.

A voice of calm perfection filled her mind, *"YOU ARE SAFE NOW, MY PRECIOUS CHILD. BUT YOU MUST GO BACK. DEKRIOT, THE ABOMINATION OF THE ABYSS, DESIRES NOTHING BUT THE DESTRUCTION OF ALL. DO NOT LET THE DEMON DECEIVE AND ENSNARE YOU. STAY TRUE. YOU HAVE MUCH YET TO DO."*

Chapter 21
Far Afield

(Year 522 -R.C.-)

The hum of bees as they danced among the daisies, coneflowers, and bleu bells mixed with the rustling leaves, squealing axels, and horses' hooves as they clopped down the road. A light breeze tussled Betal's hair and caressed his face. The deep shadows of the forest beyond the road's edge seemed to beacon him, promising sights and smells only dreamed of. He loved it.

"Why are you smiling?" Mangin asked while astride her horse.

"What?" Betal replied.

"I said, why are you smiling? We're going at a snail's pace. At this rate, it'll take over a week to get to Cross Corners instead of a day."

"Well, Dithiyar is fragile. He can take only so much."

"That's horse-dung, and you know it," she said. "So, again, why are you smiling?"

Betal shrugged. "The farther I've gone is the new lowland fields."

"Oh, come now. We've been to Hill Top in the south and roamed the pastures. Hells, One time, we even went all the way to the foot of The Talendor Mountains."

"I remember. Their jagged white tips cut into the clouds." He shook his head. "But those were just pleasure rides. This is different. It's a blessing from The Lord, and I plan to enjoy every second I can."

Mangin laughed. "Well, you're easy to please, aren't you?"

His smile slipped and he lowered his head. Easy to please? I can think of one thing that would please me more.

He glanced at her out of the corner of his eye. Dressed for a long trip, she looked amazing. Her hair hung loose about her shoulders in copper waves, her gray slacks, and black boots hugged her legs, and she'd buttoned her green top to her neck. "What would please you?" he asked.

She scowled. "For that old man to stop dragging his feet. It's bad enough it took that fool Cruchfield three days to get everything ready, but now Dithiyar's complaining we're going too fast. The delay is keeping me from my future."

At first camp, she stalked to the old priest's coach to talk. Betal couldn't hear them, but her face was flashing from rage to evil joy. When she finished, the old man scuttled away, white-faced, to where the guards erected his tent.

The smile danced across her full pink lips as she strolled back to Betal.

"What was that all about?" he asked.

"Oh. Nothing," she replied. "I just told him if he didn't stop dragging his ass, he'd not make it to Gate Hall." She chuckled. "Would you believe he had the gall to ask me for a favor as soon as he stepped out?"

She paused and gave him a quick look over. "You look quite lovely today, by the way. That red coat goes well with your eyes, and those boots are quite sharp. I do believe the road suits you." She gave him a wink and sauntered away toward where Cobb stood at their camp's perimeter.

Their relationship still baffled Betal. Cobb's eyes burned pure hatred at Mangin as they talked, yet he obviously enjoyed the way she touched him and whispered in his ear. The man hated her, yet lay with her many a night. It made no sense. Why bewitch someone you know despises you?

Betal caught sight of Adel as she eyed Mangin and Cobb. She spun and stalked to the other side of the camp, her face red. Betal wondered which Adel was angrier with, Cobb or Mangin.

Once they set up camp, Betal chose to eat with the rest of the men rather than alone in his tent. He made his way to the center of the camp where they'd set up a kettle over an open fire. It appeared to be some kind of stew.

The man tending the fire, Betal couldn't remember his name, paused at seeing him. "Is there something you need, M'Lord?" the man asked.

Betal sniffed. "That smells wonderful."

"I do the best I can with what I have."

"Pour me a bowl, my good man."

The man's eyes went wide. "You want to eat this?"

"Certainly. Why not?"

The man shrugged and handed Betal a shallow bowl and large spoon. He nodded to another at the fire—Betal thought his name was Keven—who looked at Betal with hooded eyes and filled the bowl without saying a word, making sure not to spill any.

"Thank you." Betal nodded and stepped away to find a place to sit to enjoy the simple meal.

Adam Killington, one of the elder guards and a good friend of his father, waved him over to sit next to him on a downed tree near the edge of the camp. "Eating with the rest of us, I see," the older man said with a smile. "So, what do you think of your first day on the road?"

"It's exciting," Betal replied with verve. "It's all so new. I love it."

"Well, give it time. It'll wear on you, believe me."

"Is travel usually this slow, though?" Betal asked. "Mangin thinks we should be at Cross Corners by now."

"Hardly. If it were just two people on horseback, probably. But with most of us on foot, and the wagons so heavily laden, we want to take it easy. We don't want to overstress the horses." Adam hesitated. "But, I must admit, we're going even slower than we should."

"So Dithiyar is slowing us more than we should."

"Well, Dithiyar doesn't seem to be taking too well to the road. But, I imagine his old bones are just not used to it. Give him time. He'll come around."

Betal wasn't so sure. Dithiyar might have been older than the hills, but he was still spry. No, Betal thought. The old man's sluggishness seemed more out of reluctance than exhaustion.

After they finished their meal, Betal took a stroll around the camp before heading to his tent for the night. They'd set up in a large cleared space by the side of the road, with the five wagons in a rough circle around the outside and the middle left for the tents and cooking. As he made his way, Betal caught sight of Cobb, staring daggers at him from behind one of the wagons, but Betal ignored him. His days of fearing them were long past.

As he passed near Mangin's tent, he paused at what he heard.

"That's it. Work out the sound," Mangin said.

"T hhe—" Adel started.

"This is 'the.' T H together makes a thhh sound," Mangin said.

"The g... r... at—"

"The Great Lord..."

Betal stepped back, his eyes wide. She's teaching her how to read?

Mangin enjoyed playing at being tough and cruel. So why take her time to teach a peasant to read? For the girl's betterment? He doubted it.

Betal worried about Adel's future. If the young woman was going to stay with Mangin, she may come to some harm in Gate Hall. However, if she returned to the village, news would spread about being so close to Mangin. Many would alienate her for it.

With a yawn, Betal decided to worry about it later, and headed for bed. Before he entered his own tent, he felt... something... brushing his mind. He froze and scanned the camp, but saw nothing out of the ordinary. If it had been Mangin trying one of her tricks, he'd have felt a disturbance in Chaos, but there was none.

Snapping up some defensive wards, he crept to the edge of the camp. If there's some hedge mage with a band of brigands trying their skill on me, they're in for a nasty surprise. He caught motion out of his left eye, something gray. He hunkered down next to the wagon and searched the area, but saw nothing. After a couple of minutes, he sighed.

Maybe it was Mangin.

With a shake of his head, he stood and turned for his tent but stopped. Some twenty feet into the woods, next to a fallen tree, stood a large gray wolf, its yellow eyes gazing into his, without blinking. Several seconds passed as they stared at each other before the wolf's tongue lolled out. It slowly turned and loped into the depths of the forest.

"That was odd," he said aloud.

"What's odd?" Adam asked behind him.

Betal jumped. He hadn't heard the man approach. He shook himself and told the elder guardsman what he saw.

"Wolves have always been thick around the village. They typically keep their distance and rarely harass the livestock." He patted Betal on the back. "Don't worry about it. I'll let the lads know, and we'll keep an eye out for the pack. But I seriously doubt they'll bother us."

"Really? Even here in the wilds?"

"It was probably just curious." He patted Betal again. "You sleep well and I'll see you in the morning. We'll have breakfast together, and I'll let you know if anything comes of it."

Betal thanked him and headed back to his large, plush tent. He witnessed several of the men bunking down out in the open, or under the wagons, and it gave him pause.

And here I thought I was going to be "sleeping rough", he thought with a frown.

He, Mangin, and Dithiyar would sleep in small four-post beds, on thick-carpeted floors, with a multitude of lamps. Even the temple servants accompanying them slept on cots in small tents. Meanwhile, everyone else had to make do on the hard, cold ground.

Betal considered joining them, but realized it would be silly. He wanted the men to like him—he tired of being an outcast—but how would his sleeping out in the open accomplish that? It wouldn't.

Besides, why shouldn't I live better? He was on his way to being a full priest of The Great Lord. He had his calling, and they had theirs. Yet, he still felt guilty.

A light rain fell as he entered his tent. Feeling eyes on his back, he stopped and peered into the forest. Deep in the woods, a pair of golden eyes stared back. He shook his head and continued inside. After stripping, he climbed under his think covers and extinguished all his lamps with a hint of Chaos.

The soft titter-tat of the rain on the canvas roof helped him drift off to sleep as a strange name floated through his mind: Zara.

Zara ghosted away from the human's camp through the flittering moonlight, her gray fur blending into the darkness. *I must reach him*, she thought.

A white wolf approached. "We head out."

"Yes, Shin-Ja," Zara said.

"The thing's moved on toward the river to lick its wounds." Shin-Ja shook herself as if trying to throw off water. "Even after the pack reduced that thing, those pathetic humans couldn't finish it. So we return to the hunt."

Zara couldn't fathom how the thing still lived after all these years. "How much longer do we have to do this?"

"Until it's dead! It killed my mate and pups. The Mother granted us this extra time, and one day, it will be weak enough for us to kill. Only then will I willing go to the Mother's embrace."

Zara glanced back at the human camp.

"No more fawning over your humans." Shin-Ja said with contempt.

"I was just trying to—"

"No!" Shin-Ja snapped. "No more humans! They took my boy from me—my last, precious pup. They can all die for all I care."

"But Veil—"

Shin-Ja growled. "Don't you dare say his name. He's gone because of you. My pup is gone. The pack is gone. You hear me?"

Zara's ears wilted. "Yes."

Shin-Ja trotted into the darkness.

With one last look toward the human camp, Zara followed the older wolf. She worried about Shin-Ja. Veil's mother grew more erratic and violent with each year.

Chapter 22
To Cross the Cunning

(Year 522 -R.C.-)

A sharp swaying woke Daylin. She couldn't open her eyes; they were too heavy. Yet, she heard roiling, churning water. *Am I on a boat?* she wondered.

"She's going to be all right," a female voice said in the darkness. "She simply needs a bit of rest."

"Thank you, Sarah," a man said at her side.

She realized someone held her hand when they gave it a squeeze.

"When she comes to, don't let her overexert herself, Ellis," Sarah said.

Ellis? Why is Ellis holding my hand?

"We love her nearly as much as you do." Sarah paused. "But that goes without saying, doesn't it?"

"Um, yes… of course. Thank you, Sarah." Ellis gave her hand another squeeze.

He loves me? She considered the possibilities before discarding them. *Well, of course he does. He's practically my brother.*

"Dirge. Dirge! You heard Sarah. She's going to be fine," Ellis said. "Go tell the rest. I want us in a tight circle when we get to wherever Evan is taking us, and I want a strong watch set."

"Consider it done," the gruff swordsman said, followed by the sharp swaying again.

I must be in bed.

She floated off to sleep, the question drifting through her mind as she did. Did Ellis see her as more than a sister?

Daylin awoke to the sounds of joyous laughter, along with singing and the playing of instruments. She opened her eyes to the familiar pale blue sky and fluffy white clouds painted upon her wagon's ceiling. She turned her head and saw Ellis sitting on his bed, gazing down at her with his brilliant blue eyes. A broad smile split his face, accentuating his high cheekbones and dimples.

She suppressed a sigh. *It's not fair for a man to be so beautiful.*

"Good morning, lazy bones," he said as he touched his medallion.

"What happened?" She sat up.

His smile slipped. "You lay back down."

"I think I've slept enough, thank you." She got into a sitting position and swung her legs over the side of the bed, but needed to grasp the overhead cupboard to steady herself.

"Sarah will have my hide if you fall and hurt yourself."

"I'm fine," Daylin insisted as she waited for her head to stop spinning. "What happened?"

"You tell me. Once that thing went back inside a tavern, you passed out."

"What thing?"

"The thing we felt in the streets," Ellis said, his face filled with concern. "I caught sight of it only for a moment."

"What was it?"

"I don't know. It was short and wore dark black robes. I didn't even get a look at its face." Ellis grunted and shook his head. "I'm just glad it went away."

"Me, too." She put a hand to her head and took several deep breaths. It seemed to help. "I was trying to keep the horses calm so they didn't hurt themselves. I don't think I could have kept it up for much longer."

"Well, it worked. Thank you. You gave us quite a scare. You hit the ground pretty hard. Dirge near went white, saying he couldn't hear you breathing."

"I wasn't breathing?"

"That's what he claimed. Said you grew real cold, too. Sarah said it was just his imagination, 'cause by the time she got to you, you were breathing fine."

"I remember the cold." Daylin clutched herself and shivered. "Darkness and cold stretching on forever."

"Do you remember anything else?"

"Not much." She gently shook her head. "Just… light; light and warmth. 'Stay true,' the light said."

Ellis's eyes grew wide. "Ukase spoke to you?"

Daylin shook her head as she closed her eyes a moment. "No. Nothing like that. I'm sure it was just Sarah talking to me."

She slipped out of bed on unsteady feet. She wobbled a moment before falling forward. Ellis jumped up and caught her, one arm at her shoulder and the other about the waist. She didn't flinch; didn't feel repulsed. She gazed up into his eyes and relished his warm embrace.

"Are you sure you don't want to stay in bed?" His voice was soft and playful, and he had a sprightly twinkle in his eye.

I could lose myself in those eyes, she thought, lost in the moment. She felt her belly rumble as though tiny puppies frolicked within. She asked softly, "Are you trying to get me into your bed now?"

His smile fell away, and a hint of panic sprang forth in his eyes. He took a step back but kept his hands where they were as though to steady her. "Ah, no. Of course not. I wouldn't think of it. That would be just… weird."

A year ago, it would've felt weird to her, and wrong, but now she wasn't so sure. His gentle touch mixed with the compassion in his eyes caused the puppies to romp even harder. She suppressed a sigh when he took his hands away.

Does he love me more than a brother? She needed to know.

As she opened her mouth to ask, there was a knock on the door, followed by Dirge's stern voice. "Evan is back with news."

Daylin scowled. *Damn that gloomy man!*

"Coming," Ellis said toward the door.

"I'm coming, too." Daylin tried her best to tug the wrinkles out of her dress.

"Are you sure?" Ellis asked, his face filled with concern.

Daylin softly swatted him away and opened the door. "I told you, I'm fine."

The head guardsmen's eyes went wide a moment upon seeing Daylin exit the wagon first, before returning to their customary severity. "What are you doing up? Mistress Sarah was adamant you stay in bed till we're ready to cross."

"Sarah can be cross all she likes, but I'm fine. Though I could use a hand down if you insist on thinking I'm an invalid."

He took hold of both her hands, his gray eyes filled with apprehension, as he helped her down the stairs. "I would hate for anything to happen to you."

Daylin smiled at the doting man. Dirge often acted like a concerned father, and she loved him for it. "Where did a man with skin as dark as yours come up with eyes that light?"

He looked away. "From my mother."

Daylin knew he was holding back. She felt a heady mixture of loss, guilt, and remorse from the man, but chose not to press.

"Evan wants to speak to you regarding our crossing," Dirge said to Ellis.

Daylin scanned the camp when a sudden chill ran up her spine. Her eyes immediately snapped to a small person in a dead black robe coming their way, seeming to glide rather than walk. She squeaked. "Priest!"

Dirge whirled about with a hand to his sword hilt, but Ellis clasped the burly man's wrist to keep him from drawing. "Wait."

Ellis stepped in front of Dirge and Daylin, and addressed the stranger. "Can I help you?"

Stopping less than ten feet away, the stranger lowered his hood. The thing—Daylin could think of nothing else to call it—stared at her with blood-red, catlike eyes. Its hands and face glittered in the sun from the green and gold scales covering it, and a slight stink of sulfur drifted on the breeze.

Daylin felt like shrieking, but it came out as a peep. It was the thing from the street, the thing that pulled her into that nightmare of darkness and cold, and while not as strong as before, the evil emanating from it still made her feel as though maggots crawled beneath her skin.

"I bid you good day." The thing's unearthly voice crackled and popped like scorched leather twisted into knots. "I am sorry if my presence caused your animals any undue stress earlier. Most here are used to me, and I tend to forget how... upsetting my presence can be. I have restrained it, so you need not worry about it happening again."

"What do you want?" Ellis asked, obviously trying to keep his composure.

"My Master, Kenja, would like to bid you welcome, and asks if you would do him the honor of performing for him."

"Your—your Master is a priest, I presume?" Ellis kept an even tone.

Daylin didn't think she could do half as well as she trembled.

"Of course," the odious little thing said with a smile as it tilted its head from side to side.

"How did your Master know of our coming?" Dirge asked, his voice hard as iron, as his hand flexed on his sword grip.

"He didn't," the thing hissed. "I simply know that my Master would want me to invite you."

It again tilted its head to the side. "Your reputation precedes you. We have long desired to witness your amazing show. You are crossing the river, I presume. My Master does not like boats, you see, so you will need to come to the heart of the city to meet him. Until then." It bowed its head slightly and moved on, silent as the void.

Once the thing was out of sight, Daylin whirled toward Ellis. "We have to get out of here." Her heart hammered away in her chest.

"I will not have this discussion again." Ellis turned, and with a scowl, walked away toward a break in their customary wagon circle.

"Don't you dare walk away from me." Daylin charged after him with Dirge on her heels.

As they reached the inside of the circle, she grabbed Ellis by the arm and yanked. "I'll not go back to them! You hear me?"

Ellis clasped her gently by the arm and walked her back to their wagon. "You're getting back in bed."

Several members of the troupe witnessed the altercation, but turned away and gave them their privacy.

"The priests still want me, but I'll not let them take me. I'll kill myself first. I *swear* it." Her eyes burned as tears streamed down her face.

"Stop that. You'll do no such thing." Anguish filled Ellis's eyes, and he engulfed her in his arms. "I swear to you, I won't let anyone take you. I'll die first."

"As will I," Dirge said behind Ellis.

He held her in his strong arms, a balm that eased her pain and fear. She gently pushed him away once her tears stopped—it felt far too good in his arms and she was still mad at him. She wiped away her tears with her sleeve and sniffled.

"Besides," Ellis continued, his voice soft and soothing, "Chaos wants me. Not you."

"They do still want me." She stared off into the distance. "One does for certain."

"Who?" Ellis asked.

"A priestess named Celeste. She took over Ruddick's house after Vir and I fled." The memory of the woman drew a shudder. Celeste had wanted Daylin with a passion long before Ruddick died. "Vir and I spent months dodging her hunters. It wasn't until we found that fallen tree that I felt safe." She gazed into his eyes and smiled a little. "You know... my campsite you stole?"

"We stole nothing," Dirge said.

Daylin shook her head and waved him off. "Oh, stop it, grumpy pants."

"Be that as it may," Ellis said. "That's far to the south."

"But—"

"I'm telling you. We've nothing to worry about. No one around here is looking for us. We've passed paladins before, and they didn't give us a second look. Right?" Ellis reached up and touched her hair a moment before pulling his hand away sharply.

He cleared his throat and continued. "Ukase has led us here, and it is here we'll cross."

"How do you know it's Ukase? How do you know it's some old forgotten God of Order?" Daylin couldn't shake her doubts.

Ellis rolled his eyes. "Who else could it be?"

"What if it's something else?" Daylin asked with a shake of her head.

"Like what?" Ellis shrugged.

Daylin hesitated a moment. "What if it's Chaos? I can't put my trust in forgotten gods. I've had my fill with gods."

"I know it to be Ukase," Dirge intoned with a scowl. "And you watch your tongue, little one. I'll hear no blasphemy from you."

"Enough, you two," Ellis said. He paused, but shook his head. "It's not Chaos. I felt him speak through me."

"But how do you know it's Ukase? You're far from orderly. None of us are." She gestured toward the swordsman. "Except for Evil Eye, of course."

"Evil?" Dirge said with affront.

"Yes, Evil Eye. Because you're giving it to me right now, and I don't like it."

"I said that's enough." Ellis paused and seemed to look inward. "If it was Chaos, it would have led me straight to his people; not away from them. He led us to you. Ukase knew we needed to be together. And now He says we must cross here."

He turned and stared east, across the river, his eyes tight and his lips pursed.

Daylin chewed her lip while eyeing Ellis out of the corner of her eye. She took a step forward and lightly placed her hand on his forearm.

"What is it? I know there's something more you're not telling me."

Ellis turned and placed his hand on hers. Closing his eyes, he lowered his head a moment before peering into hers. "It's the vision—the one outside Kirks Knob." He paused and took a deep breath. "I have to go into The Lands of the Dead." He told her everything: about the land, the spirits, the tower with the great, ominous, pulsing light therein. "Something's going to happen there, and I'm a part of it."

He actually has to go into that horrible place? She shivered, her heart going out to him. "Thank you for telling me."

"Thank you for not pulling away." He reached out as if to touch her face, but snatched it back.

Damn these puppies, she thought, clutching her middle.

Daylin turned away to compose herself, and saw Sarah and Angharad approaching, arm in arm. *They're such a beautiful couple,* she thought with a smile.

Sarah strode toward them in a long, bright-green dress highlighting her short, dark-red hair and blue eyes. The sight of Angharad brought a usual pang of jealousy. The woman's golden-blonde hair glowed in the sun, and her eyes seemed to smolder. She wore a short white dress exposing much of her ample bosom, lithe arms, and shapely legs. A narrow waist accentuated her broad hips.

How does she make them sway like that? Daylin wondered with a little chagrin, knowing she couldn't compare to the stunning actress. Daylin's breasts were too small, she had no hips, and her limbs were more like sticks.

Once they approached, Sarah asked her with a frown, "And just what are you doing up, young lady?"

"Good morning to you, too, Sarah," Daylin replied.

The healer turned to Ellis. "I told you, she needs to stay in bed for the rest of the day." Sarah extended an arm toward Daylin. "Look at how pale she is. She looks like she could swoon at any moment."

"Oh. I don't know." Angharad looked Daylin up and down with a dimpled smile. "I think she looks positively radiant. I mean, look at her. She's glowing."

Daylin's cheeks burned as she turned her head away, yet she couldn't help smiling.

Sarah nodded her head. "True. The fresh air does seem to agree with her. As does something else, I suspect," she added with a grin. "All right, ten more minutes. Then it's back to bed with you."

Sarah turned to Angharad and patted her hand. "Speaking of which, I should see to Dandle. Who knows what kind of trouble he'll find in this place."

"No more trouble than you, I expect," Ellis said with a laugh.

"Oh so true." Sarah chuckled.

"And I need to see my Tom," Angharad purred. "He's probably feeling a bit neglected, I suspect. I need to remedy that." She kissed Sarah and the two went on their way.

"I worry about her," Ellis said.

"Who?" Daylin asked.

"Angharad," Ellis said. "She was trying to hide it, but she's troubled with one of her melancholy spells."

Daylin realized he was right. She'd been so preoccupied with the woman's appearance she hadn't noticed the darkness emanating from Angharad. On top of that, the woman's smile seemed forced, as though painted on, and her eyes held a hint of sadness. "I'm sure Sarah is doing what she can to help." She grinned. "In every way she can."

Dirge grumbled, "Those two need to put an end to that. It's sordid."

"Enough, Dirge." Ellis frowned with his brows drawn. "I've told you before; whoever folks bed, it's their own business. Do you think ill of me when I bed a man rather than a woman?"

"I would never think ill of you." Dirge said. "But, it is against God's will."

"Don't give me that," Ellis said. "My feelings are a part of me. If bedding a man were wrong, it would feel that way. But it doesn't."

Dirge twisted his mouth as though he ate a sour plumb. Looking down, he added under his breath, "And if you're going to lie with a woman, you should marry her first."

Ellis laughed. "I'm not the marrying type." His eyes flicked toward Daylin. "But if I was to marry—be it man or woman— that choice is mine, not yours."

Did he just... Daylin took hold of herself. *Stop being silly.* With a grin, she then poked at Dirge. "Come now. I'm sure you've bedded a lass or two in your time."

Guilt surged through the large, dark man as he took a half step back.

Her eyes went wide. "Really? Dirge, I must have details." Daylin hopped on her toes. "Who were they? What were they like?"

Dirge's face went stony. "I don't want to talk about it."

"Oh, please do." She giggled. "I know you've done it. I can feel it, you know."

"I said I don't want to talk about it." Dirge's eyes took on a haunted look.

Ellis patted him on the shoulder. "You need say nothing."

Daylin knew the large man was hiding something. Waves of love, shame, and remorse emanated from Dirge, and she desperately wanted to press. She glared at Ellis. *You may not want to hear his secret past, but I do.*

Ellis scowled. "No more, Daylin. Anyway, you need to get back to bed, and I need to see Evan about the crossing."

Dirge spoke up. "Evan said we may not be able to cross for a week. He also said the crossing may take up two days."

"A week?" Ellis shook his head. "Wait. If you knew this all along why didn't you tell me?"

"The two of you were having a conversation," the big guardsman replied without a hint of sarcasm. "It would have been rude to interrupt."

Ellis closed his gaping mouth. "I've gotta see Evan. 'A week' my ass!"

Daylin felt ambivalent as Ellis stormed off. She knew their being stuck for a week on that side of the river upset him. Yet, she couldn't help but feel happy about it. Much better to sit on the west side of the river than be over there, surrounded by priests; well, so long as she didn't run into that little monster, anyway. Even thinking of it was like rubbing an angry porcupine across her skin.

As she turned to mount the wagon, a friendly and familiar presence entered her mind. "I am coming, Mother. I will protect you."

"Bucky!" She clasped her hands. "Why d'you change your mind?"

"We feel your pain. Kylee tells me that since I am not afraid of boats, I should come with you, to protect you. That you need me."

Tears streamed down her face. "I do, Bucky. I do very much. You're my pup."

"I be there soon, Mother."

She wiped her eyes, climbed into Ellis's chair atop the wagon, and stared across the expanse of the roiling river to the main portion of the city.

Even with Bucky, they may not have enough to shadow the troupe. They'd needed more. Another wolf would be a boon to them.

"Maybe Evan's right." She sighed. "Maybe I'll find a wolf on the other side."

Chapter 23

A Trail

of Ash

(Year 522 -R.C.-)

Calidos Flint lounged at the kitchen table, eyeing the Master of the village of Fars Glen. The smell of smoke hung thick in the air as he sipped a cup of tea.

"You know," he said as he put down his cup and toyed with the drawstrings of a sack sitting next to his chair. "I've been after this man for longer than I care to remember."

"Y-yes," the Village Master stammered. "I understand. But, we've not—"

Calidos cut him off. "When I lost him all those years ago..." He paused and cocked his head. "What's your name again?"

"G-Gareth, M'Lord." The heavyset man mopped the sweat from his brow.

"Gareth," Calidos said with a nod. "As I was saying, when I lost him all those years ago, my men were convinced it was The

Great Lord's will. After all, when a grunkin kills your best tracker, what can one think?"

He took another sip of his tea. "But something told me to push on. So after we returned to Glennen, I had my men fetch Jantos's body. I wanted proof of how he died, and who better to give it to me than Asan?"

"I'm sorry. Who—"

"And it was Asan who told me the truth. A grunkin didn't kill Jantos, a wolf did." Calidos raised a finger in the air. "Ah, but not just any wolf; one strong in Spirit."

He leaned forward and lazily gestured toward Gareth. "You see, The Lord wasn't trying to drive me away. The Tree was." He smirked. "I mean, when will that damned Tree realize it lost?"

"T-tree, M'Lord?"

"Yes. Surely, you simpletons have heard of The True Tree? Spirit is its very essence."

"I… I don't understand, M'Lord."

"Don't you peasants know anything? You've never heard of The Great Game of the Gods?"

"N-no."

"It doesn't matter. The point is, The Tree—along with Time and Fire and all the rest—lost The Game." Calidos pointed at the fat man. "But, what I don't understand is how The Tree could have any influence in the world. It's locked away in the prison along with Time."

"P-prison?"

"Stop distracting me." Calidos shook his head. "Where was I? Ah, yes. So, if The Tree was trying to push me off the child's trail, which meant The Great Lord still wants this child dead. Correct?"

Gareth opened and closed his mouth like a fish gasping for air.

"But where was I to look?" Calidos waved his hand. "I scoured the south. I searched every Traveler there and came up empty. After a while, Hannibal himself, the High Priest of the South, called me to task. He said I was being too 'fervent' in my search. He stripped me of my men and bade me stop."

He snarled. "What would that fat sack of suet know about being 'fervent?' Edis, The Great Lord of Chaos himself, gave this task to me. Who does Hannibal think he is to deny *me*?"

"I... um... I..." Gareth licked his lips, his eyes flitting to the open window as crackles and pops drifted in from the town's inn Calidos set aflame upon his arrival.

"Several years passed," Calidos went on with a wave of his hand, "before word came to me of a great troupe of Travelers, crisscrossing the Westlands. 'The greatest show in the world,' they said. Well, I'd picked through every troupe in the south to no avail, so I figured maybe they were hiding him."

He leaned forward once more and tapped the table. "But do you know what really tipped me off?"

Gareth protested, his eyes wide and his face pale. Sweat seeped through his gray tunic, and his lank, brown hair plastered to his broad forehead.

"They said this *Grand Traveling Show* had a woman who talked to wolves."

Calidos stood and stalked across the kitchen, causing the Gareth to jump in the chair. "Well, I knew what I had to do. I sailed here with as many men as I could get. I spent months tracking this Grand Traveling Show. It wasn't easy; Travelers are as common as weeds here. But, at long last, I finally found their trail at Timsdale."

He stopped pacing and smiled wickedly. "Oh. How the rabble shrieked when I put them to the question. You people are always so tightlipped about him."

Gareth's jowls wobbled as he frantically tried to deny it.

Calidos ignored him. "But enough squealed about seeing wolves lingering near town while they were there."

Retaking his seat, he grinned at the portly, trembling man. "I can tell by the look in your eye you doubt my word."

"No, M'Lord! I do not doubt you—"

"It's all right." He waved his hand absentmindedly. "Michael—the Master at Timsdale—he didn't believe me either."

Calidos tipped his head to the side as something occurred to him. "Did you know I love fire? I do. It's my specialty. All those blessed by The Lord have one, you know, and mine is fire." Holding out his hand, he used the slightest hint of Chaos to ignite a small ball of flame in his palm. "I *dearly* love it. But the funny thing is, the further north I go, the closer I get to the prison—The Lands of the Dead—the more control I have over it."

Concentrated on the blaze, he pulled at both ends. The flame wavered and shook, and slowly drew out to a single, white-hot line of pure fire. He let it wink out of existence and continued.

He held up his hands. "What does this say about me? I'm not one to turn my back on The Great Lord. I'm not one of those fools we crushed in the south who worshiped Ukase. But what does it say about me that the further away from the Lord's influence I get, the more focused I become?"

His thoughts turned inward a moment before he focused on the Village Master once more. "I showed this little trick of mine to Michael's wife. After that, he talked. He told me everything I wanted to know. Actually, he told it to his smiling wife."

Calidos tilted his head again. "I see you still don't believe. I have her head in this bag. Let me show you."

Gareth's face paled as Calidos reached into the sack and grabbed the woman's head by her long, blonde hair. He pulled it out and showed it to his host.

"No! Lord, no! Cassy," the man shrieked, his eyes wide as he reached across the table.

"Oh. That's right," Calidos said as he took a quick glance at the head. "This is your wife. Not his." He set the head on the table, facing the Gareth, her neck charred and cut clean from when he'd severed it with fire. "I understand you have children. Is that right?"

Calidos Flint wore a snarl as he and his twenty men rode away from the smoldering embers of Fars Glen. He reveled in the aroma of soot, scorched hair, and charred flesh. The shrieks of the people and their animals as they died were a symphony to his ears. He'd enjoyed torching them nearly as much as he had Timsdale. How dare those peasants try to obstruct him in his righteous campaign?

"Cross Corners," he said as he stared off into the distance.

In a little over a week, he'd be at the river. Travelers were notoriously slow, and there he'd catch them at the water's edge with nowhere to run. After all this time, Calidos was finally closing in on the child he'd missed Cleansing.

"I'm coming for you, Ellis," he growled. "And I will burn you to ash."

Chapter 24
Cross
Corners

(Year 522 -R.C.-)

He loped through the empty forest, the wind whistling through his whiskers. *I have to find it… whatever it is.* He skidded to a stop and cocked his head. *Or is it a who?*

He shook his head and continued it down his body, all the way to his bushy tail. His long ears twitched as a twig snapped deep in the gloom. The long black hair at the nape of his neck bristled.

"Who's out there?" his mind cast into the gloom.

A harsh scent stung his nose as something brushed his mind. Feelings of grief, agony, and loss flooded him from the stranger so strong he raised his head and bayed in sorrow.

Betal's eyes snapped open, the dream evaporating, leaving a slight sense of grief.

"What was that about?" He shook his head as he rose from the bed. Other than a little stiffness from his small travel bed, he felt great.

He poured water from the pitcher next to his mirrored nightstand into the large porcelain bowl atop the table. He washed his face and teeth, and using his favorite white-bone handled razor, shaved himself smooth. He picked out black pants and a loose gray shirt from his travel chest. After a quick check in the mirror, he put on his best pair of riding boots, and stepped outside.

The rest of the camp was already out, and about their work— breaking down the camp, checking the animals and wagons, and making breakfast. The temperature felt cooler than he expected, but he decided not to go back and put on a coat. The day before grew warm, and his coat grew uncomfortable.

Killington leaned on a nearby wagon, awaiting him. "All was quiet last night. The boys saw no troubles about and no wolves either."

"How long do you think it will take to break camp?" Betal asked as they fetched their breakfast of eggs and sausage, prepared for them by Betal's servant.

"Not long. An hour at most," he replied as they sat on a pair of stools. "We should be away shortly after that. Provided everyone is up and ready to go, that is."

It took much longer than an hour.

The sun stood well past the horizon when Mangin strode up to Betal in a loose, cream-colored blouse, and long scarlet skirt. "Where is that old lump of shit? I'm sick of waiting." Her eyes burned.

"You mean Dithiyar?" Betal shrugged. "I don't think he's up yet."

Her face twisted into a scowl. "That pompous—"

She marched toward the elder priest's tent and placed herself directly at the opening. "Get up, Dithiyar. We need to get moving."

The elder priest did not respond.

"This doesn't bode well," Betal said to Killington, who grunted in reply.

Mangin gathered a fair amount of The Lord's Breath and sent a large pulse into the tent. A loud boom quickly followed.

Dithiyar shrieked. "How dare you!"

"Oh. I'm sorry. Did I wake you?" Her false saccharine voice oozed with anger.

"I am sorry, Mangin," he said from within his tent. "I didn't sleep well on this rickety bed. I'm quite sore. If I could just have a little more—"

"If you're not out here in five minutes, I'm setting your tent on fire."

The bedraggled priest stumbled out of his tent in less than three.

Mangin berated him from the moment he stepped out to the moment he was ready to ride. Her castigation continued throughout the day. When only an hour passed and Dithiyar requested a halt for lunch, Mangin's ire grew even greater.

They ate as they rode.

Come late afternoon, with several hours of sunlight left, Dithiyar demanded they stop for the night. "I cannot continue," he cried out the window of his coach. "We must stop. My back cannot take all this bouncing and jolting."

With a sigh, Mangin relented. They found a lightly treed spot to stop, but couldn't create a centralized camp like the previous night, and the guardsmen were furious about it. A split camp required more of them to man the watch.

Betal kept an eye on the woods from time to time, but he saw no wolves after the first night. However, they still haunted his dreams.

The next morning was the same as the first with Dithiyar waking late and dawdling the entire time. Mangin became so cross at the delay she slapped the old man across the face. The smack reverberated about the campsite.

As the day wore on, the thinning forest gave way to low rolling, grass-covered hills. A short time later, Dithiyar again demanded they stop early. Betal expected Mangin to fly into a rage, but she didn't.

"You are a pathetic, worthless piece of shit who should just go off and die already," she said with a snort and walked away.

A guardsman named Abner erected Dithiyar's tent. "We shouldn't be stopping," the guard said as he struggled with one of the two inner poles. "We could be in the Corners by nightfall."

"Just shut up, you simpleton, and finish your job." Dithiyar sneered at the man from his well-padded chair. "It's not for you to say when or where we go."

Abner spat and threw down the tent pole. He marched to within inches of the old priest. "I am sick of this shit. Ukase take you, old man! If you want your tent up, do it yourself." With that, he stormed off toward the center of camp. But he didn't get far.

Dithiyar took hold of Chaos and channeled it into Abner's midsection.

The guardsman stopped, clutched his belly, and his face turned white. Soon, Abner doubled over groaning, which quickly became a scream as blood and spittle spewed from his mouth. The clothing about his midsection turned to ash and fell to the ground, and his belly roiled like a maggot-filled carcass.

Betal stared at Dithiyar, his eyes wide. The old man had created a small mass of Chaos that expanded and consumed the screaming guardsman from within.

The guard's scream turned into a gulping sound as his upper torso separated from the now dissolved center and toppled to the ground with a splat. The liquefied mass of human flesh splashed about the dead man's legs, which, miraculously, remained standing as if rooted in place.

Dithiyar let go of the Chaos mass and stood tall, smiling wickedly at the rest of the men in the camp.

Betal looked to Mangin, who merely shrugged and walked away.

Seething, Betal stalked up to the old priest. "For someone who is claiming exhaustion, you're looking awful spry. I know for a fact what you did requires some measure of strength."

Dithiyar's face flushed. "Watch your tongue, *acolyte*, or I'll—"

"Shut up," Betal snapped. "You're not my master and never were. You're part of my past. Nothing more. I have a future awaiting me, and I'm tired of you delaying it." A growl escaped his throat. "Do you understand me?"

Dithiyar's mouth gaped like a fish on dry land. Closing it, he lowered his eyes.

Betal continued. "We'll be up at dawn and on the road an hour after that from here on. And if you dawdle, I will bind you to a horse where you'll remain, night and day."

Betal took a step, then stopped. He eyed the priest over his shoulder. "Oh. And if you even *think* of doing that again to anyone, I will do it to you. Only I can make the masses much smaller—minutely smaller—and spread them out about your entire body." Betal growled once more at the now trembling priest before marching toward his tent.

He did his best to avoid eye contact with anyone out of guilt. *A man just died, and all I can think about is myself.*

He hadn't particularly liked Abner. He'd been a good friend of Cruchfield, and one of many who wanted to see Betal die on the day of the *incident*. But the man deserved better than he got. He also felt embarrassed over his threat. He'd never hurt anyone in his life—not intentionally—and he was threatening Dithiyar. The threat wasn't idle, he'd meant every word, but if he followed through, he'd be no better than the old priest.

Why do I feel I should be better than this? He could do whatever he wanted. Selfishness was at the heart of Chaos. But did it have to be?

He spied Adam, eyeing him from across the camp. The man pointed at the cook pot, but Betal shook his head. *No dinner tonight, my friend. I need to think this over.*

As he reached his tent, Mangin sauntered around from behind it. "Masterfully done," she purred. "I do believe you've... motivated him far better than I ever could." She gazed up at him, her green eyes smoldering. "I do love a masterful man," she breathed as she slid up to him and lightly placed her hand on his chest.

The blood roared in his ears and his breathing grew heavy as she parted her lips, tilted her head slightly, and slowly leaned forward...

"I think I'll go see Cobb," Mangin said with a grin. She winked, slowly turned, and strolled away, her hips swaying heavily.

Sighing, Betal went inside.

The following day, well short of noon and with the road winding its way through the hills, the city of Cross Corners came into sight below them. Betal had never seen the like.

The large, sprawling city spread out from the wide Cunning River like half a star. It sat hard against the river and spread out toward and around the four roads leading up to it. Buildings hugged tight to each wide road. Across the river lay a smaller town with several large docks jutting out in the river like crooked fingers, and a wide, heavily trafficked road stretched into the appropriately named Westlands beyond. Dozens of ferries crisscrossed the river while boats drifted up and down it. To Betal, the tangled mess looked like two herds of sheep trying to cross a valley at the same time.

Two things struck Betal the closer they drew to the city—the noise and the stink. Penned-in pastures for animals brought to market filled the outskirts. The cacophonous bleats, bays, and mewing of the animals hurt the ears, and the smell of shit and rot stung the nose.

"How do they stand it?" he asked Mangin, riding at his side.

"They're peasants. Who cares?"

Betal shook his head.

The road sloped down, and the buildings became a mixture of ramshackle shacks and multi-story buildings in various stages of disrepair and water damage. Most of the tall buildings either leaned drunkenly out over the street or rested against each other, and around one in four looked to be under reconstruction or abandoned as piles of rubble.

"Why would people even want to live in a place like this?" The stink of decay, filth, and the chamber pots people tossed out their windows—regardless of what lay below—nearly had Betal in tears.

"What's the matter, Betal? Not a fan of the unwashed masses of the East Warren?" Mangin laughed. "Don't worry. Once we reach Old Town, it gets better. The roads are cobbled and clear of slop. The wealthy hate the stink as much as you, so they pay urchins to carry their refuse to the river."

"I don't feel like waiting."

Betal reached out, grasped Chaos, and spun it around him in a wide circle. Faster and faster, he spun his rope of The Lord's Breath until it caused the air to swirl and spin all about them.

People stopped and stared at the sudden gusts picking up dirt and debris, and whipping it all around. He spun out dozens of smaller filaments to gather the surrounding dust threatening to choke them and pressed it into the now swirling vortex. When Betal felt satisfied, he flung it all high in the air, looking like a small tornado, and sent it over the river where he dispersed it.

Though a small amount of the fetor persisted, Betal felt satisfied.

Mangin laughed. "Well, this certainly is an improvement. But do you think the peasants will actually notice?" She reached out and patted his knee. "It's much more pleasant now, thank you."

She surveyed the area. "I wouldn't be surprised if the temple is in a tizzy over trying to figure out what in all the hells that was."

She laughed again, her musical voice as sweet as ever.

Betal gazed at her as they moved on. *A man could grow old and die happy while listening to her voice.* It hurt having to be so close to her all the time. Yet, when she wasn't there, he ached even more.

The transition into Old Town was like a knife's edge as the road went from dried mud to paved stone. Gone were the ramshackle and wobbly wooden structures, and in their place, tall buildings of brick and stone, all on stone foundations ranging from five to ten feet high.

"Why the tall foundations?" he asked.

"It's because of the random floods, when the river tops its bank," she replied. "Old Town dates back to before The Time of Chaos. They were crafty if a bit too methodical for my taste. I mean, just look about. Too many straight lines, too rigid, too orderly. There's no style. No flow. Everything has its place. It's boring."

Betal disagreed. He found Old Town clean, neat, and built to last, with smaller lanes and alleys that crisscrossed the wide road, all meeting at right angles. Shops, inns, and taverns sat on the lower foundations with a wide walkway in front of each establishment.

Mangin pointed down the road. "Do you see that large building straight ahead there, in the center of town? That's their temple to The Lord." She put on a smirk. "It's just as I said:

everyone in their place, all separate and tidy. It's a wonder the local sect puts up with such rampant Order."

They traveled another block when Betal saw the doors to the temple burst open. Two dozen or so men in various types of armor poured down the stairs and sprinted toward them. A tall man in flowing robes of gray, red, and blue followed the soldiers. A short, stooped man completely hidden in black robes glided along in the tall man's shadow.

The men spread out down the streets, their heads swiveling in all directions, searching. The tall man in the robes, on the other hand, locked eyes with Betal and marched directly toward them. The man drew upon Chaos as he came closer.

Betal hung onto the Chaos he'd gathered, stopped, and waited for the priest to come to him. Mangin and the rest halted as well.

The young priest stopped a few yards away. Long blond hair framed his gaunt face, and his dark eyes held arrogance and suspicion as he addressed Betal. "Who are you, and what do you want here?"

"Kenja, why so rude?" Mangin asked in her willowy voice.

The priest looked at Mangin for the first time, and his eyes widened in shock. "Mangin! I'm sorry. I didn't see—"

Mangin scowled and stared hard at the priest.

"That is, it is good to see you again. You travel with a large party. Going to war, are we?" Kenja's face held an uncertain smile as his eyes traveled back to Betal. "And who is your... friend?"

Mangin's eyes still smoldered, but her voice oozed false adoration. "Kenja, this is my dear, sweet friend, Betal. He's a fellow acolyte of The Great Lord. We travel to Gate Hall; to my father."

Kenja eyed Betal with incredulity. "*This* is The Beast of Cool Winds? His reputation does him a disservice."

Kenja gave his head a small shake. "We felt a large disturbance in Chaos nearby. We thought a small Storm was forming in the city. They sent me to disperse it. The men are to deal with grunkin. Yet, I see no Storm. Do you know what caused it?"

Putting on a big satisfied smile, Mangin nodded toward Betal. "That was just the *Beast*, here. He didn't care for the stink in the East Warren so he felt it necessary to disperse it."

Kenja's head whipped to Betal, his eyes wide with shock. "Surely you jest?"

Betal said nothing and kept his eyes fixed on the young priest. Betal didn't like the man for some reason. It wasn't his manner or look, or even how Kenja had addressed him. The man had a darkness to him Betal didn't trust.

Dithiyar approached. "Enough of this *drivel*. You," he pointed at Kenja, "take us to the temple. My bones are sore from all this travel."

Looking to Mangin, he continued. "Tell the rest to find someplace to stay along the North road."

"Who are you to bark at me, old man?" the young priest said with a sneer.

Dithiyar ignored the question and continued trudging toward the temple.

Mangin shrugged. "That's just Dithiyar, our resident crotchety old ass."

"Dithiyar? Dithiyar Mardoon? *The* Dithiyar Mardoon?" Kenja's eyes were wide, and his jaw dropped. "I thought he was dead." When he received no response, Kenja shook his head and motioned for the rest to follow him.

He spoke to the little man at his side. "Take their caravan to the temple stables, then set up the rest at *The Over Reach Inn*."

Betal and Mangin dismounted and followed their guide toward the temple.

In front of the temple, the road opened into a large square, paved in red and black brick. A bazaar filled the space, except where the roads intersected. The shouts of people selling their wares, and patrons haggling over the prices, filled the air. At the temple stairs, they handed their horses' reins to the obsequious fellow shadowing Kenja.

Betal's eyebrows rose at the sight of the little man's green and gold scaled hands. He turned to Mangin as the... thing... walked away with their horses and the rest of the wagon train. "Who and what was that?"

"That's Raaz," she told him with a wave of her hand. "He's Kenja's personal assistant. He's half-demon."

"Half-demon," he replied incredulously. "I thought that was impossible. No human mother could survive the pregnancy, let alone the birth."

"He's the product of a lesser demon and a Tebu. The Forest Folk are strong; she survived the conception and pregnancy. But you're right, none survive the birth."

Unnerved, Betal changed the subject. "So, you've met Kenja before?"

"Oh, yes. I come and see him occasionally. He's really quite a dear. Don't mind him if he comes across a bit short at times. He's just the jealous type."

"Jealous of whom? Me?"

"Of course, silly. He's the kind of man who doesn't like to share me with others." She laughed at the bemused look on Betal's face. "Come now, sweetheart. Who wouldn't be jealous? Your power is obvious to all who matter."

"He's jealous of my being powerful?"

That didn't make sense to Betal. Kenja struck him as the type who was too proud of their own power to think someone might have more.

"Well, yes, there's that. But Kenja probably thinks we're lovers. Not that I can blame him. You're tall and quite handsome. Who wouldn't want to have you whenever they could?" She kissed him lightly on the cheek and strolled up the temple stairs.

Betal closed his eyes and suppressed a sigh at her lie. *I'm not handsome.*

Mangin was the only person to call him that, and she only did it to tease him. Betal held no illusions as to what he was, and no one would ever want a monster in their bed.

Chapter 25
Enlightenment

(Year 522 -R.C.-)

Betal followed the others up the temple steps. Kenja opened the large, brassbound doors and led them all into the chapel.

Betal stared. Dozens of everyday citizens worshiped The Lord and bore sacrifices at the various altars, braziers, and idols spread throughout the room. "It's full of people."

"You sound surprised," Kenja said with an eyebrow raised.

Betal nodded. "I am. I've never seen so many disciples of The Lord of Chaos before."

"Our old home was hardly a bastion of the devout," Mangin interjected.

Kenja led them through the chapel to a set of double doors where Dithiyar waited. "What's taking so long?" the old priest snapped.

Kenja shook his head and addressed a priest in blue and white robes standing next to the door. "Joden, take our guests to the master suites, and make sure all their needs are met. I'll inform Master Rendell of their arrival." He opened the door and strode down the corridor without looking back.

Joden nodded. "Mangin, it is wonderful to see you again." He turned his eyes to Betal. "And who is your friend?"

"This is Betal. He's my dearest confidant."

"I am sure he is." The priest's mouth quirked. "If you will follow me?"

Joden led them down the broad corridor, tiled in a chaotic array of small, multicolored tiles. Their boots echoed off the iridescent walls, lined with tapestries and alcoves containing various works of art. They took the stairs to the third floor, and down another large corridor ending at a set of gold-bound doors.

He walked in a short way, turned, and bowed his head. "These are the master suites. You will be well taken care of, I assure you." He pointed to a thick, red, velvet rope next to the door. "If you require anything during your stay, simply pull the rope and someone will take care of any and all of your needs."

Betal went to the far side of the huge central room. Hand-sized windowpanes stretched from the ceiling to the floor along the entire wall, with a pair of glass-paned doors opening out to a balcony overlooking the city square at its center.

He touched the glass. "Amazing."

Mangin turned to him. "What?"

"The glass; it's flawless. No bubbling, no warping. How did they do it?"

She scoffed and waved her hand. "It's just like the rest of this district. Old and boring."

Joden interjected. "We actually have no idea how old the building is, or what they used it for in ancient times. All the windows in the temple have wards built in that protect against both physical and mystical attacks and are soundproof as well."

"Thank The Lord," Mangin said. "The last thing I need is to hear the babble of those hawkers."

"Where's the bedchambers?" Dithiyar snapped.

"The bedchambers are through those doors." Joden indicated the two sets of gold-bound doors on either wall. Large fireplaces separated each pair.

"All four are ready for use. Each has a large bed, writing table, and a lounge. The temple library is at the other end of the hall, past the stairs. Feel free to read anything you wish, either there or in your room. Just know there is a ward placed upon each, barring you from taking them out of the temple."

"All I want right now is some decent food and rest," Dithiyar grumbled while heading for the room on the far right. "Be sure they knock before bringing it in," he said without turning and slamming the door behind him.

Mangin laughed heartily. "Pathetic."

Joden smiled, his eyes shifting between Mangin and Betal. "Will you require only two of the rooms?"

"We'll need three," Mangin said with a grin. "Oh. Our things are in the caravan in the stables. Also, I'll need someone to go to… what did he say its name was? Ah, yes. *The Over Reach Inn*. I need you to fetch a young woman named Adel. I'm tutoring her, and I wouldn't want to pass up the opportunity to utilize such… wonderful accommodations."

Yes. I'm sure you wouldn't, Betal thought as he returned to the center of the room and sat in one of the several comfortable chairs surrounding a low, round table.

Mangin took a quick look at the door Dithiyar went through. "Though I must say, a meal does sound wonderful. Bring me Adel, as quickly as you can, and have her bring two meals with her." As an afterthought, she added, "But nothing hot, mind. It'll likely grow cold by the time we get to it." She winked at Betal before going to the outermost room on the left.

Betal scowled. *So much for getting a room with a window.*

As Joden turned to go, Betal jumped up. "Hold on. I'll go with you. There's someone I want to talk to at the inn, and I've no idea where it is."

The priest nodded. "As you wish."

As they walked down the hall, Joden spoke up. "If you do not mind my asking, where do you hail from?"

"We're from Cool Winds. We're going to Gate Hall. Mangin's been called home to join the sect, and I am going with her." Betal cocked his head at the priest as he missed a step. "What is it?"

Joden hesitated. "I make it my business to know who resides in all the temples in the region. I have, of course, met Mangin before. And I know Dithiyar Mardoon is the head of the temple there, and by the look of your ill-tempered comrade, I can only assume he is the Old Crow himself."

"The Old Crow?"

Joden waved his hand dismissively. "It is a name they often call him." He eyed Betal. "That leaves you. I had assumed you came from the south, but you say you come from Cool Winds. It is widely known 'The Beast' resided in Cool Winds, but no one ever really says *what* 'The Beast' is. I must say, I expected something quite different."

Betal scowled. "So I gathered."

They didn't speak again until they were out in the bazaar and headed north. Joden kept glancing at him out of the corner of his eye, his face a picture of uncertainty.

"What is it?" Betal asked.

A few moments passed before Joden spoke up. "I find you quite the enigma."

"How's that?" Betal watched a pair of children run by in little more than rags.

"Your power of The Lord's Will is undeniable. Now, anyone with that much strength should be someone to fear. Yet, I do not fear you, and that puzzles me. In fact, I find myself liking and trusting you." Joden pursed his lips. "I find the latter quite unnerving."

That gave Betal pause. He knew the effect he had on those back home, but they were only commoners. "The Lord works in mysterious ways."

Joden continued. "You were raised in isolation, so I say this to you in good faith. Trust no one. I know it may seem oxymoronic considering what I said before, but it is the truth all the same. I was raised in the temple at Gate Hall. I learned much there. From our first days, we learned 'to trust someone is to tempt death.' I have seen firsthand the truth of that."

Betal chewed at his lip.

Joden stopped again. "Heed my words. Trust no one and give as little information as you can. Information is a weapon, to be used both for and against you. So, I suggest you not be so forthcoming to others in the future." Joden chuckled and continued his walk to the inn. "As I am being with you."

"I see what you mean. Thank you," Betal said. They continued their way in silence—Betal had much to consider.

Three blocks north of the square, on the northeast corner, they came to *The Over Reach Inn*, a nondescript building of four stories. Unlike the other inns, *The Over Reach* possessed a much larger front patio and the upper three stories overhung it by fifteen feet with ornate columns anchoring the overhang.

Patrons occupied only three of the two dozen tables – men and women in plain but clean clothes huddled together, deep in conversation. At one table, three men sat at their ease in fine linen shirts and silk coats hanging open. One wore his black hair at shoulder length and sported a small beard. As he drank from his pewter mug, he lazily fondled a large pearl in his left ear. The other two looked to be brothers, both clean-shaven with the same sandy blond hair, cut short.

Upon seeing Joden and Betal, the eyes of the two apparent brothers went wide, while the dark-haired man merely frowned, but he quickly wiped it away. He leaned to his right and whispered something that caused the others to laugh.

"Who are those men?" Betal asked as they entered the inn.

"The two brothers are brigand captains, Marc and Fen Kendrick," Joden replied matter-of-factly. "They run one of the larger groups calling Cross Corners home. Most of the highwaymen in the region use the city as a base, and most of them work independently. But not them; they have some kind of loose affiliation. The dark-haired man is Dillon Slade; a member of The Brotherhood."

"The Brotherhood?"

"Yes. They are assassins who worship Aza'zel."

"Aza-who?" Betal cocked his head.

"Aza'zel—The God of Death. You see, The Brotherhood are very dedicated, and are known for hunting very particular prey."

"What kind is that?" Betal asked.

Joden chuckled. "Let us just say if someone wants a certain member of the clergy eliminated without it looking obvious, then Dillon Slade is the man to see."

"He hunts priests?" Betal shook his head. "Why does your High Priest not do something about it?"

Joden turned to stare at Betal, his eyes wide and a smirk on his face. "Are you truly so naïve? Betal, political assassination is common among the pastorate. And The Brotherhood are not a simple group of local killers. Their presence is known and felt in the farthest reaches."

"But, again, why put up with it?"

Joden shook his head. "You must understand, Betal. Not everyone has the strength you do. So, they take other methods to improve their own standing."

He patted Betal on the back. "You are headed to a very dangerous place, my friend. Remember, trust no one, and always watch your back."

They crossed the inn's common room and approached the proprietor on the far side. "Good afternoon, Allen. I am here for a young woman by the name of Adel. She is a member of a caravan that arrived quite recently. What room is she in? Oh. And my friend here is wanting to see..." He turned to Betal.

"Adam Killington."

"Ah, yes," the innkeeper replied with a deep, gravelly voice. "The group from Cool Winds. They're all taking supper in the dining hall."

"Thank you, Allen." The priest handed him a silver coin. Motioning to Betal, he headed down a hall at the far end of the bar.

As Betal followed, he realized something; he'd no money. Joden was right. He'd been much too naïve. *I'll have to talk to Mangin about getting some coin when I get back.*

They passed several doors on either side of the hall before Joden opened a set of double doors at the end. The noise of conversation and clatter of utensils washed over them as they entered.

Joden called out, his voice booming, "I am here for a woman named Adel."

The dining hall silenced.

Betal pointed to Adel at the far side of the room, sitting next to Cobb at one of the long tables.

As she stood, Cobb grabbed her by the arm and yanked her back down. "What do you want of her?"

"Mangin Karados desires her company," Joden replied with a hint of a smile.

Cobb's face darkened. "No. Not tonight. Tonight, she beds with me."

"But—" Adel began.

Cobb cut her off. "I said no! You spend every night with her. We've a good bed here, and I intend to use it. I don't care if you can read or write. What good is it in the fields? It's useless."

Adel shook off his hand. "Who the hells are you to tell me whether or not I can learn?"

"You don't need to read to raise our young or keep the home. I'm tired of this useless learning. You're done with it."

She stood with her head held high, and again, pushed away his grasp. "I may be your woman, Cobb, but I'm not your slave." She stepped over the bench and approached Betal and Joden.

Cobb lunged for her. "No!"

Using Chaos, Joden shoved a large mass of air that took Cobb in the chest. He flew back and careened off the wall.

"Mangin Karados has spoken, and I do as she asked. And so shall you," Joden said, crisply. "Come along, young woman. I do not have all day."

As Joden ushered Adel out of the room, Betal looked to Killington sitting near the door to the hall. "Adam, would you join me in the main room? There're things I wish to discuss regarding where we go from here."

With an uncertain look toward the Cruchfield table, Adam stood and joined Betal in the corridor. Without a word, Betal led him toward the front.

Once in the common room, Killington spoke up. "Forgive me for asking, but why would you want to speak with me about the travel plans? Cruchfield's in charge of the guard, and he's made it clear that his son is his second."

Betal sat at the nearest table and gestured for Adam to join him. "I just wanted to talk. And after what happened in there, I thought it might be easier on you if the others thought this was something other than a social visit." He shook his head. "Besides, we both know what they think about me. Cruchfield wouldn't listen to a word I say. He'd likely spend the entire time simply trying to figure a way to kill me."

Adam nodded and sat. "Very true. Well, let's have a drink and you can tell me what's on your mind."

Betal twisted his mouth. "I appreciate the conversation, but unfortunately, I can't join you in drinking."

"Why is that?" Adam asked.

Betal laughed. "I've no coin. It never occurred to me, until a few minutes ago, I'd need it. Back home, if I needed something, I just asked the staff for it. I never had to buy anything in my life. It's no wonder the people hate me."

Adam laughed. "Not everyone hates you, my boy. And no need to worry about the coin. I'll cover it." He waved over a serving wench.

A young woman with long, brown, flowing hair approached. Pale legs flashed under her short blue skirt, and her white blouse opened down the front.

Adam ordered them both an ale.

"Would you care for anything to eat?" she asked in a soft, high voice. To which Adam declined.

Her eyes went to Betal. She took him in from head to toe and licked her lips. "And you, sir? Is there nothing I could do to... *satisfy* any of your appetites?" Her large, dark brown eyes seemed to smolder.

"No. Thank you," Betal said politely while shifting in his seat, and waved her away.

She frowned, looking crestfallen, and went to fetch their drinks without another word.

"Did I say something wrong?" Betal asked Adam.

Killington grinned. "I'd say she's upset you didn't take her up on her offer."

"What offer?"

Adam's eyes went wide. "She offered you *herself* as a meal." He chuckled. "Hells. If she looked that way at me, you'd be drinking here alone."

"But, she made no such offer." Betal looked askance at Adam when the man laughed. "Adam, she didn't."

The older man laughed even harder.

"I say she made no such offer!" Betal slammed his hand on the table. "Who would? Who'd offer themselves to a monster without being forced?"

Killington sputtered. He stared at Betal, his mouth hanging open. "You can't be serious?" His eyes grew large. "You are serious." Adam sighed and leaned across the table. "Betal, you're a very good-looking man. And a powerful one, at that. Whether people know who you are or not, they can see it.

He leaned back. "My young friend, you're no longer in Cool Winds. Out here, no one knows you as 'The Beast.' And even if they do, there's many who'd find that attractive. Listen, Betal. You've the world at your feet. Don't let life slip past you for not seeing it." He gave a pointed jab toward Betal. "And you're not a monster, whatever they call you. Forgive me for speaking so, but your father would have words with me if I didn't set you right."

The bar maiden came back with their drinks, and Betal took another look at her. *Could he be right?*

She set down their drinks and accepted the coins from Adam. As she turned to walk away, she gave Betal a smoldering smile, winked, and headed to another table.

Betal's jaw hung open. *But, I'm 'The Beast.'*

"So," Adam said, taking up his mug. "What did you want to talk about? Obviously not a woman."

Betal picked up his own pewter mug and took a sip of the dark brown ale. "Nothing, really. I just wanted to talk. Mangin's going to be busy with Adel, and I'm in no mood to deal with Dithiyar. I just wanted the company of a friendly face for a while."

"Well, my boy, my time is your time."

Two hours later, with a slight buzzing in his head, Betal made his way through the crowded bazaar, deep in thought. Adam gave him quite a lot to think on. A dozen yards from the steps of the temple, Betal caught the toe of his boot on an upturned paving stone and tumbled to the ground. He sat up with a curse, staring at his scuffed-up hands.

The surrounding crowd backed up with a sharp intake of breaths and formed a wide circle while talking in hushed tones.

Betal stared at them with an eyebrow cocked. *All I did was fall*, he thought. After a moment, he realized they weren't looking at him.

To his left, only three feet away, a man lay face down with a crossbow bolt in his back.

Betal's mind snapped into focus. He scanned the crowd and the roofs of the surrounding buildings, but saw nothing out of the ordinary. He quickly grasped Chaos and wove a shield about himself. *That should've been me.*

Betal wished he could have done something for the poor man, but Chaos wasn't meant for healing. It was much too complex and intricate, and one would just as likely kill someone as cure them. When someone needed healing, they went to either a hedge mage and their minor magic, or apothecaries with their herbs.

Betal stood and slowly made his way to the steps of the temple, his head swiveling, searching for the would-be assassin. He readied several nasty spells to take care of them. The shield he wove about himself caused the air to ripple, and the people scattered. They now knew him to be a priest as well as the likely target.

By the time Betal mounted the stairs, no one was near the body. He stopped and gave it a quick look. The man's clothes were intact, his purse still tied to his belt, but the crossbow bolt was gone. He cursed himself for not recovering the bolt. It might have led him to the assassin.

He quickly made his way up the stairs and into the temple. He dropped his shield and crossed the mostly empty chapel to the door to the inner sanctum. It disappointed him to see someone other than Joden manning the door.

"Where can I find Joden?" he asked the acolyte who pointed him in the direction of the main library.

Betal sprinted down the corridor, the sound of his boots ringing loudly off the walls, and up the wide stairs to the third floor. He started down the hall to the library when he saw Joden halfway down the hallway to his suite.

"Joden, wait," he called out, sliding to a stop next to the priest.

"Betal, what has you in such a lather?" he asked with a smile.

"Someone just tried to kill me."

The smile slipped from the priest's face. "Tell me everything."

Betal relayed, as calmly as he could, everything from the moment he left the inn until the moment he entered the temple.

"Come. Let us have a look from your balcony."

The suite's central room was empty upon their arrival. They made their way to the far wall, opened the door to the balcony, and stepped out. Betal quickly re-wove his shield and pointed to the spot where the attack had taken place below. The space was still clear of people, but the body was gone—only a large pool of blood remained.

"Too late, as I suspected," the priest intoned. "I will send out a squad of guardsmen to ask questions, but I do not expect them to find anything."

They went back inside. "It is as I told you, my friend; your life will now be far more interesting." Joden started for the hallway, but quickly turned. "Oh. I nearly forgot. I was sent to inform you there will be a dinner in your honor at The Great Hall in two hours' time."

"Thank you, Joden. If you don't mind, please inform Dithiyar. I'll go tell Mangin."

"I thank you for the honor," he replied sarcastically with a smile.

Betal crossed the room to Mangin's door. She'd placed a ward about it, so he sent a pulse into the room and waited. A few minutes passed with no response, so he sent another, much stronger one.

Mangin flung open the door, stark naked. "What do you want?" she shouted. Her breasts heaved, and she glistened with sweat. She ran a hand through her wild, fire-red hair and moderated her tone. "What is it, Betal? I'm in the middle of something."

Betal did his best not to stare, and his cheeks burned. "I—I just wanted to let you know we're invited to dinner in The Great Hall in two hours."

She cocked her head and put on her best devilish smile. "Well, I did just finish eating, but I'm sure I'll be peckish again by that time. Thank you, Betal." She started closing the door but stopped. "Unless there's something else?" She glanced at something in her room and pursed her lips. "No. Never mind. I think not. Not yet, anyway." She laughed and shut the door.

With a shake of his head, Betal turned and headed toward Joden, who appeared to be talking to Dithiyar through his door. He hadn't reached the center of the room when a thud and a crash came from the other side of the old man's door.

Joden jumped back, looked to Betal, and laughed. "It would appear Dithiyar is not interested in attending the dinner."

He approached Betal. "Well, I will leave you to get some rest. Someone will come to let you know when it is ready and escort you if you so wish. If not, The Great Hall is on the second floor at the end of the main corridor."

After Joden left, Betal sat in one of the large, comfortable chairs in front of the fireplace. His earlier buzz was returning, and he still felt a little shaken from the attempt on his life.

Who and why would someone want him dead? The latter was the more important question. If he could figure that out, it might lead him to the former. He came up with no answers by the time a young acolyte came to take them to dinner.

Chapter 26
Intersecting
Ideals

(Year 522 -R.C.-)

Mangin lounged in a padded, high-backed chair near the end of the long U-shaped dining table. While fiddling with the sheer cotton dress hugging her form, she cast her gaze about the Great Hall. The room glowed warmly from low hanging chandeliers running down the center and mirror-backed candles along the walls. Servants came and went from a pair of doors behind her, bearing food and drink.

Having found the pheasant crisp and moist, she tried a bite of the diced pork. Frowning, she turned to Kenja. "Whoever prepared this did it a disservice with the spices." She took a sip from her crystal glass. The exquisite wine—dry and robust—washed out the pork's aftertaste.

Including Betal, Dithiyar, and herself, twenty people lined the table; all but two of them were priests. It surprised her Dithiyar even showed. He'd appeared at the last minute in his usual huff, taking the seat next to Master Rendell Morgan. Morgan wore layered robes of gold, red, and blue. They hung loosely over his overly large frame, and gold rings sat on each of his pudgy fingers. Around Morgan's neck hung a thick gold chain with two large medallions. One signified his leadership of the Council of Merchants—which oversaw the running of the city—and the other proclaimed him High Priest. The other priests all wore their finest silken robes, each one a multitude of mishmashed colors typical to followers of Chaos.

Mangin hated robes, finding them far too bulky and concealing. Oddly, all their robes were of the same fashion and cut. She pursed her lips. *Yet another example of excessive order.*

Devin Reich, the captain of the city guard, talked quietly with Thevron Drocks, the temple's paladin. Each wore tight leather pants and linen shirts, but past that, their similarities ended.

"Drocks is quite fascinating," she said to Kenja. "Have you ever seen someone with skin so dark before?"

When Kenja didn't reply, she glanced at him and scowled as he stared daggers across the table at Betal.

She'd idly considered taking him up to her room after the dinner. His drab, gray robes complimented his eyes and allowed his high cheekbones to stand out. But Adel was still there. Kenja was a great lover, but he had a cruel streak, and she did not intend to share her angel with the likes of him. The more she thought about it, the less she felt like taking Kenja to bed ever again. There she sat, all but offering herself, and he only wished to pay his attention to Betal.

She sipped her wine. "If you're so infatuated with him, go see if he's interested. He might say yes, I don't really know. I'm not sure where his predilections lie. I've never seen him with a woman or a man." She sighed and shook her head. "The locals were much too frightened of him, and he's not the type to force himself on anyone."

When Kenja still refused to respond, she tilted her head. His reaction to Betal was fascinating. Commoners seemed to either take an instant like or dislike to her dear friend, but it was the first time she saw it from a fellow devotee of The Great Lord.

She changed tactics. "Tell me, Kenja, why did you think Dithiyar was dead?"

He cocked an eyebrow at her. "You don't know?"

"Know what?"

"Dithiyar Mardoon aided Lord Heartless during The War of Power. He's over five hundred years old."

"Five hundred years? I knew the crotchety bastard was old, but…" She shook her head. "It would appear I must have a talk with our dear Dithiyar."

"So, I understand you're tutoring some commoner. Adel, is it?" Kenja took a long pull of his own wine, his eyes locked on hers over the rim of the glass.

"Wonderful," she said, beaming. "She's a very talented tongue." She leaned back and crossed her arms, but kept her face calm. *If you even think of doing anything with her, I'll take your head.*

"Is that so?" He grinned. "I thought you were just teaching her to read?"

"Well, she's proven to be quite sharp and I want to see if she could become my clerk." Wondering where he was going, she smirked. "Since when are you interested in my clerical affairs? If I didn't know better, I'd think you're jealous."

Laughing, he replied, "I'm hardly the jealous type."

"So true." She did her best not to laugh. Kenja was incredibly possessive as well as ambitious. It made for a dangerous combination. She'd have to keep Adel even closer to ensure her safety.

Through the thick conversation about the table, Betal said something that drew her attention. "What was that about Travelers?" she asked. She dearly loved the traveling shows.

"Reich was just telling me a troupe left town only a few days ago. They had over twenty wagons."

"Yes. They were quite unusual, and not just for their size." Reich's voice grumbled as though he chewed rocks. "They crossed the river from the Westlands and made camp north of town, but only stayed two days. Most motleys stay as long as two weeks to attract as many patrons as they can."

"I've heard of them," Thevron Drocks interjected. "They're of some renown in the Westlands. They've traversed it for some twenty years and are always well met."

"What's their name?" Mangin asked.

"Concord's Grand Traveling Show," he replied with aplomb.

"I've never heard of them," Dithiyar mumbled around his wine glass, his fifth of the night.

"It seems this is their first time crossing The Cunning," Master Rendell said. "They took two days to do so. I wonder why they crossed at all."

A young priest tore her gaze from Betal. "Perhaps they wore out their welcome over there. Some people just aren't as accommodating as others." She turned back to Betal and ran a hand through her long black hair with a small grin.

Frowning, Mangin crossed her arms again, her leg kicking under the table, as she glared at the young woman.

"I just want to know why they only stayed two days," Reich asked with a frown.

"Perhaps if we run across them on the road north, we will ask them," Mangin said as she thought of multiple ways of disabusing the black-haired woman of her obvious intent.

"I hear their animal trainer has a pack of wolves for pets," the woman dared to add.

"Wolves?" Betal sat up, his eyes keen.

"Yes," the sniveling young woman said, sitting forward with her right hand extended on the table. "Do you like wolves?"

"Actually, that's not quite true," Reich interjected. "There's a woman who has a pet wolf. I've seen it myself. But it's only one. The rest are simply dogs. She lets them run wild—even the wolf—and keeps none of them in cages."

Sitting back, Betal seemed to look inward.

"Betal has an affinity with wolves," Mangin said, her eyes locked on the dark-haired priest.

"Is that so?" Kenja murmured, sipping his wine.

"Yes. It's said they heralded his arrival into the world," Mangin added.

Lowering his head, Betal tapped his fingers on the table. "That's not exactly true, Mangin."

"Come now." Shaking her head, Mangin smiled. "The villagers say it was the cries of the wolves that drew them to where they found you."

"Is that true, Dithiyar?" Drocks asked.

The old priest simply nodded in reply.

"I don't care for wolves." Kenja inspected his nails. "They're too structured, too orderly. I understand they live in families with a distinctive hierarchy, from pack leader to the most worthless."

"That's true," Drocks said. "I've watched them—cloaked, of course. I've never liked them either. There's a feeling about them I just don't trust."

"You're all ones to talk about something being too orderly," Mangin said. "All of Old Town is nothing but straight lines and strict districts. How do you put up with it?"

"It's good for business," Master Rendell said.

"How is that?" Betal asked.

"There are more forms of power than that of The Lord," The High Priest replied. "The power of commerce is nearly as powerful as Chaos; perhaps even more so in The Reach. Chaos is waning in the Westlands. No more than three of four villages have priests in residence, and there are too few paladins to take up the slack. Most linger in Gate Hall."

"I'll be sure to let Hogar know that," Dithiyar said into his wine.

"He knows my opinion, and shares it." The High Priest scowled at Dithiyar. "It's said The Lands of the Dead are stirring. Things are creeping out."

"I've never heard of any such thing," Scoffing, Dithiyar waved his hand.

Rendell turned to him. "You never crawl out of your hole."

"I don't have to take any more of this; certainly not from the like of you." Dithiyar jumped to his feet, his chair crashing to the floor behind him. Downing the rest of his wine, he threw the glass to the floor. "Heartless should have destroyed this city like he did Ravenwood."

Mangin giggled as the old man staggered off. *Oh. How the mighty have fallen.*

"What's Ravenwood?" Betal asked.

"It *was* the home of Heartless before he became The Champion of the Lord," Master Rendell said. "As I understand it, he took exception with some there. They treated him poorly before his ascension and then mocked him afterward." He took a drink. "Now the only thing remaining of the city of Ravenwood is a vast wasteland of Chaos."

"Apparently, some go there just to see it," Mangin said. "The Lord's Wonder, they call it—those who survive the grunkin, that is." She laughed. "How could a fool like Dithiyar ever have the honor of working beside Lord Heartless?"

"I imagine," Master Rendell replied, "all his strength now goes to keeping himself alive."

A wicked grin crept across her face. *I'll have to see what I can do about that.*

Betal returned to his suite after the dinner, feeling sated. The food was amazing, both in variety and taste. Wavering slightly, he stopped to steady himself – he'd also enjoyed several glasses of their wine. Staring out the window, his jaw fell open. "It's dark out?" He was one of the last to leave the dinner, but he hadn't realized it had gone on so long.

The sounds of Mangin and Adel in the throes of ecstasy emanated from her room. "Why didn't she ward the room? I guess she *wants* to be heard tonight."

Betal shrugged and took a seat to gather his thoughts. He had a wonderful conversation with Master Rendell near the end. Betal found the man quite fascinating, with so many views of not only Chaos, but of the way of the world. His opinions on how to govern a region were so diametrically opposed to the doctrines of Chaos they bordered on heresy. But perhaps the man was right. There was very little violence in the city. The City Watch kept a tight control on any such activity as well as any major thefts that might occur. They did the same with the surrounding farms. The people lived with a modicum of safety, free of the roving band of marauders plaguing other towns. Ironically, those same marauders also lived in the city, and used it as a base of operations. The heads of the three largest bands actually held seats on the merchants' counsel. "It's like the wolves and the sheep all living together."

Frowning, he still couldn't shake the thought of that wolf on their ride west. "It's like the thing *wanted* me to see it." Worse, it also seemed to be trying to communicate with him.

"That's enough for tonight." He shook his head, wanting an early start the next day. It was their only chance to catch that band of Travelers. "Maybe that wolf-woman can tell me something."

Betal got up from the chair and made his way to his room. Upon opening the door, he froze. A single candle bathed the room in soft light, and a woman lay in his bed. Grasping Chaos, he spun a shield before him and filled the room with light, then flung the sheets off the woman.

Squealing, she raised her hands toward him. "Please, My Lord, I mean you no harm. I-I was told you'd enjoy my company. Y-your friend, Mister Killington, he said you'd appreciate me." Her eyes were wide as her naked form trembled.

Betal recognized her. "You're the serving girl from the inn." He relaxed and shook his head. Releasing Chaos, he threw the room back into near darkness. "It's dangerous to let yourself into someone's room."

"I apologize, My Lord," she said. "But I just couldn't help myself."

As his eyes adjusted to the dim, she slid out of the bed and sauntered to him. Her long brown hair hung down past her shoulders, partially covering her ample breasts.

Her swaying hips drew him to her downy nethers. His eyes snapped to her face when she slowly undressed him. He took hold of her hands at his belt. "I don't know if we should—"

She kissed him, her lips meshing with his, and he felt his body go limp—well, not all his body.

"Come, My Lord." She drew him to the bedside and undid his pants, then took down his drawers. "I know this will be your first time, but I'll take good care of you."

Betal fell back on the bed with the lithe young woman straddling him. When she kissed him again, he returned it with fervor. *Perhaps we won't get off to such an early start tomorrow after all.*

Dithiyar stalked back and forth across his room. It had been several hours since the dinner but he still fumed over Rendell Morgan's comment. "How dare that pompous bastard speak to me that way?!"

Grasping a vase, he hurled it at the door. The vase shattered, adding to the pile of objects he'd launched earlier. "I deserve better than this. I was there in the beginning. I was the one Heartless came to, to learn the ways of Chaos." He slumped into the bedside chair. "Damn you, Twitch. Damn you for leaving me behind."

Chapter 27
Revelation

(Year 522 -R.C.-)

The warm morning sun awoke Mangin. She enjoyed the sight of the city at night and hadn't closed the drapes the night before. She lay naked under a thin sheet. An equally unclad Adel clung tightly with her head on the crook of Mangin's arm.

Mangin brushed the blonde hair from Adel's face and smiled as the woman's eyes fluttered open.

"Good morning, my darling." She kissed Adel on the forehead. "How did you sleep?"

The lithe beauty stretched and smiled back. "Wonderfully. I've never slept in a bed so comfortable before. I think I could get used to it." She idly ran her fingers up and down Mangin's stomach and chest. "I could get used to doing other things in a bed like this as well." With a twinkle in her eye, she leaned over and nibbled Mangin's breast.

Mangin laughed and pushed Adel away. "Now, now. None of that. I expect we'll be getting an early start, so you need to get back to the inn and pack."

"I never unpacked," Adel replied. She sat up, slid her hands up her sides, and cupped her breasts, her eyes riveted to Mangin's.

"Is that so?" Mangin couldn't help but think of the possibilities. She shook her head. "Be that as it may, you need to be going."

She rolled out of bed and slunk to the other side where she gently pulled Adel to her feet. As the young woman passed, Mangin swatted her on the behind, causing Adel to squeal and giggle. The girl liked a good spanking, and Mangin was more than willing to oblige—the redness from the night before had already faded.

"Go back and let everyone know we'll be leaving soon."

Adel put on a slight pout. "Fine. But I'm going to miss this bed." She sighed as she dressed and left.

Mangin's smile slipped as the door shut. "I have to do something about her."

She'd not lied to Kenja about wanting to train her to be her personal clerk. The woman was smart, as well as subtle, when she needed to be. The way she handled Cobb was proof enough of that. However, Gate Hall was going to be a very dangerous place for Adel. She possessed no talents for the arcane arts, and that made her vulnerable.

Mangin held no illusions about her future life. Gate Hall was a pit of vipers with everyone grasping for power and leverage. She may know how to manipulate the mind, but her training from Dithiyar had been woefully inadequate when it came to politics. Her mother's books and papers were helpful, but they weren't enough. And the rigid politics they played at The Corners was nothing compared to those at the citadel where they embraced The Great Lord with fervor.

In time, someone was sure to try to use Adel against her. "I have to keep her safe."

With a shake of the head, she put it aside and stretched. "I'm as hungry as a wolf."

The statement made her think of Betal.

With a smile, she exited her room, not bothering to put on a robe. She strolled to the front door, pulled the cord to call the porter, and crossed to the glass door leading to the balcony. She opened it and stood there a moment, letting the full glory of the morning sun seep into her skin, but also thrilling at the contrasting chill of the air.

She heard the door to Betal's room open behind her. *Perfect*, she thought.

She put on her best smirk and slowly turned, ready to greet him and revel in the distress her state of undress would cause. Her smile melted and her eyes hardened as a young woman quietly backed out of Betal's room. The woman's long brown hair was disheveled, and she looked as though she'd rapidly dressed.

Mangin marched to the central room. "And just who are you?"

The woman squeaked and spun around. Her jaw dropped open as her eyes traveled up and down Mangin. She snapped her mouth shut and dropped her gaze. "Pardon, madam. I didn't see you—"

Mangin cut her off. "I asked your name. I also want to know what you were doing in Betal's room."

"I—I'm Jena, madam." She glanced to Betal's door. "I'm sorry, madam. I wasn't told you two were exclusive. Not that we did any—"

Mangin cut her short with a harsh laugh. "Don't you dare try and lie to me. I know the look of someone freshly sexed."

Stalking forward until standing only inches away, Mangin loomed over the young woman. She took the time to get a better look at the girl. She was quite lovely, albeit far too short.

Mangin considered taking the girl for herself, but the girl had just spent the night with Betal, and Betal belonged to her. With a snarl, Mangin gathered Chaos. *Will he still find you pretty without a nose?*

A thought occurred to her. "Did you make him happy?"

The girl trembled, and she eyed the floor between her feet.

Mangin released the Chaos and smiled. "No need to be afraid, child. I'm glad he finally lost his innocence. It's good for a man to gain some experience in how to please a woman." She cocked her head. "And for his first time to be with someone so lovely…"

The girl didn't reply.

With her right hand, Mangin stroked the young girl's cheek. "There's no exclusivity here, child. What's your name again?"

"J-Jena, madam."

"Jena. What a sweet name. Tell me, Jena: from where do you hail? I don't recall seeing you at the temple before."

"F-from *The Over Reach Inn*, my lady. Adam Killington bade me come here and… visit Lord Betal."

Mangin sighed. "Oh, Adam. What a thoughtful man."

She cupped Jena's chin and raised her face to look her in the eyes. "When you see our dear Mister Killington, tell him Mangin sends her thanks." She bent down and kissed the young woman on the cheek.

Jena shook even harder.

"Again, child, there's no need to fear." She gently turned Jena and urged her toward the door. "Now run along and do as I ask."

After the door closed, Mangin took a seat in the lounge chair directly in front of Betal's door and waited. An hour passed. The porter came with her breakfast and went—she ate heartily. Finally, Betal opened his door and stepped out, wearing only a robe.

"Jena?" He jumped at seeing Mangin sitting there regarding him… still naked.

A thrill raced through her at his jump. She stood and sauntered toward him, her hips swaying. "Good morning, my dear."

His jaw dropped and his eyes widened. He became so engrossed in the treasures she displayed, he unconsciously let his robe fall open, exposing his arousal.

Oh, very nice, she thought as she glanced at his manhood and her jealousy over Jena fled. Betal belonged to her, and nothing else mattered. *That's right, my love. One day this'll be yours, when you learn you need to* take *it.*

"I'm afraid Jena's gone." She leered and nodded at his stiff member. "It's good to see you, too, Betal."

He jumped and snapped his robe closed. "What do you mean she's gone?"

"She's a wonderful choice for your first dalliance. Quite captivating." Mangin licked her lips. "I even considered tasting her myself."

"What did you do to her?"

She laughed. "Nothing, Betal. As much as I'd have liked to. I just asked who she was and sent her on her way."

"Oh, all right." He shifted his feet. "Did she... say anything about me?"

Mangin chuckled. "Men."

He looked at her quizzically and shrugged. "I just wish she'd stayed till I woke up. I'd really like to see her again," he added under his breath.

"Oh? One night wasn't enough?" Mangin chided.

"No," he said with a hint of wonder. "We had such a wonderful conversation."

Her brows shot up. "Conversation? Betal, I'm disappointed in you. And here I thought you'd ravished her all night."

"Well... we did have a lot of fun." He dropped his head, grinning. "She said I was her wolf."

It seems I'm not the only one seeing it, she thought. "Did you howl?" she asked.

He blushed.

"Betal. You animal."

To her amazement, he grew even redder. He shifted his feet and added, "We talked, too. A lot."

Mangin turned and headed back to her room to dress. "Well, you can talk to her again when we get the men on our way out of town."

"No, no. We're not leaving," he said absently. "Not yet."

She stopped dead, turned slowly, and stared at him. "What are you talking about?"

He stood taller and puffed out his chest. "I said we're not leaving yet. I want to stay a couple more days. I need to get to know her more."

Mangin scowled.

Betal shook his head and walked toward her. "You don't understand, Mangin. This woman is different. She's funny and kind. And... and she wasn't scared of me. I told her what happened back home. She said she felt sorry for me, but she felt it made me a better person. A stronger one."

Mangin's jealousy rekindled. "Is that so?"

"Yes. She respects us—the priesthood—and harbors no hatred of The Great Lord."

She sneered. "Betal, she's a whore. Killington paid her to fuck you last night."

"I know. She told me." He pulled a pair of silver coins from the pocket of his robe. "She gave me the coin so I could return it to Adam. When I asked why, she said she wanted me to know she didn't want it." His face broke into a radiant smile. "She didn't want the silver. She just wanted me."

"She wants you?" Mangin growled, her face a thunderhead.

The very idea was ludicrous to Mangin. No one just wanted her. No one sought her out. When she wanted someone, she had to take them, like Cobb. None of those stupid peasants would willingly bed her. Her only other option was with those like Kenja—covetous people with an agenda who wanted her for her power and position.

Mangin stalked toward him. She opened her mouth, raised her finger... and stopped. She closed her mouth and turned away, her anger gone in a flash.

She'd never known a man who wanted her, but she did a woman. Ever since Mangin had opened Adel's mind—ridding her of her silly fears and misconceptions—she'd come to Mangin willingly, wantonly... lovingly. She'd not asked Mangin of anything. True, Adel wanted to learn to read and write, but that had been Mangin's idea. And quite often, Adel would spurn her tutelage times, wanting to make love instead.

"Love?" she said to herself. She'd never considered the possibility with anyone beyond Betal, or herself.

"You think she loves me?" he asked.

She ignored his question. "You're right, Betal. You need get to know her better." She spun around and gazed up into his silly, innocent eyes. "You need to know her true feelings, Betal. Find out what she says is true. Just because she gave you the coin, doesn't mean she isn't playing a game."

"You think she was lying?"

"Find the truth!" She sighed. "You're right about staying. A couple of days more won't make a difference. It's not like we're on a schedule, after all."

"Thank you, Mangin."

His beaming smile made her feel a little guilty. Because, if Jena truly cared for him, Mangin would be forced to change the girl's mind, and that would likely break Betal's heart. Mangin wasn't about to lose him to some Cross Corners barmaid whore.

Mangin had room in her heart for both Betal and Adel. After all, she was nothing if not flexible.

As she turned to go, Betal spoke up. "Wait. Since we're staying, there's something you need to know." He told her about the attempt on his life the day before.

"This is serious. The Brotherhood aren't allowed to conduct business in the city. I'll have to bring this up with Reich. In the meantime, I'll send for Worm. He can guard our door at night and watch over me when I'm out."

"You think they'll attack us here in the temple?"

"It's what they do, Betal."

She turned toward her room and asked him over her shoulder, "Would you please summon the porter? I'll have a message for him." She smiled. "I'll have Worm bring Adel. We need to keep working on her studies."

And I need to thank her, she thought. A ghost of a smile played on her face, and love filled her heart.

Blood and gore dripped from the jaws and claws of the grunkin as it moved away from the human's farm on the outskirts of Cross Corners. Powered by its rage and pain after finding its true prey out of reach, it slaughtered the humans and all animals it found there.

The grunkin knew it shouldn't be able to differentiate between life forms. It hated life, especially its own, and sought to end all other life it found. But something had touched the grunkin, cursing it even further than The Lord of Chaos already had. A vast dark being granted it consciousness and bade it to destroy certain beings before all others.

The grunkin hated the dark being. It didn't want to know its past—that it had once been a man with a family. And it didn't want to remember slaughtering that family. But it did what it was told until it made the mistake of not killing all those wolves. Their counter attack had crippled it.

However, in the end, it didn't matter. The grunkin finally found someone the darkness sought, someone also connected to The Lord of Chaos, and it would soon rip him to shreds. Perhaps then, the darkness would let it die.

Chapter 28
The Wolf

(Year 522 -R.C.-)

Betal stared at Mangin's door in disbelief. He'd never seen that look on her face before. *Am I missing something about those two?*

With a shake of his head, he pulled the cord for the porter and raced to his room to dress. By the time he had finished, the porter awaited him. He told the man about Mangin's missive and went to the balcony door.

"Would you care for breakfast?" the man asked.

Betal said yes, grasped Chaos to weave a shield, and walked out to the balcony. He wasn't taking any more chances. A short time later, the porter returned with his food.

Betal ate on the balcony, deep in thought. He knew Mangin liked to mess with him, but she had a good point. Was Jena just playing a game by giving him the money? It was possible, but he still didn't think it was so. However, thinking and knowing were two different things.

The truth was, he didn't even know how he felt about Jena. He knew she made him feel special. Like a normal person. She'd opened his eyes in so many ways. Like how the life of the commoner always teetered on the edge of destruction, and how it often drove them to live every day as if it were their last. She'd said most had little to nothing if they lived outside Old Town. Jena grew up in the West Warren where her entire family had died when their house collapsed.

"If Allen hadn't taken me in at *The Over Reach*, I'd have died, too," she'd told him. Her eyes were like dark-brown pools pulling at him.

And then there was the way she touched him. Subtle and yet, demanding. She made him feel like he was in complete control, yet guided at every step. She'd grunted and moaned, laughed, and cried. She was amazing, in every way.

He shook his head and went back to eating. *Am I thinking with my heart or my cock?* There was only one way to find out.

After finishing his breakfast, he walked to the large mirror at the end of the room, next to the door to the hall, and inspected himself. His loose white shirt was clean and pressed, and his black pants fit snug, tucked in his freshly blackened boots. His hair was in a slight state of disarray and he needed a shave, but chose not to. She liked how he looked last night so that should be good enough.

He donned his rose and onyx coat from the rack by the door. He wondered a moment if the gold stitching running down the sleeves and at the collar might be a bit too much. He smoothed out the front to calm himself. It wasn't working. With a deep breath, he opened the door.

The temple teemed with traffic. Though in a hurry, he did his best not to jostle anyone on his way. As he crossed the chapel, Joden greeted him with a smile. "Good morning, my young friend. And how is the new day treating you?"

Betal couldn't help but return the smile. Joden never seemed cross; at least not in the short time he'd known him. "Good morning, Joden."

"I trust you had a pleasant night. You had some very lovely company, after all. If she had spent the night with me, I know I would be quite jovial."

"You heard about that?"

Joden laughed. "I am the one who escorted her to your room."

"Do you know if she made it back to the inn all right? If too many know she spent the night, it might put her in danger."

Joden looked at him quizzically. "What would make you say that? I was at last night's dinner, and you made no enemies that I know."

"I'm talking about the person who tried to kill me last night."

"Oh, yes. I let the guard know and informed The High Priest. The Great Lord may love the discord, but the Council, not so much. They do not like anything that detracts the business of the square."

"Thank you."

"Think nothing of it." Joden grinned. "Well, you go and get your little woman and give her a kiss from me."

"Hells no. She's mine." Betal headed to the front of the temple. He heard Joden laughing as the temple door shut.

Betal stood a moment at the top of the stairs. He grasped Chaos, wove himself a shield, and headed at a trot toward the inn, feeling buoyant. The sun seemed brighter, the sky a more radiant blue, and all about him, the air seemed to be abuzz. He'd never felt so wonderful, and he owed it all to Jena.

About halfway to the inn, he caught sight of Adel and Worm coming his way. She waved and smiled as she approached him. "I understand you're the one to thank for our getting a few extra night's sleep in a comfortable bed, rather than in the rough."

"Yes," he replied. "And you are welcome. You haven't seen Jena come this way, have you?"

"Who?"

"She's a serving girl at the inn. She's short, well not short so much as petite, with long brown hair and beautiful brown eyes."

"Why, Betal. You sound positively smitten. I take it she's the other person I need to thank?" She laughed. "Well, you just be careful. I know it's easy to fall with your first, but take it slow. You don't want to scare her off. And, no, I've not seen her, but if I do, I'll let her know you are looking for her." She paused. "Although something tells me she already knows."

She headed off toward the temple, but turned and added after a few feet, "Who knows, Betal. If you play this right, you just might talk her into joining our little party." She turned and ran toward the temple, laughing, with Worm tagging closely behind.

Betal continued to *The Over Reach*, thinking on what Adel said. "Get her to join us?" He hadn't thought of it before, but it sounded like a great idea. It'd be a wonderful way to get to know her.

Adel may have been toying with him a little, but she had a point. He needed to take it slow. Jena was a special woman, and he'd do whatever it took to get her to see him in the same light.

A short time later, he reached the inn and bounded up the stairs. Half the tables out front held folk taking their breakfast. Among them was Dillon Slade. The dark-haired man seemed deep in thought and didn't look up as Betal made his way to the doors to the inn. The man may have seemed oblivious, but Betal had a feeling Slade missed nothing.

Entering the inn, he noticed Allen wasn't behind the bar. He approached the new bartender, a bedraggled man in his late thirties, and asked if Jena had come in yet.

"No," the man told him. "She works in the afternoon. She's still most likely at home. She'll be here soon. Would you care for a drink while you wait on her?"

"Yes. That'd be fine. I'll have a wine, red." He fished out a silver coin and tossed it on the bar. When he'd told Mangin the night before about his lack of coin, she laughed and gave him a pair of fat purses filled with both gold and silver.

As Betal waited on his drink, he noticed a pair of skulls mounted on boards above the bar. When the man gave him his drink, he pointed to them. "Why do you have skulls above the bar?"

The man eyed Betal a moment before replying. "The Ghost brought them in; told me to mount them as a reminder. I had no idea what he was talking about, and I didn't care, neither. I just did as he told me."

"The Ghost? You mean Hogar?"

The man nodded and shuddered. "When The Ghost tells you to do something, you do it. It was a good couple of months before people would even come back, 'cause of the stink."

Betal thanked him for the drink and went back outside to wait for Jena on the patio. He stepped through the doors and looked for a good table to wait for Jena. Dillon Slade was gone—not surprising. Betal gave a quick look around and took a seat at the nearest table, trying to enjoy the morning sun, slowly sipping his wine.

He couldn't stop thinking of Slade. The man was the head of a group that killed priests, and only yesterday, someone had tried to kill *him*. Had Slade been behind it? And if so, who put him up to it?

In less than a quarter hour, six of his caravan's guards exited the inn, led by Killington. He stopped short, his eyes wide at the sight of Betal. "My boy, what are you doing here?" He continued before Betal could respond. "Me and the boys would like to thank you for the extra respite. We're taking a walk about the town. Would you care to join us?"

The rest looked less than pleased at their leader's request.

"No. Thank you, Adam. I'm waiting for Jena."

"Who's Jena?"

It was Betal's turn to look surprised. "The bar maiden who works here." When Adam shrugged, Betal continued, "The one you sent to my room last night."

Adam shook his head. "Lad, I sent no one to your room."

Betal's jaw dropped. He told Killington about seeing her in his room, and her saying Adam had been the one to send her there.

"Betal, on my life, I sent no woman to your room." The man smiled. "Wait. Is this the lass who served us last night; the pretty one?"

"Yes. But, why would she say you paid for her to come?"

Killington laughed heartily. "I wouldn't worry about it, my boy. By the sounds of it, you just likely scared her. She probably said it so you wouldn't burn her to a crisp, thinking her a thief."

Adam turned to his fellow guardsmen. "Lads, you should have seen her; long brown hair, big beautiful eyes, and the nicest bosom I've seen in some time. She was quite a handful, by the look of her."

Betal's cheeks burned.

Adam laughed even harder. "Wait She wasn't your first, was she? Well, hells. No wonder you're waiting on her."

The men joined in with the laughter.

Betal scowled. He'd thought Adam was his friend.

Adam shook his head. "No need to get upset, my boy. I meant no harm or disrespect. It's good to see you in better spirits, is all.

Lord knows we all felt the same as you after our own first go at it."

The guardsman patted him on the shoulder and started to leave, but halted. "I mean it, Betal. It's great to see this little lass has made you happy. But, don't go falling for her too hard, now. She'll likely break your heart. The first ones always do." He bid Betal a good day.

Betal frowned and sat back. Everyone was urging caution regarding Jena. Were they right? Was he going too fast? A part of him agreed with all the criticisms, and it told him to slow down and think it through.

Maybe I should just go back and send her an invitation to dinner.

His thoughts evaporated when she came bounding up the stairs. Her hair was in a long braid hanging down her back and her burgundy blouse was so tight it accentuated her full figure. Her skirt was deep green, loose, and hung less than half way to her knees, leaving her bright white legs to flash in the morning sun.

She looks even more beautiful than last night, he thought. His heart beat wildly, and his manhood burst to life.

She stopped at the top of the stairs, her eyes wide. When he stood, a smile bloomed upon her face. She hesitated, then ran to him, flung herself into his arms, and soundly kissed him.

"Why are you here?" she asked, her breath rushed and heavy after their kiss. "After the conversation I had with your priestess friend, I didn't think I'd ever see you again."

"What did she say? She didn't hurt you, did she?" He caressed her cheek.

"No. She didn't harm me. She just wanted to know who I was, and what I was doing in your room." She cocked her head to the side. "Are you two lovers?"

Betal knew Mangin's temper and jealousy well. What she was jealous of, though, was still a mystery. "No. It's nothing like that. We're just friends."

He took a short step back and cupped her chin gently in his right hand. "As to why I am here, well, you didn't say goodbye this morning, and I wanted to give you a kiss upon rising." He leaned forward and gave her a light kiss upon her lips.

He pulled back, and his smile faltered a bit. "I had to see you again."

He gazed deep into her eyes, trying to gauge her response, afraid he was being too forward.

His heart sank as she stepped back and her smile fled. "I'm sorry, Betal." Tears formed in her eyes, and she turned away. "I didn't wake you because I knew you were leaving today, and I hate goodbyes. I know it's silly to feel this way after such a short time, but I can't help it."

She turned back to him, drying her tears with the back of her hand. "I wanted my last memory of you to be sweet. But now you're here to get your people and leave, forever." Her tears flowed once more. "And now I have to watch you go."

Betal let out the breath he didn't realize he was holding. He smiled and stepped toward her. He, again, cupped her chin, raising her face so he could gaze into her eyes. "I'm not going anywhere."

"What?"

He leaned down and kissed her softly on the lips once more. "I decided we're staying a little longer." He kissed her harder, and she emitted a slight whimpering moan. "You're not going to get rid of me that easy."

She threw her arms about him, clinging as if she'd never let go. "Thank you."

She ran and told the barman she was taking the day off. The man glanced at Betal by the door and nodded. Betal nodded back. He took her hand as they left to enjoy their glorious day.

She showed him the city from one end to the other. They shopped at the bazaar, and ate several small meals at inns, bistros, and tearooms, all about the town. She wanted to show him everything there was to see. They canoodled, be it in the back of a quiet dining hall or out front on the patio of the teahouse. She took him out the back of a high-priced inn and had him ravish her right there against the side of the building. Her cries of lust brought onlookers to see what the distress was. Betal didn't care if they watched. She was all that mattered.

The light was fading when they made it back to his room at the temple. On their way in, Betal asked the porter to bring them some wine and cheese—he expected they'd build up quite a hunger and thirst.

Two hours later, the porter came with the refreshments whilst the two of them were in the throes of passion.

Lying on his back with Jena between his legs, Betal waved at the man holding a large tray. "Thank you. Just place them on the table near the *door*—" His eyes shot to Jena. "You bit me."

She grinned. "You weren't paying attention."

He grabbed her by the shoulders and pulled her up to him where he kissed her soundly. He rolled them both over so he lay on top. It wasn't much longer before his climax ended that particular session.

Betal lay on his back, thinking on the future, with Jena curled up beside him, her head resting on his shoulder. His friends told him not to rush it, but he'd made up his mind. "Come with me, Jena. Come to Gate Hall."

She gazed up at him with her big brown eyes, and it only confirmed his feelings.

"I want to be with you and only you. I can't stay here. My place is at the sect house, and I want you there with me." He placed a kiss upon her forehead. "Please say you'll come with me."

She smiled, her eyes beaming. "Yes, Betal. I'd love that. I want nothing else in the entire world." She crawled up his body and kissed him hard.

Betal knew she was the one—his reason for living. The Great Lord may well have plans for his future, but from that moment on, they'd include Jena.

His thoughts flashed back to the night before, and he chuckled.

"Are you laughing at me now?" she asked, pulling away. "You'd better not be laughing at me."

"No. I'm not laughing at you, my love." He ran his fingers through her hair. "I was just thinking about last night and how frightened you seemed. You weren't scared at all, were you? You're too bold to be frightened that easily."

When uncertainty crept across her face, he reassured her, "It's all right. I'm not angry. It's just that… well, I know Adam didn't send you. He told me so." He sighed. "I must admit, it caused me to do some thinking, though."

"That's a relief." She laughed, pushed herself up, and got out of bed. "Would you care for some cheese?"

"Yes, thank you. I'm famished." He sat up and scooted so his back rested against the headboard.

Jena returned with the tray and sat at his side. She took up the slightly curved, serrated knife, cut a piece off the soft cheese, and handed it to him with a smile.

He reached out for it with his left hand. "That looks wonderful."

Her smile slipped as she slashed his wrist. The blade cut deep and blood sprayed. She lunged at him with the knife. He twisted to get out of the way, but the blade sunk into the right side of his chest.

Pain blossomed, and the world seemed to slow. He watched as she wrenched the knife out and stabbed him again. He grunted as the blade struck a rib and slid to the side, its serrated edge gouging his flesh. Not satisfied, she slashed him repeatedly across his chest. When he tried to push her away, she sliced his arm. Then she took aim at his neck.

Out of instinct, he brought up his right hand. Power surged forth, and a bolt of Chaos flew from his palm, striking her in the shoulder. She screamed as the blast threw her from the bed. Panting, he scrambled after her. His heart pounded, leaving trails of blood on the sheets, walls, and floor.

She lay in a heap, gasping for breath, her skin ashen. The arm holding the knife, the knife taking his life, lay against the wall— the blast had torn it off, and blood fountained from the wound.

He dropped and took her head in his shaking hands. "Why? Why did you do this? I loved you! I'd have given you anything!"

His tears fell onto her face as she whispered, "Must kill the wolf. Must kill the wolf. Must... kill... the wolf..."

Life left her eyes.

Betal sat back and cried, knowing he'd soon join her in death. Chaos did many things, but it couldn't heal.

His breathing slowed and his vision blurred at the edges. He tingled, feeling cold to the bone. His consciousness slipped, detaching, as though no longer in his own mind. The wounds no longer hurt, yet he still felt them.

The blood seeping from his wounds pooled on the floor and intermingled with Jena's as he shared her fate. The dark red contrasted sharply with the while tiles. It flowed down the grout lines as it spread, creating intricate patterns.

Well, this is interesting, he thought, examining the gashes in his chest and arm. *That's not right. It's not supposed to look like that.*

He thought of how it should look—the skin whole and hale with the pink hue of life rather than the gray before him.

The slashes started to close.

He stared in wonder, thinking his mind played tricks on him as the wounds sealed and his blood ceased to flow out. His heart beat stronger, his breathing returned to normal, and his vision cleared.

He touched his skin with a trembling hand. There were no scars or blemishes. It was as if the attack never happened.

How? Why? He shook his head. *The Lord must still have need of me.*

He gently placed Jena's head on the floor and stood on wobbly feet, staring down at her. She was still beautiful... and he'd killed her.

Weak from the loss of blood, he staggered across the room and sat on one of the well-cushioned chairs. He couldn't bring himself to look at Jena, so he stared at the closed door to the central room. He needed to think.

She hadn't attacked him out of fear, or even hatred—her face had shown neither. She'd just looked like a butcher going about their business. Is that what she was? Had it all been a rouse?

"Kill the wolf?" he muttered. *What did that even mean?*

His thoughts went back to the wolf on the road to Cross Corners, and to all his odd dreams. Was there more of a connection to wolves than he knew? And why did people want to kill him over it?

His face firmed. They'd leave at first light and travel hard. Somewhere down the road was a Traveling Show with a woman who talked to wolves.

"Maybe she can tell me."

Dillon Slade seethed as he rode away from Cross Corners. His long hair and cloak flailed behind him, and his eyes stung from dust as he urged his horse for more speed.

"Damn you, Jena!"

Why hadn't she stuck to the plan? Now The Brotherhood was forced to leave The Corners because the fool woman broke the edict. After a time, he'd be able to bribe their way back in, but for now, they had to lie low.

In a way though, his departure was fortuitous. The day before, he'd received a letter from the regional head of The Brotherhood, demanding his presence at Gate Hall. And when the High Slayer called, you went. The man spent most of his time in the south, and it was said he could actually commune with Aza'zel—unlike most Brotherhood members.

Dillon shuddered, thinking about the High Slayer. He didn't relish having to tell what happened, but he wasn't about to lie. One did not lie to Talic Sern.

Chapter 29
Making Camp

(Year 522 -R.C.-)

The clack of the horse's hooves on hard-packed road and the squeaks and creaks of the slow-moving wagon mixed with the tweets and chirps of the birds flitting within the trees and bushes lining the road. The sun neared its zenith within a bright blue sky, and the scent of flowers filled the light breeze. Yet, Daylin noticed none of it. She chewed her lip and fiddled with the wagon reins as she eyed Ellis out of the corner of her eye. He sat next to her, deep in thought, his troubled eyes staring off into the middle distance.

"What's wrong?" she asked.

He didn't reply.

"Angharad was wondering why we left Cross Corners after only one day."

He remained silent.

"You don't have to worry, though. I told her it was my fault. I told her all the priests made me nervous."

In truth, the young blonde wasn't the only one who asked that question. It was on everyone's mind. They'd spent only one day and night at the city before hurrying on, and many of the troupe openly grumbled about all the folks who didn't get to see their shows.

She forced a laugh. "I told her not to worry. I said we'd be back that way as soon as we were done at Gate Hall."

She knew his real interest wasn't Gate Hall, but the thing pulling him beyond it. But now as they headed north, Ellis slowed their pace, and she didn't understand why.

"What's wrong, Ellis?" She reached out and squeezed his left arm. "You can tell me anything. You know that."

His head jerked toward her, his eyes wide, looking haunted. "What? Oh, nothing. Just… thinking."

His painted-on smile didn't fool her. "Ellis…"

He sighed, his eyes seeming to go inward again. "Fine. Something's pulling me, something new, and I don't understand it."

"What do you mean?"

"The rope tied about my throat—pulling me so hard across the Westlands I thought I'd choke—is now tugging me to go back." His eyes filled with uncertainty. "It's like my head's going to pop off."

"Is it some place you have to go?" she asked.

"No. It's a man… I think."

"A man?"

He nodded. "I had another dream last night. A new one."

Her throat tightened.

"It was so much more vague than usual. It led me to the heart of those cursed lands as usual, but I wasn't alone."

"Is this man supposed to go with you?" she asked.

"Yes, him." He lowered his head. "And others."

"Do you know who he is?"

"No. But I'll know him when I see him."

Daylin chewed her lip. "You said it was pulling you back. Does that mean we have to go back?"

He shook his head. "I don't think so."

"Then let's wait," she replied with a shrug. "Whoever this man is, he's obviously behind us on the road. I say we make camp and wait for them to catch up with us."

"Yes. That makes sense. But what do I tell the rest? They don't like the slow pace as it is."

She smiled at him. "You're making it too hard for yourself. Just tell them you have one of your 'feelings' that this is the right thing to do."

Ellis smiled—the first true one she'd seen out of him in some time. He leaned over and gently kissed her on the cheek. "What would I ever do without you?"

She swung her head away, feeling her cheeks growing warm. "Stop it. You're being silly."

"Could you get one of the dogs to fetch Evan?"

With a nod, she concentrated, sending her thoughts to Bristle, screening them out front. Looking through the large dog's eyes, she had Bristle stop in front of Evan with one paw at the ground and one in the air. Evan nodded and came riding, knowing Ellis wanted to talk to him.

A few minutes later, the scout arrived. "What is it, boss?"

"I want to make camp. Possibly for a couple of days. I need you to find us somewhere appropriate."

"So soon?" Evan shrugged. "Well, there's a nice spot I passed only a short way ahead. There's a bridge crossing a fair-sized creek. On this side of the bank, there's a nice open space big enough for us. It looks well used, so I'm guessing it's a common way point."

"Excellent," Ellis said. "Have Dirge tell the rest. Then head back and make sure the area is secure."

"I'll have the dogs check it out as well," Daylin added.

Ellis again smiled and patted her on the knee. "Thank you."

Damn these puppies, she thought, giving the reins a shake to get the horses started again.

An hour later, as they pulled into the open ground, Ellis circled the wagons. The dogs had found a small, secluded campsite just inside the far tree line. It looked like the kind brigands use to set an ambush on anyone camping there. The dogs said there was human scent, but it was at least a week old. Ellis didn't want to take any chances.

At nightfall, Ellis and Daylin readied themselves for bed. As Daylin stepped out of the changing room in her nightgown, she felt her cheeks redden. Ellis sat on the end of his bed, still fully dressed, leaning forward with his head down. Staring at him, the wagon seemed smaller. The air felt heavy and filled with an energy she didn't understand. It was as if a thunderstorm were brewing just under the roof.

As she stepped forward, he looked up at her and smiled. She dropped her head as the puppies ran roughshod in her stomach.

Ellis stood and approached her. He cupped her chin and raised it so they were looking eye to eye. He stroked her cheek with his thumb, his blue eyes never looking so big.

She quivered.

"I want to thank you again." His voice was as soft as a caress. "I meant it when I said I wouldn't know what to do without you. You're my rock. You never question my visions, and you don't think I've gone mad like most would." He chuckled. "Even though I'm not so sure of that myself."

His hand gently pulled her face forward, and he leaned in.

She panicked. "I need to go for a walk!"

Pulling away, she spun and burst out the door into the cool night in only her nightgown. It wasn't until she stepped on a small, sharp rock that she realized she was still barefoot. With a curse, she considered going back for her slippers and a cloak, but thought better of it. If she went back now, she wasn't sure if she was ready for what would happen.

What am I doing? she thought while wandering about the camp.

It was a normal night in the troupe. Even though it was well past sundown, only half had called it a night. They sat around large fires, quietly talking, singing, and playing their instruments. It was normal... except for Ellis trying to kiss her. And now she threw away her chance, one she wasn't certain she wanted in the first place.

What were these feelings? Was it love? Lust? Or something else altogether? She envied the interrelationships crisscrossing the camp. They all had someone to care for them, and in many cases, multiple people. She needed to talk to someone she knew and trusted, who could help her with that kind of conundrum. She needed to talk to Sarah.

Sarah was not only one of the most gifted performers, but she was also a skilled herbalist and the unofficial camp counselor. She had a wonderful ear and always seemed to know just what to say. Having seen so much of the world, and being in several relationships, the young woman understood the ins and outs of the human heart.

Not seeing Sarah about any of the fires, Daylin headed for her wagon. She mounted the steps and knocked. Daylin was in such a tizzy she only waited for Sarah to say, "Yes," before opening the door and entering. She halted with a slight squeak, her cheeks reddening.

Sarah was lying naked upon the bed, her arms and legs entangled with Angharad's.

"Oh, my. I am *so* sorry. I didn't mean to interrupt you. I don't know what I was thinking." She spun about to leave.

Sarah called out, "No. Come back. It's all right." She disengaged from the blonde and rushed to Daylin's side. "What's wrong, honey? I've never seen you so out of sorts."

"What are you doing out in the cold in just your shift?" Angharad added. She jumped up, pulled the blanket from the bed, and wrapped it around Daylin, pulling her back in the wagon.

Daylin didn't think she really needed the blanket. It wasn't that cold outside, and the wagon's interior was quite warm—the sheen of sweat covering both women was proof enough of that. Nonetheless, she let them usher her in and onto their bed.

"You really don't have to do this," she said with her head down, desperately trying to hide her burning face.

"Oh, hush," Sarah said as she gently rubbed Daylin's back.

"Let me get you a cup of tea." Angharad crawled across the bed to their stove.

Neither one pushed her. They just gave her time to gather her thoughts, and she loved them all the more for it. She accepted the tea from Angharad. "Thank you."

"Now tell us what's wrong," Sarah said.

Daylin shrugged. "I just needed to go for a walk."

"Oh, hogwash," Angharad said with her hands on her hips.

Daylin sighed and took another sip of the tea. "Fine. I left the wagon because Ellis and I got in a fight. Well, we didn't get in a *fight* so much as he did something I didn't like. Well, he didn't actually *do* anything, so much as he was *going* to do something. At least, I think he was."

She threw up her hands. "Oh, hells. I don't know if he was going to do it or not. Part of me wanted him to do it, but another part of me was put off by the very idea."

She picked up steam, rambling away, but couldn't help it. "And the part of me that wanted it scared me! I mean, I've never even done that before! What if I was bad? What if my being bad drove him away? What if I liked it more than he did? What would that say about me? What if—"

Sarah broke in and cut her off. "Honey, honey, slow down. Take a breath."

Once satisfied, Sarah continued, "All right. That's better. Now, what exactly are you talking about? What did Ellis do?"

Daylin lowered her head in shame. "He tried to kiss me."

"Tried to kiss you?" Angharad's right eyebrow twitched. "What are you talking about?

"Well, I've never kissed anyone before," Daylin said.

Angharad looked even more bewildered. "But, you two have been lovers for years—certainly as long as I've been with the troupe. Now you're telling me in all that time he's never kissed you?" She shook her head in disgust. "I never figured Ellis to be the apathetic type, certainly not with you."

Daylin pulled her head back. "What?"

"It doesn't make sense," Sarah added. "I've seen him with people in the towns canoodling aplenty, and he certainly seemed to enjoy himself. Everyone I've spoken to has said Ellis is passionate—that's why they love him so much. Why wouldn't he be that way with you?"

Daylin's head swiveled between the two. Shocked, she dropped her hands and spilled some of the tea on herself. She yelped, quickly put the teacup on a shelf, and blew on her hands. "What? Lovers? We're not lovers! Who said we were lovers?"

"Everybody, my dear," Sarah said in a soothing tone while grabbing a towel for Daylin. "It's all right. There's nothing to be ashamed of. You make a wonderful couple. You're lucky to have him."

"But that's just it," Daylin pleaded. "I don't have him. No one has him. We're not together like that. We never have been."

Sarah and Angharad shared a shocked look of disbelief, while Daylin continued, "He's happy with his occasional townie, and I… well, I've never had a lover. I've never even kissed anyone."

"You're messing with me," Angharad said. She saw the distress in Daylin's eyes. "No, no. I believe you. It's just a surprise. You mean… you've never been with… anyone?"

"No," Daylin replied. "No one ever wanted me. Well, except for Ruddick, but I don't think that counts."

"What do you mean?" asked Sarah. "Who's Ruddick?"

Daylin scowled. "I'm surprised you hadn't heard. He was a priest. I was his slave as a child. Some nights, when he got drunk, he'd come into my room, lie on me, and stick his thing in me until he was satisfied. His breath always stank of brandy and onions. Till this day, I can't stand the smell of either."

"Oh my. You poor thing." Angharad grasped her hand and kissed it.

Sarah rested her head on Daylin's shoulder. "I'm so sorry, honey."

"It's noth—" Daylin's throat caught. "I mean, there's nothing to…"

She wanted to tell them she'd put behind her long ago. Only she couldn't. Her eyes welled up with tears as she curled up in their arms and cried. Sobbing, she saw it all again: the excruciating experiments, the musty stink of the straw-covered cage floors in the basement, the loneliness of having no one care about you even when surrounded by Ruddick's other child slaves. But mostly, she remembered the snarling face and stench of the grunting monster as he repeatedly took her.

After a time, with soft words and soft touches, the two women coaxed out all her tears. Sarah gently put her hand beneath Daylin's chin and wiped away Daylin's tears. "That's better, sweetheart. You don't have to worry about that ever again. Ellis would never do that to you."

"I know." Daylin sniffled. "I didn't think he was going to force himself on me. It's just that… well, he'd been so down for so long, and when I helped him decide to wait here, it was like the clouds came away from his eyes. He'd never looked at me that way before." She dropped her head again. "No one has. I mean, why would they?"

"What are you talking about?"

Daylin pouted. "You just don't understand. You're both so proud and beautiful. I'm nothing."

Sarah's mouth quirked. "Come now—"

Daylin cut her off. "No. It's true. You're flawless, both of you. You're so beautiful, with lovely figures. You actually have breasts and waists and hips. Hells. Sarah, you have the most amazing butt I've ever seen! And what do I have? I've got this tiny chest and no hips. My arms and legs are so gangly they look like they belong on one of Johnathan's marionettes. Whenever I put on a dress, it looks like I'm wearing a sack." Daylin closed her eyes and shook. Hearing herself admit her shortcomings only made it worse.

Angharad caressed Daylin's cheek, her eyes sad. "You have nothing to be jealous of. You're so beautiful."

"I am not."

"Yes; you are. You've a lovely face, your hair is like silk, and your eyes…"

Daylin frowned. She hated her cursed eyes.

"You must believe me," Angharad said. "I've seen the way people look at you. Hells. I'm willing to bet once people find you aren't exclusive with Ellis, they'll come pounding down your door."

"We definitely aren't exclusive. We aren't anything. He's like a brother. I think." She shook her head. "I swear to you, for all the time I've known him, I've never really been sure how I feel about him. I love him, dearly, as I would a brother. And he's always treated me the same way. So, it surprised me when he looked at me like a lover rather than a friend."

"Do you now think of him as more than a brother?" Sarah asked.

"I'm not sure," she replied. "Part of me gets so jealous when I see him with other women or men. I yearn to be touched the way he touches them. Yet, all the same, I'm so happy for him. You must understand. No one knows him like I do, not the real Ellis. He's so lonely all the time. He feels so separated from the world. It's like—" She shrugged. "It's like he doesn't think he even belongs here. Till this very day, he feels responsible for his parents' deaths. So, I'm happy when I see him with his lovers, that he's connecting with someone. Even if it's a brief one."

Sarah seemed to think for a moment. "Let me ask you something. So, when he tried to kiss you—and believe me, he was going to kiss you—did the thought repulse you?"

Daylin shook her head. "No. I wouldn't say that. I just wasn't sure I wanted it."

"Was it the thought of kissing him, or just kissing a man?" Angharad asked.

Daylin thought about it. "I'm not sure. As I said, I've never been kissed before, and it scared me."

Angharad glanced at Sarah with a mischievous smile. "Well, there's a way we can find out." She reached out with both hands, took Daylin by the face, and kissed her, oh so gently, on the lips.

Daylin's eyes went wide. A slight moan escaped her throat as she closed them and let the kiss linger. *I didn't know anything could feel this soft.*

Angharad released the kiss and sat back with a smile. "Well?"

A giggle burst out of Daylin. "It was... lovely. Thank you. But, to be honest, it didn't make me feel... well, like I see the look in Sarah's eyes when you kiss her." She frowned, hoping she wasn't hurting Angharad's feelings. "I'm sorry."

"Oh no, dear. It's all right." The blonde giggled. "Don't feel bad. I'm glad you enjoyed it. You're a wonderful kisser. And you're so lovely. Please don't think otherwise. You do yourself a disservice."

"So, do you think you'd like to kiss a man?" Sarah asked.

Daylin grinned and nodded.

"You just weren't sure it should be Ellis," Sarah added. "Am I right?"

"I guess so." Daylin frowned. "The fact is: I don't know if he truly wants me, or if it was a moment of weakness."

"How do you undress for bed?" Angharad asked.

"I do it in my wardrobe," Daylin replied.

"Next time, undress in front of him," Angharad said. "If he's truly interested in you, he'll let you know. Believe me." She grinned.

Daylin blushed. "Oh. I don't know if I could do that."

She sighed. "So what should I do? Just kiss him and see if I like it?"

Sarah seemed to think a moment. "I say no. If you go back and kiss him tonight, and you felt nothing special, you might ruin your friendship. For all we know, it was just a moment of weakness."

Sarah held her head up high and spoke as though she were making a decree. "I say you go back and tell him you're flattered, but you'll not kiss him tonight." She held up a finger. "In fact, tell him I said so. Tell him I said you're to wait at least two days. After that, you may kiss him. And if the kiss makes your blood boil…"

"What?" Daylin asked when Sarah didn't finish.

"Then you rip each other's clothes off," Angharad said. "And make love like you should have been."

They all fell about laughing.

"Thank you, for being my friends," Daylin said with a beaming smile and tears in her eyes.

They hugged each other and made their goodbyes. As Daylin opened the door, Angharad called out. "*Wait.* I don't want you going back there alone." She stuck her head out the door and whistled loudly.

"What?" Daylin tilted her head. "You think I'll need a guard at my side when I tell him?"

"Gods no," Angharad replied. "It's the grunkin I'm worried about."

"What grunkin?"

"You haven't heard? There's a grunkin in these parts. The folk back at Cross Corners told me about it. For years now, there's been something killing people off by themselves. And, apparently, it's been mostly women."

"Yes." Sarah nodded. "It attacked a farmstead just a day's ride back up the road. It killed everyone, including the livestock." She shuddered. "I talked to the man who found them. He said it's been stalking these parts for years."

"Is it The Beast of Cool Winds?" Daylin asked. Stories about The Beast had circulated for as long as she could remember.

"No," Sarah said with a shake of her head. "That's a man, from what I understand, a powerful priest. No, this is an actual grunkin."

Daylin stood on the top step, peering out to the darkness, trying to pierce the veil of night, to no avail. "I'll have the dogs keep an eye out."

One of the guards approached the wagon.

"Derek," Angharad said. "I want you to escort Daylin back to her wagon. Apparently, not everyone's heard about the grunkin."

The guard stared wide-eyed at Angharad's still naked form.

She clapped her hands. "Snap out! Now, as I said, I want you escort Daylin, and you're to wait for Ellis to talk to you. I'm sure he'll have instructions once he's heard what Daylin has to tell him." Smiling wickedly, she added, "And if you do a good job, I might even give you a kiss for keeping our darling Daylin safe." Giggling, she ducked back into the wagon.

When Daylin made it back to her wagon, she saw Ellis pacing back and forth in front of it. He was shirtless with his mother's bronze medallion about his neck, looking gorgeous. She quelled her butterflies.

He ran up to her. "Where have you been? You scared the life out of me, running out like that!"

As he reached out to her, she held up a hand. "Stop."

He pulled back. "Look, I'm sorry. I'm so sorry for what I did. I don't know what I was thinking. I—"

She cut him off. "We'll talk about it when we get back inside. First, I just heard from Sarah and Angharad there are reports of a grunkin in the area."

His eyes went wide. "Hells. Why didn't I hear about this before?"

He turned to Derek. "Fetch Dirge. I want fires ringing the outside of the wagons, and I'm doubling the guard. I also want men with bows on the roofs."

He turned back to Daylin and lowered his eyes. "I guess stopping here wasn't such a great idea after all."

"No, stopping was the right thing to do," she said. "It's what felt right to you, and I agreed. Besides, the thing's been roaming about the region for years. What worries me is the most recent attack was only a short way from here."

She marched past him into the wagon, and he followed. Once the door closed behind them, Daylin spun about. "We need to talk."

"Oh, yes. About that. Look, Daylin—"

"I will not kiss you, Ellis," she said matter-of-factly.

He looked taken aback and crestfallen.

She marched to the front of the wagon and turned to face him. "I will not kiss you, Ellis Concord. Not yet, anyway. In fact, Sarah says we're not to kiss for at least two days."

Ellis pulled his head back. "Sarah? What's she have to do with this?"

"She said we have to wait two days. After that? We'll see if we still want to kiss each other."

He cocked his head to the side with a grin. "So, you do want to kiss me?"

"I did." Her mouth quirked. "All right. Fine. Yes, I do want to kiss you. But Sarah's right. We should wait. If this just turns out to be some momentary thing, it could ruin our friendship. And I won't risk that. Do you understand me?"

Ellis smiled, his eyes beaming so strong it caused her butterflies to act up again. "Yes. I do." He grabbed a shirt, pulled it over his head, and grabbed his crossbow from a cupboard.

"What are you doing?" she asked.

"I'm taking first watch. You go get some sleep. I'll try and not wake you when I come back." He headed back out the door, but paused and looked at her over his shoulder. "Sweet dreams, Daylin Dragonvein."

She heard him chuckle as he walked down the steps. "Two days, huh? I think I can last that long."

I hope I can, she thought.

Those two days seemed an eternity to Daylin. But she was happy. For the first time in what seemed like forever, Ellis had something on his mind other than his visions. There were no sightings of the grunkin from either the guards or her dogs, and to her amusement, the entire troupe was abuzz over the goings on between her and Ellis.

After the initial shock wore off regarding she and Ellis not being a couple, many took bets as to which would come first: their having a tumble in the sheets, or her kicking him out of his own wagon. She spent much of the time talking with the women of the troupe. She wanted to know what it was like, being with a man. Sarah told her it should help her overcome her fear, that she needed to take control of what the priest had done to her all those years ago.

"You have to put in your mind," Sarah said, "That was not sex. It was something that happened to you. Sex is something wonderful you engage in and experience."

The funniest and perhaps most embarrassing thing, though, was the number of women in the troupe who kept flirting with her. When she asked Angharad, the blonde replied, "I just wanted to make sure you weren't attracted to women. You know, for your own good."

On the midafternoon of the second day, Daylin walked across the camp in a dress Sarah had made for her. It was yellow, with short sleeves, a tight waist, and hung to her knees. She fussed about the open front, showing a good deal of the little cleavage she had to display. She'd finally decided what to do with Ellis. At the end of the evening, after they had their dinner by the fire, and with everyone watching, she was going to grab him and kiss him soundly. Then, regardless of how it felt, she was going to take him to bed and have her way with him.

She was almost to Ellis when Henry, her best scout next to Bucky, called out to her mind. All flirtatious thoughts fled. She sprinted to Ellis, who talked with the two jesters, Dandle and Maxie, Strong Tom, and Jonathan, the marksman. "A caravan's coming," she shouted.

Without waiting for them, she dashed to the road, worry eating at her gut.

Chapter 30
Chaos Joins
the Show

(Year 522 -R.C.-)

Betal rode out in front of their caravan with Mangin at his side, and Adam, who led the vanguard, was not happy about it. Betal didn't care. He tired of choking on the dust from the back. It hadn't rained in weeks, and the heavily traveled road was awash with grime. Besides, he wore his favorite red coat—the one with the silk trimmings—and didn't want it to get too soiled. He needed to stand out today for some reason.

Next to him, Mangin looked resplendent in a dark green dress cut for riding. It was full length, from the top of her neck, to the midpoint of her polished black boots. Long white lace tipped the full puffy sleeves, extending over her white riding gloves. The tight dress fit her form so well it left little to the imagination. With her red hair flowing in the wind, she sat atop her horse, looking like a goddess awaiting her worshipers.

Betal caught movement off the right side of the road. At first glance, he thought it was the wolf again. He'd seen one the night before as they made camp, a full day's ride from Cross Corners.

"Just a dog," he said to himself. *It must belong to a nearby homestead,* he thought. It looked far too healthy and well fed otherwise.

The dog took one good look at the caravan and dashed up the road and over the oncoming crest.

"Honestly, Betal, your dourness is scaring off the wildlife now." Mangin laughed. "Seriously, my dear, you must smile more. At this point, you're likely to scare off any local brigands before I get a chance to play with them."

Betal suppressed a sigh and put on his best smile. "Is this better?"

She rolled her eyes and shook her head.

He didn't feel like smiling after Jena. He kept playing the moment over and over in his head. *How'd I miss it?* he wondered. Not that it mattered. He'd given her his heart, and she tried to kill him. He doubted he'd ever really know why. It almost seemed premeditated. The look in her eyes as she lunged at him with the knife... It wasn't some sudden madness, as Mangin had suggested. She'd looked determined.

Thinking about her last words, he muttered, "Must kill the wolf?"

"It was just a dog, Betal. Not a wolf," Mangin said. "Not that I care if you want to kill it or not, but I doubt you'll find it. It's likely deep in the wood by now."

"I don't want to kill some farmer's dog. I was just thinking about what Jena said."

"That again? Seriously, Betal, you must snap out of it. So some harlot tried to stick a knife in you. It comes with being blessed by The Great Lord." Though trying to sound nonchalant, anger still filled her voice over it.

At *The Over Reach*, she'd confronted the barkeep regarding Jena. Mangin jerked him into the air with Chaos. When he claimed ignorance, she crushed him, causing blood to explode out of the barkeep's mouth and neck. When she dropped his body behind the bar, it had made a "shlock" sound, like a bag of rotten apples.

Mangin continued. "Once we reach the citadel, you can expect much worse. Remember, the higher you climb, the more perilous is the perch upon which you stand. Assassinations, though rare, are always a danger."

The comment gave him pause. Assassination? Was it possible someone at the citadel somehow got wind of his coming and planned to take him out before he got there? He asked what she thought about the possibility.

"You may have something there." She smiled warmly, grasped Chaos, and caressed his cheek with it, her eyes both loving and possessive. "I'll have to keep a closer eye on you than I thought. I may even have to keep you at my side both day *and* night."

The touch sent a chill through him and created a stirring in his loins so strong he wanted to take her right there beside the road and be damned with the consequences. He came back to reality when they crested the hill.

Mangin nodded her head down the road. "It appears we've caught up with your traveling show."

His eyes snapped back to the road ahead. At the bottom of the hill, hard against the upcoming creek, lay a large open field filled with a double circle of wagons. People filled the center of the circle, many of whom were running out to the road. Their clothes were a hodgepodge of colors and styles. So much so, The Lord must smile broadly at the sight of them. Several men stood atop their wagons with bows out.

"Why the bowmen? What need have they to protect themselves?"

Mangin chuckled. "Perhaps it's your sour face?"

As they approached the group in the road, Betal checked out the two, up front: a man and a woman. The man was of middling height with blondish hair and blue eyes. His clothes were simple, but of a very fine cut. And for some reason, his eyes held shock and bewilderment.

He's no performer, Betal thought. His stance looked all business.

When he looked at the woman, he found it difficult to take his eyes off her. Quite pretty, with long brown hair and blue eyes, she had a slim body with slender legs and delicate arms. She wore a short-sleeved, yellow dress open at the front. Her skin was like porcelain, and her high cheekbones made her exotic. His gaze went back to her eyes, and he gasped. They were now *brown*. He stared as her eyes shifted again, to blue, to yellow, and back to brown.

His father told him when he was an infant his eyes shifted color in the same way. *Is she a gift from God?*

As Betal pulled his horse to a stop, the man spread his arms wide. "I am Ellis Concord, and I welcome you to Concord's Grand Traveling Show!"

The man's announcement washed over Betal. He simply couldn't tear his gaze from the woman.

"If you'd like," the man continued, "we'd be more than happy to perform for you, my lords."

She must be the one, he thought. He spoke the first thing that came to his mind. "You're the one who talks to wolves, aren't you?"

She frowned, and her gaze fell to the ground in front of her.

"Am I wrong? Please, you've nothing to fear. I heard about your amazing talent back at The Corners, and I pushed the caravan hard to catch you. There are things I must speak with you about."

The man, Ellis, stepped in front of her and addressed Betal, his eyes holding a challenge. "I am sure Lady Daylin would be happy to talk with you. When she desires it."

Betal returned the challenging stare. "You're headed to Gate Hall, I presume?" When Ellis nodded, Betal smiled. "Excellent! We'll travel with you."

He turned back to Daylin and smiled. The first real one he'd felt in some time. "I'll not miss a chance to speak with Lady Daylin. We'll take dinner in my tent this evening. Is that agreeable?"

Through her delicate brown locks, he saw her face turn rosy. She chewed her bottom lip and rapidly bobbed her head.

Betal nodded in return and turned his attention back at Ellis. The man had a look of resolve in his eyes, like a difficult task he wasn't ready to face. "Tell me, Show Master, why the bowmen on the roofs? Having trouble with bandits?"

"We heard news of a grunkin in the area, so we're simply taking precautions." With an elaborate bow, the man waved his arms to the left in a grand gesture. "If My Lord and My Lady—I'm sorry. I didn't get your name."

"Mangin," she purred.

Her eyes bored into Daylin, before switching to Ellis where they took on a look Betal knew all too well. Mangin was planning to play, and it seemed her first toy would be The Show Master.

"My Lady Mangin," Ellis said. "If you'd please follow me? We'd love to put on a show for you."

Betal turned to Adam. "Have them set up camp next to the show. If they need more room, just let me know, and I'll help clear space."

As Betal started for their camp, a tall, dark haired man, dressed in a motley of colors spoke to a woman at his side. "My Gods! Have you ever seen anything more beautiful in your life?"

"Honestly, Dandle, your appetites are boundless," the cherry-haired young woman said. "But I'd tread lightly with that one. She's the look of a predator about her. You'll likely get burned."

"I'm willing to bet the pleasure would be more than worth the pain," he replied.

She laughed, kissed his cheek, and ambled over to Daylin as she made her way into camp.

Betal chuckled. *They're both right.*

Daylin's legs felt weak. She didn't know what had come over her. All she could think of was the man's eyes.

"So, who are they, do you think?" Sarah asked.

Daylin jumped. She'd not noticed her friend approach. "What? Oh, um, I don't know."

"By the looks of them," Sarah said, "I'd say they're powerful merchants. Or perhaps a lord and lady from the south. They're certainly an attractive pair."

"His eyes are the most beautiful things I've ever seen," she said absently.

"Truly?" Sarah said with a grin.

"It's like I was looking into his soul." Daylin's cheeks burned.

"He is, indeed, quite lovely with those high cheekbones and strong nose."

Daylin nodded, but her fascination went beyond his looks. His initial pronouncement that he knew of her... curse distressed her. But when he'd continued, his voice changed, turning so soft and kind that she couldn't deny his request.

"And those lips," Sarah went on. "They're made for kissing."

To her embarrassment, Daylin nodded. Only minutes before, she was ready to kiss Ellis and give herself to him. Yet now, her thought centered on this man, this stranger. "I don't even know his name."

Chapter 31
Wicked

(Year 522 -R.C.-)

Ellis stewed in their wagon over the idea of Daylin having a private supper with Betal—he'd learned the man's name a short time before. It sounded familiar for some reason. Logically, the dinner was a good idea. Daylin could find out more about the man. Which was imperative. The moment Betal came into view, the ever-present tugging about his neck ended.

His elation soured as they drew near. Betal was rather handsome, and he radiated power and authority. He had the kind of eyes Ellis liked—deep and brooding—though, for some reason, he thought they should be gold, not brown. And his smile was sweet, with lips made for kissing. Unfortunately, the man only had eyes for Daylin. The woman, on the other hand, while stunning, filled him with dread. She also emanated authority, but unlike Betal, Mangin knew it. Her cocky air and mischievous smile said she could have anything she wanted. On top of that, an aura of mayhem and death emanated from the entire group. It was as though the embodiment of death was standing behind him, and they were all now marching toward doom.

His mind went back to the comely young man. *Why is he important? He didn't even give me a second look.*

Daylin stood before a full-length mirror, fussing over the dress she'd picked out for the dinner. It was white and hugged her tightly, with a cut that, in his opinion, was far too deep, and a too-short hem as well.

"Would you stop pouting?" Daylin said with a smirk. "It's not very becoming."

He scowled. "I'm not pouting. I just don't trust him."

"You don't trust him? You don't even know him yet," she replied while checking her reflection. "Besides, didn't you say he's the one you were waiting for?"

"Not knowing him is exactly *why* I shouldn't trust him." He tempered his voice and continued. "As to him being the one, it means nothing. The problem is I don't know *why* we had to wait for him." Adding under his breath, he said, "Besides, I didn't like the way he was looking at you."

"What do you mean you didn't like—" Daylin spun about, her mouth hanging open. "You're jealous."

"I am *not*."

"Yes you are," she said with a smile. "You're jealous that a handsome man looked at me."

"He's not *that* handsome," he muttered.

Daylin threw up her arms with an exasperated sound and turned back around.

"And he was staring at you like a starving wolf. He was practically foaming at the mouth."

"A wolf?" She paused and then shook her head. "Regardless, he's handsome, and you know it. Just because he's not your type doesn't mean he's not good looking." She giggled. "Unless you're just jealous he wants to have dinner with me and not you."

He looked away, his cheeks burning.

She adjusted her hair in the mirror. "To be honest, I'm surprised you even noticed him at all with the way you were staring at the redhead's tits."

His eyebrows furrowed. "I was *not* staring at her tits."

"Oh, shut up. Everyone was staring at her tits. You want her, and you know it."

"I wouldn't get within twenty feet of that one if I had the choice." He scowled again. "I'm serious, Daylin. That woman is powerful and dangerous. She had an aura about her—they both did."

She, again, turned to face him with concern. "What are you saying? Have you had some kind of vision about them; something we need to worry about?"

"No," he said, but quickly continued as she shook her head and turned back to her fussing. "It's not a vision. It's just a feeling, especially about her. I'll not lie to you, Daylin. She frightens me."

"Then I'll do my best to avoid her." She reached into her pouch, pulled out a jade and pearl encrusted black choker, and clasped it about her neck.

It looks beautiful on her. In fact, I've never seen her look more beautiful. He shook his head, trying to banish the thought. Doing his best to sound nonchalant, he said, "That's pretty. I don't remember seeing it before. When did you get it?"

"It's a gift from Angharad. She said she wanted to thank me for allowing her to be my first kiss."

His eyebrows shot up. "You kissed Angharad?"

"Uh huh." She nodded, taking an elaborate gold, silver, and pearl hair chain and draped it on the back of her hair.

Ellis grimaced. "And what was *that* a gift for?"

She whirled about with her hands on her hips. "Honestly, Ellis, envy does not become you. Unless you've forgotten, I do not belong to you."

"I never said you did. I just think…" He didn't know how to finish.

"You think what? That I should be alone?" She threw up her arms. "Hells, two days ago, you wouldn't look at me twice, and now you're acting like you don't want me to be with anyone. Oh, and if you must know, it is from Sarah. She gave it to me because she cherishes me as a friend and wants me to look my best tonight. And, no, I did not *bed* her for it, if that's what you were implying."

He started to lie, "I never—"

She held up a finger and stared daggers at him. Stalking toward the door, she flung it open. "Now if you don't mind, I have a dinner date. Not that it's any of your Chaos-loving business." She slammed the door behind her, cursing as she stormed away.

"Good one, Ellis." He put his head in his hands and groaned. "It's like I can't think anymore."

Ever since their caravan set up, he felt a black aura about them. Only now, it encompassed the troupe's camp as well. Those two were bad, he had no doubt. The problem was he'd sensed something even worse. As a black coach near the caravan's middle rolled by, he felt an evil presence—something black and wicked—and whatever it was, he wanted no part of it.

Mangin strolled amongst the artists as they put on their shows for her and her companions. They were all so bold and beautiful she was giddy with the possibilities. The only traveling shows she'd seen were a pair when she was young. They'd come to Cool Winds and were quite pitiful—especially when compared to what she was seeing all about her now. Concord's show had four different acts performing at the same time among the wagons, and it was apparent they could easily put on four times that many if the crowd was big enough.

One of the troupe's jesters roamed the center, engaging whoever seemed uncertain of where to go next, all the while juggling colorful balls that seemed to be on the verge falling to the ground about him. The fool saw she was looking at him and headed her way. She really wasn't in the mood for the antics of his ilk. She remembered the fools from the other shows when she was young and never found them funny—at least not until she finished *playing* with them.

"Good evening, my lady," the fool said, his balls spinning about his head.

She ignored him and walked on.

Her rebuke didn't sway him. "Is there anything I can help you with?"

She pursed her lips. She'd be amongst those people for some time to come, it appeared, and she didn't want to scare the others off before she had her fill of them. But she also wanted to rid herself of the pest. Grasping a modicum of The Lord's Breath, she sent a blast of wind directly into the fool. The gust shoved him back several feet and sent his balls flying. To her surprise, his initial shock and fear turned to determination.

Ignoring his balls, he removed his ridiculous, multicolored hat, and boldly approached. "I humbly beg your pardon if I've done anything to upset you." His mouth quirked into a seductive smile. "But are you sure there isn't anything I could do for you?"

His implication sent a thrill racing through her. Never in her life had anyone ever been so brazen. Not sexually, anyway. She liked Cobb because he defied her, challenged her, but she knew he still hated her and despised himself when they had sex. Yet, there stood a man so brash and proud he'd approach her even after knowing she was a disciple of The Lord of Chaos.

She took hold of Chaos, gathered up his balls, and started them spinning over and about her head. Several times, a ball came close to striking the man, but he never flinched—not once. Impressed, Mangin gave him a good look. He was quite handsome with a strong, lithe body, and well-turned calves. "What's your name, jester?"

He bowed. "I am Dandle the Jape, the jovial one with the golden cape." The bright gold cape was hard to miss as it clashed with his multicolored shirt and tight, striped pants.

"Who was that woman I saw you talking with when we arrived?"

"That would be my dearest Sarah, my lady," he said with a twinkle in his eye.

"So, you're a couple then?"

A wonderful thought occurred to her.

"We're coupled, yes, but it's not an exclusive pairing."

"She's quite stunning," Mangin said with a smile. "Bring her with you tonight. I'll be expecting the pair of you after sundown."

She lazily ran a finger up his chest and cupped his chin. When he leaned in for a kiss, she stepped back and walked away, letting his balls fall about them. It was something she had learned from the jester's mind she'd played with in her youth—always leave them wanting more.

Chapter 32
A Dinner Date

(Year 522 -R.C.-)

Betal sat on the edge of his chair in his tent, his left leg bouncing up and down as he scraped his right thumbnail over the edge of the nail of his middle finger. He'd so many questions for the young woman and didn't want to scare her off by being too forward, too brash.

As Lynda laid out the fine porcelain, crystal goblets, and gold utensils on the oaken dining table, Betal scanned the tent one more time. The candle light filled the room with a soft, golden glow and a pleasant, clean scent. Two high-backed, padded chairs sat across from each other, and the place settings were in order. It was perfect. Now, all it needed was his guest.

As if his thought summoned her, Daylin announced her arrival outside the tent. "May I come in?"

"Of course." Betal stood, doing his best to keep his voice from quavering, and nodded to Lynda.

The servant pulled aside the flap, and Betal nearly gasped as Daylin breezed into the tent like an angelic creature of light. Her short, tight, white dress accentuated every curve of her lithe form, and the alabaster skin of her exposed chest and long, slim legs shimmered in the candlelight. She wore a wide, jeweled, black choker about her delicate neck, and gold and silver chains adorned her hair. Her flushed cheeks glowed, and her eyes sizzled as she gazed at him.

She's the most beautiful woman I've ever seen, he thought.

"Please, come in." He smoothed his shirt and ran a hand through his hair. He'd not wanted to be too intimidating, so he chose a simple pair of black pants, and white shirt, along with his best tan traveling coat and knee-high boots. He now felt underdressed. "Let me get your chair." He strode around the table and held out her chair. He didn't know why he was doing it, but it felt right.

"Thank you," she said after hesitating, and took her seat. "I want to thank you for the invitation, Lord Betal."

"Just Betal," he said, as he took his seat. "We're just two people sitting down to dinner, nothing more." He immediately wanted to take it back. Far from wealthy, even he saw the opulence of the setting, especially the two gold candelabras set at either end of the table.

"Betal," she accentuated his name. "I wish to thank you for the invite. I'm sorry. I already said that, didn't I?" She smoothed her dress and checked the chains in her hair. "What was it you wished to talk to me about?"

He smiled. She was nervous, but not intimidated. She didn't bow her head in reverence, but instead, looked him in the eye and held herself with grace. "We'll get to that in a moment. We should have dinner first."

He nodded to Lynda. "Lynda, the wine, if you please."

The servant hesitated for a moment, a slightly shocked look upon her face—apparently unused to the courtesy. She stepped forward, filling each of their glasses, and with a nod, left to fetch their first course.

Daylin chewed her lip, her eyes flitting about the tent.

"Is everything all right?" he asked.

"Um, yes." She held her hands slightly above the table, rubbing her fingers together. "I'm just—well—I'm not used to such—that is… it's all so pretty."

He frowned. "Yes. Yes, it is."

Dithiyar might never make small talk and try to connect with a mundane, but Betal felt he had to. He knew they'd never live near as well without the help of commoners. He smiled again. *Of course, this woman is far from common.*

They gazed at each other over their wine glasses, neither one speaking. He found himself at a loss for words. Her grace and beauty reminded him of Mangin, and the strength in her eyes made him think of Jena—the two most beautiful and dangerous women he'd ever met.

The thought of Jena caused him to scowl, so he shook it off. "So how long have you been with the show?"

"Most of my life, since I was a child." She took a sip of her wine.

"That long?" He sipped his own. It was a fine vintage, but he hardly noticed. "But you weren't born into the show? Where'd they come across you?"

Her face darkened.

Several moments passed, and she still hadn't replied. "I said, where'd they come across—"

"I heard your question, and I'd rather not talk about it." Her eyes smoldered.

His curiosity piqued. He put the question off until later. He set his glass down. "I'm sorry. I didn't mean to bring up a sore subject."

Several minutes passed, and neither of them said a word. He fiddled with his nails, while she twisted her glass between long, slim, supple digits. *Even her fingers are pretty*, he thought.

Lynda entered the tent, breaking the tension. She held a large platter filled with bowls of food: greens, buttered beets and carrots, squash, berries, along with a pair of roasted quail on a small platter.

The cook's outdone himself.

After Lynda placed servings on both their plates, she said, "I'll return with the roasted pork and beef."

Daylin stared at all the food, her mouth slightly agape. "Do you always eat like this?"

"Oh, Lord, no."

"Then…" She gestured at the food. "Why?"

"Well…" He stared into her amazing eyes. "You're worth the effort."

She lowered her head, her face blushing. "You don't even know me."

The silence returned as they ate, so Betal took it upon himself to try a different tack. "So, what do you do in the show?"

She glanced up, her fork raised halfway to her mouth. "I put on a show for the kids, mostly. I have my dogs jump through hoops, balance on small barrels, walk on their forelegs. Things like that." She delicately put a forkful of squash in her mouth.

I never thought I'd envy a fork. He shook the thought away and smiled. That was his opportunity to ask her about wolves. However, his smile slipped. "Wait. You're saying you only do the dog shows for the kids? What about the adults?"

"Nothing," she replied through a mouth full of greens.

"Surely you jest." When she shook her head, he looked askance. "You don't dance or sing or anything?"

"Nope. Just my dogs." She popped half a beet in her mouth and closed her eyes. "Mmm."

When Lynda brought in the platter of pork and beef, both smothered in rich gravy, Daylin's eyes popped back open. "Oh my gods. That smells *amazing.*"

Betal sat back and watched as she accepted large portions of meat.

She took a bite and squeezed her eyes shut a moment. "Oh. It *is* amazing. Thank you so much, Lynda. Please tell the cook it's all so, well… amazing." She giggled and took another bite.

"Thank you. I'll do just that," Lynda said with a smile. She glanced at Betal, gave him an approving nod, and left.

He watched Daylin eat. *She must be ravenous.*

He took a few bites himself, relishing the wonderful mixture of spices in the beef gravy. "Is this your first time on this side of the river?" he asked as he cut another slice of beef.

"Yes," she replied through a mouthful of pork, swallowed, and took a sip of her wine. "But Ellis thought it time to grace the good folks on this side as well."

She put her fork down and sighed. "I hated leaving. It's so lovely and diverse there. But Ellis was right. We're doing the people here a disservice by not coming sooner. Besides, the more who see us, the greater the fame we'll have."

They continued to talk as they ate. She made little jokes and regaled him on their exploits out west.

Unable to take his eyes off her, he paid little attention to his meal. He found her intelligent, with a quick wit and a delightful sense of humor. "Ellis is a fool."

Her fork stopped half way to her mouth. "What are you talking about? He's not a fool. He's the smartest man I've ever known." Her eyes smoldered.

Betal took a sip of his wine to steady his nerves. "I mean your talents are being wasted. Well, perhaps not wasted. Entertaining children is a wonderful thing. I just—I just mean you could do so much more. You're funny, and smart. Your voice is so lovely. You've a body meant for dancing… and a face to make the gods envious."

Raising her napkin to wipe her mouth and hide her blush, she refused to meet his eyes. "I thank you for the complement, but I'm hardly all that." She used her other hand to fuss with her dress.

"You're that and more." His heart hammered and his skin prickled as he reached across the table and took her hand. "You're the most beautiful woman I've ever seen."

Her blush spread to her chest. She stared at her hand in his as if never seeing such a thing before. "Again, I—I thank you. But I'm far from pretty. I mean, most in the troupe are far prettier. For goodness sakes, what about your woman? She's stunning."

"Not compared to you," he said. "And Mangin's not my woman. We're not lovers. She's simply a friend." He frowned. "Perhaps my only friend."

"I know how you feel, believe me." Lowering the napkin, she gave his hand a slight squeeze, and peered back into his eyes. "I've known the people of the troupe for most of my life— they're like family. But until recently, Ellis was the only one I could truly call my friend."

He felt emboldened. "Friend? So, you and Ellis aren't pair-bonded?"

"No." She, again, dropped her gaze.

"That's good to hear." He reached across the table with his other hand and gently lifted her chin. "Because, I'd dearly love to see you again."

"But you're seeing me now," she said with a grin.

It turned to a frown. She pulled her hand back, squared her shoulders, and looked at him hard. "I don't know if you are just trying to manipulate me, but you invited me to this dinner to ask me something. What was it?"

"I'm not sure I should now. I've a feeling it's a sore subject, and I don't want to upset you."

Her back stiffened. "Ask anyway."

Betal pursed his lips and sighed. "Back in the city, I was told of a woman who worked with a large traveling show. They said she could talk to wolves."

"And where did you hear this?"

"From a guest at a banquet."

"And where did *they* hear it?"

"He said he saw you with a wolf, and it did what you wanted without your having to talk to it or giving it any signals." Though not told that, Betal felt it was true. "And right before we joined you, I saw a dog on the road. It acted strange and then darted away. By the time we topped the crest, you were already in the road waiting for us."

She eyed him a moment. "I've no wolves." Before he could interject, she continued. "No *wolves*. Not anymore. The one this person saw was, most likely, Bucky. He's only half wolf. The others refused to cross the river." Her voice became iron. "The answer to your question is, yes, I can talk to wolves. I can talk to wolves and dogs, and just about any creature that's smart enough. It wasn't something I was born with. And the reason it's a sore subject is when I was a child, I was a slave to a priest. He used me, abused me, and experimented on me."

His heart sank. "I'm sorry."

"I don't want your 'sorry,' and I don't want your pity. Hells. I don't even know why I'm telling you all this! I guess I'm just tired of hiding it all."

"What happened?" he asked. "Please, tell me."

She took a deep breath and told him about Ruddick, and Jasper, Celeste, and Vir. "We spent a long time hiding from other priests until Ellis and Dirge found me. The troupe took us in, and, in turn, we protected them."

"What happened to Vir?"

Her eyes flared, but quickly softened, as did her face. "He got old. He wasn't young to begin with. One day, he told me he loved me and he was proud of what I'd become. Then he just left. Wolves are pack animals, they live for their family, but they often go off to die alone." Under her breath, she added, "We all die alone."

Betal didn't know what to say. There was nothing *to* say. Many didn't like The Great Lord and his disciples, but Daylin had reason to despise them. How would she react when she learned *he* was an acolyte of Chaos? He frowned, knowing the answer.

"I should go." He rose from his chair. "Feel free to finish your dinner. I'll return after you've gone."

As he passed by her, she grabbed him by the hand. "Why did you want to know?" Sorrow and fear filled her face. "Please, tell me. There's a reason, I can see it in your eyes." She stood in front of him, still holding his hand. "I opened up to you—a stranger. I faced my fear and told you what very few know. Please, tell me why it was so important."

He sighed, awash with guilt. *She's going to hate me if I tell her everything.*

"I asked, because I think I've some kind of connection to wolves. I just don't know what. I've seen them several times while on the way here, lurking in the forest, staring at me." He corrected himself. "Well, I've seen one, anyway. For all I know, it's always the same wolf."

"What did it do?" she asked.

"It's strange. Several times now—usually around dusk—I'd spot it staring at me from beyond the edge of camp."

"That's all?" She frowned.

"No. A few days ago, a woman tried to kill me." He hesitated and lowered his head. "Someone… very close to me."

Daylin gasped. "Why?"

"I don't know. I think it was political. I—I was forced to defend myself." He had difficulty keeping the scowl off his face. "As she died, she said, 'must kill the wolf.'" He shook his head. "It still makes no sense."

She reached out and touched his cheek. "You loved her, didn't you?"

"I thought I did."

She seemed to ponder something. "Is there anything else you can tell me about the one in the woods?"

He shrugged. "I got the feeling it was... trying to... talk to me."

"Well, it may have been," she said, her voice like a caress. "Wolves are smart. They do their best to avoid people, but some wolves are special, like Vir. They're much more intelligent. They're as smart as we are, if not more. Maybe it was one of those. Maybe it saw something special in you and was simply trying to communicate." She moved closer until her chest touched, the heat seemed to sear his skin. "You've a very old soul, I think. Maybe this wolf saw that.

Her other hand reached up. "I want to kiss you, Betal."

He bent down, and their lips met. She tasted of honey and smelled of lilac. It was so sweet his heart almost broke from it.

How could he ever tell her the truth? He had to lessen the blow, somehow. "Please don't take this the wrong way," he said softly. "I know you've been sorely treated by the followers of The Lord."

She frowned and turned away.

He squeezed her hand. "Your hatred is *more* than valid. I don't blame you one bit for that. What that man did was... was wrong."

Betal didn't understand what he was saying. In a world of The Great Lord of Chaos, how was anything wrong? You did what you wanted and paid the consequences. Yet, deep down, he knew his words were true. Some things were simply wrong.

He continued. "But please believe me when I say not *all* followers of Chaos are like that priest. Not all of them think of bringing only pain."

Doubt filled her eyes. "I don't know, Betal. I just don't know." She gazed up at him and smiled. "But I'll try."

She caressed his cheek. "And yes, I too want to see you again."

She rose on her tiptoes, kissed his cheek, and slid across his body to leave. As she opened the flap, she turned back. "Thank you, Betal. That was my first kiss from a man, and it was wonderful. I hope there's more in the future."

Betal leaned against the storage wagon, brooding as two of the guards broke down and stored the dining table.

"So, how was dinner?" Killington asked. When Betal didn't answer, Adam added, "That bad, eh?"

Betal ran his hand through his hair. "I just have a bad feeling about this."

"Come, now. You can tell me. I didn't see her storm out, so it couldn't have been all that bad."

"The dinner was nice—uncomfortable at time, but nice."

"Come on, son," Killington said with a smile. "Out with it."

Betal levered himself off the wagon. "She was stunning—*is* stunning."

He told Adam about everything, except the details of her enslavement to the priest—he wasn't about to break that confidence. "What do I do? As soon as she finds out who I am, she's going to hate me."

Adam rubbed his chin, glancing at Betal out of the corner of his eye. "Does it matter to you?"

"Yes," Betal replied. "And I think it scares me more than anything."

"What are you talking about? Are you in love?"

He took a deep breath and exhaled. "I don't even know what love is. I thought I loved Jena, and she tried to kill me. I thought I loved Mangin, but I'm just a toy to her."

"Mangin?"

"Yes." Betal held up a hand. "Don't get me wrong. She's my best friend, but I know her, and I know how she really feels about me.

He shook his head. "Daylin is the most captivating woman I've ever met, and if I lose her... I don't know if I can get over it."

"Betal, you just met her. She's pretty and all, but—" Adam shook his head. "No, no. I can see it in your eyes." He clasped Betal on the shoulder. "I'll not tell anyone in the troupe you two are with the church. My word on it. But, it will come out, eventually. After that, all we can do is hope for the best. I'm willing to bet if she feels the same about you, she'll give you a chance."

Betal hoped it was true. But he also knew The Lord was fickle, and he loved to torment others.

Chapter 33
A Matter of Darkness

(Year 522 -R.C.-)

Flickering candlelight danced on the canvas walls as Mangin lounged in her bed, her limbs twisted amongst her two new lovers. Aromas of incense, sweat, and sex filled the tent as her heartbeat returned to normal.

"You were amazing," Sarah said while idly playing with Mangin's hair. "I wish Angharad could've been here to share it."

"In due time, my sweet," Mangin cooed.

Sarah sighed. "I just worry about her so."

Dandle lifted his head to see over Mangin. "She's not responding to the herbs?"

"No. Not the herbs nor Whisp's treatments," she replied.

Mangin's brows furrowed. "What are you two going on about?"

"My lover, Angharad. Earlier today, after seeing Daylin off, Angharad fell into such a deep darkness, and nothing has helped." She gazed into Mangin's eyes. "She suffers from debilitating bouts of melancholy and I'm frightened for her."

Mangin's mouth twisted at the mentioning of that woman, Daylin. Betal's reaction to her piqued Mangin. But as Sarah continued, Mangin became intrigued in their conversation. "Has she always been like this?"

"For as long as I've known her." Sarah shook her head. "But it's been much worse as of late."

Mangin untangled herself from her new lovers. "All right. Everybody up."

"What's wrong? I hope we've not offended you." Dandle's voice was cautious.

Courageous and smart, Mangin thought. *This one has real potential.*

"You two are taking me to see this Angharad." Mangin stood, clapping her hands together. "Come now, quickly. I want to get some sleep tonight."

Mangin threw on a blue silk robe and arranged her hair as her lovers scrambled into their clothes. They exited her tent and crossed the campsite, as the air filled with music, singing, and laughter from Travelers who'd yet to call it a night.

As they mounted the steps to Angharad's wagon, the door opened and a wizened old man exited, shaking his head. He stopped and stared at Mangin, his eyes growing wide, but quickly looked away. "If, if you'll excuse me, I'll be going to bed now." He stumbled down the steps and hurried off.

"Who was that?" Mangin asked.

"That's Whisp," Sarah replied.

He must be a hedge mage, Mangin thought with contempt.

Putting the man out of her mind, Mangin stepped into the wagon. A single candle, casting a sickly light into the gloom, lighted the interior. A golden-haired woman lay in a bed built into the wagon. Wrapped in a housecoat, she faced the wall in the fetal position.

"Just go away," she squeaked.

Mangin grasped Chaos and scanned Angharad's mind, finding a layer of blackness, as though a dark cloud enveloped it. "Fascinating."

She turned to her new lovers. "You two wait outside."

She shut the door and sat on the edge of the bed. "What's your name, my sweet?" Mangin already knew, of course, but she needed the girl talking to continue her scan. When the blonde cried, Mangin asked again, more firmly. "What is your name?"

"What does it matter?" the girl sobbed. "You'll end up hating me just like everyone else. Everyone hates me. Why do I keep trying? Why should I help someone when no one'll help me?" Her shoulders shook as she bawled.

Mangin delved deeper. She spun a fine web and sunk it into Angharad's mind. She needed to isolate the darkness, and see if it was, indeed, a thing of the mind... or something else. She shifted her web to-and-fro, until finding what she sought.

It is a blackness. But also a lack of light.

Mangin pulled her net, tweaking it ever so slightly, and spun it tighter to encase the dark cloud. She slowly squeezed the darkness; pulled and squeezed, pulled and squeezed, until the darkness was only a tiny speck, and light pulsed throughout the young woman's mind. Soon, the pulse grew into a blossom of light, cascading and flowing with a healthy glow.

Pleased, Mangin turned her attention to the dark speck, but found it had moved. She refocused her web, trying to catch the darkness like an angler in a net, yet it kept moving as though it held an intelligence.

"Come here, you little imp," she muttered. She needed to be careful how she attacked the foreign entity. If she moved too quickly, she may well tear the girl's mind.

Finally, she latched on. It spun and vibrated, trying to wriggle free, but she held fast. She examined the darkness a moment. Something about it seemed... familiar. As she drew it out, the darkness latched onto her web. It seeped into the filaments and flowed toward her.

Mangin panicked.

She yanked her threads out of Angharad's mind—heedless of any damage it might cause—and released The Lord's Breath. As the blackness dissipated into the ether, Mangin heard a hollow chuckle.

She wiped the sweat from her brow and gathered herself. "How are you feeling?"

The young woman stopped sobbing, rolled over, and slowly sat up, her eyes wide. "What did you do?" she asked, her voice filled with wonder. "It's gone." She flung herself at Mangin, hugging her tight. "I don't know who you are or what you did, but I thank you from the bottom of my heart. You're an angel!"

She tilted her head as if seeing Mangin for the first time. "My gods." She giggled. "You're gorgeous." She straightened her back, holding herself high. "I'm forever in your debt. Whatever you wish of me—body or soul—it's yours."

"I am flattered. Thank you," Mangin replied. "As for you being in my debt? No, I don't think so. You're a free woman, and I wouldn't want it any other way."

Angharad looked baffled. "Why did you do it, then? Why help me if you've no need of me?"

Mangin brushed golden hair from the lovely woman's face. "Your lover, Sarah, brought you to my attention, and I thought I could help." Gently, she kissed Angharad's cheek.

"You must allow me to do something." Angharad stroked Mangin's face, slid to her neck, and continued down to caress her breast.

Mangin pulled away, piqued. "I told you, it was a gift. You owe me nothing."

Angharad frowned. "I'm sorry. It's just that—I feel so full of life. It's like a weight has been lifted from my soul—a blackness I never thought I'd escape from." Smiling sheepishly, she lowered her eyes as her cheeks reddened. "And you're so beautiful. I couldn't resist."

Mangin pursed her lips at all the possibilities with the stunning woman. *No*, she thought. If she did anything with Angharad now, it'd be no different from what she did with Cobb.

She shook her head. "I assure you, I want nothing. Your feelings of euphoria are natural. You're alive and you wish to make love. But not with me. Not now. I'll send in your two friends, and you three can celebrate until you're sated."

She stood and took the blonde's hand. "We'll talk again in a few days. And after that time if you still feel a desire for me? Well, we'll see." She kissed Angharad's hand and left.

As she sauntered away from the wagon, her friends rushed in. Their cries of joy, quickly followed by their elation of life and love, brought a smile to Mangin's face. She'd learned so much from these people. Never again would she have to bewitch someone to know their carnal lust.

Unless that's what I want, she thought with a giggle.

The grunkin snarled, saliva dribbling from its second maw. It eyed the redheaded woman in the circle of wagons, yearning to sprint through the underbrush and rip out her throat, but the ever-increasing compulsion from the darkness beyond forbade it. It had three targets in the camp, but that woman wasn't one.

The humans were vigilant. The grunkin didn't know how to enter the camp and slay whom it needed to before the humans would kill it. It desperately wanted to die, but the will of the dark being was too strong to deny. It would have to lure them out so it could do its job.

Chapter 34
Discoveries

(Year 522 -R.C.-)

As Daylin ambled home in the crisp summer morning air, the birds sang louder; the flowers smelled sweeter, and the grass felt like feathers beneath her unshod feet. Her dreams had been sweet and funny, and one was quite erotic, filled with kisses from Betal while they made love. She'd never been happier in her life. She climbed the stairs to her wagon and opened the door.

When she entered, Ellis sat on the edge of his bed with his head in his hands, his clothes looking as though they'd been slept in. His head snapped up. "Where the hells have you been!" He shot up and marched toward her. "I said, where th—"

Daylin held up her right hand. "*Watch* your tone." She eyed him hard.

Ellis blinked and stepped back. "Where have—" He cleared his throat. "What happened? Where've you been all night? I've been worried sick."

She clicked her tongue. "Dirge lent me his tent, if you must know. And from your tirade, I'd say I made the right choice."

"Tirade? I just wanted to know where you were."

Brushing by him, she strode to her wardrobe. She pulled out her pouch holding the choker and hair chains and put it in a small drawer. Her slippers, which she had been carrying, went on the bottom. She started to close the door, but recalled something Angharad had said. Leaving the door open, she undid the buttons of her dress.

"Would you talk to me?"

The dress slipped from her shoulders and pooled at her feet, leaving her nude. She'd not worn a slip as the dress was simply too tight.

Ellis made a choking sound. "What the hells are you doing?"

"I am undressing. Isn't that obvious?"

"But I'm standing right here!" He took a deep breath. "You can at least do it in the closet like you normally do. What's gotten into you?"

She felt his eyes on her bare back and bottom. "I'm tired of hiding in here. And I'm tired of this conversation. If you wish to stay and leer at me, so be it. If you wish to leave, then go. Either way, do so quietly. This rant of yours is ridiculous and is beneath you."

She slowly turned around to face him. His eyes went wide, and with a curse, he bolted for the door. She chuckled as the door slammed, but it quickly turned into a sigh. She wanted to see how he would react at seeing her naked and got her answer.

If he truly loved me and wanted me, he wouldn't have left. But instead of staying and ravishing her, he fled like a frightened child. "I guess it's a good thing I didn't kiss him."

By midmorning, they were finally on the road, and Daylin felt so uncomfortable it bordered on unbearable. She tried to engage Ellis several times, but he wouldn't even look at her.

Near noon, he spoke, his voice sounding forced. "So, what did he want to talk to you about?"

She considered ignoring him. She considered telling him it was none of his business. She seriously considered lying and telling him Betal had propositioned her. Instead, she chose to be civil. "He wanted to know if it was true that I could talk to wolves."

"Why?"

She pursed her lips. "He thinks he's being followed by them."

"So, he's insane." Ellis turned his head and spat. "Or is he just paranoid?"

She ignored his disdain. "I told him the wolf was simply curious, but it reminded me of Vir."

"Don't go and tell him too much," Ellis replied, his voice was sharp and biting. "The last thing we want is for him to have too great an interest in you."

"Don't you dare tell me what I can and can't do," she said in a low, soft snarl.

"I'm telling you, I don't want him—"

"I don't give a *spit* what you *want*." She stabbed a finger at him. "We had this discussion last night. You don't own me. You've no right to tell me what to do. It's not like you even want me. You just want to order me around like you're my father. Well, guess what? You are not." Shaking, she closed her eyes and took a deep breath. "I'm sorry, Ellis. I shouldn't have said it that way, but you know it's true."

She shook her head, angry with herself. "I know you're lonely; I've always known. You can't hide it from me." She paused. "Look. I know you won't take a lover within the troupe and you won't go near the redhead, Mangin. But I understand she has a handmaiden that's quite pretty."

He didn't respond.

"Betal has a body-servant named Lynda, who's lovely. Also, there are also plenty of men in their party. Several of them are quite handsome and might be interested."

Ellis scowled, keeping his head down and his eyes on the road. "So now you want to be my whoremonger?"

"Stop that! Stop feeling sorry for yourself." She adjusted her billowy, sky blue dress, and changed the subject. "Do you have any ideas as to what's happening next? Any new thoughts on Betal?"

After grumbling something, he spoke up. "No. None. Were you able to find out anything about him?"

She blushed. It was the whole reason she agreed to the dinner in the first place, but somewhere along the way, it had changed, and nothing she'd learned would be helpful to Ellis. "No. I'm sorry. It just sort of slipped my mind."

"What in the seven hells do you mean it 'slipped your mind?' Did you become distracted when he picked his teeth?"

She took several deep breaths, trying to calm herself again. "I guess I did. I was so mad at you when I first went. And he kept asking the most innocuous questions." She sighed and shook her head. "You don't understand, Ellis. There's just something about him. He has this way of disarming you and putting you at ease. I didn't even realize it until we were almost through with dinner."

"Yeah. Right."

She looked at him. "I'm not trying to betray you. I just think you should give him a chance."

Still glowering down the road, he remained silent for several minutes.

"Ellis, talk to me."

He spat and wiped his mouth. "Did you fuck him?"

Daylin slapped him across the face and jumped from the wagon. Ellis was setting a good pace, so she hit the ground hard. Her ankle buckled, and she rolled off the side of the road into the tall grasses. Slightly dazed, she got up and limped south, away from the lead wagon.

Once Ellis brought the wagon to a complete stop, he jumped down and sprinted after her. She'd hobbled past the next wagon in line when he'd caught up with her. "Are you out of your damn mind?"

Ellis grabbed at her arm, but she pulled it away and kept trudging, the pain in her ankle getting worse with each step.

He continued after her. "Are you trying to kill yourself? How could you be so stupid?"

She kept moving. As she passed Jeanette's wagon, the singer called out, "What are you two doing? What's going on?"

When Ellis got hold of Daylin's arm and spun her around, her ankle gave, sending her tumbling to the ground.

When Daylin hit the ground, Jeanette gasped. "Oh gods. Are you all right?"

Daylin grabbed her throbbing ankle and swatted at Ellis when he tried to help her. "Go away. You've done enough already."

As Ellis stepped back, Dirge rode up and jumped off his horse. "What happened? Is everything all right?"

Ellis pointed at Daylin. "She jumped from the damned wagon while we were still moving."

Daylin sat, curled up into a ball, and clasped her aching leg, trying not to cry out in pain, anger, and frustration.

Dirge knelt. "Lynette, are you—" He cleared his throat. "Are you all right, Daylin? Did you hurt yourself?" He gently pulled Daylin's hands away and examined her ankle. "It's starting to swell." He picked her up, cradling her in his stone-hard arm, and carried her further down the wagon-line.

When Ellis followed, Dirge stopped and glared over his shoulder. "You go back to your wagon. I'm taking her to Sarah." He started walking again, and added over his shoulder, "We'll have words when I come back."

As they came abreast with Sarah and Angharad's wagon, Sarah ducked inside while Angharad and Dandle stayed on the driver's bench. Sarah lowered the back steps and ushered them inside. "Place her on the bed. I'll see to her." She glanced at the ankle and waved at Dirge. "Now, off with you. Go deal with whoever did this to her."

Daylin blushed. "I did it to myself."

"Why ever would you do that?" Sarah replied while going through various drawers, pulling out bandages and salves. She placed a healthy pinch of herbs in a cup and added some tea from a kettle. "The tea's not hot, I'm sorry, so it'll be a bit bitter. But it should help with the pain."

Sarah started to apply the white salve to Daylin's ankle, but stopped. "Your feet are filthy. Where's your shoe?"

Daylin shrugged. "I don't know. I guess I lost it in the fall."

Sarah tisked. "I'll give this a quick wash first. In the meantime, tell me what happened."

Angharad came back, took a seat, and picked up Daylin's hand, giving it a light squeeze. "It's all right, honey. Just tell us what happened."

Daylin blushed. Doing her best to keep the quaver out of her voice, she told them everything, about Ellis's attitude and their fight the night before, and about Betal and their wonderful dinner. She tried not to gush over him too much, but found it difficult. She finished with her spending the night in Dirge's tent while the man was on guard duty.

"I didn't go back because I wanted to give Ellis time to cool off," Daylin said. "I guess that was the wrong choice."

"You did the right thing," Sarah said as she patted dry Daylin's foot. "What happened to cause you to jump from a moving wagon?"

"Because Ellis is a jealous ass," Daylin said with scorn. She told them of their quarrel, and their words on the road.

"Oh. I am so sorry, my dear." Angharad hugged Daylin. "I'm sure, in time, he'll come to his senses. Until then, feel free to stay with us."

"Thank you. You've no idea how much this means to me." Daylin kissed Angharad's hand.

"So, are you going to be seeing Betal again?" the delicate blonde asked. Daylin nodded while sipping the cold, bitter tea. Angharad smiled. "So our gifts worked their charm."

"Oh yes. Thank you again. They're so lovely. I'd like to wear them when we have dinner again tonight." She frowned for a moment. "Unless Ellis hasn't come off his snit by then. I may need Dirge to fetch them for me."

"You have no worries there, my dear," Sarah said as she applied the salve, and wrapped the ankle.

Angharad ran her fingers through Daylin's hair. "We have many more dresses and baubles to adorn you with. We'll have that young man weeping with desire before the night is done."

With a giggle, Angharad continued, "I had a wonderful night as well. In fact, it was the singular, most glorious experience of my life."

Daylin cocked an eyebrow. "What happened?"

"I was in such a dark place. The melancholy was so strong I thought I'd never return. Everything was muffled and shadowed, like a blanket of darkness was smothering me." A dimpled smile bloomed on Angharad's face. "And then she came, swooping in like a goddess from the night. She reached into my mind. I felt her caress and soothe it, and she pulled me out of the gloom."

Daylin's eyes narrowed. "What?"

"It's all gone," Angharad replied. "The darkness is gone. She healed me. They always said it can't heal, but she healed me." She laughed and clasped her hands together. "After she left, I went for a walk under the stars. I jumped and cavorted and galloped and skipped. I tripped and danced and went to everyone's fire. I walked backward and played hide and seek with whoever would play like it was the only game in the world. I felt like a newborn colt ready to face the world."

Daylin's eyes went wide at the rant. "What are you saying?" She pulled back as her blood turned cold. "Who healed you?"

"Mangin," Angharad said, dream-like, staring off into the distance. "She is a priestess. She is a priestess of Chaos, and she healed me. And she wanted nothing in return."

Daylin stared to shake.

"She's such an amazing woman. She's one of the good ones." Angharad gazed at Daylin. "The men of the caravan say Betal is one as well. And if everything you've said about him is true, he must be a good one, too. It makes sense. There must be good ones as well as evil."

Daylin's face flushed. "Betal?"

"Yes." Angharad frowned, her face filled with concern. "What's wrong? Daylin. Daylin..."

Angharad's words warbled and thinned. Daylin's ears rang, and the room spun; it whirled and twisted until all went black.

Chapter 35

A Name from the Past

(Year 522 -R.C.-)

Dirge fumed as he stalked across the camp to Sarah's wagon. He'd told Ellis he never wanted to hear him speak to Daylin like that again, and if he did, the boy would have welts to remember it. "I taught him better than that."

If Dirge had ever done something like that with Talic around, his old master would have—

Dirge stopped with a scowl and shook his head. He'd not thought of his father in quite some time. "He's *not* my father. I *have* no father."

Dirge examined the camp as he continued. It was now one camp rather than two separate ones; yet the vehicles from the newcomer's group were so plain compared to the troupe's that they stuck out like pearl onions in a barley soup. The people were intermingling as well, going from wagon to wagon, and open cook pot to open cook pot, sampling what everyone offered.

Dirge didn't like what he saw. There was too much intermingling. In addition, there was something about the young lord and lady he didn't trust—especially the woman. She reminded him of the old City Masters back in Tuilar.

Once he reached Sarah's wagon, he mounted the stair and knocked on their door.

"Just a moment," Sarah said.

She then spoke to someone in the wagon. "It's all right. You're just confused. Those herbs shouldn't have done that. They must have been far stronger than usual. They should've only taken the pain away; not rendered you unconscious."

"No," he heard Daylin reply. "It wasn't that. It was me. When you told me about Betal… it's just… It's nothing."

"Oh. It's all right, sweetie," Angharad said. "I know it can be frightening. The priests, by and large, can be a cruel bunch, but they are not all bad."

Dirge's head shot back at the mention of priests.

"Aren't they?" Daylin spat.

"No. Not all," Sarah said. "After all, just look at Whisp. He was one of them, and in a way, he still is. Yet you'll not find a gentler and more caring man."

"But he's not a priest," Daylin said.

"You don't have to be afraid of them all," Sarah said.

"You know how I feel about them," Daylin said with anger in her voice. "How long have you known? Was it before I even had dinner with that—thing?"

"No," Dirge mumbled, his hand shaking. "By Ukase, tell me they're not saying what I think they are."

There was a hesitation before Sarah replied. "Dandle told me—probably around the same time as your date."

"And you didn't send warning?" Daylin shouted.

"Well, you didn't seem to care back at Cross Corners," Sarah said. "Besides, it's been so long that, well, Dandle thought they must have forgotten by now."

"You don't understand," Daylin said. "You *can't* understand."

"What don't we understand?" Angharad asked.

"It's Ruddick! It's what he did to me. That monster was a priest, and he used Chaos to torture and twist me into what I am now, a *freak*. Everything it touches becomes a freak."

"You're not a freak," Sarah said.

"Don't touch me!"

Dirge couldn't take anymore. He pounded on the door. "Daylin, it's me."

"Dirge, help me!"

Dirge heard a thump as he yanked the door open. Daylin lay on the floor in front of the door while Sarah sat on the bed. Angharad sat against the far wall, her eyes filled with fear.

"What in God's name is going on?" he asked as he knelt to Daylin.

"Please, Dirge," Daylin implored. "Just get me out of here."

Dirge gingerly picked Daylin up, being careful not to bump her bandaged foot. "When I return, I'll have words with you two." He seemed to say that a lot today.

Daylin clung to him, trembling. "Please, just go."

It was the second time that day Dirge held her lithe form in his arms. He did his best not to notice how soft she felt, how her body heat radiated into his chest. "I'll take you back to your wagon."

"No," she replied. "Not there. Just, take me to your tent, please."

He peered into her tear-filled eyes. "My—my tent isn't set up yet. We'll go to Whisp's. The old man hasn't stuck his head out for quite a while. He's even had Strong Tom driving his wagon for him. But I'll make sure he sees you."

She nodded and laid her head on his chest.

He berated himself for enjoying it. He'd no right to that feeling, now or ever.

"Dirge," she said softly. "Who's Lynette?"

Dirge stumbled. "Um, what?"

"You called me 'Lynette.' Who is she?"

He hammered down his feelings. "She's no one."

Once he reached Whisp's, he hammered on the door and berated the old man until he let them in. Dirge told Whisp about her injury, and the old man directed him to set Daylin down in his padded chair.

"Why didn't you take her to see Sarah?" Whisp asked.

Dirge told him what had happened, along with what he overheard.

"I see." Whisp eyed Daylin as she stared off into the distance.

He quickly opened his cupboard, grabbed a cup, and added a pinch of powder from a pair of boxes. He filled the cup with water and waved his hand over it. Within moments, the water was steaming.

"Here, lass." He pressed the cup into her hands. "This will help with the pain, and help you rest."

Daylin drank the cup without even looking at it. Once she finished, her eyes drooped, and she was asleep soon after.

"That should have her out for at least an hour," Whisp said as he retrieved the cup and put it away.

Dirge knelt before Daylin and patted her hand. *I'll protect you. I couldn't protect her, but I'll die before I let anything happen to you.*

Standing, he confronted the hedge mage. "Did you know about this? Did you know they were priests?"

"I suspected, yes. Why did you think I've not left my wagon?"

Dirge scowled. "Why didn't you send warning?"

"I told you I wasn't going to step out of here. The woman already suspects me as it is—I didn't get my wards up fast enough at Angharad's."

Dirge shook his head. "Considering where we're going, you'd better get over your fear. And soon. We'll have need of you."

The old mage's face became a thunderhead. He opened his mouth to speak, but stopped. His anger melted from his face, and he lowered his eyes. "You're right. I should have said something. I'm sorry."

He removed a box filled with odds and ends from his other chair and took a seat. "And yes, you're right. I can't lay up here forever. Once we reach Gate Hall, someone's bound to find out who I am. In a day or so, after I make the appropriate preparations, I'll approach them."

Dirge pulled his head back. "Why?"

"To garner favor for when I return to the sect. The politics there are dangerous, and I'll need all the help I can get. I don't know who that woman is, but she's powerful."

"You intend to stay there?"

Whisp waved his hand. "Gods no. I'll need to find out all I can to help us escape when the time comes."

He pointed at Dirge. "But mostly, I'll approach the woman to find out who they are. We need to know all we can. In fact, I suggest you talk to some of their retainers and guards to find out what you can as well."

"How will I know who to trust? I'm not much for— falsehoods."

The old man grinned. "Yes; your type doesn't do well with lying. Just approach those that seem like-minded. They'll look sullen and sour, like you."

Dirge nodded. In his youth, back in Tuilar, he'd learned well the look of a man who held serious misgivings for Chaos. He had a good idea of whom to approach first.

"I'll return." He glanced at Daylin. "Take good care of her."

He left before the man replied.

Once he hit the ground, he waved for Lem to bring him his horse. "Pass the word. Daylin is fine. She's sleeping. I'll tell Ellis and we'll head out."

He rode to the front. When Ellis demanded to see Daylin, Dirge shook his head. "We need to get moving, and now. You can see her tonight. We're vulnerable all spread out like this. Now, get these wagons moving."

Dirge could tell Ellis didn't like being ordered about, but he did what was right and flicked the reins.

Once the wagon train was moving, he rode back along the line until he reached the point where the troupe's wagons ended and the priests' began—unlike the arrangement while camped, their guard insisted the two groups travel separately. He approached the leader of their guard, a man named Cruchfield.

The man had a look of disdain and distrust on his face as Dirge approached—something the man seemed to hold perpetually. "What do you want, Traveler?" Cruchfield asked with a sneer.

Dirge nodded to him. "If I may, I would like to have a word with you. I understand you're someone… worthy of trust. That is rare these days." Dirge didn't know for sure, but he suspected. Cruchfield reminded Dirge of many of his compatriots back in the old days.

The man's eyes widened. "I thank you for the compliment."

"It's not a compliment when it's true. Men of conviction are hard to find." He extended his hand. "My name is Dirge."

"Erin." He took Dirge's hand. "Erin Cruchfield."

Erin tilted his head. "You're different from the rest. Tell me, why are you with them? You don't strike me as the type to take to Chaos like most of your kind."

Dirge considered his response. "I've sworn myself to their leader, and I'll follow him to my death. He's a good man, if a bit too brash at times. These are good people. They're not like any other Travelers you'll come across."

"You're a man of honor?" Cruchfield's eyebrows rose. "That's indeed rare. What do you ask of me?"

"What can you tell me of... *them*?" Dirge kept his voice lower so as not to carry.

"You've not heard of them?"

Dirge shook his head. "We know very little on this side of the river."

"Dithiyar is the priest in our village—"

"Dithiyar?"

"Yes." Eric pointed backward with his thumb. "You've not seen him because I don't believe he's even stuck his head out of his coach yet. Not even to relieve himself."

"The black one?"

"Yes. The woman's name is Mangin. She's an acolyte. We're taking her to see her father. Apparently, he's the high priest at Gate Hall."

Dirge whistled as he kept an eye out for anyone getting too close.

"Indeed. She's a spiteful *bitch* who loves to twist people's heads. I can't wait to be rid of her and headed back home."

"What of this Betal?"

Cruchfield snarled. "You mean The Beast?"

Dirge snapped his head toward the guardsman. "What village are you from, again?"

Once they stopped for the night, Daylin headed back to her wagon. She admitted to Whisp part of her fight with Ellis had been her own fault. "I need to make amends. He's my best friend, and I don't want to lose that for anything."

"That's good," Whisp said. "But I don't want you going by yourself. Your ankle looks much better, but I want you to stay off it for a day or two."

He pulled open the door to the driver's bench. "Have a guard fetch Dirge, would you, please?"

A few minutes later, Dirge knocked on the back door with a crutch in his hand. "I got this from Sarah. I had a talk with her. She and Angharad said they're very sorry for upsetting you."

Daylin scowled. "I don't care what Angharad has to say. That priest was in her head. For all I know, she's nothing but a puppet now."

Whisp raised his hand. "Well—"

Daylin's hard stare cut him short. She turned back to Dirge. "Would you help me down, please?"

"Thank you, Dirge." She tested the crutch under her arm then limped back home and up the stairs. As she reached the top, Ellis flung open the door. With his face filled with relief and remorse, he threw his arms about her, hugging her tight.

"I'm sorry," she said, thinking he might never let her go.

"No, I'm the one who's sorry. I had no right to say that." He pulled back. "Please tell me you forgive me."

She smiled. "Of course I do."

He helped her inside, and she took a seat on her bed. He sat across from her and stared into her eyes, seemingly at a loss for words. She smiled and reached out her hand toward him. Relief filled her when he gently took it.

"I'm sorry. I only want the best for you," he said.

She smiled and squeezed his hand. "I know. I just don't want to lose you as a friend."

Dirge spoke up, startling Daylin.

"We must talk." The swordsman sat next to Ellis. "I spoke with the head of their guard, Erin Cruchfield. He said they're from the village of *Cool Winds*."

Ellis frowned. "What else did he say?"

"He said the man in the black carriage is a priest named Dithiyar, and the other two are only acolytes, not full priests. The woman, Mangin, has strong family connections. Apparently, her father is the head priest at Gate Hall. As for the man…"

He looked deeply into Daylin's eyes, his voice hard as iron and his eyes burning with hatred. "He's the one we've all heard about. He's The Beast of Cool Winds, the living embodiment of The Lord of Chaos."

Daylin's eyes went wide and her jaw dropped.

"Are you sure?" Ellis asked.

Dirge nodded. "Are you all right, Daylin?"

She didn't know what to think. Betal wasn't just a user of Chaos, but a *thing* of Chaos. She shook her head. "I guess I expected something different."

"What do you mean?" Ellis asked.

"I expected horns and a tail," she replied.

Instead, she saw him as a man who projected a great caring for others and filled her with a sense of… something. *Is trying to lure me into some kind of wicked, cruel game?*

"Not all monsters have horns and tails," Dirge said.

Daylin trembled. Would that monster try to devour her, or enslave her like the woman had Angharad? Perhaps he already had, because any time she thought of him, her heart beat faster, her skin tingled, and her loins felt warm.

She thought about their kiss: sweet, yet firm with more than a hint of hunger.

With a shake of her head, she cursed herself. *Stop it, fool!*

The two men had continued their discussion, and Ellis said something that caught her attention. "What did you say?"

"I said we can't let him know how much this upsets you," Ellis replied.

"Who? That *monster*?"

"Yes. I'm talking about Betal. The next time you see him—"

"*Next* time?" she shouted. "I'm never seeing that thing again!"

"You have to," Ellis said.

"Never!" She jumped to her feet. Wincing in pain, she sat back down. "Do you hear me? Never again."

"We don't have a choice," Ellis said.

"*We?*" Daylin shook her head with her eyes wide.

Dirge interjected, "Why must she continue to interact with that… thing?"

"Because," Ellis said, "the only reason he's here is to talk to Daylin. If she refuses to see him again, he'll leave, and you know it."

She scowled and lowered her head.

"There's something else," Dirge said. "I believe Cruchfield wants Betal killed."

Daylin's head snapped up—appalled at the idea. She scowled at her reaction. *Why should I care if he's killed?*

"What makes you think that?" Ellis asked.

"He asked if I could, 'get rid of him.'"

"What did you say?" Daylin asked.

After a moment, Dirge answered. "I told him I couldn't."

Daylin let out a breath she hadn't realized she was holding.

"Good," Ellis said. "Because we need him."

"*We* need him?" Daylin shook her head. "I told you, I want nothing to do with him."

"Daylin." Ellis's eyes firmed. "We can't take the chance. You *will* see him again."

"Yesterday, you wanted to know if I'd bedded him, and now you want me to go back." She snarled. "So, do you want me to bed him now? Do you? Would that make things better for *you*?"

Ellis stood. "Daylin—"

"No! Just get out." She climbed into her bed and faced the wall, trembling. "The only thing I *need* is to be left alone."

Chapter 36
The Road
North

(Year 522 -R.C.-)

They'd been heading north for two days—two slow, glorious days. Initially, Mangin expected the Traveling folk to shun her once they learned who she was. But as word spread about her aid to one of their own, the fear vanished, and their thanks, blessings, and requests for her time *and* pleasure poured in. Their sexual appetites were like nothing she had ever known. Mangin was a sweet, exotic fruit, and everyone wanted a taste.

Crossing the center of the camp, Mangin came across Betal watching the Sartan Brothers practice their dueling and going over lines. She asked Betal, "Thinking about taking up the sword?"

"No," he replied, even more sour than usual. "I was just thinking."

"Oh. About what?"

He glanced out of the corner of his eye. "You'd only laugh if I told you."

"Come now, sweetheart. You must give me more faith than that." She loved to see him sweat and squirm, but not today. He was far too somber and solemn to suit her mood.

"I don't know." Betal shook his head and started walking.

Mangin made a ticking sound with her tongue and followed. "You're too serious, Betal. Just look about you. These people are amazing. I've never had so much fun in my life. I now understand why The Great Lord loves them so. These people revel in life and challenge death daily. They're walking on ropes high in the air, throwing knives at live targets, eat fire, swallow swords, and juggle axes. They're all so beautiful and precious that I want to keep them about me forever."

"Then why don't you?"

Mangin sighed. "Because it's their freedom, I love most."

Betal glanced at her. "Freedom?"

"Yes. My life before me is, more or less, set. I'll go to the sect and rise or fall as I might, while theirs is a life that's seemingly without end."

"Well, you do seem to enjoy having your way with them."

"Yes. I do," she purred. "These people are astonishing. They want me, Betal. They actually *want* me."

"What do you mean?" Betal asked.

She pursed her lips. "Come now. Don't try to fool with me. You know very well what I mean. Everyone back at that piss-pot we used to call a home hated us. The only way I could enjoy myself was if I made them do it."

"What about Adel?"

"My poor Adel. I feel so sorry for her."

"Why?"

She didn't reply. Mangin hadn't given Adel a reading lesson in several days, and the girl felt left out.

Spotting Angharad on their stage built right into their wagon, she stopped and watched as the group rehearsed a new play Sarah came up with only a day before. They weren't in any kind of elaborate costumes as they spoke their lines, but Angharad's blonde hair shone in the sun.

"Is she the one you helped?" Betal asked. "The one with the pretty dimples?"

"Yes," Mangin replied. Happy that Angharad stopped looking at her like an adoring puppy, Mangin decided tonight she'd dine with the lovely woman, and taste what was undoubtedly the finest dish in the entire troupe.

"Why d'you do it?" Betal asked.

She looked at him with one eyebrow raised. "Why not?"

He shrugged. "I don't know. It's just not like you."

"She suffered from a dark melancholy. In one of my mother's books, a portion posited such things were of the mind, rather than the spirit world." She shrugged. "It was a perfect time to find out."

"And what did you find out?"

"There was something there." She shuddered. "Something dark and malevolent."

"I see," Betal said, obviously not listening. Instead, he stared at the Traveler's lead wagon, shook his head, and stared walking again.

Mangin cocked an eyebrow. "So what's on your mind, truthfully?"

He snorted. "I was wondering if every woman I'll ever meet will either fear me or hate me. And am I always going to be alone because of it."

She did her best to suppress a smile at his silliness. "So who wants to kill you now, my pet?"

"Most of the people here, I suspect. But presently, I think Daylin does."

Mangin scowled. *Again, with the dog-woman.*

He shrugged. "Our dinner was amazing, but now any time I go near her, she runs the other way. Hells, one time, Ellis walked me to their wagon. She cursed him out and slammed the door." He shrugged. "Maybe we should just go on. I'm sure you're eager to get to the city."

"I am. But, as I said, I'm enjoying myself too much right now."

"All I know is she hates me." He sighed. "Maybe it's for the best. The last woman I took a liking to tried to kill me."

Mangin rolled her eyes. "I know you're lonely, but give it time. One day, you'll find someone." She smiled mischievously. "Just remember, a woman wants to be *pursued*. They're your prey and deserve your attention.

She wondered if he caught on, but doubted it. "As to this Daylin woman, she has good reason to fear you. You're Betal, the very breath of the Lord. Everyone should fear you *and* challenge you. This Daylin is just a commoner. She's nothing you need to worry about. If you want her, take her. Otherwise, forget her."

She grabbed his arm, pulling him up short. Stepping close, she placed a hand on his chest, raised herself up, and brought her lips toward his. With a look of desire, he leaned into her.

She smacked him on the cheek. "No getting fresh with me, you understand?"

His eyes went wide and his jaw dropped open.

With a laugh, she dashed away. Glancing back, she saw him start after her, but stop after only a few feet. *Oh well,* she thought. *The game goes on.*

As she made her way to the edge of camp, she thought about Betal and his fascination with this woman, Daylin. She was skinny, far too pale, and according to most of the troupe, preferred the company of her dogs to most of the people. "What does he even see in her?"

She strolled through the double ring of wagons and stopped. Not ten feet away, sitting against one of the wagon wheels, was Daylin.

Mangin gazed at the lithe woman and cocked an eyebrow. *She is rather lovely,* isn't she? The woman possessed a pastel look, soft and sweet, with a kind of sadness as well—the kind poets pen sonnets about. Perhaps Betal saw in her something much like himself—something somber and solitary. Mangin frowned. That would not do. Betal was hers, not some pathetic washed-out dog-woman.

Mangin sauntered over.

When Daylin noticed Mangin approach, the young woman's eyes widened. She sprang to her feet and hurried away.

"Stop," Mangin snapped. Grasping Chaos, she snared the woman. "I would have words with you." She gently lifted the girl and turned her around. Even whiter than before, fear filled Daylin's face, but her jaw held firm. Her eyes shone with anger and determination. Mangin couldn't help but respect it.

"What do you want?" Daylin said through clenched teeth.

Mangin released the bonds. "I wish to talk with you, my sweet. I've not seen you since the day we met, and I wanted to get to know you." She tilted her head. "I understand you hate all things Chaos. Why? It's obvious The Lord blessed you, so why resent him so?"

Her brows furrowing, Daylin took a step back and lowered her head. "I don't know what you're talking about."

Mangin moved closer, put her finger under the woman's chin, and lifted it. "I do believe you've the most beautiful eyes I have ever seen," she cooed. "And your skin is so soft and supple. I can see why Betal likes you."

Daylin jerked back. "He does *not* like me. He got the information he wanted, and now he wants nothing from me. And I want nothing from him."

"Of course he likes you, my dear." Mangin softly took Daylin's face between both her hands.

The shy ones require subtlety, she thought. *Like whispering to a new colt before you bridle it.*

"He finds you intriguing and lovely, and I am forced to agree. You might be the most exotic creature in this entire troupe." Mangin leaned in and placed a soft kiss upon Daylin's lips.

The girl snapped her head back as if burned. "What are you doing? I'll not be your plaything like the rest." She whirled and marched away again.

Mangin snarled. *I'll have this little thing whether she likes it or not.* She grasped Chaos and once again encased the girl, whirling her about. Spinning a net, she grasped the woman's mind. At least, she tried to. As soon as she placed the net, it melted away.

Mangin's eyes went wide and her jaw dropped. "What did you do? How were you able to do that?" She smiled with sudden realization. "Is it part of your gift?"

"Do what?" Daylin spat back, struggling at her bonds. "Let me go!"

"Enough, Mangin!" Betal shouted behind her. "Release her."

Mangin glanced back and smirked. It seemed Betal followed her after all.

"I mean it, Mangin. Let go of her. Now," he growled.

A thrilling chill ran up Mangin's spine. She needed to figure how to get him this emotional when she *played* with him.

Perhaps then, he'd finally lose control and take her like he should. "As you wish," she said blithely. "She's of no concern to me." She let the dog-woman go.

Betal went to Daylin, his voice like a caress, "Are you all right?"

Mangin made her way back toward the camp, her eyebrows furrowed. "Play with her all you want," she said under her breath. "Just don't forget to whom you belong."

Chapter 37
The Grunkin

(Year 522 -R.C.-)

The last two days for Daylin had not gone well. Following her accosting at the hands of Mangin, Daylin felt an absolute wreck. She refused to leave the wagon. She had no appetite, and when she did eat, it was difficult to keep it down. And sleeping through the night was impossible due to nightmares of Ruddick experimenting on her again. Only now, Mangin stared over his shoulder, laughing. She dreamt of Mangin chasing her, looming larger than a tree with demonic green eyes, and no matter how hard she ran the priestess always gained. In another, Sarah and Angharad, danced on marionette strings with a gigantic Mangin as the puppeteer. They danced and sang the praises of their new master while trying to help the Chaos priestess latch those same strings onto Daylin.

The last one truly hurt. The two came by the day before, but she sent them away. They'd lain with that witch. Also, everyone said Mangin had been in Angharad's mind. Daylin couldn't trust them anymore.

Daylin shuddered, still feeling when that woman touched her with Chaos. It was a sensation she'd never forget, thanks to Ruddick funneling it into her when she was a child. The woman tried to touch her mind. It hadn't worked, but Daylin knew the woman would try again to find out why.

Ellis wasn't helping matters, hovering over her, constantly asking if she was all right, and trying to spoon-feed her when she refused to eat. One moment, he'd look at her like an older brother, and the next, he'd gaze at her like a would-be lover.

Then there was Betal. Strangely, after he'd made Mangin leave her alone, the only pleasant dreams she had were of him. They'd repeat their dinner date, with her chatting away like a brainless fool while he sat there and watched. His eyes drew her in until there was nothing else. They engulfed her, and it put her at ease. She lay in bed, feeling a panic overcome her, then think of him, and the panic abated. He was a beacon of light, burning away the darkness. She no longer feared him, and it worried her.

Or, at least, it should, she thought.

Sighing, she rolled over. It was deep in the night and she couldn't sleep. Ellis's shallow breaths and slight snore a few feet away was like a balm. She might no longer think of him as a possible lover, but she always felt better when he was near.

She closed her eyes and tried to let herself drift off when a mental yelp from one of her dogs filled her mind. Bucky was off to the east, patrolling the night, when he smelled a wrongness all about.

What's wrong, Bucky? she thought to him. She sent out her mind, connecting it to Bucky so she could witness the world through his senses.

Bucky's hackles raised at the wrongness of the smell. He scanned the darkness when his ears picked up a rustle to his right. As he swung, a flash of something white raced toward him. He tried to jump away, but something snapped hold of his right-rear leg, its sharp fangs sinking in. Bucky yelped in pain as it threw him into the air and slammed him back to the ground.

Daylin bolted up with a scream, hugging herself and shaking, as she felt his life-force slip away.

Ellis was there in the matter of moments. "What's wrong? Another nightmare?" He held her tight.

"He's *gone*," she cried.

"Who?"

"Bucky." She told him about the attack.

"What was it?" he asked.

Tears streamed down her cheeks. She didn't want to say it. "G-grunkin."

"Shit." Ellis stood, hastened to the door, and stuck his head out. "Evan! Roust everyone. A grunkin just killed Bucky!"

He hastily dressed, grabbed his bow, and knelt next to Daylin. "I'll take care of it. Call in the other dogs and have them and the rest set up a perimeter just outside of the wagons. Have them bark if they see it approach." He gave her arm a squeeze and left.

She spent the rest of the night shivering and crying. Bucky, her only remaining connection to Vir, was gone. It was as if Vir died all over again.

They doubled the guard on the camp that night, but nothing else happened. In the morning, Dirge led a dozen men to the location she said she had last felt Bucky. They returned a short time later. Ellis, with Dirge at his side, told her they'd found Bucky's remains.

"It broke his neck when it slammed him to the ground," Dirge said. "It ripped apart The back half of his body and cast about."

"Dirge!" Ellis glared at the stoic, dark-skinned man.

"No." Daylin waved him off. "It's all right. At least I know he didn't suffer."

"There's no doubt it was a grunkin," Ellis said. "We found putrid white fur, and from its tracks, it seemed to have only three legs."

She shivered in her blanket. "What happens next?"

"For now, we hang tight and keep a hard watch," Dirge said.

Ellis touched her shoulder. "I'll stay here with you—"

"No," she cut him off. "I'll be fine."

"But—"

"I said I'll be fine," she insisted. "I just want to sleep. Please."

Ellis frowned, but nodded, and the two men left.

Daylin spent the next two hours switching between sending away well-wishers and mentally checking on the rest of her dogs. She sympathized with her pack; they shared her grief.

They howled and cried when they weren't snarling in anger, filled with a desire to hunt the creature down.

It was near noon when yet another knock came to her door. "Please go away," she croaked. "Thank you for your sympathy, but please, just go away."

The stairs creaked, and there was a pause. "Daylin? It's Betal. Please, let me come in."

Without knowing why, she leapt up and threw open the door—

And there he stood, as tall and as beautiful as ever. She flung herself into his arms and held him tight. His arms enveloped her as he gently rocked her back and forth. She wanted to berate herself. She should hate the man. She hated his God, and his friends—she hated everything he stood for. But for some reason, she couldn't bring herself to hate *him*.

"I never thanked you for helping me with that woman," she mumbled into his chest. "I was so scared and didn't know what to do."

"It's all right. Everything will be all right," he said in hushed tones. "I'll make sure Mangin stays away from you." He pulled back and wiped her tears. "Now, tell me what happened last night. Your friends haven't been very forthcoming. I'll help in any way I can."

Daylin told him what happened to Bucky.

He held her even tighter, still speaking softly, "I'll take some of my men and track it down. This thing has terrorized the people in this region for far too long. It's time to kill it."

She gazed up at him through her tears. "Why?" When he looked at her quizzically, she continued, "Why would a priest want to kill something created by Chaos?"

Betal smiled. "Because it's the right thing to do."

Her head spun. "Who are you? Who are you, *really*?"

He tilted his head. "What do you mean?"

"Never mind." She buried her face into his chest once more. "Just hold me."

With one arm wrapped around her back, he caressed her hair while rocking back and forth. After a time, he kissed the top of her head and took a step back, delicately extricating himself from their embrace. "I need to get going. We'll need to do this while we still have enough daylight."

She leapt forward, grasping him by the head, and kissed him. She didn't want it to end. Nevertheless, she backed up and stroked his cheek while gazing into his eyes. "Be careful, please."

He stroked her cheek in kind. "I promise." He turned and descended the steps.

Ellis stood a few paces away with a sour look on his face. Betal approached him and said, "I'm going after that thing. Keep an eye out for it here, just in case." He turned back, smiled at her, and left.

"Who the hells does he think he is, telling me what to do?" Ellis mumbled as he stalked off after Betal while calling for Evan and Dirge.

"Please don't do anything stupid," she whispered. "Either of you."

Dithiyar sat in his tent, with a book in his hands, stewing— he'd long before given up on actually trying to read. His plans were crumbling before him, his machinations to re-ascend to the heights of power, all for naught. Within the matter of days, he'd lose Betal, and end up back in that worthless village to rot until the end of time.

"They can all die for all I care," he said to himself again for the umpteenth time. "I don't know why I just don't turn around and go back."

"Because I don't want you to," said a deep, ominous voice.

Dithiyar dropped his book with a shriek.

Hogar seemed to materialize in the middle of his tent as he unwrapped his camouflaging cocoon of Chaos. "Surprised?" He chuckled, his crimson eyes seeming to burn with fire. "You needn't be. I've shadowed you ever since the village."

He strolled to the tent opening and peeked through the cracked opening. "What's your take on these Travelers?"

"I haven't," Dithiyar said. "What do I care about a bunch of performers?"

Hogar turned and strode until he loomed over Dithiyar. "You should. Something about them bothers me. Most troupes are small, have no organization, and break up within a couple of years." He gestured to the tent flap with his head. "Not this bunch. There's something sinister going on here. They're far too orderly to be truly favored by The Lord."

"What do you think it is?"

"That's what I want you to find out." He pointed his black, gauntleted finger at Dithiyar. "You've spent far too much time sulking. Go out amongst these people. Find out what's going on. Apparently, a grunkin is nearby and several of them have decided they want to hunt it down. For some reason, Betal is helping them." He shook his head. "Why he'd even bother, I've no idea."

He looked to the tent wall as though peering through it. "Perhaps it's these people. They make me itch. I sense a remnant of Ukase amongst them. One or more must be followers, and I want to know who."

"How am I to do that?" Dithiyar asked, cowering in his chair. "I have no way to sense such a thing."

"I don't care how you do it," Hogar said. "Oh, and I especially want you to look into a woman named Daylin," he added. "The one Betal's been playing with. It seems she has some ability to block Mangin's mind control. Find out how she does it."

Dithiyar shrugged. "Again, how?"

Hogar snarled. "*Just do it.* I'm going to the Westlands and hunt for answers there. When I get back, I expect news from you." The paladin vanished.

It took a while for Dithiyar to stop shaking. He pushed himself away from his desk, picked up his cane, and limped toward the door—though not needed, it put people off their guard. He knew he didn't dare dawdle because Hogar was likely still near—or possibly, even still in the tent—so he went out into the midafternoon sun.

They set his tent up alongside the rest of his retinue. Ever since Mangin's altercation with the woman who managed the dogs, relations between the two camps had cooled. There was no open hostility, but Travelers seemed a bit on edge and kept to themselves at night.

He set out to walk the camp, and everywhere he went, the Traveling People stopped what they were doing and stared at him. Moreover, every time he tried to engage someone in conversation, they backed away, albeit politely. It was as if he were a stray, snarling dog and they didn't know what to do with him.

How am I to learn anything like this? he thought with a grimace.

It angered him, seeing so few guards with a grunkin on the loose—too many had joined in on the hunt. It surprised him Betal went off to hunt it down. That young man never seemed to take a liking to many of The Lord's blessings. He wondered if Betal was jealous as though only he was worthy of The Lord's praise.

After an hour, Dithiyar gave up. It was unlikely Hogar still stalked him—if he even had in the first place. But Dithiyar wasn't one to take chances. So, he went out of the circle of wagons. *Maybe I'll find someone lingering out there.*

As he wandered around the outer circle, he saw a scrawny young woman with dark hair, walking along the edge of the road next to a tall, hulking man as escort. She was in a simple yellow flowered dress, something rather tame compared to the rest of these vagabonds. *She must be the one Hogar was referring to.* When she glanced his way, he pressed himself up against the wagon and sneered. *Never let them see you coming.*

Daylin walked the outer ring of the wagons, keeping an eye on the tree line some hundred feet beyond. The wagon had become stifling, and she wanted to take a walk. Ellis had asked Lem to guard her door, which made her laugh at the time. However, she didn't find it funny when he followed her around.

"I'd hate myself until the day I died if something were to happen to you," Lem had said.

It was the first time in days she didn't feel afraid. At least not for herself. Two men she cared a great deal about were out there, hunting a monster that wanted nothing but to kill. Mangin still worried her, but not as much as before. Whatever the priestess had tried on her, failed.

I don't need to be afraid of her anymore, she thought. Well, that wasn't completely true, but at least she needn't worry about the woman twisting her mind.

She ambled through the tall grass on the far side of the road—Lem only a few feet behind—and chewed her lip while thinking about Betal, hoping him and Ellis would be all right.

Please don't let anything happen to them, she prayed to The Mother. Years before, Vir said The True Tree looked after her. She dearly hoped that were true. *Please, look after them.*

"Well, what have we here?" a man said behind her, his voice smarmy and thin.

Daylin jumped and whirled about. Only a few feet away, stood a bent, shaking, old man in black robes, leaning on a cane.

"So, you are the one they say talks to dogs," he said. "And how did you come by that? Was it a gift from The Great Lord?"

"Who are you? Where did you come from?" She took a step back. He made her skin crawl.

"I am Dithiyar, a servant of The Great Lord of Chaos." He snarled and stepped forward. "And you are a peasant who will answer my questions."

Lem drew his sword and stepped in front of her. "Back off, little man."

The priest casually flicked his hand to the side. Lem whirled through the air with a scream and landed some twenty feet away with a thud.

"Lem," Daylin screamed.

"You will answer my ques—" The old man jerked his head toward the deep grass.

Daylin sensed a mind in the grass. It was intelligent, but animalistic, predatory... and psychotic. There was also a coldness to it, something black and evil reminiscent of the little man with the scales back at The Cunning. *Could it be him?* Her skin crawl like maggots writhed beneath it.

Steeling herself, she searched, trying to pin the mind down, but it kept skittering away like water on a hot stove. One moment, it seemed far away, and the next, within arm's reach. She caught movement out of the corner of her eye, tearing toward her through the tall grass. Covered in grayish-white fur, it shrieked, sending a shudder down her spine.

The grunkin!

Trembling, she didn't have time to be scared. She only had time for thought.

Chapter 38
Shining Like a Beacon

(Year 522 -R.C.-)

Daylin snatched the mind of the lunging grunkin. It flailed and thrashed, trying to escape, but she held tight. The grunkin crashed to the ground and slid to within feet. Shaking, she stared at the thing in disgust, nearly retching from its stench. *This thing killed Bucky!*

The priest gasped. "What did you do? How did you do that? You're controlling it, aren't you? How? Damn it, woman, tell me!"

"I don't know," she said, straining to keep the thing down.

Led by Strong Tom, the guards came running with bows drawn.

"Kill the damn thing," she screamed. "I can't hold it for much longer!"

"No!" The priest flung out his hand.

The bowmen loosed. Five shafts sunk into the grunkin, quickly followed by five more. But it still wouldn't die.

Two wolves, one gray and one white, sprinted out of the tall grass and attacked the beast. The gray dove for its underbelly while the white clamped its jaws around the grunkin's throat. With a shake, the white ripped off the grunkin's head.

"Damn you," Dithiyar screamed. The priest let loose a blast, striking the white wolf's hindquarter, snapping and melting its leg. The wolf yelped and crawled off into the high grass as the gray sprinted for the trees.

"No," Daylin cried. "Why did you do that?"

Dithiyar ignored the question as he eyed the dead monster, his jaw slack. "The Lord made grunkin to be uncontrollable—to destroy at a whim. Nothing can control them." His head turned to Daylin. "Until now." An oily smile bloomed on the priest's face. "The Lord takes, and The Lord gives."

She shied back, a tingle running up her spine. "What are you talking about?"

The priest stepped toward her. "With you, I'll sit at Heartless's side once more."

"No." She took a step back.

"All I have to do is copy your gift and we'll have an army of grunkin. The reign of Chaos will never end."

Thoughts of Ruddick flashed through her head. "Copy?"

"You must come with me." The priest clasped her arm.

"No!" She yanked it away.

The priest snarled. "I don't have time for this."

The air solidified around Daylin, cocooning her, and lifting her into the air. "Help!"

The bowmen turned their aim to the priest. "Put her down," Tom shouted.

The priest flicked his hand. A glowing ball of multicolored, gelatinous ooze rocketed through the air, striking the ground in front of the men, and exploded. Men screamed as dirt blasted them off their feet.

Daylin thrashed. "Put me dow—" The cocoon choked her.

"Keep your mouth shut, unless you want to lose your tongue," the odious man said as he hurried toward the horse line. "I don't need you vocal—just alive."

Daylin's eyes searched the tree line hoping to spot Betal and Ellis, but nothing moved within the forest. She thought about calling her dogs, but knew the priest would kill them.

"I know someone at Gate Hall who can open you up for a cost, but it will be worth the price to know how you do it."

In her mind, she was once again eleven years old, at the mercy of Ruddick and his horrific experiments. Tears streamed down her face. *Where are you Vir? I need you.*

"This isn't good," Betal said. "Are you sure?"

"I'm sure," the troupe's tracker replied. "The tracks circled the camp three times. But now they're angling toward it."

Ellis approached with the swordsman at his side. "Are you sure, Evan?"

The tracker looked between Betal and the Traveler leader. "Yes. I'm certain."

Betal scowled and waved to Adam. "Let's go. We don't have much time." He dashed through the trees. *Lord, I hope we're not too late.*

They exited the woods on the far side of meadow, across from the camp. At the edge of the road, several men lay on the ground near a smoldering crater. Dithiyar raced in the opposite direction, dragging a hovering Daylin.

"What are you doing?" Betal bellowed.

The old man cursed and shot a ball of Chaos at them.

Betal grasped The Lord's Breath, batted the ball aside, and sprinted for the old priest. "Stop!" He sent a bolt of his own at Dithiyar's feet.

With a wave of his hand, Dithiyar shimmered from head to toe. The bolt struck him, and vanished, absorbed into the priest's new iridescent armor.

Betal tried to grab Dithiyar with Chaos, tried to push him over, and even tried boring through the Chaotic shielding, but nothing worked. It simply drew the power in, making it all the stronger. "It's like Hogar's armor," he panted. He considered blasting at the ground in front of the old man, but that might harm Daylin.

Dirge sprinted past with his sword drawn.

"It won't work," Betal shouted. "That shielding will eat your sword!"

The dark-skinned man simply murmured and ran all the harder.

Dithiyar laughed and sent a bolt at the swordsman.

Dirge dodged it.

Another bolt flew.

Dirge spun out of the way and kept running.

Dithiyar snarled and fired again. "Die, you worthless shit!"

Feet from the priest, Dirge dove to the side as a bolt whizzed past his head. He rolled, leapt to his feet, and hacked at Dithiyar's arm. With a crack, the blade flashed bright white with magic, and slashed through the mystical armor.

Dithiyar shrieked as his arm fell to the ground and blood fountained from the stump.

Betal's mouth fell open. "But, how?" He tried to copy the magic from the sword. He thrust both hands forward, pulling from his own will. A brilliant beam of white blazed and struck the old priest in the face. Dithiyar crumpled with a fist-sized hole through his head.

The cocoon about Daylin vanished and she tumbled to the ground. Betal stood tall, looking like a hero out of a story. She yearned to run to him, but the cries of the injured white wolf were too heart wrenching. She dashed to it, reaching out with her mind, but the wolf snarled and snapped at her.

"It's all right," she said as she approached. "I'm here to help you. Calm yourself."

"No," the wolf screamed. "You all deserve death! You stole my pup! You stole my Veil! I didn't have enough time with him, and you took him from me!"

"Please, I don't understand."

"Humans only know death and pain, and you *took* him. I'll never see him again."

"Just let me help you." Daylin stopped a few feet away, not daring to get any closer.

"Please, Great Mother," the wolf whimpered. "I just want to see him again before I die. That's all I ask."

Betal stared at the smoldering hole in Dithiyar's head. *What in all the hells did I do?* With a shake, he searched for Daylin and found her sitting on the ground near a wolf.

"I'm here to help you," she said it as Betal ran up. "You need to calm yourself."

He knelt to Daylin, and searched every inch of her for an injury, but thankfully saw none. "Are you all right?" he asked, laying a hand on her shoulder.

She gazed up at him, her eyes filled with both joy and sorrow. "I'm fine. Thank you." Her eyes went back to the wolf. "But, she's dying."

Betal examined it. "Did you call it?"

"No. I don't know where she came from. Dithiyar hurt her when she killed the grunkin. But she won't let me help. She's so full of pain and anger." Daylin shook her head. "She keeps talking about a lost pup."

"It's not the gray one from the road, thankfully." Betal stood to get a better look. "It looks familiar though. Where have I seen it before?"

The wolf lifted its head, their eyes met, and their minds connected. Her name popped into his head: Shin-Ja.

Images and emotions struck Betal, along with Shin-Ja's cries of remorse… that suddenly turned to elation.

His memories flooded back, memories of a time before he was human.

Veil opened his blue eyes and sighed. There was nothing like waking to the security of your mother's fur, her heartbeat a comforting rhythm in the darkness of the den which every passing day seemed smaller and more confining.

Why do I need to stay down here? he wondered. Old enough to sleep outside like his cousins, he enjoyed the flavor of fresh meat over the taste of her milk, and he loved to explore and run and play. But his mother insisted he stay put.

Yawning, he stretched, and shook himself, then Cast his thoughts to his mother, Shin-Ja. "May I go and play?"

Lifting her head, she gazed at him with a grin. "Yes, you may, but don't venture too far." Love flowed with her thoughts, but so did caution. "I don't want you to leave my range. Do you hear me?"

"Yes, Mother." His tail wagged so hard his entire rear swayed as he scrambled out of the den.

Shin-Ja woke with a start. Something had disturbed her sleep, haunting dreams with a feel of premonition. Her ears pricked when she realized Veil had not returned. *Where is that pup? It doesn't take this long to explore the glade.* She reached out with her mind to find Veil and grew more alarmed the further out she had to go. When she finally found him, her stomach wrenched— he was far to the south. *It's too soon.* She clawed her way out of the den, snarling. *He's not ready yet.*

Lakota, the pack leader, greeted her at the entrance. "Good dayspring, Shin-Ja."

"How could you?" she snapped. "How could you let him go off that far?"

"Calm yourself," Lakota replied. "I did not send him off alone. Zara is keeping a nose on him."

Shin-Ja bristled. "Zara? She's only a yearling."

"She is more than capable. She does not make the same mistake twice and has a good sense of discipline."

"But they're headed south. You know what lies in that direction." She dashed off.

"He must find out sometime, Shin-Ja. You coddle the pup too much. You know who he is and what he's to become."

"I'll not lose him. Do you hear me? Not him!"

"You cannot stop the inevitable," the pack leader Cast to her. "Only pain lies in that life."

She ignored him. Laying back her ears, she pushed for more speed—the wind ruffling her snow-white fur with every bound. *I'll not lose him.* Thoughts of the bloody, broken bodies of her mate and other cubs flitted through her mind, making her want to howl. *He's all I have left.*

Shin-Ja panted atop High Hill. Her sense of Veil, at first crystal clear, was now hazy and stunted. She felt them to the south, vague and distant, but couldn't make contact. She'd followed the two by scent thus far but feared she'd lose that as well. Something masked them. Her hackles rose as anxiety rippled through her. It smelled of the minions of destiny shaping things.

Please, Mother, she prayed to the True Tree. *Don't take him yet. It's too soon. I haven't had enough time with him.*

Her heart hammered as she dodged around trees and leapt over logs. As she neared the forest's edge, she finally caught sight of them, and her connection with their minds snapped in.

"Stop," she screamed. "The both of you; stop this instant and don't move one step more!"

Thank you, Mother. Thank you for not taking him today.

Veil jumped at the strength and of his mother's Cast. One moment he and Zara were alone in the world and then there his mother was, strong in his mind and sprinting toward them. Feeling her anger, he sat, his ears wilting.

Zara sat next to him. "It would appear our adventure is over for the day."

As Veil stared into the distance, a chill ran up his spine and his mind drifted. *Why do I feel so strange?* His eyes wandered to a large tree near the edge of the forest. It pulled at him as though something there wanted to talk. Cocking his head, he scampered toward it. The tree grew more fascinating with each step. Sitting next to the trunk, he stared deep into its branches. The world seemed to grow thin, and something brushed his mind.

He cocked his head the other way. *It's almost like it's trying to Cast to me.*

The brushing became a prod.

It is *trying to Cast to me!* He shook his head. It made no sense. *Maybe if I open my mind a little more—*

"REMEMBER!"

His hair stood on end, his legs quivered, and his mind opened further. A massive jumble of images, memories, and revelations flooded him. He blinked at the onslaught, not contemplating it all. "Mother," he Cast out. "I think I understand now. It's all coming to me."

"Great Mother, no," Shin-Ja said. "I feared this would come."

"What do you mean, you feared it?" Zara asked. "This is a wonderful day, for all."

Veil sat in awe. With his mind jumbled and unclear, he found it difficult to focus, but he was sure of one thing, he was more than a wolf. He could change into whatever he wanted.

I'm supposed to do something too. At least, I think I am. "Mother, do you think—"

New scents and the sounds drifted on the wind, and he forgot what he was about to Cast. With the investigative exuberance of youth, he dashed to the forest's edge. His mother screamed in his mind to stop, but he didn't. He couldn't. He had to see what lay beyond the forest.

There, in an open field, the strangest creatures scrambled about only a few bounds away. They didn't look at all like prey, more like playful hunters. *Are these the humans everyone said they were strange and dangerous? They don't look that scary to me.*

They ran about on their hind feet, tackling each other, and then running away, like wolves at play.

Maybe they're distant kin, he wondered, watching with fascination. *They're so strange. How can they smell with faces so flat? And where's their fur? I wonder how that would feel.*

He examined them closely, studying the way they looked, and the way they felt in his mind. Taking it all in, he focused the impression on himself, willing it into being.

I wonder if—

Dizziness struck, rocking him as though he'd taken a blow to the head, and then the world ripped away. Vision going black, he tumbled to the ground while frantically trying to Cast out to his mother, but her mind was gone. The last thing he heard was her howls of anguish as he changed.

Betal staggered, holding his head with eyes wide. He stared at the wolf in disbelief. "Mother?"

Shin-Ja cried out, "Veil!"

He stumbled forward, using Chaos to tear off his clothes. Within three steps, Betal changed from a man, to a massive, black wolf. He dashed to her, nuzzling her neck, and licking her face. "I'm sorry, Mother. I'm so sorry. Please, forgive me." He whimpered.

"Oh, how I've missed you," she said, her tail wag little more than a few flops. "Don't cry, my sweet. All is well now. I finally found you, my lovely pup—my precious one. That's all that matters. The Mother granted my wish."

Her thoughts weakened.

"No! Please, Mother. Don't *go*." He pushed his face into her fur, desperate to feel the security he knew as a pup.

"The Mother calls me." She licked him. "You must do what you came here for. Awaken, my sweet Veil. Everything depends on you."

"I don't know what that means!" His whimpers turned to cries.

"I'll always love you." Closing her eyes, Shin-Ja's life slipped away.

Veil lifted his massive head, howling his pain and remorse at the sky. They turned to ragged screams as the wolf, Veil, regained his human form.

Crying, Betal cradled his mother in his shaking arms. Shin-Ja died in peace and happiness, her love for him shining like a beacon to banish the night.

To be continued in

Chaos Reigns, Volume 2:
The Tower of Time

Glossary

Adel Floweret {a-Dell} – The lover of Mangin Karados and Cobb Cruchfield.

Angharad {Ang-aR-ad} – A member of the Portrayals Theater Company.

Aza'zel {a-Za-Zeel} – The God of Death.

Beast of Cool Winds, The – See Betal.

Betal {Be-Tal} – an acolyte of Chaos living in Cool Winds.

Brotherhood of Assassins – Assassins and worshipers of Aza'zel.

Calidos Flint – Priest of Chaos from the Southern Region.

Channeling – To manipulate the power/essence of ones god.

Chaotic Prison – See Lands of the Dead.

Cord (AKA Daniel Conduin) – The father of Ellis Concord.

Council of Taneer – Godlike individuals who oversee the city of Taneer and The Great Games.

Dithiyar Mardoon {Dith-i-yar} – Chaos priest at Cool Winds, former teacher of Lord Heartless.

Dirge – Sword master, Travelers lead guardsman, and anointed "Warrior of the Righteous" of Ukase.

Daylin Dragonvein {Day-lyn} – Animal telepath, empath, and dog trainer for the Travelers.

Dekriot {Dek-rIot} (AKA The Abomination) – Ultimate demon of the abyss.

Edis – Name of the Lord God of Chaos.

Ellis Concord – Head of Concord's Grand Traveling show.

Erin Cruchfield – Cool Winds Head of militia and commander of the caravan to Gate Hall.

Gabriel – The Arbiter and Champion of the Council of Taneer.

Great Lord, The – See Edis

Great Soul Stone, The – The crystal latus where all souls derive before life and return to after death; nestled in the roots of The True Tree.

Grunkin (AKA Chaos Beast) – A creature mutated by the Lord of Chaos.

Gunther Karados {Gun-ther Care-a-dose} – Mangin's father. Head Priest at Gate Hall.

Heartless, Lord (AKA Twitch) – The Champion of the Lord of Chaos and master of the world during the reign of the god of Chaos.

Hedge Mage – One that draws on the essence of life that emanates from the world.

Hogar (AKA The Ghost of Death) – Paladin of Chaos who roams The Reach.

John Simmons – Leader of the village of Cool Winds and Betal's adoptive father.

Lands of the Dead (AKA Chaotic Prison) – A prison where time stands still for everything except roving bands of incorporeal soldiers and Timekeepers (prieasts) to Kala, the God of Time.

Lord's Breath (The) – The essence of the Lord of Chaos that priests and paladins channel.

Mangin Karados {Man-jin Care-a-dose} – Chaos acolyte trained in Cool Winds.

Marsha Lewins (AKA Tasha) – Ellis's mother.

Mother, The – See The True Tree.

Raaz – Half Demon lackey of Master Rendell Morgan.

Reach (The) – A region in the central part of the content of Bindane, just south of the Lands of the Dead.

Ruddick {Roodick} – Chaos priest that experimented on Dalyn as a child.

Sarah – A member of the Portrayals Theater Company and troupe herbalist.

South (The) – A region in the southern-central portion of the content of Bindane.

Taneer, the Eternal City – The city at the center of, and yet outside of, the matrix of the multiverse.

Tebu – Also called the Tree-folk, or Green-folk; denizens and protectors of the wilds.

Travelers – A traveling group of entertainers.

True Tree, The – The first. The creator of life and the multiverse. The creator of the Great Soul Stone.

Twitch – See Heartless, Lord.

Ukase {oo-case} – The Lord God of Order.

Vir – Wolf friend of Dalyn.

Whisp – A hedge mage of minor magics and illusions, and former acolyte of Chaos.

Yurken {Yoor-keen} – Large humanoid creatures created by minions of the Lord of Chaos during the first Great War to be used at shock troops.

Acknowledgments

I wish to thank everyone at the Writing at the Ledges group; Randy, Colleen, Rosalie, Lori, and well, the list goes on and on. Thank you all.

I wish to thank my many friends at the Meet up - Lansing Writers & Readers Guild for their help in the proofreading.

I also wish to thank my folks, Jerry and Barb for your years of love and support.

A special thank you to Angharad for the use of your name. We'll never forget your talent and heart. We miss you, and will keep you in our hearts, always.

I especially want to thank my wife Sarah. I couldn't have done it without you, my loving Angel Eyes.

About the author:

G. S. Scott works at a civil engineering firm in Grand Rapids, Michigan. He enjoys writing all types of fantasy stories and poetry. He is active in local writing groups and is an avid gamer. He enjoys local theater with his playwright wife. They share their home with their sweet and cuddly cat and hyperactive dog.

Also by G. S. Scott:

True Tree Chronicles book one:

Cleansed

~~~~~~~~~~

Sorrow's Heart

(A True Tree Chronicles Origins Story)

~~~~~~~~~~